SURVIVANOIA

SECOND EDITION

Baroness Von Smith

Burning
Giraffe

SURVIVANOIA by Baroness Von Smith

Cover by Jason Helmer

Chapters six and seven originally appeared on the website Once Written as the short story "The Comic Who Couldn't Laugh"

Second Edition
Published by Burning Giraffe Books
www.BurningGiraffeBooks.com

ISBN: 978-0-9981881-2-6

for Charles, Hawkeye, and Joe

INTRODUCTION TO THE SECOND EDITION

The ability
to update her fiction
is the privilege
of the modern author.

It is also her curse.

B.V.S.

W.N.Y.
August 2018

SECOND INTRODUCTION TO THE SECOND EDITION

I started writing this book in the late '90s. I intended it to be set, say, next Tuesday. But next Tuesday in the '90s is not today's next Tuesday.

Survivanoia was started before smartphones and Google; when slam poetry was nascent; when it was Minesweeper everyone played not Minecraft; before Al Gore invented the Internet. Should all these things be updated?

I decided no. I decided this when, at the gym, I caught the first hour of *The Fifth Element*. The film, while carrying the mark of the decade in which it was made, holds up as being set in the future. I believe *Survivanoia* does as well. I appreciate the gentle irony of this sort of "futuristic nostalgia." I think Dacianna Von Worthington would, too.

B.V.S.

W.N.Y.
August 2018

SURVIVANOIA

I

The Inventor and The Instigator

(Friends)

CHAPTER 1

Encludsmo Stuckhowsen had a landlord who spied on him. Though knowledge of this fact in no way affected his routine, he fully anticipated that one morning he would be hauled away for the crime of doing nothing by a handful of imminently practical-looking men. It never occurred to Doctor Stuckhowsen that the spying landlord might instead lead to his emancipation, self-reclamation, even perhaps that ultimate indulgence: his Americanization. The Doctor lacked the audacity to conceive these things, just as the knowledge of his spy failed to en- or outrage him, lead him to set traps, or alert the authorities.

Doctor Stuckhowsen remained certain in the knowledge of his spy, though he had no tangible evidence. Occasionally he'd peer at his leftovers, examine his ice cream, certain there had been more last night. Or perhaps a book lay askew on the coffee table that The Doctor felt certain had been aligned when he'd left.

A spying landlord wasn't a foreign situation to Doctor Stuckhowsen, a foreigner himself to these free United States. But it did seem an odd thing to him, given that he rented a condemned shack beneath the freeway overpass. He lived under the section of highway where the 110 and 105 freeways converged and in front of an impossibly enormous billboard that said: PUT CHEESE ON STUFF! The billboard towered thirty stories above him, the legs of it blocking The Doctor's view from his rear windows.

That someone would rent such a place seemed unlikely only to those who didn't grasp the severity of the housing situation in Los Angeles and/ or were unaware that Dr. Stuckhowsen's roots lay in an obscure Eastern European country whose inhabitants cared not who was in charge but only that the bombing stopped. Once a person fully comprehended these two contributing factors and their ramifications, it became perfectly logical for this little scientist to hand over twice the monthly payment of a midsized sedan (which he did not have) to live in a boarded-up shack under the freeway.

The Good Doctor didn't care where he lived anyway. He dedicated his waking hours to research. He tended no garden, harbored no pet, dated no woman. He'd never bothered to pry the 2x4s off the windows, never swept the grime from the stairs.

He had come to America speaking almost no English but was extraordinarily good at math. He graduated from UCLA with three separate but related doctoral degrees, only slightly improved English, and exactly one friend. Something—his lacking language skills, perhaps—saw him still unemployed a year after graduation, living off a modest lump-sum payment the school had given him in exchange for rights to a patent. A less ardent man would have felt exploited.

Most of Doctor Stuckhowsen's American encounters had been neutral. People tripped over his first name and occasionally asked if he was related to some composer. Mostly when they asked him this they looked ready to beat him to a pulp, which made him happy to tell them that he was not. Seldom was he in public, anyway. He did most of his laundry in the kitchen sink, acquired much of his furniture from the curb, and usually cut his own hair.

He shopped sporadically, when he remembered that he needed food. He'd wander through the market, fill a red carry-cart with canned fish, potatoes, cabbage. In the same strip plaza as the market was a thrift store, where he bought black pants and tweed jackets. One Saturday he'd found a stash of aprons. Not white—blue-striped, longer than standard, with a center divided patch pocket: THE GARDENA BUTCHER SHOP HAD CLOSED. He bought all seven of the aprons then stopped at the dollar shop for elbow-length rubber gloves. Yellow. Dr. Stuckhowsen didn't own a lab coat.

There was a single thing he splurged on: a restaurant which he frequented. Romanian. Not his homeland but similar foodstuffs: organ meats, overripe cheese, ruby wines, and black vodka. Twice a week The Doctor walked there, a mile each way. He walked with a purposeful, pronounced swing, like a skiing monkey with too-short trousers and white socks, clutching an ever-present umbrella despite his Los Angeles address. He ate by himself, chatted with the proprietors in their native tongue, and read Russian science journals off the Internet from his laptop. Occasionally, Emil the Hungarian stopped in and they played chess. But they were equally skilled and usually stalemated. The Doctor always left a considerable tip.

It never occurred to Encludsmo Stuckhowsen to be frustrated, dissatisfied, or sad. When he grew tired of a project, he put it aside for a time, taking up another in its stead. He never concerned himself with whether a thing offered a market; he researched for research's sake.

One day he received a notice from his bank—overdrawn. Dr. Stuckhowsen wasn't certain what this meant. He gathered his umbrella, strode the mile to the restaurant. The girl who stood behind the counter was the daughter of the proprietor. The proprietor spoke to her in Romanian but she responded, always, in English, which inadvertently made The Doctor feel stupid, made him feel obligated to attempt English.

"Oh, the usual?"

"Naw, naw, please, the telephonic device may I use please? Here call, not a lengthy distance."

"The phone? Sure, Doctor."

He called a number scribbled on his hand, the number of the only true friend he'd made in college.

"Please is Mister Tyson there?"

"Encludsmo?"

Silence.

"Encludsmo, it's Annie! Antoinette."

"Oh! 'Allo, Ah-knee."

Fond laughter. "I'll get Ty for you."

Tyson arrived on the phone; they talked briefly. "Get yourself a meal while you're waiting. I'll pay. I'll pay!" He hung up.

The Good Doctor did indeed get himself a meal: thick black sausages in a wine-based gravy, slightly sweet, roasted beets and potatoes, and a soft bread with a crisp, sweetish crust. He was mopping the last of the gravy with the bread when a familiar voice spoke his mother tongue.

—My friend why haven't you called me?

Encludsmo smiled as he turned and stood. Behind him, Tyson wore the same earth tones as he had in grad school, and the same Timberland boots, and his unruly chestnut hair still fell just over the top of his wire-rimmed glasses. The old friends hugged.

"Odd to hear my language," Encludsmo said in English.

—You didn't answer my question.

The sound of his native tongue soothed him and he responded in kind. —Just busy, he replied. —We're all busy.

Tyson insisted on paying Encludsmo's tab and purchased a bottle of Romanian wine as well. He then led them to his silver Camry.

—Antoinette misses you.

—And I her! And especially her cooking. And how is your little girl?

—Not so little. Seven now. In school and growing like a weed!

—Seven! Seems impossible. Oh, turn here. And here.

—Here? There's no road.

—It's dirt, but it's okay. I made this road, had to blast it out myself when I first moved in.

"Good Lord, man! You live here?"

Encludsmo blinked at Tyson. He examined his crooked, boarded up abode, which looked bleaker than usual in the sharp glare of Tyson's head-lights, then blinked at Tyson again.

—Sure. The roof does not leak. No one bothers me.

Tyson gestured to the towering billboard. —Do you?

Encludsmo glanced at the sign, sighed heavily, shaking his head.

—American cheeses.

He got out of the car, charging toward his front door as always, while Tyson gingerly picked his way through the lawn, a lengthy, brown fire hazard that had long ago consumed the walkway.

Encludsmo fussed in the doorway—three locks, to protect the research—while Tyson glanced along either side of the house. He pointed to stylized, spray-painted letters, big and bright against the dirty white aluminum siding. "Taggers."

Encludsmo shrugged.

Inside, a yellow bulb warmed the cramped living room. Homier than the outside, the living room boasted an antique coffee table and matching end tables, a battered, overstuffed leather chair, and a sagging but cozy couch covered with a thick, white afghan. Bookcases lined the walls, a chess set waited on the coffee table, and two easels held framed paintings of scenes from Encludsmo's homeland.

Tyson plopped onto the squishy couch. —You need to move.

The Doctor frowned, paced, waved away his friend's suggestion with annoyance.

—Then you need a dog. Maybe a fence. An alarm system.

—What I need is money.

The Doctor showed Tyson the letter from his bank. Tyson squinted at it.

—This is your checking.

—Okay.

—Where's your savings?

Encludsmo's face flushed and his heart picked up. —In a bank? I have none.

—Bring me all your mail from last month. You keep it, like I told you, right?

Encludsmo didn't take time to respond. He jogged into the kitchen and retrieved, from under the sink, a brown paper sack half full of envelopes.

—From the last year.

—Not much, Tyson observed. He then enviously noted nothing addressed to "resident." He peered at his friend's address.

"110 and 105 Interchange! Lower level?"

The Doctor blinked again. —Is that not a reasonable address?

—I suppose if mail gets to it. . . .

Encludsmo shrugged, gestured to the bag.

Tyson shuffled through the letters, found one postmarked from Pennsylvania with a name he recognized: Lucretia Stuckhowsen.

—How is your sister?

—Crazy. More than ever, read for yourself.

Tyson scanned the letter. —She writes to you in English?

—To practice, I think. I won't tease her, obviously. Also, she believes it will help me to learn.

Curly, slanted letters told Tyson, "I got a deer repeller today, a thing with a motion sensor that you fill with water. When it senses somebody come near it, it sprays them. The police tell me this is legal. Unlike the electric fence and barbed wire. The hardware store won't take either of those back, by the way. I guess I'll use them to wrap Christmas gifts this year."

—Her English is good, Ty said.

—Too bad mine is not.

—Sounds like she's having problems with her neighbors.

—Her problems are in her head. This is a good country for her. They do not put the crazies to death.

Ty returned his attention to the bag. He pulled an envelope from it, ripped it open, and grinned triumphantly at the paper inside. —Look here. This is your savings. You have a bit of money yet.

—How much?

Tyson gave him the figure. Roughly two months' rent.

—Not so much.

Tyson raked his hands through his hair, gazed at Encludsmo, who took an uncomfortable step back in reply.

—Tell me what you're working on these days.

The Doctor's face brightened at the mention of his research. —Come see!

He led Tyson to what would have been the bedroom, were it not serving as somebody's laboratory.

—Here is a contention serum. That over there is—

—Finished?

—Not yet. I have Emotion Potion that's finished.

—What's it do?

—Makes whoever drinks it feel warm or chill, depending on the emotions of the people around them.

—Maybe. What else? What about the contention serum? How soon?

—Two weeks? Maybe two months. Oh, it will be wonderful! It's nearly done. It makes people not want to have.

—Not want to have? Like, things?

Encludsmo nodded.

"So it makes them content. Ah. Content-shun. What else?"

"Finished? The pretentiometer, he is done."

"What's he do? It do?"

Encludsmo struggled for words, fell back into his own language. —Measures the level of pretentiousness in a room.

Tyson frowned slightly.

—Pretense is a form of lying, Encludsmo explained. —There is a direct and calculable correlation between pretentiousness and deceit, which in turn makes future deceit calculable, predictable. Not just how much but when and about what types of things. It's very easy really, you simply take the contrapositive of the area under the—

—Don't waste your breath on me, my friend. Math is one thing I'll never understand.

—Math is merely another language. You already speak seven, why not eight?

—Some languages are harder to master than others. We're not all as bright as you.

Tyson pulled his wallet from his coat pocket, rifled through it until he found one of his business cards. —Go here.

Encludsmo studied the card made to look like stamped metal. "Survivanoia? What means this?"

"It's a made up word. It's a weird place. They make weird stuff."

—Like?

—Sofa coffins, bulletproof jogging suits, gas masks in fashion colors. They distribute things, too, like radiation pills and anti-anthrax pills and baby coffins. They developed the West Nile virus vaccine. Just now they're working on treatments and a vaccine for that new disease, Flower Flu. The one where you wake up blind?

Encludsmo squinted. "They were in paper this week past."

"Survivanoia was?"

"Yes, that blindness disease. Ad claims you have treatment already. Not surprising, if sickness truly derived from plants. We share only 40% DNA, so not many places to look. Lawyer says people dying for no reason. Want to class-action sue."

Tyson's brow creased. "In the *Picayune*?"

—No, the arts paper, the *Bi-Weekly*. And it could be a contrivance, anyway. I understand LA is the land of litigation. There was no article, just an advertisement.

—What section? In the back?

Encludsmo retrieved the article for his friend, apologizing for having been the bearer of bad news.

"Well, like you said, maybe it's fake. A gimmick of some sort."

Encludsmo grinned. —Still, I am surprised to find you working at such a strange, dark place.

"That's what a PhD in languages will get you. A crappy job in customer service. Anyway, they're looking to expand. New company president. Just brought in a new person to head up R and D. A product like yours might be something they'd want."

He salvaged the restaurant sales slip from his trouser pocket, scribbled on the back of it. —See one of these people. The Baroness speaks German.

—My German is terrible.

—It's better than your English.

* * *

Something about him must have appealed to somebody, since they gave him an appointment the same week he called. That Friday, Dr. Encludsmo Stuckhowsen took the long, awful trip up north two valleys to Survivanoia in Valencia. Three buses and as many hours later, he stepped onto the street in a land so green and plush he couldn't believe he was still in Greater Los Angeles.

His appointment was with Baroness Dacianna Von Worthington. She met him in the lobby and they walked together up a white spiral of stairs with a silver railing. She seemed impossible—impossibly tall with wine-colored hair twisted into an impossible braid that bounced gently against her hips as she made her way up the stairs in front of him. Encludsmo seldom noticed a woman's hips.

Sunlight charmed her office—a large square room decorated like the office of a lawyer/big game hunter. An imposing white bear guarded her enormous desk. Built-in bookshelves were crammed with thick volumes and bejeweled by extravagant knick-knacks. Like the buzzing Jacob's Ladder, which made The Doctor smile.

He attempted small talk; she offered him wine and they spoke at length and with matched knowledge and enthusiasm, especially about wines of his region of the world. This segued into climate change, then Flower Flu, then something seemed to click and she wanted only to know about him and his invention.

He explained his device to her, in German, which she did indeed speak fluently, though no accent betrayed her English. Halfway through his presentation, she stopped him. The Doctor began to pack his borrowed briefcase, discouraged, but she instructed him to sit. Moments later, a man appeared in her office. "Scally," she called him: tall, dark, and somehow familiar. The Baroness translated to this Scally person everything The Doctor told her about his pretentiometer.

While she talked, her fierce, violet cat eyes blazed. She was a force, a presence, a tree on fire. Tall, broad, curved. Dr. Stuckhowsen liked her, trusted her. Her smile reminded him of Ty's. He hadn't mentioned Tyson, as his friend had cautioned him that it might do more harm than good. But in this woman, despite her fortitude or perhaps because of it, he sensed a similar benign permanence. All this struck him like a hidden thing discovered and lent him a strange lightness in his belly.

He carried this lightness with him. Three buses, three hours. Back in his neighborhood, twilight darkened the streets, made them blue and cool and eerie, and dogs yelped and howled in The Doctor's wake. But the black monstrosity that he discovered following him remained silent.

He'd noticed it as he stepped off the bus—a large, living shadow hunkered down beside the scratched, graffitied plastic of the bus shelter. It didn't growl or bark and The Doctor thought little of it until he heard its feet padding against the street in his wake. It spooked him, this dog the size of a large sheep, the color of asphalt, except for his brown feet, padding along behind him like a friendly, hellish companion.

The Doctor ducked inside a coffee shop. The sugary smell inside reminded him that he was famished, and he wasted five dollars on an espresso and a slice of cake . . . then tasted it and no longer considered the spent money a waste.

He sat in the front window. People trotted past, weighed down by laundry, by children, by internal woes. Outside, two men in rags shared a drink from a bag wrapped in brown paper while they played dominoes.

The Doctor noticed, on one of the rag men's hats, a metallic silver S, enclosed in a metallic diamond—Survivanoia's logo. After he'd researched the company in preparation for his interview, Dr. Stuckhowsen had found this little silver S an ubiquitous presence in Los Angeles.

"Armageddon is over," one of their slogans proclaimed. "We lost." Another said, "The revolution was yesterday."

The Doctor had spent a good bit of time on the Survivanoia website. Among the items available for purchase were lead-lined baseball caps, "For safe and happy gun-firing holidays! What goes up must come down! Don't let your New Year be wrecked by a stray celebratory bullet! Don't have this Fourth be your last! Good protection for up to .38 caliber."

The Doctor also found the sofa coffins Ty had mentioned. He thought perhaps he'd misunderstood his friend, but there they were. Like a sofa bed, but folding nearly inside-out, into a plaid-lined, wooden, vaguely coffin-shaped thing. "Serves you in both life and in death! Inexpensive! Prevents the need for your loved ones to cover you in newspapers and stomp you into the ground upon your expiration. Why waste money on a beautiful wooden box you'll never even get to enjoy? Think practical. Think Survivanoia Sofa Coffins!"

The Doctor was unsure where his invention, his little pretentiometer, would fit with these self-proclaimed post-apocalyptic products. But the woman, the Baroness, had seemed excited and promised him a response within a few weeks.

The Doctor stared through his own reflection, out at the dark street. Nobody looked up at him, though he knew he was quite visible now that evening had faded to night; nobody slowed his pace to even glance in the window, and even the rag men's attention stayed glued to themselves and their too-loud laughter and their game.

But the dog. The dog sat by a lamppost, head cocked, ears pointing. Everything was pointy—pointy ears, pointy snout, pointy tail. The Doctor guessed him mostly German shepherd. Crossbred with something to make him bigger and darker and possibly to take the signature shepherd curve out of his back. His brown eyes gazed velvety from his dark face. The Doctor remembered how hungry he'd been. He ordered another piece of cake and filled his coffee cup with water.

The dog gobbled the cake, drank the water, and tried to eat the cup. Dr. Stuckhowsen headed up the street and the behemoth followed, keeping pace beside him, looking now left, now right. At the end of the street, the dog gracefully jumped the guardrail, then waited for The Doctor to lumber his way over the corrugated metal band. The two of them picked their respective ways down the embankment at an equal pace, and by the time they'd reached the bottom, they seemed to have struck a deal. The dog would guard Encludsmo, and Encludsmo would feed the dog.

He held open the door to the house, but the dog lay down on what would have been a porch if The Doctor had had a porch instead of an uneven stack of concrete blocks at the entry to his house.

Inside, that familiar feeling overtook him: that someone had been here. He'd mentioned it to his friend Ty, but Ty thought him paranoid. —How could someone know when to come? Outside of your visits to the restaurant, you're always home.

Encludsmo had protested that his visits to the restaurant were fairly regular, that a person could watch him and know; it wouldn't be so difficult, really. Tyson didn't concede. What did The Doctor have that anyone would know to want? Standing in the center of his living room, he now puzzled this same question.

The dog made Doctor Stuckhowsen feel protected. So he left the front door open while he prowled through his dark house, snapping on lights in his wake. Nothing seemed out of place. No books askew on the coffee table, nothing missing from the kitchen, no imprints on the couch from someone sitting to peruse his magazines.

In the lab, everything seemed to be where he'd left it. He'd left it a mess. He'd spent the week dredging through all his notes and compiling a comprehensive presentation. He could simply have discussed the little device, but Tyson suspected they would want something written, something he could leave behind with them. And he'd been right.

The Doctor stooped to retrieve a page of notes from the floor by his desk and spotted it: a smashed beaker. Clean, no chemical hazard, but shattered on the floor. The Doctor's eyes hooded. Had there been an earthquake? Never could rule that out. And he'd been far enough away today that he might not have felt it. He swept up the glass with the lab broom and wandered back to the living room, brooding.

—Feels bad, he said to himself. —Like a warning. Like doom.

The dog stood, barked, once and deep. The Doctor blinked at it, made his way to the porch.

—Doom?

The monstrous animal barked again.

Doctor Stuckhowsen perched next to it on the concrete, stretched out a hand and tentatively patted its head.

—Then I really am in trouble.

* * *

Being responsible for a belly other than his own had The Doctor shopping less sporadically, doing everything with more intention. As the hills crisped from green to brown and temperatures crept from double to triple digits, The Doctor's life began to assume that of a person who in fact cares for something.

Doom loved canned fish as much as he did. He also enjoyed the cheese and sausages at the Romanian restaurant, where, until an incident, the dog would lie on his feet, while The Doctor played chess against the Hungarian.

Watching the dark animal's overt contentment one evening made The Doctor consider something. That night, he was up until the day broke new, back working on his contention serum. He'd been at a standstill with the project, but this time he felt confident he'd done it, found a way to make people feel satisfied. Without giving them cancer. Or rickets.

After he woke the next afternoon, as he fixed himself some coffee, a commotion sounded from outside; the grating of tires on his gravel lot, the rumble of a car engine, a loud curse, and, finally, "Jesus Christmas! Look at the size of that thing! Encludsmo! You've got a demon on your porch!"

Encludsmo checked his pocket watch; it was two in the afternoon. A peer through the boards out the front window revealed Tyson at the bottom of his concrete blocks. Encludsmo undid his three locks and opened his door.

—What is wrong?

Ty gestured, slowly, at Doom who stood sentry with his head cocked, making no sound.

—No, he is fine. Doom! This is my friend.

The dog relaxed and Encludsmo coaxed his friend past the animal and into the house. Tyson plopped onto the couch and stretched his long legs across it.

—That's quite a watchdog you got yourself!

—Not much of a watchdog. He never makes any noise.

—Protection trained, Tyson said. —They don't bother to bark, they just eat your head.

Encludsmo frowned and spoke in Tyson's native English. "More than the dog is wrong with you. What are you doing here at such an hour as this? A working hour."

"Working hours are for working people. As of one this afternoon, I no longer belong in that category."

Encludsmo raised an eyebrow.

—They fired me, Ty explained.

—Why?

—You won't believe why! Doesn't matter anyway. I came mostly to double check that you didn't mention my name, you know, at your interview.

Encludsmo dropped into his recliner, tossed his hands in the air. —I will not take their money! I will keep my machine.

"No! No, you take all that they give. You ask for twice what they offer! I mean it. And get royalties, too, don't get screwed, like at the university. Have you heard anything from the Baroness yet?"

Encludsmo suddenly found the floor very interesting.

"You forgot? How could you!"

—I did not forget. At first I checked each week. But the phone mail confuses me. When American numbers are spoken, what numeral the name corresponds to is lost on me. I seem to always push the wrong ones.

And there was an incident at the restaurant with some strangers and the dog some weeks ago that cost the proprietors some money, so that I felt bad asking to use their phone.

Tyson sat upright. —Let's go check now. My cell phone is in the car.

—You're avoiding your wife.

Ty slumped again. —No. I'm avoiding an empty house. Annie's out of town until Friday.

—Have you been drinking?

—No.

—Maybe you should start.

—Got any vodka?

Encludsmo shook his head, smiling. —We could get some, if you'd like.

Tyson sighed. —I guess not.

He eased from the couch. —Thanks for the invite, though. I should go. I don't mean to encroach. Bring me some paper and I'll write down how to check your voicemail.

Encludsmo happily obliged. —Tonight is when I usually go, you know, on Tuesdays. I'll check tonight.

—I'll come tomorrow.

Tyson gave his friend a hug, and Encludsmo patted Doom on the head while Ty slipped past the beast. He headed back to the lab where he kept himself busy until nightfall. Then he put on his tweed jacket and claimed his umbrella from its hook on the wall by the door. He closed the door and locked its locks. Doom stood and stretched and waited for The Doctor to lead the way. But Dr. Stuckhowsen waved a finger.

—I can't take you along and then ask to use the phone. Not after what you did.

Doom stared at him. He made a whiney sound.

—I'll bring something back for you.

When he stepped off the makeshift porch, the dog followed him. Twice more he led the animal back inside the yard, reasoned with him, and tried to leave. Finally, he unlocked all the locks again and went inside. "C'mon. Come!"

Doom didn't come; instead he fell back on his haunches and whined again, like he knew he was being duped. But The Doctor called him again and he obeyed. As The Doctor closed the door, he saw the dog settling down behind it, looking as sad and lonely as Tyson had.

The Doctor had the restaurant to himself for nearly half an hour; only the English-speaking girl was present. He ate hurriedly, still feeling anxious about asking to use the phone. He felt a wash of relief when Emil the Hungarian arrived, just before The Doctor's dessert.

"Where is your monster?"

"Guarding the house."

"Good. Then the only bloodshed tonight shall be on the chessboard."

Emil ordered a plate of sausages for himself and a bottle of wine for them to split. Three bottles later they stalemated their second match, while the proprietor's daughter fell asleep on a stool behind the counter.

"I think we must both find other partners, learn new strategies," Emil said, pulling on his llama wool sweater. He dug a paperback from a tattered messenger bag and retreated to a corner table, bidding The Doctor goodnight.

Dr. Stuckhowsen packed the carved wooden chess pieces into their box. The daughter came, yawning while she wiped the table, asked, "Did you need to use the phone?"

The Good Doctor felt himself blush. "Yes, very much please."

"You're still waiting for an answer, then?"

"Yes."

The girl shrugged, gestured to the black phone by the counter. "Good luck."

Dr. Stuckhowsen followed the instructions Tyson had written for him, entering his password and mailbox number, and finally pressing one to listen to his message.

A man's voice identified himself as Sydney Scalinescu from Survivanoia. "We've reviewed your instrument and, unfortunately, decided to go with a similar product offered by another engineering team." The steady, almost sing-song voice told The Doctor that Mr. Scalinescu was dictating, reading his reply into the phone.

He said something about this other design being more easily reproduced, apologized, and wished The Doctor the best of luck in placing his invention elsewhere. "Any notes, calculations, or similar material you left in our possession will be mailed out to you before the end of this week. If you would like to discuss this further, call me at . . ."

The Doctor hung up. He didn't bother to note the phone number. He left his usual hefty tip, collected the bag of spare meats for Doom, called out a farewell, and slipped out into the night.

Outside, the air held a sharp chill, a steep contrast with the eighty-plus temperatures the day had offered. It reminded The Doctor that he did, indeed, live in a desert.

He made his way through the cold, dark streets. Blue street lights caught him, then let him go again, leaving him to be enveloped by the moonless night's inky blackness. Occasionally a dog's startled bark sounded. The closer he got to his house, the fewer the streetlights. The Doctor found the darkness comforting. In darkness, everyone is equal.

He walked the long street to the embankment at its dead end, at the bottom of which sat his house. He didn't head down the dusty hillside, though. Instead he stood, gazing up at the freeway. Even at this late hour, it hummed with cars, buzzed with lights. He squinted at two small figures balanced among the barbed wire shrouding the freeway signs, spraying wide swatches of color onto the state-mandated green. What had Tyson called them? Taggers?

The Doctor had inspected his house after Tyson had pointed the painting out to him. He hadn't minded; it added some character to what Encludsmo felt was a sepia world. He sighed, wishing the taggers would climb the cheese sign.

—What is this about? he muttered to himself. —This unhappiness?

The very concept eluded him. He pondered the odd feeling he found in himself, the lump in his stomach, the sadness tangled with the dull anger that seemed to go through his body leaving him electric. Over what? Why?

But an odd sound pulled him from his ruminating. A snarling and . . . yes, a man yelling. Well, no, screaming. Horrific sounds, though soft and distant as memories through the roar of the freeway.

Dr. Stuckhowsen clutched his umbrella and marched down the hill. Outside his house, he found an automobile—a shiny, neat vehicle from what he could tell in the dim light. The door to his house gaped open. From it shone a single beam, a line of illumination, as from a flashlight.

He raised his umbrella, cleared his throat, and approached the door. "Here is the living place for Doctor Encludsmo Stuckhowsen! I am asking you that you at one time leave or I am telephoning the—"

Doom came to the door. The light beam trapped him and displayed to The Doctor his crimson-stained jowls and chest and paws. The Doctor slowly eased past the animal, snapped on the light switch next to the door, and gasped in alarm.

The coffee table lay upside down. A man lay across it, sprawled at a most disturbing angle with a terrible red chasm where his throat should have been. The Doctor took a single step closer. The man's throat had been ripped out, chewed. His glassy eyes stared off toward the kitchen and his dark hair fell across his cheek. The dead man clutched a spiral-bound notebook in his hand, its pages covered with unintelligible scribbles of non-English notes and impossible calculations.

Dr. Stuckhowsen pried his notebook from the slaughtered man's hand. He shivered, swallowed back a wave of nausea, and took a deep breath. Behind him he heard his dog panting. He spun round and faced the animal.

—Doom! You've eaten my landlord!

The animal cocked his head at The Doctor.

—Good dog!

He patted his pet's head and thumped him on the back as he'd seen other dog owners do.

—But they will come for you. Put you in jail. This we cannot have.

The Doctor's gaze found the flashlight. He switched off the overhead lamp and made his way through the house with the help of the inconspicuous, battery-driven beam. While the dog busied himself with the bag of leftovers from the restaurant, The Doctor moved swiftly from room to room, jamming a suitcase with clothes, filling a cardboard box with notes—some in books, some on napkins—and collecting the bag of mail. Didn't need the authorities finding out about his rabid sister. They might blame her for the mess on the floor.

He knelt down beside his dead landlord and searched through the man's pockets. He found a wallet, some hard candies, two condoms, and finally, car keys. Outside, he shoved his belongings into the car's trunk. He called for Doom. The animal formed a black shadow in the dark doorway then galloped across the yard to the open, waiting car door. He flopped onto the back seat as if this had been his plan all along.

—Wait here, The Doctor instructed. —I have two more things.

Inside, he now sensed the metallic blood smell. He moved in a wide arc around his slain landlord to his laboratory. There, he plucked a single sample vial from the wooden rack, its cool glass reassuring in the dank gloom. He tucked the vial into the pocket of his tweed jacket.

Finally, he retrieved a small metal box from under the lab bench and stole back through the house. Outside, he locked all three of his locks then got behind the wheel of the car.

He got lucky—the car was an automatic. He pointed it in the right direction and pressed the gas pedal, driving haphazardly up the road he himself had fashioned from a pile of dirt and landfill. Once he was off his property, he took the metal box and headed back on foot, toward the house.

But he kept going. Up to the base of the enormous billboard. A lattice-work of scaffolding greeted him there, waiting to be climbed. And climb it he did, to its midpoint, more awkwardly even than might be anticipated due to his dragging the box along with him.

He unlatched the box and from it drew two of the four remaining patches of explosive, a roll of duct tape, and a considerable length of fuse. Sweat stung his eyes as he worked and exhaustion threatened to plunge him to his death, but something in him overrode it: a new, strange vehemence.

He recognized, distantly, that at the moment, and for the first time he could recall, he served a purpose outside the realm of science, was taking action that did not serve research. He didn't pause now to wonder why.

A short while later, Doctor Encludsmo Stuckhowsen headed south on the freeway under which he had lived for so many years. Behind him, the very earth let loose an ominous, terrible thud, which nearby residents would first mistake for an earthquake.

There in South Central, at the intersection of the 110 and 105 freeways, this billboard—a colossal monstrosity people drove past daily without ever seeing—this gargantuan thing of metal and wood crumpled and fell, col-lapsing onto a boarded-up house covered in gang symbols.

The Doctor, from the car of his dead landlord, felt the rumble of earth and steel, and he smiled. An unfamiliar, self-satisfied smile.

—Always did hate that sign.

CHAPTER 2

Tyson Woolritch sat in his silver Camry, wondering idly if the planet had finally hit the tipping point. This was in part due to the six solid lanes of traffic, and in part because of the red sun scorching the parking lots of competing gas stations and convenience stores, its mean, white glare blinding the men and women unlucky enough to walk in LA. Bigger, faster, more. . . . But better?

He peered through the windshield and searched for his joggers. There. The blonde came toward him, pink shorts and a pink running bra gleaming as she headed south on the six-lane street. The other runner he caught sight of in his review mirror, her long copper hair fierce against the bright morning. The joggers remained a constant thing in a world that seemed ever more rickety.

The light changed and he eased his car forward. Five, seven, twelve cars turned off Roscoe and onto Balboa, then . . . red again. Northridge was residential as Los Angeles neighborhoods go, meaning more than two blocks of houses existed between main thoroughfares. Still, on weekdays, thousands of people traversed those thoroughfares at the same time, making for a twenty-minute mile each morning and every damn night. What else to do but gaze at strangers?

The joggers passed on opposite street corners, the red-head running across the Wendy's driveway, while the blonde sprinted through the 7-11 parking lot. The copper-haired girl's ponytail flipped and whirled like a gymnast's ribbon, blazing against her black bra.

Tyson had never seen her in anything but black and her T-shirts depicted skulls and monsters. But today she clutched her shirt in her fist, allowing Tyson to once again marvel at the incongruous masterpiece on her back: a tattooed angel taking flight, lovely as any Michelangelo.

The seraph's wings dazzled in gold-tipped white, her gown an open-sky blue. The angel's hair matched the runner's, billowing down the length of the runner's back. Tendrils of copper showed below the woman's black sports bra. Tyson had seen the jogger, and, in the scorching summer months, her remarkable tattoo, nearly every workday for two years now. The drawing captivated him equally with each viewing. But today its ethereal charm lasted only moments, eclipsed by concern for an old friend.

Encludsmo Stuckhowsen had phoned the night before. They saw each other seldom now, with Encludsmo's former annual holiday visits having been reduced to phone calls a couple years back. Thus a call in late summer made Tyson anticipate something afoul. He hadn't been wrong.

His friend, an award-winning PhD scientist, was living in a condemned house beneath a freeway overpass. Worse, the man's bank account was depleted to the point where even this dubious shelter might be taken from him. An insultingly inappropriate lifestyle for a man so brilliant.

Tyson had gone through his inventor friend's current projects and sent Encludsmo to his own employer, the peculiar engineering firm Survivanoia. The company was expanding their research department, so Encludsmo's chances of employment in some capacity seemed good. But Encludsmo's living conditions concerned Tyson. Should he invite his friend to stay with him? Could Encludsmo survive in Northridge?

Then there was the awful advertisement Encludsmo had shown him. . . .

A horn sounded and Tyson realized the light had changed. He responded appropriately, turning onto the freeway ramp, then waited there for another stoplight to allow him access. His drive to work was "in the right direction," meaning out of the Valley. On the opposite side of the freeway, cars streamed south in a thick ribbon of gleaming metal. By now, 7:30, they no longer flowed but crept. Head south, young office slaves.

But Tyson headed north.

A mere twelve minutes from the time he hit the freeway, he pulled into his company's generous parking lot, where corrugated steel roofs protected the employees' cars from the worst of the sun's vicious heat.

SURVIVANOIA, a creepy-lettered sign above the entranceway said: PURVEYORS OF THE POST-APOCALYPSE. Despite his admiration for the company, office jobs didn't generally agree with Tyson. It seemed to him that corporate cultures spawned the same cliques as high school. Cubicles had replaced the classrooms and managers the teachers. But a dress code still prevailed—polo shirts and khakis; jeans on Friday with loafers.

And just as in high school, Tyson ignored it, choosing instead a dark linen dress shirt and a pair of Timberland hiking boots, worn under crumpled earth-tone corduroys. He kept his unruly hair at mad scientist length and still wore glasses when even his optometrist had done corrective surgery on him.

He passed through the retina scan and an angular metal sign in the foyer informed him that THE REVOLUTION WAS YESTERDAY. Another said ARMAGEDDON IS OVER ... WE LOST. He rolled his thumb over a scanner to enter the elevator, reminded as always of *Star Trek*. On his floor, the second, the door opened silently to a cool blue sea of cubicle walls and filing cabinets. His department—customer service—was farther down, its walls and cabinets sea foam green.

Harker, Chaz, and Julio worked from five until two, EST business hours, and so were always there when Tyson arrived. Upon spotting him, they lunged down the cubicle aisle, a three-headed six-legged monster.

"We have a new ... girl," sniggered Harker.

Chaz followed suit: "Yeah, maybe you can show her the ropes."

"I'm telling you," complained Julio in his slight Spanish accent, "it's weird. Like a hooker wearing sneakers."

Tyson snatched his UCLA mug from his tidy desk. "Can you at least let me get coffee before you start with the goon squad routine?"

"You don't understand," Harker giggled.

"Yeah, Melvina is not your everyday girl."

Julio made a face and wandered back to his cubicle. "Even the name is phony. I think we're being punked or some shit."

Tyson squinted against the tightness in his forehead, predicting a headache. "Melvina?"

As if summoned, a voice responded, gravelly. "That's me! I'm new." A flutter of lavender and yellow streaked through the cubicle alley, an outstretched arm seeming to pull it forward. Melvina snatched Tyson's hand and pumped it like she was filling a water bucket.

Melvina did not walk with a sway or a roll in the hips. Melvina was not effeminate, not small in stature, no nervous first-day giggles. Tyson was hard-pressed to find anything feminine about Melvina. He saw stubble on Melvina's chin. But then caught a certain twinkle in Melvina's eye.

"Miguel says to come see you about getting trained," Melvina told Tyson.

"Oh? Oh! Yeah. How about some coffee for starters?" Tyson held up his mug.

"Great! I'll get my cup and meet you in the breakroom."

Melvina strode off. Julio leaned on his cube entrance, frowning. Chaz and Harker doubled over in silent laughter, slapped each other on the back. "Better close your mouth there, Professor."

"Or Melvina might stick something in it!"

Tyson glared silently at the lot of them, lest he say something irrecoverable. He still had to work with these people.

Of course, they misinterpreted his silence.

Harker's eyes widened. Chaz's mouth formed an O.

"We didn't—"

"—not our gag—"

"—started this morning—"

"Go ask Miguel."

"Yes, ask me." Miguel, all five-feet-seven of his skinniness, stood with his arms crossed and a regretful smile on his handsome Hispanic face.

"Who's training the new person?"

Miguel nodded. "Come with me, Professor."

Tyson followed Miguel, sighing inwardly at the predictable nickname. He supposed they meant it as a compliment—after all he had a PhD in languages—but on bad days it only drove home the LA-mortgage worth of student loan debt and his inability to maintain a job.

Once in the safety of his glassed-in office, Miguel spoke in the gentle-but-firm tone people usually reserved for relatives. "I know it's probably awkward for you," he said. "But just be diplomatic. Melvina's credentials are fantastic and she was hand-picked. She identifies as a woman. Treat her accordingly."

Tyson squinted again. "Can I ask—"

"No. Don't ask, just do, and do right. It's not a big deal, don't make it one."

"Can I ask about an unrelated topic?"

"Depends on the topic."

"Did you see the ad in the *Bi-Weekly*? On Sunday?"

Miguel nodded. "The class-action business for the people whose relatives died of Flower Flu? Don't worry about it."

"Don't worry about it?"

"We've been sued before." Miguel waved a hand, dismissing the entire legal system. "It won't go anywhere. We're certainly not planning on downsizing."

Tyson wanted to know if it were true, the claim that his company was withholding the cure to a deadly virus that killed people in a violent, torturous way. Flower Flu purportedly had been derived from the Venus flytrap and manifested in the way of autoimmune diseases, so that the body digested itself from the inside out. For some reason, unknown or at least undisclosed, the disease seemed to target Hispanics, though New

Orleans had experienced an outbreak shortly after the virus manifested in Los Angeles.

Why would a company purposefully withhold the cure to something so nasty? And if it weren't true, why wouldn't they respond immediately to accusations of such criminal negligence?

Were Tyson the boss, this question would have consumed him. No work would be completed, certainly no new employees hired, until he had answers. But Miguel didn't seem to know and quite obviously didn't care.

So Tyson spent the day as he did with all the new hires: trotting Melvina around, introducing everybody. "This is Melvina. She is new in sales." He tried not to catch anyone's eye and ignored the double-takes and stuttering.

Melvina either didn't notice or did a great job pretending, and instead barraged Tyson with friendly questions: *How long have you worked here? What* exactly *do they make? What exactly do you do? Do you like it?* They were well-meaning but, like his "Professor" moniker, made Tyson uneasy. Especially that last one.

His wife's rocket lab supplied some product to Survivanoia, and she'd suggested the place to him for possible employment after he'd quit his third translating job and been fired from Berlitz. Tyson just couldn't be interested in French or Spanish. Russian had lost its appeal once he got Cyrillic down pat.

He was a purist regarding languages, interested only in those like Encludsmo's, with no traceable roots or origins and no sister languages. The obvious place for him was a university—those final bastions devoted to curbing the human hunger for an answer to *why*. But so far none of the local universities had had openings, and Annie's career was not something Tyson would ever ask her to sacrifice.

So he worked for this odd place, whose perverse humor, at least, granted him a crooked smile. They sold gadgets and novelties for profit to pay for the real science. They developed, manufactured, and distributed their CWG line—Constant War Gear. Items like bulletproof cat and dog vests, radiation-resistant jogging suits, gas masks and barbed wire in fashion colors, as well as more practical things such as radiation pills and sensors.

Similarly, the company designed and sold a furniture line, HABITAT, which included, among other things, sofa coffins, panic beds (*why waste an entire room when your bed can do the job?*), and tables sized from nightstand to dining room that performed a cornucopia of tasks, including filtering your water and alerting you to poisons or allergens in your food (*personally programmable!*).

Tyson acknowledged the world view required to market such things. The hardcore research, though, was largely kept under wraps and instilled in him admiration and wonder. The West Nile Virus and Avian Flu vaccines had been developed by Survivanoia's research teams.

Currently, he knew, they were working on Dense Food, nutritionally-concentrated rations to fight starvation. Unlike Nomnasto, whose genetically-modified staple foods were developed for profit, Survivanoia's science, the real science, seemed guided by humanitarianism. Perhaps even—dare Tyson think it?—compassion.

"I like what they do here," he told Melvina and left it at that.

He led the new hire to the courtyard, where Melvina gasped at the garden and Tyson had to admit he'd been stunned when he'd first seen it as well. The courtyard was housed in the U formed by the building. The office/production facility had been constructed recently, as specially designed by Survivanoia engineers. The layout, a horseshoe with the hallway running the center of each wing, ensured that every workspace had sunlight.

The square was fashioned after a Persian garden: laden with fruit trees, adorned with a shallow pool in the center, and home to a handful of strutting peacocks.

Melvina put a hand to her chest when they entered it, and said in a reverent, husky whisper, "My god, it's gorgeous!"

They wandered in silence for a while. The thick scent of sweet roses and the crisp fragrance of crisp lilies made Tyson almost light-headed. He sensed his breath slow, felt the soothing cool of the garden embrace him, an organic relief much more gentle and calming than the smacking, utilitarian cold of an air conditioner.

Melvina whispered again, "I can't even hear the freeway."

Tyson paused, listened. Heard the cooing of the colorful birds, the rustle of lizards he knew were there but never saw.

"You're right," he said. "It's spooky."

"It's like a movie set! Or, or a house in Beverly Hills, or someplace like that. I can come here every day?"

Tyson smiled, pleased that someone else appreciated the place. "Both the cafeterias have entrances. Most people seem to forget about it in a few months."

"I won't!" Melvina promised. "I'll work out here if I can."

Tyson left the new employee under a fig tree with a stack of reading material.

Back at the cubes, the boys were winding down to leave. Harker played his daily round of Minesweeper while Chaz answered email. The area reeked of fast food and Julio sucked soda from a FUIE cup with its snarling star.

Julio noisily sucked air through his straw. "Settle a bet, Professor. Which bathroom does Melvina use?"

Tyson sighed. "How should I know?"

"It's the one by the photocopier," Harker said, as a mine exploded and ended his game. "Isn't it?"

Chaz snickered. "Figures. The newly-installed handicapped, unisex toilet. You'd think we knew he was coming!"

"She," Tyson corrected.

They ignored him.

"You owe me lunch, though, don't you?" Julio tossed the empty cup into his trash can.

"Maybe they get money for hiring freaks like that," Harker mused. "You know, like how you get a bonus for hiring the handicapped?"

"Like this company needs more money," Chaz scoffed.

"Well, why else would they hire him?"

"Her," Tyson corrected. Again. *These* guys were who Miguel needed to talk to, to tell to be diplomatic.

"They say it's the new company president," said Julio.

Tyson's curiosity overrode his annoyance. "What's the new president?"

"All the weird stuff that's been going on. The underground wing being built for R and D—"

Tyson dismissed that. "Have you seen any digging? That's just gossip."

"—the virus that we cured but won't release—"

"That's a media contrivance."

"—and she threatened Geo."

Tyson waved that away, too. "Geo deserves to be threatened. If it happens enough, maybe he'll turn into a human being. Besides, she also got us the new benefits package, right? That's not only normal, it's positive."

"What about the clown suit meetings?"

"Okay, yeah. That's a little weird," Tyson conceded to the recently confirmed-by-witness rumor that for quarterly meetings the managers were now required to dress in clown suits.

Harker picked his nose with a tissue-covered finger. "Did you know that her Hummer has rattlesnake seats?"

"Whoo-wee!" said Chaz, "I do like the kinky girls!"

"Did you know we're being sued?" Julio's knowledge of this surprised Tyson.

"Because of her?" he asked.

"I dunno. Some cure we supposedly have. For that Flower Flu? Where you wake up blind?"

Chaz tossed his hands in the air. "That's what I just said!"

"That's some scary shit, man. I hope we're not holding back any kind of cure for that fucking disease."

Harker's eyebrows squinched together. "We have biologists here?"

"They chain them up in the basement." Tyson managed not to roll his eyes.

"Well how am I supposed to know?"

"You work here!"

"Fine, then is it true? Professor? Are we withholding some lifesaving cure developed by enslaved biologists?"

The question caught Tyson off guard. *Was* it true? Who was this Baroness, this seemingly insane new company president? Could she be taking the corporation in the ugly, but profitable, direction of so many pharmaceutical companies?

"I'll bet it's true," said Julio, halting Tyson's reverie. "I'll bet you *lunch* it's true."

"I actually think what Ty said, it's a media conspiracy."

"Contrivance."

"Whatever. You're on. Then we'll be even, bitch!"

Tyson envied them their levity. He wondered how they'd go about finding out . . . if they'd expect him to investigate for them. He concurred with Julio: he too hoped they weren't holding back any kind of cure for that fucking disease.

* * *

Antoinette, Tyson's wife, was already out back grilling steaks by the hot tub when Tyson got home. He watched her tuck a lock of chin-length, chestnut brown hair behind her right ear before jabbing the thick slabs of meat with the BBQ fork, flipping them against the grill to sizzle and spit.

"You're home early." He slid his hands around her waist. She tilted her head and he kissed her neck, happy that she was plump again, done with that stupid dieting business. He preferred her with a little belly. He'd been just the tiniest bit disappointed when the wedding pictures came back; she was so beautiful with her heart-shaped face and her big blue eyes, but just a shade too thin in his opinion. He liked her better now.

Tyson nuzzled his wife's neck. "What's the catch?"

"We go into lockdown tomorrow."

"Testing your rocket already?"

Annie nodded. "We'll be celebrating if it works and holed up if it doesn't." She worked for Jack Parson's Labs and headed the design team engineering some new type of hybrid fuel rocket that Tyson didn't understand. Still, he gloated inwardly and not for the first time that his wife was a real-life rocket scientist.

"Where's Zoe?"

"Zoe is over at Rachel's house."

"The one with the pool?"

"Bingo. And she phoned that she would like to eat there and spend the night, to which I said yes and no respectively."

"Uh-oh, no sleepover? What happened?"

"First, it's a weekday, and I frown on that."

Tyson rolled his eyes. "I don't know about this year-round school thing. Shouldn't she have a summer?"

"That's irrelevant, because she doesn't. Welcome to California. And she brought home a C on her science exam. I know it's only second grade, but I'm a scientist. I can't. No. At least a B, I told her. So she'll be home by dark. How about you?"

Tyson didn't mention the Flower Flu or the class action. These were too horrific. Instead, he told her about Melvina, who was merely problematic.

Annie raised an eyebrow. "I don't see a problem at all. If she says she's a she, who is anyone to say otherwise?"

Tyson agreed, but, "I just don't think she's . . . *trying* very hard."

Annie laughed. "Oh my god, Tyson! That's maybe worse than if you were just appalled by the entire concept. It's so . . . judgy!"

"You think *I'm* judgy, you should hear the boys."

"I'd rather hear German opera."

"I *like* German opera!"

"And I don't judge you for it."

Tyson rolled his eyes.

Annie kissed him. "The important thing is: does Melvina do a good job? Is she kind to animals and does she leave a decent tip? Those are the things that matter in this life."

"I know that! I'm not saying I care. I just don't understand is all."

"So just accept. Trust me, it's easier."

"From a scientist, no less."

"Not too much of a scientist, apparently, given that my child is practically failing second-grade science."

"Maybe she's going to be a writer. Then you'll have to just accept it." He winked at her.

"You're right. Let's drink too much bourbon and climb into the hot tub. Maybe I'll call and tell Zoe she can sleepover after all."

* * *

"Do you think people think they're talking to a woman?" Chaz yawned openly, reminding Tyson of a corpse.

Tyson howled inwardly. *Why is this even still a concern of yours? Don't you have a hobby you could talk about? Or a TV show? Or maybe you could just SHUT UP!*

But the words would be lost on his coworkers. He responded mildly, "If she answers their questions, who cares?"

He'd been avoiding the boys since Tuesday, when they'd sung "Devil with a Blue Dress On," every time Tyson came in earshot, as prompted by Melvina's multi-blue tank dress and matching shawl.

Three weeks had sped by. Melvina took to the phones fearlessly and with ease. She was bright and friendly, caught on quickly, and was humble enough to admit when she didn't know something.

The issue of the mysterious class action and the Flower Flu vaccine had been forgotten, and the boys were back to more important things.

"Plans for the weekend?"

Harker grumbled, "Ahh, my kids wanna see that new animated thing."

"Yeah, mine too." Chaz's tone matched his friend's. "But I'm making the wife take 'em."

"It's not bad, actually," Tyson said, rolling his chair into the cube aisle. "I enjoyed it. Zoe loved it. She jumped when the crows attacked, giggled at everything the blue jays did—"

Chaz rolled his eyes. "Yeah, yeah. Your life *is* a goddamn Disney movie. What about you, Julio?"

Julio grinned. "I thought I'd go see the animated thing, too."

Harker shot a paper clip at him. "You bastard! When are you going to settle down like the rest of us? You think you can just go on having hot hoochie sex till you die?"

"That's right!" Chaz pointed an accusing finger. "It's time to have some kids and buy a house you don't like!"

Harker gawked at him. "You don't like your house?"

Tyson rolled back into his cube. Their familiar litany bored him. He gazed at his photograph of Annie from the week they'd spent in Wildwood, New Jersey. Zoe couldn't get over the saltwater taffy or the suckers, wound like braided rugs, as big as her head.

Behind him, his office mates fell into bitter laughter. Tyson wished his phone would ring. Instead, Harker popped his head over Tyson's cube wall. "Chaz is food slave today. You want anything?"

"I'm good, thanks."

He opened his lunchbox and proudly displayed his sandwich.

Harker smirked. "Your wife packs your lunch?"

"Only on Fridays."

Chaz's head came over the cube wall. "That's nice. Kinda weird. But nice."

Tyson gazed from him to Harker. "Did you ask Melvina?"

Chaz slid back out of view.

"You work with him," Harker countered. "You ask him."

"Her," Julio corrected.

Harker fell into his usual giggle fit.

Tyson swore at him.

"C'mon, Professor! You think Melvina looks like a woman?"

Tyson hesitated. Did he?

It had been three weeks now. And come to think of it, that cinnamon-musky aftershave had been replaced with something lavender. There seemed to be make-up involved now and hair products, maybe? There *was* still, sometimes, the hint of a five o-clock shadow. And those gaudy dresses hanging awkwardly from Melvina's fading-linebacker body.

Some people did not, in fact, have the ability to hold two opposed ideas in mind at the same time and still retain the ability to function. Tyson sometimes worried that he was one of them. But, as long as he didn't over-think it, actually, Melvina's persona no longer seemed incongruent with the pronoun.

But *some*times, words speak louder than actions.

A week—the week Annie was out of town, down in Florida, awaiting the re-entry of her successful prototype hybrid rocket, and Zoe was with her grandparents—and a half later. Tuesday. Lunch. He couldn't even blame the boys—they'd gone out without asking if he wanted anything. So he visited the Survivanoia cafeteria.

"What a spread!" Melvina was saying to some awkward fellow from production. "I just started eating in here last week. I had no idea it'd be so good!"

Tyson stepped in line just behind Melvina, who scooped a mountain of homemade macaroni and cheese onto the cafeteria tray. Tyson reached for the salad tongs, smiling at Melvina's enthusiasm. "Careful, that stuff will put hair on your chest."

That's how simply it happened. A casual, silly joke. Something he would have said to any other woman and it would have been funnier for the irony.

Melvina didn't take it that way.

As during a car wreck, when everything seems to slow, Tyson saw every crease and wrinkle as Melvina's face contorted into a mask of betrayal-fueled animosity. The plastic tray and its mound of mac and cheese hit Tyson dead in the chest. Melvina, to Tyson's dismay, started *crying* before she spun and *click-clack*ed away in her kitten heels. Then the spell broke and Tyson grew aware of the laughter and mockery surrounding him.

"Tone deaf" was the phrase Miguel used. Not his word. "Not Melvina's either," Miguel was quick to note. "A group of young engineers has filed a petition against you." It seemed one of them had found Melvina crying in the bathroom and the rest had witnessed the triggering event. Melvina blamed hormones. The engineers were not so forgiving.

Tyson didn't fight it. He opted out of any Performance Improvement Plans, having a long and mostly bad history with such programs. Instead, Tyson quietly packed his desk and left his fifth job since graduation.

* * *

At roughly noon on Wednesday, Tyson's phone rang, pulling him from his TV-and-tortilla-chip-induced stupor. He wasn't able to find the receiver before his voicemail picked up. Once the stuttering dial tone indicated a message, he checked it: Encludsmo's rough English came through, shouting as if he thought the machine were far away. But then Tyson heard the background and realized his friend was calling on a cell phone.

This concerned Tyson. All of it. He'd just seen Encludsmo yesterday, stopping there before heading home. Encludsmo had been confused about how to use his voicemail and was awaiting an answer from Survivanoia on the purchase of one of his inventions. For his friend to call him again so soon meant something was amiss. The Doctor seldom used even a conventional telephone. He didn't own one. When he needed to make a call he made use of the phone at the Romanian restaurant he frequented. Where had he acquired a cell phone? And why?

"I have left living under the overpass," Encludsmo's message said. "I am fine, do not worrying. I will phone when I am again alive somewhere."

What the hell did all that mean?

Tyson put on clothes and hit the freeway.

The first indication something was amiss was the billboard. It was gone. Not blank or changed—collapsed. Encludsmo had resented the billboard, a banal salute to American cheese exclaiming simply PUT CHEESE ON STUFF! Its dimensions had exceeded those of The Doctor's house.

A dirt road which The Doctor had blasted out himself led Tyson underneath the freeway, where the 110 and 105 met. At the end of the road, half obscured by tagger symbols, had just yesterday sat a dumpy box with boarded up windows serving as The Doctor's home.

Not wanting to return to an empty house after having been fired, Tyson had come here instead. He'd met Encludsmo's new watchdog, chatted for a while, and reminded him how to check his voicemail—for which Encludsmo borrowed a phone—in case Survivanoia had called with an offer.

Encludsmo had surprised Tyson by speaking of the Baroness with admiration, describing her as having presence, as "a tree on fire." Poetic words from his logic-ruled friend. But today the house lay flattened under the giant cheese sign.

As Tyson stood gaping at the rubble, a white Jeep-like vehicle came to a creaky halt at the top of the embankment. Tyson frowned at it. Unbelievably, it was a mail truck.

A broad-faced man with a thick, black pompadour that made Tyson jealous came trotting down the hill. "You the occupant?"

"Friend of the occupant."

"Good enough." The young Filipino flashed a perfect smile and thrust a letter and a cushioned mailer at Tyson. "Like what you've done with the place," he said, then jogged back up the shallow hill and restarted his rattling Jeep.

Tyson stared after the mail truck until he could no longer hear it. Only the items in his hand convinced him that he wasn't dreaming. He peered at them, saw the mailer carried Survivanoia's return address, and the letter was from Encludsmo's sister Lucretia. He then committed a felony and opened them.

The package from Survivanoia contained scribbled notes, some of them on napkins in illegible script Tyson recognized as Encludsmo's. There was a cover letter from a Sydney Scalinescu, which Tyson scanned and understood that his friend had been turned down, though not by the Baroness. Did Encludsmo know this?

Lucretia's letter was a single page, one side, her writing a more flowing version of Encludsmo's. Unlike her brother, Lucretia spoke good English, or at least wrote it. The letter contained flight information—dates and times. Apparently she was visiting. Tomorrow.

So Tyson's friend was missing, possibly dead, and said possibly-dead friend's sister was on her way for a holiday. Oh man oh man oh. . . . Tyson did what he always did in a crisis: he called his wife.

* * *

"He wouldn't have phoned you if he were dead," Annie told him. Reasonably. "He told you he was fine. Just wait. He'll tell you where he's at once he gets settled."

"And the sister?"

"That's tricky. Was he supposed to pick her up? I mean, he's got no car."

They decided Tyson should meet her plane.

Then he told Annie about his job. He dreaded it. "Don't make fun of me." He pouted, feeling embarrassed and guilty.

"Oh baby. You know I won't."

But sometimes she did. She never got mad, though, ever, when he was fired. And she didn't this time either. She thought it was hilarious.

"*Hair* on your chest?" She laughed until she gasped for breath and complained that her sides hurt. "I do regret," she told Tyson, "that I won't get to meet Melvina at your work picnic."

Annie's humor buoyed him up through the next afternoon. He started down to LAX at 3 p.m. on Thursday to meet Lucretia's 5 o'clock flight. LA's rush-hour airport traffic is enough to make a nun find a rifle and a bell tower, but Tyson reminded himself (repeatedly) that it was for his friend.

When he got there and checked the flight number she'd written, it didn't even appear on the board. He stood in line at the service counter for the better part of an hour only to have an attractive, if weary-looking, woman tell him sorry but this was a morning flight.

So much for Lucretia's good English.

That meant she'd had fourteen hours in the city alone, during which time she'd probably discovered the crushed shell of her brother's house. What now? Tyson had no idea how to find a stranger in a city as big as Los Angeles. He'd already called his wife once, and she had long ago in their relationship relegated him to one crisis per week.

What were his options? Phone LAPD? Ha! In this town 911 put you on hold. LAPD didn't have time to deal with a lost foreigner. Unless she posed a threat.

He ended up back at the demolition site that had been Encludsmo's house. Did it appear picked over? Encludsmo and Lucretia came from an obscure country whose inhabitants cared not who was in charge but only that the bombing stopped. Lucretia might very well have a stomach for picking through burned out edifices. Tyson, however, did not.

He sighed, irritated by his own inability. He supposed the thing to do was to follow Lucretia's probable trail. He knew Encludsmo had written to his sister about his favorite restaurant, a Romanian place, to which he had walked. So it seemed logical that Lucretia would have made said eatery her next stop.

Tyson had visited the Romanian place with Encludsmo, but couldn't recall its name; it had no sign. An odd building housed it though—a long white box with a sharp-peaked roof—and this he identified. Inside proved cool and cozy, the hostess as charming and kind as he remembered, and Tyson decided to have a meal before he harassed the staff with questions about his friend.

While he was waiting on his plateful of organ meats, munching an appetizer of sweet bread and overripe cheese and enjoying their unique black vodka, his cell phone rang. Encludsmo!

Wrong.

No number displayed, which spooked him.

"This is Baroness von Worthington," she told Tyson after confirming his identity. "I'm trying to get in touch with Encludsmo Stuckhowsen."

"You and me both!"

A pause. "This is a complicated situation, isn't it?"

What the hell was she talking about? "Sure is."

"Best to meet in person, I think."

"Fine."

"Still, it would be nice for his sister to know where he is. She's here, you know."

Tyson stifled a sigh, afraid of losing the leverage he seemed to have. "He's okay, tell her that."

A silent paused answered; the Baroness must have muted the phone. A moment later she came back on line and decreed to Tyson: Ishmael's coffee, 6:00 the next morning.

"Fine."

* * *

Ishmael's—"Our Coffee's Not Good But It's Strong!"—opened at 5:00 and kept up with patronage until 7:00-ish when the line typically stretched out the door. Its South Valley location made Tyson wonder where the Baroness lived. He'd expected a café either near Survivanoia or somewhere in Brentwood. The Baroness was assuredly the Brentwood type.

Curious about his friend's sister, he had hoped to meet Lucretia, but he found the Baroness sitting at a window table alone. "I didn't see a need to get the girl up at such an hour," she explained. "She's a night person."

She sipped something iced that smelled caramel sweet. Or maybe the Baroness herself gave off that tantalizing scent; she certainly looked fantastic. Her tailored duster came to her knees over a black crushed-velvet pantsuit. Gold subtly flecked the variegated gem-tone blue duster, giving the illusion that perhaps the jacket had been formed from lapis lazuli. The blue set off her fiery hair, which she wore in a soft, complicated braid ending in a fishtail below her hips.

Tyson immediately understood Encludsmo's poetics and further recognized the Baroness as the type of woman Annie always admired. "There goes a woman without a single pair of big cotton jobs in her underwear drawer," she'd say.

Without delay, he purchased coffee and sat across from the Baroness, dumping sugar into his cup while the steam fogged his glasses. "I don't know what I was thinking buying hot coffee," he babbled. "It's been so hot outside lately you'd think I'd know better."

"It's August in Los Angeles. We can skip the small talk. Besides, you're too smart."

Tyson felt himself blush. "What makes you think that?"

"You're an American who speaks Luci's native tongue."

So the sister was Luci now. Well, he could comprehend that; something about the Baroness put him instantly at ease—in the dangerous way of opiates.

"Encludsmo's English was never good," he explained. "His advisor sent him to my department to improve his English. But I was more interested in learning his language. I wanted to communicate better with him, have conversations—we had a lot in common. And his language is interesting to me, since it's challenging."

"As opposed to?"

"French, which is just like Spanish, which is just like Italian. Or all the Germanic languages or anything Cyrillic, right? You get the heart of one, you get the gist of them all."

The Baroness stirred her icy drink. "Just how many languages do you speak?"

"Seven."

"How many if you don't lump them together?"

Tyson, never comfortable in the spotlight, ran a hand through his hair and stared at the table. "Seventeen."

"Nothing on your resume indicated this."

"It was irrelevant."

"This is the era of globalism. Everything is relevant."

Tyson squinted at the table some more, trying to determine just what his former company president was getting at and how to respond intelligently.

The Baroness saved him. "I know Miguel fired you from tech support," she said. "But I have other departments that could use a translator. And super-genius scientists are always welcome." She slid her card across the table. "You said you expect your friend to call. When he does, ask him to contact me. If I get him, I'll come get you too."

"Is this blackmail?"

"No, it's a bribe. Is that a problem?"

He looked at her face now, into her amazing violet eyes which he suspected could lie convincingly. He frowned, gulped some too-hot coffee. He understood that he had the upper hand.

"Did you hire Melvina?"

"Yes."

"Why?"

"I have my reasons. They don't include getting anybody fired."

"I did nothing but stand up for her. I didn't have a problem with Melvina."

The Baroness shrugged. "The world judges us by our words. But the universe judges us by our actions."

Tyson gazed at her. His eyes hooded. "Why do you need Encludsmo so badly?"

The Baroness sat back in her chair, met his gaze, bit her crimson lip like some femme fatale. "Let me tell you a story," she said. "My father is a winemaker. He owns three vineyards. At one time he owned four."

"In 1986, in Moldova, Gorbachev ordered hundred-year-old vineyards to be systematically eradicated. When news that this would happen reached my father, he traveled there to stop it. Of course he could not. His friends later told me that he sat in the middle of his desecrated fields and wept, not for himself but for Mother Russia and Moldova and Georgia as well, for their jointly defiled histories.

"But some vineyards remain, they survived. Why not his? It is rumored that the director of Ukraine's Magarach Wine-Making Institute in Crimea hanged himself rather than fulfill the orders to obliterate his ancient vines. My father felt guilty for years that his had been destroyed, until he realized that even if he had hanged himself, it would have done nothing. The soldiers obeyed their command and my father was not informed soon enough to buy them out."

She paused, gazed at the table, took and held a breath then let it out slowly, seeming to force a welling memory back down. "Our country," she continued, "though known today for its wine, does not have hundred-year-old vineyards. *Our* country is known, is *renowned* in the scientific community for its intellectual prowess. Because you are The Doctor's friend, you don't smirk at that."

Tyson shook his head. "Not at all. America makes a greater number of scientific discoveries in a year than all the other countries put together. I know that. But I don't know that people would hang themselves for it. To preserve it, I mean."

"Possibly not, no. Not the average person. But the average person possibly would not sacrifice himself for anything not his own. So, just for the sake of argument, let's forget the *average* person."

Tyson pulled the worn newspaper clipping from his wallet. He unfolded it with care, pressing it smooth against the table, and turned it so it faced the Baroness. "Does your interest in Dr. Stuckhowsen have anything to do with *this*?"

To his surprise, the regal woman smiled. "If only that were our worst problem," she lamented.

"What do you mean?"

"I mean I wouldn't be chasing down an unknown, wayward scientist for a cure we already have."

Tyson mulled her equivocation. "But we're being sued. Or at least we were. Now suddenly we're not?"

She blinked, still smiling.

"It's true, then. And something even worse is true, too. Something you need Encludsmo to solve for you."

Her violet eyes beseeched him, told him clearly she had a much longer, uglier, more threatening story that she couldn't divulge. Finally, she spoke again. "I'm giving you early, distant warning."

* * *

The drive back from Ishmael's brought him to the mall intersection at the same time driving to his job used to, but facing the opposite direction. He'd spent the fifteen or so minutes lost in the vivid imagery of the Baroness's story; a hanged official, determined soldiers, a man on his knees weeping in a burned out field. Were they lies? The woman herself embodied contradiction, simultaneously so grounded yet so wraith like. Permanent, yet otherworldly. Not so much a ghost as a goddess. Who could know?

He stopped for his light and found the copper-haired girl with the angel tattoo running toward him for a change. In his rearview he found the blonde. Both women held their heads high, bodies straight with determination against the smog and the heat and the strain. They passed each other, as they did every morning, but now Tyson had a new perspective and this serendipitous situation granted revelation.

The blonde's yellow, ladder-back tank top covered very little of the tattoo Tyson had never known she had. Just as her clothes changed with the season while the copper-haired girl's seemed to be lifted from Morticia's closet, so contrasted their tattoos.

On the same shoulder, the opposite image: a devil woman, a demon succubus, inked in sickly green and bruisey purple, her batwings as hideous as the angel's were beautiful, and equally painstakingly rendered. The demon leered over the blonde's shoulder, gazing into the distance and seeming just about to head there, to launch up with great clawed feet and feed on some unsuspecting innocent driver.

A strange sense of well-being overtook Tyson. A moment of aha. Like when he'd been struggling to learn algebra and suddenly one day, just when he'd about given up, all the pieces fit together. He could subtract X from both sides and not change the equation. A punk rock girl could have a guardian angel needled into her body, while a cheerful housewife bore the mark of a female beast. A woman could navigate the world with a firm grip and a bit of facial hair.

As he turned onto his street, he noticed that the air felt cooler, realized fall was on the wind, and began to believe that perhaps the world could in fact be saved by this purple-eyed devil. Tyson could simply tell his friend that his company president was in search of him. Relay everything the Baroness had told him and let The Doctor decide what to do about it.

And if the world didn't get saved? Well, Tyson, like the Baroness's father, wouldn't be well-connected enough to bother hanging himself.

SURVIVANOIA

II

(Departures)

Cracked Looking Glass

The Comic Who Couldn't Laugh

Rough Passage for Biiiig Mac Daddy (Part 1)

CHAPTER 3

Vonnie Upchurch couldn't turn her head, so she could only see the nurse who was changing her eye tape in her peripheral vision. Vonnie's eyes couldn't blink, so the nurses had to put these horrible sticky drops in them and then tape them closed. Only between tapings did Vonnie get to see anything.

She recognized the voice, though, and had seen the woman's face before—striking, even at a good ten years senior to most of the other nurses. She had the thick, black wavy hair for which Vonnie had always envied Filipino women.

The nurse finished taping her eyes and patted Vonnie's arm. "There you go, *balasang*." She stood and Vonnie heard her swish across the floor in her near-silent shoes.

The nurse made friendly chatter with the assistant, a Spanish-speaking girl Vonnie knew to be heavyset with big brown eyes. She heard the meds cart roll by in the hallway and it occurred to her that her hearing had intensified.

"Is this that poor famous girl?" So the meds nurse was new. Her accent said Filipino; similar to a Spanish accent but more . . . bubbly.

"Yeah. She's easy."

"Pretty."

"It's a waste."

"Maybe not. Maybe that's her glance backward, and she'll learn from it. You know what they say. *'Ang hindî marunong lumingón sa pinanggalingan ay hindî makararating sa paroroonan.'*"

Vonnie had no idea what this parable meant, but the other nurse responded with a low, skeptical "Mmmm...." Something about the sound—Its resonance? Its doubt?—left Vonnie simultaneously hopeful and lonely.

The nurses all thought Vonnie couldn't hear because she was in a coma. She was in a coma because ten days ago she'd taken a bottle of Xanax and a bottle of some painkiller and a bottle of some unlabeled stuff belonging to her husband which, knowing her husband, was probably illicit. She'd washed all these down with not quite 750 mL of vodka while watching Empty-V's live airing of her husband's concert.

Bagga Chips' newest album, titled *BITCH!*, was comprised of a litany of ferocious hatred set to a heavy metal beat. Over double bass drums and screaming guitars he rapped—or shouted—to the world, or at least his fans, his version of their rocky marriage. She'd watched the performance like a football game, poured the pills into a glass bowl like so much colorful popcorn, and sat in front of the TV swallowing them one by one.

Which was why she now lay pinned to a hospital bed by her own cruel body, unable to move—even to blink or squeeze the hands of crying relatives—but with all senses fully functioning.

God love the nurses, she thought. *God love them for their lack of sympathy.*

But then the voices retreated, they all left for what Vonnie assumed was nighttime, and the floor went deathly quiet. *No pun intended.*

Having nothing else to do, Vonnie mostly thought about stuff. Her life and her place in the world. She felt an odd tranquility for the most part, tinged just slightly by sadness. Sometimes she wished she could read a book or watch a movie. But after the first couple days she resigned herself to her situation and began thinking of her own life in movie form. Where would she start? What single moment defined her?

Two moments. Same scene. Standing on my back porch tugging at my father-in-law's shirttail.

Yeah. For Johnny Cash it was when his brother sawed himself in half. For Edward R. Murrow it was the WWII broadcast from the London rooftop. For Vonnie Upchurch it was pleading with her father-in-law that first summer of her New Jersey marriage, and then again that first summer in LA.

"Please, Dad," she nearly whispers the first time. "Please don't hit your boy."

And the ex-boxer's shoulders were rising and falling with his breath, with his rage. Frankie is a big man, six three, broad-shouldered, ham-fisted. He sets one of his mitt-sized palms against her face.

Vonnie's friend Chloe had called him, knew to call Frankie instead of the police. It is mid-April and still threatening to snow one last time. Vonnie is wearing sweat pants and one of TJ's white shirts—he's still TJ, not yet Bagga Chips—and her feet ache with cold, bare on the concrete stoop.

Frankie's dark brown eyes pity her and he shakes his head sadly. "Baby. That's not how we conduct ourselves in this family."

He kisses the top of her head then tosses open the screen door and lurches into the house before she's even able to return his embrace. Her hand just catches the tail of his stone-grey work shirt.

Chloe stands in the grassy gravel, leans against Frankie's Buick. Her pale blue eyes search Vonnie's face. She's wearing a short red dress and with her curly black hair and black boots she perfectly matches the showy car, a slut-red monster with an engine the size of Vonnie's kitchen.

"I might never forgive you!" Vonnie hisses at her friend.

Chloe steps forward, hesitates, then strides to the foot of the stoop. "There's a fine line between objects and people," she says. "And even finer between animals and people."

"So I should leave him because he got a little frustrated and shoved my dog?"

51

"He hurled your dog through a window! Your *eighty-pound* dog."

Vonnie wraps her arms around herself. She trembles with the need to cry but fights the tears. "He's working a lot, you know? Like, double shifts, three nights a week. And his band has been playing out all the time and he's been trying to fix shit around the house. He needs some sleep, okay? Jocco wouldn't stop barking."

"What happens when it's the baby that won't stop crying?"

"You know I don't want kids."

"They all say that."

"You've known me since kindergarten, I've never wanted kids!"

"You'd have them, though—"

"TJ doesn't want kids either."

"—for Frankie."

As if in apocryphal response, Frankie's voice rages from inside the house and something—big, glass—shatters. The knick-knack cabinet most likely. Full of TJ's high school track trophies, photos of their wedding, and Vonnie's recently-retired bong. They were the inverse bad-boy couple: he was the good one.

Frankie's voice poses impossible questions to his son: "Is this how I raised you? To beat up girls? Are you proud?" TJ's response is inaudible.

Vonnie cringes, shakes harder. The tears finally spill out of her. She stands shaking and sobbing, her breath ragged gasps. Chloe walks up the three steps of the square concrete porch, wraps her arms around Vonnie. Chloe is only a few inches taller, maybe five-six to Vonnie's five-two, but at this moment Vonnie feels tiny. Like a child. She allows herself to be eased to sit on the stoop, despite the cold.

"If I really thought you should leave him," Chloe tells her softly, "I'd be packing your bags. I know TJ is a nice guy. Under all that chrome and broken glass. But if you play long enough at being an asshole, eventually, you know, you become one."

Vonnie sniffles and nods.

"I figured Frankie could sort of . . . realign him. You know?"

Vonnie nodded again.

"Before he realigns you."

Vonnie shook her head. "He wouldn't."

"They all say that."

Silence. Then Chloe's voice is light again. "Remember what my mom used to always tell us?" She imitates her mother's smoke-gravely voice: "You kids'll get hemorrhoids sitting on the cold concrete like that! Get a chair like a normal person!"

Vonnie laughs, glad to be able to, glad for the break in the storm. She laughs and cries all at the same time and snot runs down her face, which Chloe is gracious enough to wipe away with the tail of TJ's shirt.

It'd been Chloe holding her then and it was Chloe holding her now. Every evening she came to the hospital and told Vonnie about her day. "I started at that Survivanoia place today. Inside sales. They sell weird stuff. My favorite so far is the Tin Foil Hat clothing."

She laughs and Vonnie relishes the sound. Chloe always had a contagious laugh.

"You know those poor people who are scared of radio frequencies and mind-control rays? Survivanoia has this line of clothing? Pretty fashionable actually, made with wire-core threads to absorb electromagnetic waves."

She paused and Vonnie envisioned her shrugging just one shoulder, her left, the way she knew Chloe did.

"It's pretty cool there. My boss is *hot*. He looks like . . . you remember that Faith No More band?"

Chloe had loved Faith No More in high school. Vonnie knew her boss must look like the singer.

"He looks like their singer, Mike Patton. And he drinks at work, which I think is hysterical. Oh, I met this guy in line last night at the grocery store. He doesn't have TV either! I was sort of waiting for him to ask for my phone number, but he didn't."

Vonnie wondered why Chloe hadn't asked for his.

"I thought about asking him for his, but I never know if they're married.

Oh, check it out, our company picnic is at Magic Molehill!" Chloe laughed and Vonnie would have joined her if she could. They were not good amusement park people. The last time they'd gone was back in New York, on the Fourth of July.

"Remember last time we went? On the Fourth of July? What were we thinking?"

They'd hoped for light rain so nobody else would go and they'd actually get on the rides but—

"It was like ninety-five degrees and all of frickin' Newark was there? We were talking about how things would be with Clinton gone, and I was reading *Moby Dick*? Even on the rides! Remember? The *one* roller coaster we were like *whooo*!"

And everybody seemed annoyed like they were talking through a movie or something. Yeah. Vonnie remembered.

Every day Chloe came and had these conversations, these monologues. Vonnie wondered what she'd done to be so lucky. Who gets friends like this? Friends who not just read your mind but seem to share it.

But she's not in that second defining scene, Vonnie thought. Chloe had still been in New Jersey the second time Vonnie tugged at her father-in-law's shirttail.

They're arguing, Vonnie and her husband. For a year they've been arguing about everything and nothing. This time they own the house (though it's still tiny) and it stands on the West Coast, and this time it's "Bagga" and not TJ. He's gotten signed and is just about to become famous; you can taste it in the air around him.

They stand—stand-off—in the dining room, where a sliding door leads to the backyard. Her father-in-law is visiting from New Jersey, is smoking a cigarette on the porch. Still a slab of concrete, but the back porch this time, just off the dining room.

Vonnie hisses something at her husband; she won't yell with Frankie around. And suddenly the furniture is upturned, the TV is smashed. Well, she's sure hollering now! And everything slows down, like it does in car crashes and house fires. She feels it before her words finish coming out of her mouth, the break in tension that marks the apex of TJ's black anger. Up comes his arm, crossing his snarling face and there it goes back again. His rough knuckles catch Vonnie's cheekbone. Her head snaps sideways. The force of the blow sends her sprawling.

She sprawls into the dining room chairs with a yelp and clatter. And when she gets up from her knees, it is in the dark shadow of her father-in-law. She bolts to her feet and out the door. He catches her, clutches her to him. Wipes the blood from her face with his denim shirt.

And this time she whimpers, "Frankie, please. . . . Kill him."

These memories flooded Vonnie's mind—TJ's stricken, bruised face the following morning, their counselor-aided trek back to decency, the horrible news of what happened in New York City in September, long nights on the phone to Chloe, and then that final phone call about Chloe's mom. Anyone else would have broken in half. Not Chloe. She was off-kilter when Vonnie helped her move, but even through that obscured lens her optimism showed. She'd chatted with cab drivers and made brownies for the movers.

TJ had once described Chloe as terminally optimistic. Vonnie's favorite example of this happy disease involved them getting stranded in Silver Lake just after Chloe moved west. A forgotten purse? Angry date? Something. As a result, they'd had to walk home nearly seven miles, part of it through the barrio, in heels and club clothes.

Vonnie complained and was also genuinely frightened. But Chloe waved and smiled to the non-English speaking strangers, even the ones with neck tattoos who whistled appreciatively but never advanced, except one, who gave Chloe a big red apple and a big cute smile.

"I'm happy to be able to walk," Chloe said. "You know there's people who can't."

She scored the apple with her thumbnail, paused in her stride just for a moment and cracked it into two neat, red halves.

"Somewhere right now there's a guy in a wheelchair who used to be able to walk and now he can't." She handed Vonnie half of the apple. "He got into a car crash or maybe fell down the stairs and he'll never walk again, poor bastard, he's gotta roll every place now and some places you can't roll to, no access. On those days you just know he sits in that chair and thinks about when he was whole. I gotta walk seven miles? Gladly."

Gladly.

Vonnie sputtered and choked. She struggled to sit up and her arms moved but couldn't pull her all the way.

Gladly!

A ragged intake of breath then, "Help? Please? Help." To Vonnie it sounded so small but the nurses came running, both of them followed closely by the meds nurse.

"*Balasang ko,* you're awake!" The older nurse pulled Vonnie to her and all that thick black hair covered Vonnie's face. It smelled delightful, like jasmine. The nurse squeezed her with joy. Vonnie went into another coughing fit. She gasped and choked and flailed her arms like a mad-woman. Gladly.

* * *

Vonnie switched the TV's sound off. "All these reporters? They're all saying I killed myself because I was going to have to get a job."

"They're saying you're dead? I got you Roscoe's." Chloe held up the bag and Vonnie could smell the perfect fried chicken. Chloe settled herself on Vonnie's hospital bed and unwrapped the food.

"They're saying I *tried* to cuz of the job. That is complete horseshit!" Vonnie shouted at the television. "I wanted to work. That was part of the problem! He wanted me to lounge around the house in lingerie. Wow, this chicken is good."

"I tried to get the nurses to give you the Kripsy Kreme IV but they wouldn't."

"Did you bring any?"

"Of course. Junkie."

"And then he had the nerve to accuse me of being a whore! He said I was giving it up to whoever came over and why don't I go work in porn!"

Chloe sipped her soda and nodded. "I know."

"Maybe I should have. At least then I'd have some money. You know, of my own. Those chicks make bank."

"I've heard."

"Plus you can do girl on girl, which means no penetration which means less *money*, you know, but no *penetration*."

Chloe giggled around her chicken leg. "It's good to have you back!"

"Thanks."

Chloe gestured to the TV. "What's TJ saying about all this?"

"To his credit, he's refusing to comment."

"That's something."

"At least until his publicist tells him otherwise. That guy's a real prick."

"When can you leave, anyway? I wanna take you to this improv comedy night thing I've discovered."

"I dunno. Psychiatric evaluations or some crap. They say they need to turn me over to somebody. Insulting."

"Okay, but you did try to kill yourself."

"Yeah, there is that." Vonnie suddenly fought tears.

Chloe's voice dropped. "You could have called me, you know." It wasn't an accusation, just a fact. A fact rimmed with hurt Chloe tried to cover.

"I could have called a lot of people."

"I talked to Frankie."

Vonnie sighed audibly. "I can't . . . even look at him. I feel terrible."

"Maybe think about that next time this"—she waved an arm—"crosses your mind."

"But you don't see that when you're down in it. Besides, there's not going to be a next time."

"Good. Anyway, Frankie's on a plane. He'll be here tomorrow."

A long pause while Vonnie picked her chicken clean. "What, uh . . . what did he say exactly?"

"The same thing I did."

"That I could have called him?"

"Yeah. And we both feel like we somehow let you down. Like he didn't email you enough or I didn't hang out enough or . . . whatever."

"Nobody let me down but me." Vonnie looked up and saw Chloe wiping her eyes. "I mean it. And it's not gonna happen again. I mean that, too. This is like my second chance. I'm sure as hell not going to blow it." She tossed a chicken bone into the empty take-out bag. "But I'm not sure what's next. I'm done with TJ, obviously."

"They'd probably hire you at Survivanoia. They're supposed to be getting some new company president in a few months. It's some big coup apparently, the stockholders are all up in arms, but evidently this woman— it's a woman!—she's in tight with the mystery founder-partner. They think she might *be* the mystery partner. And they say she's planning to—"

"None of this helps me, Chloe, I have no experience at anything. I can't even type!"

Chloe sniffled and grinned. "You could learn."

First thing the next morning, Frankie threw his arms around her and clutched her to his billboard of a chest. She instantly felt safe and cared for and valued. How could she have been so stupid?

Two and a half physical-therapy-and-journal-writing-filled weeks later, Chloe wheeled Vonnie to the hospital exit and they ran shrieking like teenagers to Chloe's lemon-yellow Volkswagen Gopher.

"So Frankie is staying?" Chloe asked once they got inside. Vonnie had explained how the doctors had released her into Frankie's custody.

"At least for a while. There's plenty of room at the house."

"What's he gonna do? Frankie's not one to sit around all day."

"Chloe, he drives a cab. He can work anywhere."

"They generally like you to know the place you're driving."

"The Valley is a grid. Frankie is smart."

Chloe considered this, then raised a shoulder and let it drop. "Okay, then. Over the Hill?" she asked, meaning should they leave the Valley and go to Hollywood?

"And far away!"

Chloe put the car on the 101. "What are you going to do now?"

"Let's get drunk!"

"Okay, but I meant in the larger sense."

"I have no idea. But thanks to the wonders of modern chemistry, it doesn't bother me not to know."

"Ah . . . what are you talking about?"

"In order to be released, even into the custody of my father-in-law? I had to convince the doctors that I had returned to a state of reasonable happiness and wouldn't try it again. And to aid this process, they apparently put me on Zoloft. While I was still in a coma! They IV'd me Zoloft!"

"I think the Krispy Kreme would have worked better."

"I agree! But like I said, *err'ting irie now, mon*. Where are we going?"

"Lunch at Wolfie's, shopping on Melrose, then the dinner show at Adlib's. No talk show offers yet?"

"Wolfie's and Melrose? What are we, tourists? Yes, talk show offers, but I'm not interested. I don't want to go on *Queenie* and sob about how mean TJ—"

"Bagga. You'd need to refer to him as Bagga in public forums like that."

"That right there is reason enough not to do it! Who wants to air their dirty laundry like that anyway?"

Chloe snorted. "Bagga Chips got blindingly rich airing your guys' dirty laundry, did he not? Oh, and did you know Adlibs has a new owner? It's much cooler now. And I have to put the heater on now or the car will overheat."

"The heater? Chloe, it's like ninety degrees outside!"

"Ninety-six actually, but the car is broken, I'm sorry. You wanna be stranded? On the Hill?"

"I'm just sayin'."

"I know what you're saying. I'm already well aware. Think I like it?"

Vonnie stuck her head out the window and let the breeze dry the sweat from her brow. "Are we there yet?"

Lunch was always good at Wolfie's. But Vonnie told Chloe-the-cook what she knew was exactly the right thing: "Yours is better." And she meant it.

Shopping on Melrose proved disappointing.

"I recall," Chloe said, stalking back to the car with only one bag, "there was a time when I used to find things here I liked, not just shit I thought I should be seen in."

"You got that shirt from Von Schmidtt."

Chloe gave her one-armed shrug. "I have a weakness for Von Schmidtt."

"It's your boss, isn't it?"

"What?"

"You need to look cute for your boss?"

Chloe glanced at her quizzically over the top of the yellow car. "Did I tell you about Geo?"

Vonnie hadn't yet admitted to anyone that she heard everything while she was "out." And suddenly she found she didn't want to. "You must have." She ducked inside the car. "At some point."

The last time Vonnie had been at Adlibs, the nightclub looked exactly like the renovated bowling alley it was. Graffiti-and-gum-riddled plastic tables sat on damp carpet and only a worn drape separated the lanes from the rest of the club.

All that had changed. She didn't even recognize the entrance. Inside, a young woman offered to take their sweaters and umbrellas—funny!—while another sold them tickets.

"Have you been here before?" she asked, handing them oversized yellow tickets.

"I have," Chloe told her. "But my friend hasn't."

"Adlibs amateur night," the girl chirped, "has a strict pick-a-fight, face-the-spotlight policy. This means that if you are overheard jeering or mocking a comedian, you are expected to go perform yourself. Oh, and the raffle is at the end of intermission now. Enjoy!"

They passed from the lobby to the main room, where a raised stage graced the back wall which had once been the bowling lanes. A fancy, well-stocked bar lined the front wall and midsized round tables, each with its own candle, filled the sloped floor.

"No bad seats!" Chloe picked a table near the back as if to prove her point. "They made the floor like at a movie theatre." She held a hand at an angle.

A waitress appeared and took their drink orders. While they sipped absinthe martinis, Vonnie watched a guy wearing a headset manipulate the curtains around the stage, redefining the space. "That stage is huge."

"Yeah, they do fully-staged productions here now. Oscar Wilde, Neil Simon. All comedies."

The headset guy left and a slender, tall, light-skinned black man strolled onto the newly-intimate stage. He had a happy, crooked grin and slightly bugged eyes, and just seeing him made Vonnie smile.

"I'm Jarvis Brown. Hello."

The audience responded like school children, "Hello Jarvis Brown!"

"I'm certain that by the end of the night I'll know quite a few of you by name, since we always bust *some*body and our motto, of course, is 'if you jeer, you come up here.'"

He held a wide hand out to the audience, who responded, "Hello Johnnie Cochran!"

Vonnie thought of *Rocky Horror*.

"Are we ready?"

Jarvis introduced the first comic, who was funny enough to be entertaining; at least Vonnie thought so after her absinthe martini. "And if you're reviewing the show," the stocky redhead finished, "It's S-H-A-W Shawn. I don't care what you say about me, just please spell my name right!"

A husky woman's voice came from the audience, "Are you sure you can spell it yourself?"

Jarvis was on the stage before the words were out of her mouth. "Who's that? Miss Jackson? I didn't mean to make your daughter cry. But hike your ass up onto this stage, ma'am!"

Miss Jackson was a handsome milk-white woman wearing a red dinner dress. Her ringlet curls matched her throwback humor she borrowed heavily from Mae West. After her were two more men from the stage, not the audience, and one young, skinny heckler who told three jokes as he crept toward the edge of the stage and then escaped. Vonnie laughed so hard, she cried.

"Isn't this awesome?" Chloe howled. "I love this place."

"How'd you hear about it?"

"Oh, one of the string of single-date guys brought me here. I thought it was funny and he found it childish and appalling. That's why we didn't have a second date."

"Clearly a douche."

Of course, this came out just at the moment when the rest of the crowd went quiet. Vonnie gasped, glanced at the stage from where, sure enough, Jarvis Brown grinned back. "We got us a live one, ladies and gents!"

"No no no no no! That wasn't—I was talking about her boyfriend!" She pointed an accusing finger at Chloe.

"I don't have a boyfriend."

"You're not helping!"

Jarvis Brown cocked his head in mock consideration. "Uhmmmm . . . nope! Get your cute butt up here!"

And the audience called out practiced lines. "Tell us jokes or face the rope!" "Don't make us call the comedy cops!" "Get on stage or face our rage!"

"Are they serious?"

Chloe laughed, nodding. "Yeah!"

From the front: "Just get on stage already!"

"I gotta go up there and tell jokes?"

"Sure. You're funny. Or just tell them the truth about TJ. You'll have the room in an uproar."

"Like tell them his real name?"

"Yeah or that he's from Newark!"

The girls fell into shrieking laughter just as the young comic Vonnie had not actually scorned passed their table. "Hope the audience finds you as funny as you find yourselves," he snapped.

Vonnie and Chloe stopped to glance at him, gazed at each other, and laughed even harder. Then suddenly Vonnie was up on the stage. She couldn't see much for the glare of the spotlight. She set her eyes down and to the right, like when a car came at her with its high beams on.

"So, I'm doing stand-up? Because I was kicked out of porn."

This got a laugh. And also a comment. "You're not in porn. You're Bagga Chips' slut wife!"

Her own retort surprised her. "Ex-wife. Please get your facts straight, sir, if you're going to heckle people."

"You're a cock-sucking bitch!"

She blinked at him, then snapped her fingers. "Which is precisely how I got into porn!"

The audience let out a wave of laughter. It rolled through the club and broke against the stage and Vonnie suddenly understood why TJ liked being up there.

"Speaking of Bag *of* Chips," *the enunciation earned some giggles,* "do people think that's his real name? Like, on his birth certificate?" *Louder giggles. Roll with it.* "Like his mother, after sixteen hours of hard sweaty labor, looked down at this squirming bundle of life in her arms and said, 'Bag of Chips! That's my boy! Welcome to the world, Bag!'"

Solid laughter, but shorter than I'd hoped. "His real name, alright? His actual *name* name," *it's all about delivery.* She paused, put a finger to her lips. Then glanced at the audience. "Well it isn't any better, really." *More solid laughter, yeah it's all about delivery.* "It's Thaddeus Jude." *A lot of scoffing, punch it up.* "That's a great name . . . for a monk! Or even a pro golfer. But for an angry, hardcore rapper? Not so much, huh?" *Again that wave. Ride it.*

"That's such a lie anyway, his whole urban image. He sings about being from the projects? He's from New Jersey, alright? The Garden State? How about the Boondocks State? The projects, that's rich. The Blair Witch Projects, maybe! Baby, you're from Newark. Yo?"

Another amazing wave of delight. A few more jokes and then a small red light beside the spot and suddenly the MC stood next to her, looking pleasantly surprised. "I'd say Vonnie definitely needs to come back! Let's give it up for Vonnie Upchurch, ladies and gentlemen!" And they did.

She fumbled her way back to the table where Chloe squeezed her nearly to death. "Ohmigod that was amazing!"

"I need a drink!"

"I figured you would." Chloe pointed at the pale green concoction in a martini glass, of which Vonnie promptly swallowed half.

"Was it cathartic?" Chloe asked.

"The drink or the show?"

Chloe smiled. "That guy that yelled at you? The bouncers came and got him!"

"For real?"

"Yeah, these two guys about—"

"Excuse me." A man no taller than Chloe stepped next to the girls, offered his hand. "Nice bit just now." He was dressed like his tie had gone missing and his salt-and-pepper hair was way too neat, given the late hour.

Vonnie shook his hand. "Are you mocking me? Because they make you go on stage."

"Mocking? No. I see to it that people get on stage, actually." He handed her a business card, crisp and elegant, matte navy-blue words against a cream background. BARRY BROWNSTONE, TALENT REPRESENTATIVE.

Chloe peered over Vonnie's shoulder at the card. "So you're an agent?"

"He sure is." Vonnie suddenly felt quite sober.

"You've heard of me, good." His cell phone rang, sounding like an old rotary phone, and he held up a finger to pause and detain them. "No, no, Eddie, I'm not pressing charges. I haven't even called the police. I'd just like it back." He uttered more reassurances and hung up, tossed an arm in the air. "Tell me: Who steals books?"

Vonnie suppressed a grin. "Uhm . . . bored people?"

"Screw books, they need funny. That's why I need you."

She gave a nervous little laugh. "I'm flattered, Mr. Brownstone. But you're out of my league. I'm not sure what you want."

"I'd like to exploit your schtick in ways you'd probably never think of on your own and make us both obscene quantities of money. Fifteen and eighty-five percent, mine and yours, respectively." Barry's bluntness was hilarious.

Vonnie stared at him for a long moment until she felt Chloe's elbow in her side.

"Yeah!"

"Great." Barry stuck his hand out again. "Call me and plan to come in Monday. Early afternoon. 1:30, 2:00-ish."

CHAPTER 4

"**A**nd you need an image."

"An image?"

Barry glanced up from his jotting, ran a hand through his hair. It framed his face like a mane. "I'm assuming you don't want to spend your entertainment career as Mrs. Bagga Chips. I suggest you get a stylist and go back to your maiden name."

"Upchurch *is* my maiden name."

"Good, I like a client who's responsive." His deadpan delivery, like always, made Vonnie laugh. Everybody found Barry funny except Barry. He never understood why people found him amusing, but he was happy to be a source of happiness.

"Do you just happen to know a stylist?"

"Of course."

"Of *course.*"

"A number of them. Or pick somebody you like and we'll find their stylist."

Vonnie grinned, embarrassed by her suspicion and taken yet again by her agent's authenticity. She sat back in the big round chair that sat opposite his desk and tucked her legs under her. Her Mary Janes rested on the soft shaggy carpet in front of her.

Barry's office reflected its occupant: sparse and utilitarian, yet somehow inviting. A window made up the entire front wall, and from it Vonnie could see Wilshire District from twenty-seven stories above the street. The fluffy carpeting matched the dark grey drapes. Everything else was some designer shade of white; even his desk, made from blond wood, same as the bookshelf. Only his bright red phone broke the pattern like a cherry in a sea of soothing vanilla.

He jotted things into a notebook, had been doing so for nearly forty-five minutes now. The pen, Vonnie noticed, carried the Rotring initial, but the notebook cost maybe a dollar at any drug store.

"Alright, maiden name, check. Here's Nike's card. She seems to be the favorite with the girls." He slid a colorful business card to her across his pale desk. "Next: Which talk shows do you want, which ones will you refuse, and which ones will you do but act like a see-you-next-Tuesday about?"

"Do you really care?"

"Of course I do. I'll try to get more money from the last category."

"And the ones I refuse?"

Barry looked up from his notebook, pen hovering mid-word above it. "You have some you'd refuse?"

"Sure."

He placed the pen alongside the metal spiral of his notebook, folded his hands and blinked at her. "Who?"

"Bob O'Lie-Lee for one."

"Alright. He's politics, but I see you're expressing your principles. Go on."

Vonnie unfolded her legs, slid her stockinged feet back into her shoes. "Hugh Stoic."

"He only does radio now."

"I know, and I don't want to be on the radio with him."

"Alright. Because?"

"I'm a woman."

"So is his head writer. You're also not a stripper and definitely not a

67

victim. I don't handle victims. Hugh is actually quite charming. He's smart like you can't imagine. And he's fond of you. Go on."

"Tarzan O'Doyle."

"Alright. Because?"

"His face is made of wax."

"Not his fault."

"It's still creepy."

"Anybody else?"

"I guess not."

Barry gazed at the desktop for a moment. "Do you *know* anybody else?"

Vonnie laughed. "Yes. I have cable."

Barry unfolded his hands and picked up his pen. "Just checking."

Hugh Stoic's radio show was the first talk show Barry booked her on.

"You're a real prick," she told him.

"Which is why I'm real rich. Trust me."

The entire experience buzzed past her like a roller coaster ride, a good one, the *Whooo!* one.

"Okay," Hugh told her, "when I say, 'You're kind of a see-you-next-Tuesday' you say, 'Well you're kinda dead, bee-octh!' And punch this meat. I'm gonna pretend you punched me." He grinned like a shark, gently hitting the giant red rump roast that sat on the console.

Vonnie scowled at Barry and at the Bagga Chips lyric. "Is this gonna be funny?"

"Trust me." He then demanded of Hugh, "Is this going to be funny?"

Hugh's eyes widened and his mouth fell open. "Barry! I'm scandalized!"

"That meat," he pointed at it, "is too thick to get a sound out of."

"My head is thick!"

"Now that, I'll give you."

"Barry. You know what I mean."

"Did you sound-check the meat? That's all I'm asking."

Vonnie watched the men like a tennis match. "That really wasn't what I meant. Really."

Riding back in the town car, Vonnie played with the radio and left it on some whacked-out call-in show discussing the secret breeding of a mad race of dog men.

"What do I say on the other talk shows when they ask me if I really hit Hugh?"

Barry didn't look up from his scribbling. "You heard the broadcast, right?"

"I *was* the broadcast."

"No. I mean that's what you say to them."

Vonnie frowned, but he didn't see it. "And if they push it?"

"Be vague. Nobody's going to ask you specifically 'Did you punch a chunk of meat?' Also, Hugh said he'd corroborate. His people are telling him it's a good idea. Also, he'll be addressing it before you do."

"Why's that?"

"He's got Bagga Chips on tonight."

"TJ?"

"Yes. Same person, yes."

"You didn't tell me that!"

Barry looked up. "Yes. I just told you right now."

"You know what I mean! You should have told me before."

"Alright. Because?"

"'Cause I wouldn't have gone on! I would have said no! That's like . . . entrapment."

Barry slid his pen inside his notebook's spiral. He balanced the notebook on his legs, folded his hands, and rested them on the notebook. "Entrapment is the act of tricking somebody into committing a crime and then arresting them. I fail to see how that applies here."

Vonnie smiled despite her frustration. Barry: perpetual straight man with the world as his foil. She rolled her eyes. "You know what I mean." But she smiled because she realized she really didn't care.

* * *

Chloe frowned at her car stereo. "Okay, but Barry was the one who said you shouldn't live in the shadow of your former self." She punched a button on the stereo. "You see me pressing the button here, right? And how the station is not changing?"

"Actually, Frankie said that about the shadow. And I think it was more of a boxing analogy. But yeah, Barry is sending me to this Nike so that she can transform me—oh Chloe, I hate this song!"

"Yeah. It's stuck on the classic rock station."

"I'm sorry!"

Chloe punched it off, blew air through her lips. "Anyway, sorry. Transform you . . ."

"Transform me into someone other than Mrs. Bagga Chips."

"So why has he got you in this face off with TJ?"

"I dunno. But the most aggravating thing? Is that it's working."

"If it's working so well how come I'm still driving you around? And you moved out of the big house and into a little condo? You sure this Brownfield guy—"

"Brown*stone*."

"Is he ripping you off?"

"How would I know?"

"Wow, a spot right on Ventura!" Chloe pulled the car against the curb. "What kind of a name is Nike, anyway?"

"Are you kidding? This is Los Angeles."

A bell rattled pleasantly on the glass door when they entered. The chilled air made both women sigh with relief and a petite woman of their age greeted them, smiling.

"Hi, I'm Nike Kwaad, named after the goddess, not the shoe. My parents are from the Netherlands and didn't know any better."

"I guess that answers your question, Chloe." Vonnie watched her friend turn subtly red.

Nike smiled, tucking a piece of her purplish-silver hair behind her ear. "Everybody asks, believe me."

They followed her down a hallway of closed doors that reminded Vonnie of her chiropractor's office. Nike's pine-green dress and black suede boots combined with her hair to make her look like a fairy. Vonnie found this delightful and said so.

"Thanks!" Nike laughed like a wind chime. "Your friend's got a good style, too."

They entered a well-lit room that felt something between a massage parlor and a psychiatrist's office.

"What's so great about her style?" Vonnie pointed at Chloe's green plaid Doc Martens and told Nike: "If it's plaid, she'll wear it."

Chloe shoved her into a big leather chair. "Don't hate." She took the couch, dangling her plaid feet over the edge.

"It's definitive," Nike explained. "That's what we're going to do for you." She sat in the matching leather arm chair.

"I'm not definitive?"

Nike made a cute, apologetic face. "Not really. No."

"Survivanoia makes clothes, you know. None of the stars wear them yet. That'd make you definitive. Not to mention safe from bullets, mad dogs, and tsunamis."

Vonnie turned to the mirror and looked herself over. "I don't understand why I'm not *definitive*, dammit."

Nike ran a hand through Vonnie's shoulder-length locks. "Hair at this in-between length makes you look both older and non-committed."

"I was growing it out."

"I understand. But to project confidence, we need it either past your shoulders or no longer than your jaw."

"You mean extensions?"

"Right. And we need to talk about colors. Again, this brown you've got going on here is indecisive."

"That's my natural color! Nature decided!"

Nike tilted her head and frowned, sympathetic. "I understand. I really do but. . . . Lookit, this whole stylist thing? We're marketing you. And to be marketed, market*able*, Vonnie Upchurch needs to be a recognizable brand. Like three stripes or an alligator or a bubble with eyes and . . . weird . . . centipede feet."

Vonnie's mouth hung open but Chloe laughed and laughed.

"What's so goddamn funny?" Vonnie snapped.

"I think it's supposed to be a scrub brush. Scrubbing bubbles? Scrub brush? Not a centipede." Chloe registered Vonnie's expression. "Oh honey. Whatsa'matter?"

"I don't know if I want my hair long or short and I don't know what color it should be! It used to be blonde and people liked it. Now it's brown and apparently undistinguished. Or some shit."

Nike kneeled in front of her. "Did somebody tell you this would be fun? Cuz it's not. People think that. They think makeovers are a fucking birthday present. Can I just tell you? Nothing will make you feel worse.

"First you walk away from the session feeling like a phony. Then right when you start to get comfortable with this 'new you' you realize, standing in your mismatched bra and panties on the threshold of your closet, that in order to look like that all the time, you have to spend five thousand dollars and have a make-up girl follow you around." She smiled and Vonnie felt better.

"So why do you do this?"

Nike shrugged. "I'm good at it. And it's what people think they want. And in the case of people like you, on their way to being famous, they need it. But it's not fun. It's like being asked what you want to be when you grow up. How the fuck should you know, you're ten! Or for that matter eighteen. Like we learn so much in eight years. But you still have to pick something. And today," she pointed a manicured finger at Vonnie, "*you* need to pick an image."

Three hours of interrogation later (*Heels or flats, pants or skirts, colors or earth tones, reading or watching movies, a manicure or a day in the park, jazz, rock, techno, or classical? If you could live anywhere where would it be? If you had a million dollars to give away where would it go?*) Nike knew more about

Vonnie than Vonnie had ever realized about herself. "Okay. Anything else I should know?" Nike asked.

"Yeah. I want my hair blonde. And long."

* * *

Vonnie sat in her hotel room scribbling on the letterhead station-ary and thereby reminding herself of Barry. She paused, swept her long honey-blonde hair into a low ponytail and pushed up the sleeves on her pink and white jogging suit.

The TV lit the room, its blue light glittering against the sharp S logo of her track suit. She'd muted the sound but preferred the dynamic blue to the static, dismal yellow of light bulbs. She reread her notes, frowned, crossed out her punch line and reworded it. New jokes without a single reference to TJ.

New York City and its greater area offered three weeks' worth of club gigs, and Barry had booked her accordingly. Her second and third weeks had sold out before she'd even arrived in town, and Barry had made some mention of keeping her there and getting her into a bigger venue.

"Sandra Silverfish is playing the Met and they need an opener. They want a woman."

Vonnie found Sandra simultaneously hysterical and depressing. The woman kept telling the same joke and nobody seemed smart enough to get it.

"Also, Queenie Winspear originally wanted you that same week, but they have a better-suited topic for you so you're going on Tuesday."

"Which Tuesday?"

"Tomorrow Tuesday."

Vonnie sighed. "Barry, I don't want to go on Queenie Winspear." The whine in her own voice revealed how tired she was. Tired in every sense.

"Alright. Because?"

"Because I don't want to cry."

A pause. "So don't cry. I recognize it's a daytime talk show but you're not contractually obligated to produce tears."

"Barry. . . ."

"Given your image it's probably better if you don't. Should you change your mind, of course, you're allowed to cry. This one is all up to you."

"Barry!"

"Yes?"

"Just give me the itinerary."

* * *

Queenie's eyes were a nice tawny color, about two shades lighter than her skin. They matched her hair and were set off by her green pantsuit. She set those pretty eyes on Vonnie, and Vonnie found that she wanted to tell this woman everything then cry and eat a sundae.

"First let me say, and I think the audience will agree, you look stunning."

The audience clapped at Vonnie's brown boot-cut yoga pants, cream wrestling shoes, and patterned three-quarter sleeve top, all emblazoned with Survivanoia's spiky S logo.

"I understand you have a jogging suit that recycles your sweat so you can shower *while* you run. Save some time." More clapping.

Vonnie pulled the nod-and-smile card, still not completely sold on the post-apocalyptic features of her new wardrobe—a hybrid of ideas from Nike, who recommended casual-sporty, and Chloe, who really dug her company's clothing but couldn't wear it herself. ("None of it comes in plaid.") Vonnie had felt ridiculous at first, but each time she unexpectedly caught her own reflection she thought, *Oh, that girl is pretty.* Also, everyone else complimented her.

"We'll talk more about the clothing in a minute, but first," Queenie turned from camera three to Vonnie. "You know what I'm going to ask you, right? The thing everybody wants to know." Those tawny eyes held Vonnie's. "What led you to try to kill yourself?"

Vonnie took a deep breath, swallowed her first answer—*reword it, borrow Barry's words, lighten up....* "Did you ... *hear* the record?"

A kind smile lit Queenie's face. "Even the title, really. Painful."

Vonnie gave an exaggerated shrug. "I've been thinking of calling my comedy tour *Asshole*."

The studio audience laughed at what would be bleeped out of the aired version.

"Let's discuss your response. Because that's really what your comedy is at its heart, isn't it? A response? To the cruelty of your husband?"

Vonnie, for the first time, considered this question. She apparently took her time doing so because Queenie set a hand gently on her arm. "Vonnie?"

"No."

"No, what?"

"My comedy isn't a response to TJ's—Bagga's—anything. It's just easy for me to make fun of him because I know him so well."

"But would you have been motivated to go on stage if he'd been a more appreciative husband? A more accessible husband? A less violent husband?"

"Motivated? That was a fluke." She recounted the story of her night at Adlibs, with the angry little comic she hadn't insulted and the kick she got from being on stage. "I like to think TJ—Bagga—is laughing with me. I *know* his dad is. My father-in-law?" She found a camera, "Hi Frankie!"

"So—I think many of us expected more rage. But you don't sound very angry. Would you say your comedy has been therapeutic?"

Vonnie frowned in thought. "It's easy to look at where we are and be nothing but angry. But the fact is we loved each other. You know, they market you. You get turned into a commodity and it changes you. And it's easy to lose yourself in that."

Vonnie's brow creased and she gazed at the floor. How had she not figured this out before? Again Queenie's hand touched her arm.

"I'm sorry. I just ... uh."

"You didn't realize it until now, did you?" The depth of empathy in the talk show queen's eyes made Vonnie's hatred finally break, and she knew now it was receding.

"You still love him."

"Yeah." And Vonnie didn't cry. She laughed. Again she found the camera. "I still love you, TJ!"

A collective "Awwww" from the audience.

"Well, there you have it," Queenie stated to a camera. "Coming up next, Victoria Dodds, winner of our 'Who Looks Most Like Their Avatar' contest. Then: up close and personal with Survivanoia. Vonnie's wardrobe comes from their newest clothing line. Want to catch that tsunami wave? Mountain bike in Lebanon? You can! Baroness Dacianna Von Worthington will tell us how, up next!

"But first, our in-studio audience will now reach under their chairs and find their DNA kits. During the break we'll all find out what life-threatening diseases we are predisposed to!"

CHAPTER 5

"Are you psycho?" **Vonnie winced** at Chloe's shrill words over the cell phone. Vonnie was standing outside of the greenroom wanting food, not a lecture. "*I still love you?*"

"It just came out, I can't defend it. Can we talk about this when I get back?"

Chloe expressed a few more bursts of frustration and dismay, then apologized for being crazy. "I just worry about you. Come home soon."

Vonnie agreed and hung up. As she tucked her cell phone away, she found a woman grinning at her sympathetically around a salt bagel smeared thick with lox spread.

"Best friend in a panic?" the woman asked in a low rumble, and Vonnie's anxieties fled like sidewalk pigeons. Her face must have borne the curiosity she couldn't articulate, because the woman gave a kind smile and nodded. "I've been there. Both sides. The crazy concerned friend and you, the dummy."

"I guess I did sound pretty dumb."

"Only to the inexperienced. Here's something they don't tell you in charm school. Sometimes, a person has to look back, *all the way* back, in order to reach her destination." The red-haired woman winked at her.

Vonnie cocked her head, disconcerted. Something about the sentiment resonated, left her hopeful and lonely and feeling as though she'd heard it before but only recognized it now. Her mind struggled to find the source of this déjà vu, but in vain.

The redhead waved the bagel at the sound stage. "I think you just glanced in the rearview out there today. You've still got some peering to do." She drifted past Vonnie, graceful and smooth like a guardian angel. "But not today. Get some food before you're called back on."

The woman moved toward the stage and Vonnie watched her, dumbfounded with admiration. Over six feet tall but moved like a dancer and hair the color of fine wine in the coolest braid Vonnie had ever seen—*oh Nike would* love *this woman, who* was *this woman? Didn't Chloe say something about—oh!*

"Are you the Baroness?"

The remarkable redhead turned, nodding. "Dacianna. Nice to meet you."

"You made all my clothing. I mean, not you personally but, you know."

The Baroness swallowed a mouthful of bagel and smiled. "The company sells clothing and gadgets to help fund real science. People like kitsch, so we give 'em what they want."

"You're making me feel cheap."

"It's a misappropriation, I suppose, but it's better than using science to kill people, don't you agree?"

"Uhm, yeah."

"Then don't feel cheap. Be proud! Think of it as supporting scientific research. Especially since you're famous; now everyone will want some. Probably we should be paying you to wear it. Or at least giving it to you."

"I'm pretty sure you are, actually," Vonnie admitted. Chloe had in fact pulled some kind of strings and gotten Vonnie's entire wardrobe donated.

"Oh, yeah? Say, maybe you are kind of cheap!" The Baroness stuffed the rest of her bagel in her mouth and punched Vonnie in the arm like a kid sister and Vonnie couldn't recall the last time she felt so lucky.

* * *

"I. Still. Love. You." These words dripped from Chloe's mouth as she stood with Vonnie at the LAX baggage claim. "How could you? In front of all those people?"

Vonnie pulled at one of her pigtails, opened her mouth, but only shrugged.

Chloe stared her down for a long moment. "There goes your suitcase." Her finger followed a red Briggs and Riley as it spun past on the carousel, but her eyes stayed trained on Vonnie.

Vonnie had anticipated this, of course. She sighed. "What'd Frankie say?"

Chloe blinked.

"I know you hang out with him all the time. So you might as well tell me."

"I don't hang out with him all the time."

Vonnie cocked her head. "You've got a crush on him, don't you?"

"He's older than my dad. Was." Chloe turned back to the baggage carousel, so Vonnie couldn't see if she blushed or not.

"Chloe and Frankie sittin' in a tree. . . ."

"You're changing the subject."

They claimed Vonnie's bag and headed out to the sticky-hot and very smelly parking garage.

Vonnie yanked off her fawn corduroy jacket, but her lacy cream camisole was still sticking to her by the time they found Chloe's boxy yellow car. She yawned, which made her cough. "Geez, has anyone dropped dead in here yet from exposure?"

"Sure. They use 'em in baggage inspection." Chloe's voice had an edge to it that Vonnie recognized. They got into Chloe's car, which was even warmer than the parking garage.

"Heater's not fixed yet, huh?"

"The heater is fine. It's the engine that's broken and no, it's not fixed yet. If air conditioning is so important to you, maybe you should find time in your schedule to buy your own damn car. Or: you're married to a cabdriver, for crissake." She lurched out of the parking space and squealed down the slick black ramp.

"I'm married to, and in the process of divorcing, a cabdriver's *son*."

"Whatever, you knew what I meant."

Vonnie took a deep breath, let it out slowly. "Listen. I was just kidding about Frankie."

"It's not about Frankie. Even though I don't have a crush on him, and if I do, it's not a sex crush, it's more like a Dad crush."

"Yeah. Your dad is kind of my point." She paused while Chloe paid the parking toll, refusing the money Vonnie offered her.

"I work, okay? I'm not a charity case."

"Queenie was really nice," Vonnie told her.

"Yeah, she seemed it. But they all seem nice on camera."

"I was thinking: you should go on there." A pause. "She'd take you."

"I don't wanna do that." Chloe was suddenly mumbling.

"It's good money."

Chloe glanced at her, raised an eyebrow. "Please."

"It is! And people want to know. A 'Where is She Now?' story."

"You know that's sick, right?"

"Any sicker than what I'm doing?"

"Vonnie, you're married to—divorcing—a dickhead. That's all. Like a gazillion other women. Your dickhead just happens to be famous and you happen to be clever. But your situation is commonplace."

Vonnie thought of Barry's calmness in the face of her ranting. "Alright," she prompted her friend. "And?"

Chloe glanced at her again. "And mine isn't."

"Which is why it'd be good."

"No. Nobody will connect with it and—whatsa' *matter* with you?! Does it occur to you that I don't want to get in front of a million people and talk about what life is like after being sliced out of my mother by some fucking psycho? My stepmother didn't even know for seven years! My father didn't want to tell his own wife, and you want me to tell a nation of strangers?"

"I think it might be therapeutic. Sometimes to move forward you have to look all the way—"

"Therapeutic! I'm sorry, what? Has this new career sucked your brain out your ears?"

"Chloe, look. You've never talked to anybody about your dad and—"

"Thousands of people lost family that day. There's nothing special about me."

"And thousands of people are suffering from PTSD! And those people don't have your fucked up history."

"Oh, so now I'm fucked up." She stopped the car with a small screech that lurched Vonnie forward. Vonnie was surprised to see her condo complex—Chloe drove super fast when she was agitated.

"I'm handling this in my own way," Chloe assured her.

"The Food Channel doesn't qualify as counseling."

"You know what? I really wanted to hear about your trip, and especially about the *Queenie* show, because that supercool redheaded woman on after you was my boss. My big boss. But right now? I feel like killing you. So please just get your stuff out of my car and I'll call you in a few days."

Vonnie took her suitcase from Chloe's backseat. She watched as the yellow box raced away—heater pumping, stereo blaring a Leonard Skynard song that they both hated.

* * *

"I don't want to do the TJ shtick anymore."

Barry nodded from across his desk. "The *Queenie* stunt was brilliant. Utterly unexpected. Even I didn't anticipate it."

"I've got thirty minutes of new material."

"Typed?"

"Yes."

"With you?"

"Yes." She opened her leather satchel.

"Email it to me. What else?"

"The Home Piracy Network show films on Friday. If you want to review it, you need to review it tonight."

"HPN wants the material they know. As does Buster DelGrosso. Owner of Busta' Guts Food an—"

"I know who he is." Vonnie tapped his desk with a French-manicured fingernail. "Am I contractually obligated?"

"Contractually obligated . . ." Barry mumbled the phrase to himself, rolling it off his tongue like a lemon seed. "Technically, no. They'll film whatever you perform at Busta's. They are equally non-obligated, however, to produce what they record."

Vonnie held Barry's gaze, imploring.

He relented, giving her the advice she knew he had. "Do the Busta' Guts show with the TJ material. Switch in ten minutes of the new material. That way it will look like you're doing them a favor, giving both Busta's and HPN something nobody else has seen yet. Keep it that way for the show Sunday, then reverse the ratio."

"What's Sunday?"

"Purple Dot."

Vonnie's eyes hooded.

"Just like you're thinking, yes: the same night as Bagga Chips."

"You booked me across the street from him!"

Her agent nodded.

"Barry! No."

He closed his eyes for a beat, then set down his pen and folded his hands.

"The marketing potential for both of you is enormous."

"We both already pack the house."

"Correct. And if you play Purple Dot the same night he plays the Wontspin, that rivalry will be preserved regardless of whether you change out your material."

"What if we squelch that rivalry?"

Barry shook his head, frowning. "Animosity works well."

"Jesus Christmas, Barry! Why don't you just give us switchblades and tie us together? What do you do, meet with TJ's agent over knish and say 'how can we maximize and package their hatred, real or imagined?'"

Barry blinked at her. His brow knitted and he shook his head, appearing—for the first time Vonnie had ever seen—confused.

"What?"

"I thought you knew," he said. "I *am* TJ's agent."

* * *

Vonnie squinted through the chipped paint blocking the greenroom windows of Purple Dot. "My line isn't as long as his."

"Your building is smaller." Chloe relaxed into the plush couch and munched a sliced apricot from a platter of fresh fruit that could have fed both lines of people outside.

The greenroom still smelled of fresh paint. Cream-colored walls and a sky-blue carpet contrasted pleasantly with the brown leather couches, making the room optimistic but adult.

The coffee table—vast, glass, curvy—held a silver platter slightly smaller than a coffin, overflowing with SoCal fruits.

"Right, smaller," Vonnie mumbled, dejected. She skulked away from the window, rubbing her sweating hands on her coffee-colored cords. She picked up a slice of papaya, sniffed it, set it back down again. "I've come all this way, and here I am still in his shadow."

"Did you look into getting a new agent?"

Vonnie sucked air through her teeth. "Barry's really good."

Chloe fished around the platter, found a fig, and sampled it. "Where's Frankie tonight?"

"I thought you'd bring him," Vonnie teased, and Chloe flicked a grape at her.

"Hey! Watch the threads." She ran a hand down the length of her vanilla hoodie, one of her favorites with its big hood and three-inch S-emblazoned cuffs. A switch in the left cuff turned on heater coils like in an electric blanket, only these ran off the static electricity produced by friction of her skin against the fabric.

Chloe tossed another grape. True to her word, as always, she had called a few days after their airport argument. They'd had lunch at Chloe's—absolutely mouth-watering roast duck (despite Chloe's claims of the meal still being in the experimental stages)—and on Thursday, she'd gone with Vonnie to Busta's. Then earlier that night, they'd been driven out of Club Tattoo by.... "What'd you call those people at Tattoo again?"

Chloe answered around a mouthful of grape. "The Porno Mafia? That's what Ben called them. I don't know anything about them."

"And your boss was the guy in the biker jacket?"

"With the Hawaiian shirt, yeah." Chloe grinned the way she always did when she talked about Geo.

"I think your boss is cuter than that bartender."

"That's just because you like skinny guys. TJ turns sideways and he disappears."

Yelling from outside made Vonnie look to the window. She meandered toward it but didn't look out. "Geo is skinny," she said. "He's taller than I pictured him."

"Yeah, he's like six three or six five. You're pacing, eat a cherry."

"Eating is better than pacing?"

"The pacing is making *me* nervous."

Vonnie made one more lap around the cream-colored room. It reminded her of Barry's office with its pale-blue couch and not-quite-white curtains. It should have been comforting. She relented and sat on a pale-yellow hammock chair next to the distressed-white coffee table.

"Eating might make me vomit. Doesn't Geo break your eight-year rule?"

"I changed my eight-year rule."

"Really?"

"First I bounced it up to a ten-year rule," Chloe paused to spit out a cherry pit. "But then I decided even that was limiting and therefore probably transitive. So I settled on nobody old enough to realistically be my father. Which I figure gives me seventeen years."

Vonnie set her tongue against the roof of her mouth to stop it wagging. But something in her eyes gave her away.

"What?"

"Nothing, just . . . your new rule . . ."

"What?!"

"Didn't keep you from sleeping with Frankie!"

Chloe turned redder than the watermelon in her hand. "He told you."

Outdoors, more hollering and a siren yipped. Red and blue lights splashed through the gaps in the window paint.

"We're both lonely," Chloe explained. Needlessly. "My parents are dead, his wife is dead."

"Frankie is hot."

Chloe laughed. "There's that, too. We're not, like, dating. It was a one-time thing. Well, three-time thing." She flushed again. "He's so good-looking. And so nice."

"I know it. I've known it since high school. I mean, I don't think he's hot, but I knew you did."

"See, I never thought TJ was attractive at all."

"Of course not, he's too skinny for you! They don't look anything alike, either."

"Not a bit. Weird. That's not why I was mad at the airport, though."

"I know that, too."

Chloe picked at a grape stem. "You're not seriously thinking about getting back together, are you?"

"I don't know. I still love him. Maybe it's stupid, but it's true."

"Have you heard from him?"

"No."

"What's Frankie say?"

"The same thing he told you, that TJ isn't good enough for me but he likes having me as a daughter." Vonnie shrugged, gazing at the floor. "I told him he can be my dad whether I'm with TJ or not, and we left it at that."

Chloe tossed her head back. "That's fair. But—"

A sharp crack rang from outside. Gunshot? Could have been a car backfiring, but LA always makes you think. And screaming followed this one.

Chloe snagged Vonnie by the arm and led her to the window. "Look at these people. Look at them!"

Vonnie cupped her hands around her face and peered through the holes in the paint. Outside seemed unreal, like a war or something from TV. Two trash cans had been set on fire. The hurricane fence separating TJ's fans from hers had been pushed down in places. People punched and slapped each other. And a voice filled Vonnie's head, pieces of press comments, complementing the violence like a soundtrack: "TJ is making truckloads of money off his hate . . . the potential to translate into mass misogynism . . . can they ever really make a relationship work?" Could they?

The door to the dressing room flew open and three large men with headsets stormed through.

"We're taking you out through the side. They're canceling tonight."

The guards rushed Vonnie and Chloe through the back hall, down echoing steel stairs with fire alarms and extinguishers on all three floors. Outside, a limo waited to carry them through the chaos.

The site of boxy ambulances and EMTs reminded Vonnie of the hospital nurses. The guards grabbed her and hauled her through the line of burning garbage cans and people trying to murder each other through the hurricane fence. Hollering hate-filled nothings about her and about TJ. "How can you waste your time listening to that stupid slut bitch?!" "How can you give your money to a womanizing wife beater?!"

How easy people were to manipulate. As if the lives of Vonnie Upchurch and TJ "Bagga Chips" Fallon had anything to do with anything. The guards marched her to the limo and everything slowed down like she'd heard it does in a car crash. Slowed down and went quiet, despite the screaming and pushing and burning that surrounded her.

Then the limo door slammed and Chloe sat next to her.

"Move, *move*, MOVE!" the headset guys shouted, running alongside her limo as it crept through the side lot and onto the relative safety of the street. At the corner, on the street running in front of the two venues, TJ's limo swung up next to them. Its mirrored windows nearly matched the silver tone of it, though right now they reflected fabulously the orange fires and the red and blue police bubbles and the cream of Vonnie's limo.

Her tinted windows reflected images back out as well, so that the two extended cars side by side acted as two opposing mirrors, producing an infinite repetition of each other.

Limos always reminded Vonnie of New York, and New York reminded Vonnie of TJ back when he still *was* TJ, and they met at the school holiday dance and it turned out he was in her math class and he helped her with her math homework and they watched movies and just hung out until school was done and then all that summer TJ parked his Chevelle under the overpass and she'd watch the sun set across the Hudson behind the New York skyline.

"Wouldn't it be cool to live there instead of here?"

TJ would frown at the cityscape. "Why?"

"I dunno. Stuff happens there."

"Stuff happens here, too." He slid a hand under her shirt. "Keeps me happy."

And TJ *had* been happy, content with the idea of marrying her and working in his uncle's garage, raising Irish setters or Weimaraners (he'd never wanted kids) and vacationing in Florida once a year.

Then senior year TJ met Evan. Evan who played bass and snorted speed, trucker speed he stole from his father who drove an 18-wheeler three weeks out of every month and then came home to sleep, fuck a woman who lived in the house but was not Evan's mother, and smack Evan around.

TJ started hanging out there. Playing guitar, snorting speed, then showing up at Vonnie's reeking of beer and SpaghettiOs, and they'd sneak into the basement and have hot gorilla sex, then cuddle and kiss on her dad's futon couch.

They graduated, got married. TJ kept working at his uncle's shop and she got a part-time job and went to school at night to be an X-ray technician. TJ stayed with the band, which meant he still hung out with Evan and eventually he got signed, moved to LA, made it big, backhanded her across the dining room, and wrote a record about what a bitch she was.

The two cars rode in tandem up Wilshire. A red light halted them, side by side. Vonnie waited for TJ to roll down his window, but he didn't. She waited for him to call her cell phone, but he didn't. The light changed and TJ's car veered left while Vonnie's continued straight. She watched the image of her limo peel away from the windows of TJ's, then continued to stare after the silver car as it shot off into the night, looking small and alone.

"What will TJ's next album be about?" Vonnie wondered out loud.

"Who cares?" Chloe pulled a huge green apple from her pocket, scored the top of it with her thumbnail and snapped it in half. She then raised a shoulder, let it drop.

"Well," Chloe said, handing half the apple to Vonnie, "I guess Barry got what he wanted."

"Yeah." Vonnie took a big bite from the tart apple, let it sit on her tongue while she sucked the juice from it. "Yeah," she said. "Me, too."

CHAPTER 6

Benjamin Myers, wearing only his boxers, stood in the entrance of his Spanish bungalow scratching his head and squinting at the man on his doorstep. Palm trees blazed bronze in the early morning sun. The still air, thick and stale, carried the promise of triple digits by noon, but also the tantalizing scents of breakfast from the cafés on Melrose Avenue, half a block away.

The man who'd pounded on Ben's door, dragging him to wakefulness, looked to Ben like he could use some breakfast. But despite his nervous eyes and flaring nostrils, this lean stranger had the face of a handsome boxer. Semi-famous, certainly. Mid-list? Maybe porn. Probably not, though, with those silver-grey temples. *Where'd I see this guy?* Ben wondered.

He realized the man was talking. Apparently had been.

"I'm sorry, what?"

The man sighed and shoved a hand at Ben. "This is yours."

The hand held a wallet, black and worn.

"I don't think so," Ben started. He glanced toward the bedroom where his black linen trousers lay folded over a chair. Was his wallet in them? Wasn't his wallet brown? Maybe he should check. But the prospects of leaving this wild-eyed, disheveled man alone at the threshold disconcerted him.

The man made his decision for him. "The address is yours! Take it. Take it!" He yanked Ben's hand from its akimbo post, shoved the wallet into it, and fled.

Ben slammed the door. Dust bunnies scurried across his blond wood floor, seeking shelter beneath his blocky black couch and armchair. He peered through the slats of his wooden blinds, but didn't see the man or hear a car leave, just the murmur of early yuppies and ambitious tourists. In the Talavera-tiled kitchen, the sun's sharp angle told him it couldn't be past 8:00. Far too early for a bartender whose shift had ended at 2:30 in the morning and who'd attended an after-hours that brought him stumbling through the door—womanless—at quarter past seven.

But curiosity overrode tiredness. He reheated a cup of yesterday's coffee and opened the wallet. The license was in one of those flip-out plastic things. The address indeed matched Ben's. Ben didn't recognize the guy in the photo, but he'd bought the house from someone who had rented it out, so this must have been one of the previous tenants.

Examining the picture, he decided that the madman at the doorstep must have been either blind or incredibly generous in his physical assessments. The photo guy shared the wallet bearer's high-cheekboned face but offset by blue eyes and red hair. Not grey, as Ben's had turned (nearly completely as of last year), betraying him at the comparatively young age of thirty-four. Women described Ben as "cute," sometimes "handsome," but he'd never graduated to sexy.

The microwave beeped. On his way to it, he yanked closed the yellow curtains over the porcelain sink. Who was this previous tenant guy? What was his name? Ed Bloodworth. *Blood*worth. Even his name was alarming!

Ben riffled through the rest of the wallet. Not much in it. A library card. No Norton's Food card, no video rental place cards, no photos. A bank card; maybe he could drop the wallet off at BankZilla and they could hunt Eddie down.

What unnerved Ben was the money. Hundred dollar bills. Lots of them. And some weird orange certificate things. Foreign currency? Ben felt uncomfortable touching it. He thought about calling 411, but what could he tell the guy if he did find him? No, dropping it off at the bank seemed better. Good and anonymous.

He left the wallet on his dresser. Some superstitious feeling made him check his pants to make sure he still had his own wallet, his own identification, and was still Ben Myers.

He took a shower, mostly cold. The cool water left him refreshed and sleepy, so he went back to bed. At 3:00 in the afternoon, his radio clock came on, the Clash pulling him from sleep. Thursday. Thursdays meant the comedy club. In lieu of the previous night's linen pants, he dug out a pair of brown, wide-wale cords from his drawer and put on a brick-red jersey-cut T-shirt. Safe earth colors. The cut of the shirt hid his little teddy-bear belly. The fact that he knew this about the colors and cut and didn't mind it made Ben feel old.

* * *

Busta Guts: FOOD AND FUNNY, SEE? The sign featured a typecast mobster, smoking a fat cigar, and rubbing his belly as he laughed. In fact, the drawing was a caricature of Buster DelGrosso, the unfunny comic (but shrewd businessman) who owned the place. Dark, small, and dirty with a shallow stage facing six rows of scarred bistro tables, Busta's lived off its reputation, and like so many places in Hollywood, was frequented mostly by tourists

Back in the '80s, when stand-up had reached its pinnacle, Buster DelGrosso made comics. His club had once provided the brightest new talent to the screen. As of late, stand-up seemed positioned for a comeback, and the Home Piracy Network had begun filming their half-hour specials of up-and-coming comics at Busta's, including one tonight. So who knew?

The girl showed up early, but that wasn't the only reason she stood out. People dressed tourist-nice at Busta's—khakis and pressed shirts. This chick had on a baseball jersey—Pitt—over a short plaid skirt and boots. Plaid boots. Plaid Doc Martens with gold laces that matched the writing on the jersey. Underneath the skirt were black fishnet stockings and she wore the jersey open, revealing a lace tank top.

Just enough skin, Ben thought. He hoped she didn't come near him. She did, of course.

"Bar open yet?"

"Only for you." Geez what a cliché! Ben wanted to slap himself.

"What's your special?"

"What's your pleasure?"

Her ice-blue eyes sparkled. "I asked you first."

Ben faltered. He wasn't supposed to serve his personalized drinks here. But no one else was around yet, so he wouldn't be upstaging anybody. . . .

He leaned in conspiratorially. "Sweet or sharp?"

"What?"

"If you had to choose between, say, Jaeger Meister and peach Schnapps, which would it be?"

"Jaeger."

That meant he could make her a sit-and-spin. He selected a pilsner glass, poured a half gin, half vodka base (mixed over ice), then two magical liquors that sat one on top of the other, blue over red. He set it in front of the girl, inserted a stirrer. "Watch."

He stirred it with vigor. The drink swirled and turned patriot blue. It kept spinning and the blue faded, passed to purple for just a moment, then flushed fire engine red.

The girl grinned, cocked her head of loose black curls and examined him. "You work at Tattoo."

"Maybe."

"He does," said a different woman, a swank redhead. "He makes another drink called the Kafka. It's grey, and a little city forms at the bottom, disappears each time you take a sip then reforms again, reconfigured." She dropped onto a stool and shot him a smile. "He also juggles broken bottles and breathes fire."

"Hello, Heather." Ben sort of smirked. "What'll it be?"

"The usual. And: Lacy was prowling around here earlier."

"I thought Buster banned that crowd."

"He doesn't know that Lacy hawks. He thinks she's just a starlet. Besides, she was prowling around for *you*." Heather turned to Ben's new friend. "Comedy is like acting: the porno industry snatches up the failures. Eats them up and shits them out." She aimed her smarmy smile at the girl. "Are you on tonight?"

Ben glared at Heather. "I'd introduce you two, but I don't know Pitt's name. This is Heather."

The girl put out a hand. Ben prepared Heather's whiskey sour, glad for the respite. The pornography hawks made him prickle. They stalked joints like Busta's, made good-sounding offers to fame-starved kids. "Hey baby, you're gorgeous, you're talented, you could make three hundred bucks a day working in film!" Buster had cracked some guy's skull open one night and promised to shoot him next time. So what was Lacy chasing?

Ben set Heather's drink on a napkin.

"Her name is Chloe," Heather told him and pranced off.

After Heather left, Chloe asked him, "Your girlfriend?"

"Absolutely not."

"She'd like to be." She eyed him over. "And . . . you've slept with her."

Ben felt himself flush. "Only once. We were both drunk."

"Maybe you'd like to get drunk with me some time."

Ben's face absolutely burned. He pointed to Chloe's jersey. "Did you go to Pitt?"

"No."

"Oh. I thought maybe you did because of the shirt. That's, ah . . . that's where I'm from."

"I bought this in Venice. I thought it was funny, you know, to buy a Pittsburgh shirt in California."

"Funny peculiar or funny haha?"

"Funny ironic." She sipped her sit-and-spin.

"You ever been there?"

"You couldn't pay me enough."

"How do you know if you've never been?"

"Let's just say Pittsburgh is aptly named."

"You're pretty funny." He gazed at her suspiciously. "*Are* you on tonight?"

"No, one of my friends is. Vonnie."

"Connie Anders?"

Chloe shook her head. "*Vonnie* Upchurch. The one doing the HPN show tonight."

Ben nodded, pursed his lips slightly, hoping he disguised how impressed he was. And jealous. Upchurch was the headline, the one whose special was being filmed. Former wife of rap-rock star Bagga Chips, comedienne Upchurch had taken the horrific and slanderous lyrics he'd sung about her and twisted them against him. Now half the country laughed at him. Naturally, this had gained her quick access to the talk-show circuit. Brilliant. Ben wished he'd thought up some similar approach with his own, now long-abandoned shtick.

"Want to meet her?" Chloe asked.

This struck Ben as an odd question, being that he worked for the club and it was usually him asking that question—kind of a standard pick-up line, come to think of it. "Sure."

"Good. We can all have dinner at my place Saturday night. Good?"

"Uh ... good!"

Any fantasies he may have harbored about sex with two girls—one of them a famous comic!—or watching two girls have sex with each other were squelched by Heather as they closed up.

"Neither of those women even wants to see you naked. I, on the other hand ..."

"You realize that, since you're the club manager, I could potentially sue you for sexual harassment." He winked at her.

"Oh, please do. Court would at least break the predictable cycle that has become my life. Seriously. Honey? Use a condom."

* * *

Before Chloe had the door open, she apologized. "Vonnie couldn't make it."

"I'm not surprised. Saturday is top dollar for a comic."

"I didn't think you'd make it either, Mister Bartender."

"Speaking of which." He shoved a bottle of wine at her. "That's from Canada," he said. "Eastern Canada."

"I didn't tell you what I was making."

"So?"

"So how did you know what wine to get?"

He grinned. "I'm a bartender."

Chloe had a nice apartment in a marginal neighborhood on the seedier side of Hollywood. Maybe the vaulted ceilings and hardwood floors made up for not being able to leave the house after dark without putting on some hardcore attitude.

She sat him at the dining room table—wrought iron with an inset grey marble top. Ben ran a hand along it. "This is gorgeous."

"Thrift store, can you believe it?"

In place of a tablecloth, which would have covered the beauty of the marble, she'd draped three cobalt blue runners. A metal watering can spilling over with blue and white irises rested on the farthest of these and placemats set beside cloth napkins graced the other end. Tasteful.

And the food! Duck prepared in Grand Marnier sauce with wild rice and perfectly steamed asparagus. Crème brûlée for dessert. Chloe owned a cook's blowtorch. Ben thought he could marry this girl. She had taste, a sense of humor, and cooked like a fiend!

"Why are you such a good cook?"

"*Why?*"

"You have to admit it's a bit unusual for somebody, what, twenty-five?"

"Is this an elaborate ruse to determine my age?"

"Yes."

"I'm twenty-nine."

Ben finished his wine. "You don't look a day over thirty. Seriously, not many people in their twenties cook this well unless it's their profession."

"I'm not a chef."

"I figured. So?"

"I watch Food TV a lot."

Ben sensed there was more. For the first time in their short relationship, Chloe seemed hesitant. He hedged the bet: "For a reason?"

"Do you really want to know?" She attempted a laugh. "In the past five years, my life became a bad Lifetime movie. Oh wait, that's a redundancy."

He snickered. "But yeah, I'd really like to know."

"My dad died when the World Trade Center came down. All the channels were showing it all the time. I couldn't get away from it, but I couldn't stand the silence when the TV was off. Music wasn't enough, I wanted voices, you know? People."

Ben searched her for signs of farce. Was he being punked? He didn't think so. Her speech was rushed. Plus the way she'd referred to it, not the media-catchy "9/11."

"What about the Weather Channel?" he asked.

Chloe shook her head. "It affected the weather. All that smoke and debris? So I started to watch all these different people cook. It got to be interesting. They each have their own little pet thing. And cooking, it's a form of creation, I guess." She shrugged. "I found it therapeutic. Don't laugh."

He looked at her, sparkling eyes and wide smile. Earnest.

"How about your mom?"

"My real mom died when I was born. My *step*mom died a year after my dad."

"That's rough. How'd she, I mean—"

"Let's say . . . of a broken heart."

"That's poetic." He instantly regretted his sarcasm, sensed that he'd missed a cue to drop the subject.

"Poeticism seems to disturb people less than telling them that she hung herself from the exposed pipes in the basement."

"I, ah . . . I'm sorry."

Chloe glared at him only for a moment then shrugged. "I warned you. So what about you? Any Afterschool Specials you want to share?"

Ben rubbed his chin "We'll do me next time."

"I won't do you next time." She winked at him. "I'm a third date girl."

* * *

Ben drove home happy, not even minding his broken radio. Brand new car and the radio—satellite—stopped working after two weeks. The dealer said it wasn't their responsibility, here's a voucher, go to a stereo place. The stereo places looked sideways at the car because it was a hybrid and they don't work on hybrids cuz it's an electric car, comprende? They could be electrocuted.

But he wasn't thinking about any of that. He was humming and day-dreaming about Tuesday, their scheduled second date. What foresight on his part to have accepted those passes to Alrik's art show opening! He never believed he'd actually use them but stuff like that can come in handy. Handy . . . *handy with the ladies.* . . .

Of course he figured it'd be the third date before there'd be any hands involved. He already knew just where to take her. As such a good cook, she'd be tough to impress, but when searching for hard-to-find wines, he'd recently stumbled across this Romanian place and—who was parked in his driveway?

A silver Escalade sat, motor running, across his driveway, blocking his entry. Adrenaline brought Ben its rush of anger and irrationality. Then he noticed that one of the taillights was out and sighed: Heather.

For show, he screeched to a halt inches from her bumper and flung open the door. He had not been completely truthful with Chloe. Yes, he and Heather had hooked up only once so far, but neither of them had been drunk, and it was the beginning of an arrangement whereby if both of them were free and physically needy they could use each other to fill that need. Technically, he was not yet with anybody, nor had they fucked again; they both really liked oral.

Chloe's chastity was cute, though; he found it charming, and he'd decided before he got out of his car to send Heather home.

But as he stepped from his hybrid, the Escalade darted away with a tight squeak of tires. Ben cursed after the SUV, bitter with the realization that he'd just been blue-balled twice in one night.

CHAPTER 7

"**S**o how was your wild night, loverboy?"

"You should know."

Heather raised her eyebrows at him. "How's that?"

"I appreciate our arrangement, but I'm dating. And color me crazy but stalkers make me nervous."

"What on God's green earth are you on about?"

Ben peered at his manager. She had a hand on her tilted hip and a vaguely-offended sort of frown creased her brow.

"Don't you drive a silver Escalade with a burned out taillight?"

"Silver *Explorer*, psycho. And I fixed my busted taillight two weeks ago. You told me where to go."

That's right, he had. So who the hell'd been parked outside his house? Like they were casing the place. Not that Ben owned much worth stealing, but he liked the things he did have. His couch was comfortable, his stereo kicked ass, and the bedroom furniture had been his grandmother's, which in his opinion more than made up for the dresser's mismatched hardware and circular stains. He'd considered refinishing the piece but—the wallet! Shit, he'd forgotten all about it.

What if the Escalade guy was Eddie the Wallet Owner? Ben took a deep breath. Tomorrow the banks would be open and he'd return it. He counted his drawer, liquor, and receipts, brought the numbers back to Heather's office along with an apology. She shrugged in a way that told him she was still irritated, but gave him her usual, "Break a leg at Ta-Twat."

Ben hated Club Tattoo but loved working there. Two stories of open space outfitted in pale wood, sheer drapes, and chrome faux-industrial piping, the antithesis of Busta's. So too with the clientele. Tattoo patrons ranged from over-privileged children-of-famous-people to Persian princes and their bombshell American dates. The club had a stage show on the lower level—impersonators, magic, sometimes vaudevillian stuff. Upstairs, people danced. No average citizens and no white light ever graced the carpets, dance floors, or bathrooms of the infamous Club Tattoo.

Tattoo bouncers carried sidearms. More than one of their waiters was rumored to have used his kitchen torches for things beyond the showy at-the-table caramelization of desserts, and two of the waitresses were known for having gone on to become Hollywood Madams. For Ben, all this meant two things: that he got to put on a show and that he got tipped superbly.

What Heather had told Chloe was true—the fire breathing and broken bottles. He also worked some basic magic: a cup-and-ball trick he did with shot glasses and maraschino cherries, a dollar-in-the-lemon trick. This week he planned to debut a disappearing dollar bit: "Drink Your Money Away," he'd named it. He poured a shot with the money in the glass, still visible when served. Once the patron consumed it, the cash disappeared. Ben made out on money tricks because Tattoo customers seldom carried anything smaller than fifties, and they usually let him keep the bill.

The ninth dollar drinker shook his shot glass, stared into the bottom, rubbed his finger around the inside.

"Amazing, isn't it?" a girl asked.

A girl with black hair and ice-blue eyes.

"Chloe!"

"I've been sitting here for nearly ten minutes. What's wrong, you don't recognize me out of uniform?"

The Ninth Guy barked, "Hey! Where's my Hamilton?"

Ben pulled a ten-dollar bill out of the guy's ear, handed it to him. The guy snatched it and waltzed away.

Ben frowned after him. Chloe reached around him for a handful of maraschino cherries. "Cheap SOB, huh?"

"Naw, I lost concentration at the end there. It's all about timing." He noticed the cherries, aimed his frown at her.

"Is that your way of saying scram? Get outta here kid, you bother me?"

He blinked at her. "No. Don't eat those, I have to account for them." He snagged one from her. "You're probably right, cheap SOB. So, come here often?"

"Hey Benjy Boy!" A leggy platinum blonde poured herself into a stool at the bar's far end. Blue veins bulged through the loose skin of her hands, but her face could still sell lip gloss to teeny-boppers.

Ben waved a finger at Chloe, "Just a minute," and he moved to the blonde. "What's your poison, Geena?"

"What, no kiss? Give Mamma a kissy-wissy, baby." She yanked him to her by his shirt, took his face in both her hands, and planted a sloppy kiss on his mouth. Amazingly, she left no trace of lipstick. "I hear you're making dollar bills disappear tonight."

"I hear you're making other things disappear."

Geena giggled. "Show me yours. Sorry, but you can't afford mine."

Ben poured her a shot, the money disappeared, he pulled it out of her blonde mane. She let him keep the bill and hers was a fifty. He served the small crowd that Geena inevitably left in her wake. Eventually everybody had something in his hand, and Ben returned to Chloe.

"You here alone?"

"Vonnie dragged me."

"She doesn't have a gig tonight?"

Chloe nodded. "Later. Over at the Wontspin."

Ben wondered if Chloe got paid to act as her friend's mascot, but before he'd figured a tactful way to phrase this question, Lionel burst through the swinging doors behind the bar. "Heads up! Ice! Ice, ice, baby!" He dumped a plastic busboy's tray-load of ice into the bar trough, muscles bulging around his white undershirt. "You short anything else?"

"I could use more Blue Curacao," Ben said. "And don't eat those!" He smacked Lionel's hand, which was full of bright red cherries.

"Uh-oh," Lionel sang.

"What?" Ben followed the barback's gaze. "Oh."

"Porno mafia at three o'clock."

"Why does Alex let them through the door?"

"And the fetish crew, no less."

Two women and three men reached the top of the stairs, spread out like a survey crew, like they owned the joint. Or planned to rob it. They'd have been awfully conspicuous, though. Two of the three men had slick black ponytails and black leather trench coats. The third guy's dirty-blond hair fell into his eyes. He also wore leather, a motorcycle jacket over a Hawaiian shirt, and had an eyebrow ring and a goatee.

Then there were the women. One like Elvira, but with breasts the size of watermelons. On her arm, a small, skinny girl in a plush fur leopard top and matching boyshort panties. She had boots to her knees, Halloween cat ears over her black Bettie Page cut, and wore a mesh duster that trailed on the floor. Her chest held mere cantaloupes.

Ben turned to Chloe to tell her about how the last time this crew showed up, they'd had to close the floor for a night to clean up the mess. Luckily, the club appealed to a crowd made hot by scandal and murder, especially if the death involved being smothered between watermelon tits.

But Chloe had slid off her stool and was creeping toward the women's bathroom, eyes fixed on the youngest of the men, the one with the short hair.

Lionel came swinging back through the doors again. "Boss says blow."

"Really?"

"Yeah, apparently these clowns crashed the gates. Riley's on his way up, says get everybody out, don't come back till tomorrow."

"Who's gonna finish my shift?"

Lionel shrugged. "My guess is Tattoo's second floor is closing for the evening."

"My guess is Riley sets this shit up."

Ben searched for Chloe but to no avail, decided she was holed up in the bathroom with her comedienne friend and he'd call her later. He considered hitting Fuzzy or one of the other dance clubs, but realized he was bored with that scene, was very much looking forward to Tuesday night with Chloe and the prospect of Tattoo being reduced from the slender-possibility-palace he currently pretended it wasn't to *just a job*. So, for the first night in many months, Ben headed straight home after work.

As he pulled into his driveway his headlights swept over his little house, revealing the unmistakable form of a person standing in his front room. Forgetting the public service announcements which recommend that if you should come home to find a stranger in your house, you go to another house and phone the police, Ben burst from his still-running car and lunged through the door.

A shadow slipped through his sliding kitchen door. Ben followed. In the backyard he saw someone hop the eight-foot rock wall but struggle for a grip. He lurched after the intruder. But lack of exercise got the best of him. He stood panting and sweating in the dim light as the figure slipped lithely into the neighbor's garden.

Ben put his car in the garage and headed back inside to assess the damage. The lock was busted, but nothing in the house appeared broken or missing. Perhaps he'd had the good fortune to arrive just in time? He checked the bedroom, where even the foisted mystery wallet still sat unmolested on his dresser.

But there'd been a sound as the intruder slipped over the wall, the unmistakable crunchy squeak of leather. Only certain types of people, Ben knew, wore a leather jacket in midsummer. The same kinds of people, come to think of it, who were likely to drive silver Cadillac SUVs. This, on the same night as the Porno Mafia? This was bad.

Ben didn't want to end up like the stupid amateurs trying to make it in the business. The hawks always collected a few failed actors who didn't mind, maybe even liked the work. Maybe tried to get a little too big. Like any big-money business, competition killed. The porn kings and queens regularly met up with people at Tattoo, usually men, who left the club with them and then disappeared for good. Occasionally they didn't leave the club at all. Then the Tattoo staff got to clean up the mess.

Yeah, this was bad.

Ben slept in his clothes. At 7:30 his alarm went off, but he needn't have set it. He'd been awake since dawn, staring out the window and chewing his nails. He pulsed through Melrose traffic to the BankZilla on the corner of Fairfax, where he paced outside the metal-slat gate for the three minutes it took them to unlock the door to customers.

The aging, too-skinny clerk drew away from him slightly, as if he smelled. Her eyebrows, which she had shaved and painted back on so that she appeared perpetually surprised, made Ben slightly afraid of her and indeed of the bank, as if he had walked into an elaborate trap.

"This is . . . I found this. And I have reason to believe the man it belongs to needs it very much." He explained about the address, slid the wallet under the shield of bulletproof plastic.

False-nailed fingers snatched the wallet from the metal tray and tapped a keyboard furiously. Still gazing at her computer screen, Creepy Bank Lady shook her head. "Account's closed. Has been for months. The last address we have is yours."

"What can I do?" Ben's vision tunneled.

"Try the DMV. Next in line, please."

"His license has my address."

"Then 411. Next!"

He stumbled punch-drunk out of the chilly bank and into the bright morning heat of an LA Monday. For a while he sat with his hybrid running, panting like a rabid dog. And sweating. The heat made him come to. He raised a hand to his new car's air conditioner vent and discovered that it pumped out damp, tepid air.

Ben sighed. "Alright," he said out loud to himself. "Fine. 411 it is." He headed one city-block north to the HondaWood dealer. "Why not confront Bloodworth directly?" he shouted at himself. "These people already know where I live anyway, right? Right! If they want to kill me, they will." His arms flailed in surrender, hands briefly abandoning the steering wheel.

"With some luck I'll wake up while they're hovering over my bed with a butcher knife and just hand them the wallet."

He ran a red light, a stop sign, and cut off an old lady.

Perhaps the Honda dealership's manager perceived that he was contending with a man on the edge. It took very little to persuade him that, unlike the stereo, the AC was certainly their responsibility, and they would see what they could do right this minute.

While Ben was waiting, he used the manager's phone.

"Information, what city?"

But after some key-tapping she told him, "No listing in the greater Los Angeles area."

He hung up to find the dealership manager looking apologetic and a little frightened.

"Let me guess," Ben said. "You need a part."

The manager nodded. "If you'd like, you can take the car today and drop it off again later. We should have the part by tomorrow."

"No, take it. Keep it. Call me when it's ready. If I'm not dead, I'll come get it."

* * *

Tuesday evening the sun retreated but left its heat behind. At 7:00, the squat buildings and square bungalows of Melrose blazed metallic in the low light, and the temperature still hung in the high nineties. Ben phoned Chloe and left a message. Could she drive tonight?

Nobody threatening had shown up at Busta Guts, and Ben had spent the night on Heather's couch. He considered asking Chloe to pick him up from the club, but he needed a shower, change of clothes, and the tickets for the art show, which he hoped he remembered correctly as being tacked to his bulletin board.

Back at his little house, nothing seemed amiss, making him wonder if conspiracy theories had finally taken over his better judgment. He heard the phone ring from the shower and found Chloe's voice on his machine when he got out. "My AC and stereo are broken, too. How weird is that? But my car is not in the shop, so yes, I can drive if you want."

At 9:00 precisely, Chloe pulled up in her yellow Volkswagen Gopher, wearing a mint green slipdress, a black feather boa, and black vinyl platforms. The stereo seemed healthy enough to Ben, blasting '80s favorites loud enough to rattle his front windows. But he had more pressing things weighing on his mind.

"Listen!" he hollered over a Duran Duran tune he was embarrassed to admit still made him choke up if he paid attention. "I hope you didn't split the other night because of Lana!"

Chloe shook her head, made a right onto Melrose.

"Or Josie!"

She shook her head again.

"Can I turn this down?"

"It doesn't turn down!"

Very funny, Ben thought. If she was pissed at him, why hadn't she said so earlier? He punched the down arrow, incensed. There was no way he was showing up at his friend's art show opening with some chick who— it didn't turn down. It also didn't turn off, and the next song was Led Zeppelin, which probably ranked as Ben's most hated band ever, but he couldn't change the station either.

"Your radio's broken!"

"I told you that! I also have to turn the heat on now or the engine's going to overheat!"

Ben trusted things could only get better.

His friend's opening ran out of a one-room independent gallery in Studio City in the Valley. Chloe found a parking space in the bank lot across the street. When she turned the engine off, and the full-blast heater and killer radio with it, Ben stumbled out of the car into the comparatively cool air and pretended to kiss the ground.

Chloe stood, arms crossed. "You can take a taxi home."

"I think it might be worth it. How can you drive that thing?"

"It's been broken forever, I'm used to it. Besides, how else were we supposed to get here?"

Ben stood, dipped his head. "Point taken."

"Can we go see some art now, please?"

"Well, I can't promise you that." He took her arm and led her across Ventura Boulevard to Gallery AnArtChy.

Music poured from inside the bright storefront gallery. "Sounds like they hired the Flintstones band to play," Ben said.

"I like it. That's a marimba. The marimba is a great instrument because it can be simultaneously spooky and whimsical. Unlike the poor theremin, which is always associated with monsters around the corner."

"Thank you, Professor."

"Don't mention it."

Inside, amidst the brilliant lights and dazzling paintings, Ben found his friend, the artist, Alrik. Despite the man's Scandinavian name, he stood less than six feet, talked like a surfer, and had trim, dark hair that would have looked absurd underneath a Viking helmet. His paintings, too, were quintessentially American, a high-energy blend of comic book and graffiti art. Not "moving" or poignant, but an awful lot of fun.

Chloe assembled a cheese and fruit plate for them to share, and Alrik pressed plastic goblets of wine into both their hands. But he pulled Ben aside, "There was a guy here asking about you, man. I mean he was looking for somebody else, but kinda asked about you. You know some guy name a ... Blood ... something?"

Ben's stomach tightened. "Was this guy in a leather coat?"

"Naw, business clothes. Blond hair, goatee. He left a card."

"Did he say what he wanted?"

Alrik shook his head. "Something about owing him money." He handed Ben a card, which Ben pocketed.

"Did he seem . . . dangerous?"

His friend shrugged. "It's hard to seem dangerous in a Hugo Boss suit." He sent Ben to view the show.

Ben gulped his wine, snagged another glass. He scrutinized the other visitors. They seemed divided between hip kids and Euro-trash. The kids were skinny, had spiky hair bleached at the tips or shaved heads and goatees. They wore Glitter Baby and Rock Star Arsenal gear, greeted the artist with congratulatory hugs, wolfed cheese, shied away from the wine. The others—older, darker—frowned at them. Frowned at the art. They leaned into each other to whisper in foreign snatches then broke apart in nasty laughter.

"Know any of those clowns?" Chloe asked. "They look like they got lost on their way to Tattoo."

"Listen, I hope you didn't split on Sunday because of that woman at the bar. Or the chick in the cat suit."

"None of the above. One of those guys? Was my boss."

"I thought you work in an office."

"I'm not saying I can account for it, I'm just telling you why I left."

"What's the name of your company again?"

She laughed at him. "Why, you think I'm lying? That I'm actually a porn star?"

"No. If you were you'd have a nicer car."

"Those girls make a lot, huh?" She sounded like she might be considering it in earnest.

Ben wanted to avoid a public hard-on. "Want to go?"

"I guess. Where?"

"Are you hungry?" he asked.

"I could eat."

"There's this weird place I stumbled on, serves Romanian food. I was going to wait until Saturday to take you—"

"But we seem to need something to occupy us."

Ben nodded, felt warm from the wine. "Occupy. Exactly."

"What *is* Romanian food?"

He led her back across Ventura to the car. "I have no idea. I thought you'd know, you're the chef."

"Dracula was from Romania. Maybe they'll have blood pudding."

She started the car, killing the conversation.

The restaurant proved elusive, having no sign. But an odd building housed it, a long white box with a sharp-peaked roof. Stucco, no windows—just an oversized, wooden door that could have been attached to a castle. Vaguely reminiscent of a church, sans steeple.

Chloe stepped out of the car and looked around. "I have no idea where we are."

Ben pointed up the road. "Three blocks that way is the 110–105 interchange."

The castle door opened to a long foyer and inside was cool and cozy. Dim lighting, much of it from candles, dark wood on the floors and the steeped ceiling remained exposed. At the far end of the foyer, a brunette college-aged girl sat in front of a register. She hopped off her stool when Ben and Chloe entered. "Welcome to Vlad's!" She gave them a warm smile.

"I love your dress!" Chloe spouted in admiration of the girl's floor-length black and purple velvet gown. The top fit like a vest while the bottom belled.

"Thanks! My Gramma made it."

She led them through an oversized entranceway to the main room where crisp white linen covered three rows of square tables. In the corner by the fireplace, two men crouched over a chess game while an enormous black dog slept under the table. Aside from them, Ben and Chloe were the only customers.

The girl sat them at the table farthest from the concentrating men, explained the menu and made suggestions in good, only slightly-accented English. While she was talking, an older gentleman in his shirt sleeves and wearing an apron sneaked around her to set a basket of warm bread on the table.

"Take your time. Let me know if you have questions."

Ben set the menu aside. "Apparently Romanian food is organ meats, wine, and vodka. And bread."

Chloe broke the loaf into two large chunks. "Our question has been answered."

"Ours has but mine hasn't."

"What?"

"You never told me where you work."

"I did so, on our first date."

"Tell me again."

The girl brought a bottle of wine, made an elegant ceremony of opening it and letting them smell the cork, then poured just enough in each glass to obtain their approval before leaving the bottle.

"Survivanoia," Chloe reminded him once the waitress had left.

Ben snapped his fingers. "Ah! There was a reason I forgot, which is because I wanted to, because of that whole scandal with the Flower Flu."

Chloe squinted at him. "Scandal?"

"The week I met you, in fact, some lawyer ran an ad looking for people whose relatives died of Flower Flu. She's claiming that Survivanoia has a treatment and won't release it, so she's doing a class-action suit."

"Class action. And it's 'filing.'"

"What?"

"It's just called class action."

"Oh. Anyway, I—"

"I don't know anything about this. You saw it in the paper?"

Ben nodded, feeling that something had the potential to go very wrong very soon, like a soaring kite the moment before it pitches to the ground.

"I'm not saying you're responsible. It's not like you run the place, you're . . . inside sales, right?"

"Right."

"See, I was listening. I just suffer from short-term memory loss."

Chloe's face brightened—the kite finding the wind. "So if I ask you next week, you'll remember?"

"You're pretty funny."

"You say that a lot, are you aware? But you never laugh at anything I say. You don't even smile, you just give me this sort of smirk."

Ben gave just the smirk she spoke of. "That's my Afterschool Special, as you termed it."

"Go on, I'm tuned in. I've got popcorn and everything. Even better, I've got wine."

"Really good wine, too." He helped himself to another glass. "Okay . . . I came here from Pittsburgh to do comedy. Believe it or not, Pittsburgh has a good reputation, comedy-wise."

"Vonnie confirms that, yes."

"I did pretty good out there, and I don't have that Pittsburgh accent."

"True. You haven't said 'yuns' or 'Stillers' once since I met you."

"So, I figured I had a shot. I come out here and I'm doing alright, playing places like Adlibs and getting good reviews and a word here and there from some bigger names."

"And then? Tragedy struck." Chloe mimicked a violin.

Ben tossed back the rest of his wine. He told her about how his taste buds went funny on him one day. Apples tasted salty. Then his lip tingled and went numb, and that night at the club, he laughed at somebody's joke and his face felt weird, like half of it was taped down. He ran to the men's room to see.

"Bell's palsy," Chloe guessed.

"Right. You had it?"

"A friend, briefly. They gave her some steroids and something else—antibiotics? And it went away in a couple weeks."

"Mine didn't." Ben had been saddled with a broken face for almost ten months. "So in the interest of not scaring anybody, I taught myself this smirk. It used to go along with a shoulder raise and a little snort." He demonstrated. "I thought I'd appear clever and refined. They thought I was a stuck-up prick. I got blacklisted."

Chloe's brow furrowed. "Why didn't you just tell them the truth?"

"Embarrassed! *Palsy?* Everybody makes fun of the palsy kid!"

The black behemoth under the chess table raised his head at Ben's outburst.

Ben leaned in and said in what sounded to him like a whisper, "That's the biggest goddamn German shepherd I've ever seen. Or Doberman. I mix all those pointy dogs up. That's one of the few things I can say in Spanish. I can ask where the bathroom is, call somebody nasty names, and I can say the dog is big and black."

"We seem to have gotten off topic."

"Oh, yeah." Ben shrugged. "So I took up bartending. I'm a loser, baby."

Chloe sat back. "I'm to believe that a clever, successful guy—at least when he's not drunk—traveled three thousand miles, got himself on a stage, and then let a temporary embarrassing inconvenience kill his career?"

He struggled with her words for a moment, then asked, "What *would* you believe?"

"You wanted to be a bartender."

"Nice. Thanks very much."

"What's wrong with it? You make a lot of money. You're good at it."

"Who the hell are you to tell me what I'm good at? I was funny, goddammit!"

The dog looked up again, grumbled.

Chloe folded her arms. "Funny haha or funny peculiar?"

Ben smirked. "Very clever. Touché."

"I have another friend like you, he's this great teacher—"

"Please. Drop it."

"—but he scorns teaching and continues to struggle with his painfully mediocre—"

"Will you please! Shut—"

Two huge hands shoved him backward. No, not hands—paws. Ben's chair tipped and a maw of white teeth snarled beneath smoldering brown eyes. He heard a sharp cry in a foreign language. He scrambled out of the chair, landed on his belly. Something dropped from his pocket.

The chess players circled him, he heard their bantering, saw their formal shoes. He noticed the one man's pants were two inches too short and that his socks were stark white.

Then he heard Chloe's voice rise above the chaos. "Hey! Where'd you get these?"

He squinted up at her, pinned by the weight of the dog, who stood on his back and held him gently but firmly by his neck, police-dog style. She held a wallet. Not his. A worn, black wallet. And now she rubbed his nose in the funny orange money.

"These are pollution credits," she informed him. "Stolen from my company. You're in a lot of trouble, Mister Bartender."

"That's not m—"

A growl cut him off, made convincing by its teeth. Chloe snapped the stranger's wallet closed with a flourish. "This whole wallet is stolen. I'm stealing it back."

He saw the flame of orange certificates against the minty green whirl of Chloe's dress and watched her platforms clomp out the door. A rivulet of drool ran down the side of his neck.

At least it wasn't blood, he thought, that'd come later when the Porno Mafia people came after him for a wallet they knew he had. Overhead, the distraught chess players flapped and squawked and then Chloe's stereo rose above them with that same damn Duran Duran song. "Don't say a prayer for me now . . ."

It would not be denied. His lips pulled away from his teeth, and his mouth fell open and for the first time in years, Ben smiled. Really smiled. He smiled so big he thought he must be buzzing, like fluorescent lights or a muted television.

"You're in trouble!" she'd said. He savored this. The understatement did it, pushed a hearty bark from the back of his throat, a laugh! Benjamin Myers, Bartender Extraordinaire, laughed and laughed and laughed.

CHAPTER 8

"**A**re you insured?"

Geo Rivera peered over his shoulder at the woman. Her voice, simultaneously buttery and malice-laced, matched her demeanor.

"Excuse me, what?" He spun in his office chair to face her.

"Insurance. Medical, life, car."

"Are you ... selling some?" His brow rumpled. He wondered why this woman—sexy though she may be—was going, what, office to office? Cubicle to cubicle? Didn't they have meetings for this sort of thing?

The woman, model-tall but curvy, strolled to the center of Geo's office. Geo stared in awe at her hair, a complicated wine-red braid that fishtailed below her hips. She, meanwhile, took in his office.

Being the head of the sales department got him out of a cubicle. But not being a VP meant that instead of the courtyard garden, his window faced the parking lot and the mountains beyond.

Originally, Geo had centered his desk in this picture window, facing it out to the mountains. He'd lined the walls with bookshelves and occupied the visitor chair with the giant rubber plant they'd issued him, leaving both plant and chair to stand guard off to his left. But having his back to the door incited his paranoia.

He'd tried keeping the desk in the window but facing the office. That spooked him too. Finally, he'd tucked the desk into the corner formed by the window and the right wall, kitty-corner from the office door. He'd still felt exposed, so he set the giant plant behind him—between him and the window. He'd recently requested a second plant, to locate strategically between his desk and the door.

The redhead scrutinized his cornered desk, the plant hiding behind it and the half-empty bookcases. He sensed from her the same detached disgust his mother had displayed when visiting his first college apartment. But this woman was Geo's age: mid-thirties.

He suddenly felt schlumpy. It struck him how difficult it was to make a good impression when you're sitting down. She'd no way of knowing that at six feet, he nearly matched her remarkable height. She hadn't gotten close enough to see his green eyes—eyes the girls all squealed about—hell, she hadn't even shaken his hand.

Her gaze found him. "Is somebody trying to kill you? Because this"— she waggled a finger in the direction of his desk—"is very uninviting."

First insurance, now feng shui.

Geo's cell phone buzzed in his pocket.

"I've got a lot to do," he told the woman, checking the number. "So if you want to leave your little flyers or whatever...."

The caller ID came up *unknown name* but he recognized the 323 number as Kate's, which meant he didn't want to answer it.

His attention returned to the sexy redhead. "I'll call you if I'm interested, how's that?" He tilted his head so that a lock of his dirty-blond hair fell into his eyes and tossed a toothy smile most women found alluring. He was considering giving her his business card. His other business card.

I could use this woman, he thought. He'd never seen a tall girl so well put together. Usually they were obese or the opposite extreme—all bandy-legged with linebacker shoulders; human hangers. This one would have made a perfect Venus model. No, better: her breasts were good and round and large. And that hair. Imagine it let loose! A man could get lost in that hair.

She leaned against his desk, crossed her arms, and gazed at him evenly. Geo could smell her, a blend of leather and expensive cigars. And sex. His cell phone buzzed again. Same number as before. When he looked up from the display, the woman's violet eyes caught and held his.

"I won't countenance being tailgated," she told him.

"Countenance?"

"Tolerate."

"Oh."

Her voice remained smooth; deceptively edgy. "And running your Jeep into my vehicle would be equivalent to driving into a stopped train. If you're going to continue to drive like that, I'm hoping you're insured."

Geo recognized her threat, like an offer he couldn't refuse. But he also liked the way she looked and smelled and the impossible purple of her eyes. Even her threat kind of turned him on.

"This is Los Angeles," he said in the low monotone Kate hated. She called it his Disappointed Dad Voice. "Everybody tailgates."

"Not me they don't," the woman purred. She stood, strolled to the threshold, and shot him a wicked, challenging grin.

Then she was gone.

His cell vibrated a third time. A different number appeared on the screen with the name ANTEATERS' THRIFT SHOPPE. What had Kate done? Shoplifted? Literally shopped till she dropped? Dead? Geo should be so lucky. He sighed then flipped his phone open.

As soon as he said hello, Kate came at him with her upspeak. "I understand that we're in the process of breaking up? And I know you want me out of the apartment as soon as possible? Even though I *found* the apartment?"

Geo cringed at her series of "questions." When he'd met her, it had, of course, been endearing.

He responded in Dad Voice. "What is it you want?"

"I want to know why you sent all my stuff to the thrift store!"

What on Earth was she on about? "You told me to take the box by the door to Anteaters'."

"The box by the front door. Not the kitchen door!"

Oh. That did kind of make sense.

"You did this on purpose," she accused.

Actually, he hadn't. He'd been trying in earnest to be helpful. While he didn't want to live with her anymore, he didn't intentionally want to hurt her, either. Did he? Was it unconscious? Regardless, Geo maintained his monotone. "You said 'box by the door.'"

"Why would I leave a box to go out by the *kitchen* door? This is an example of how you don't listen. When we were fighting before? And I said, 'You don't ever listen to me?' And you said, 'What do you mean?' *This* is what I mean."

Why was she calling him at work, anyway? Of course he was pretty much always at work, one job or the other.

"—my friends all tell me you're screwing your starlets? But I said—"

And Kate had put up with that, actually. A lot of girls wouldn't. Or his distraction. Or irritability.

"—and make you food and all the time? And make sure you have clean clothes and—"

Probably it would help if he got more sleep. But when? He couldn't quit this job—the movies easily paid for their own production costs, but they weren't going to pay his living expenses yet. Not after reinvestments like the new computer, and he really needed to buy lights and stop renting.

"You did this on purpose!" Kate said again. Her voice cracked and Geo knew she'd started crying. "Now I gotta buy back all my shit from them cuz they don't believe me! You should come down here and fix this. I don't have money and—"

"This is going to sound cold, Kate, but I don't have time for you right now."

He snapped his phone shut and turned it off. No more buzzing, let her voicemail and text herself into oblivion. Or at least until it took the edge off. Speaking of which. . . .

He opened his bottom desk drawer and retrieved a bottle of Don

Eduardo Silver tequila he'd purchased in Mexico. From it he poured two fingers into his coffee cup and sucked it down. Maybe in LA it was only 3:00 but it was five o'clock in . . . Chicago!

"You should really turn your desk around," a different woman told him. "You're going to get caught one day by someone who cares."

Geo spun in his chair again to face Chloe, one of his inside-sales girls, carrying a stack of multi-colored files.

"Like the Baroness," Chloe stated, trying to squelch a smirk.

Geo recovered from guzzling his exceptional tequila and coughed out, "Who?"

Chloe strutted to his desk but stood next to it and didn't lean against it like the redhead.

"I saw her leaving your office. That tall woman? She's the new company president."

"Since when?"

"Monday."

"*Yesterday* Monday?"

"Uh-huh."

"What happened to the old company president?"

Chloe raised a shoulder, let it drop. "Nobody seems to know."

"Hmm." He considered this. Grimly. "What did you need?"

Chloe told him. But he found Chloe distracting as well. Sales "girl" was a misnomer—she was almost thirty. Where the new company president dressed like a lawyer in silk and wool and high-heeled sling backs, Chloe had on a lacy button-down over flared pants and flat heeled, black Mary Janes painted with flames. A fashionable blend of cute and dangerous. A chocolate martini to the Baroness's cellared cabernet. The Baroness was complex, refined. Chloe was ripe.

"Are you listening to me?"

"Of course," Geo lied. "I'll fix it." He took the stack of folders from her.

"And I fixed the McCreery account. He did pay us. I chased that down with accounts payable and he's back with his standard monthly order again."

119

"Good."

She pursed her lips. "You're welcome."

He nodded and sent her away with his toothy smile.

Yeah. His second job was definitely getting to him. At "the other side of thirty," as they'd so graciously described it at his 36th birthday party, he found that less than seven hours of sleep left him fuzzy-headed and easily distracted. Geo seldom saw a bed for more than four hours. At least not a bed for sleeping.

Naked women cluttered his thoughts the same way they cluttered his life. Porn stars, even the amateurs he used, got to thinking they were really stars and behaved accordingly, all temper tantrums and bad manners. One thing he appreciated about his day job: he was the star here.

At least he had been. With the old company president. From his window he saw the Baroness—and how dubious a title was that anyway?—saw her stroll across the blacktop toward a yellow Hummer. The yellow Hummer she'd told him not to tailgate. It was parked next to his Jeep.

Geo snatched his car keys off his desk. He trotted around the U of the top floor, down the gentle curve of the wide steel staircase, past the retinal scanners and out the door.

He slowed once he got outside. Heat came off the tarmac in visible waves and immediately a puddle began forming in the middle of his lower back.

"Leaving early?" he called to the amazing redhead.

"Are you?" She had her own Dad Voice.

Geo smirked.

She gave her enigmatic smile, cocked her head like a curious animal. "Did you check with Scally?"

Geo waved away both the question and his boss's name. "Never."

"I'll have to take that up with him." Still grinning, she opened the door to her vehicle.

Geo noticed the near-silence. The late afternoon heat kept the animals sheltered. Not like at night, when the air filled with the cries of night birds and songs of insects that sounded like they must be as big as a person's head. Mornings and evenings, hawks perched on the streetlamps, many of the lights too new yet to have been outfitted with bulbs. The industrial park was so actively encroaching on wildlife that Geo had once found a coyote in the passenger's seat of his open-top Jeep, eating half a club sandwich he'd left there.

He glanced toward the hills, where graders and bulldozers sat perched in front of a large stand of trees. He'd hiked those mountains; Kate was a backpacker and knew the terrain. Sloped. Nothing too steep or treacherous. That's what the Baroness's vehicle was built for. Water and trenches and steep-ass mountains. But it sparkled in the drenching sunlight. Not a speck.

"How come you went with yellow?" he asked. "Shows dirt."

"I always have it cleaned after I take it out."

"I thought you'd tell me you had two of them. One for work and one for play."

The Baroness's eyes hooded almost imperceptibly, and her nostrils flared. "*That* would be excessive." She shut the bright yellow door without slamming it and rolled down her window silently. "One more thing, Geo. I expect you to change your outgoing phone message. Today. Before you leave."

Geo felt himself blush even in the heat. He'd forgotten about that message; he'd recorded it after a late night at the office with the old company president.

"You've reached Survivanoia's BiiiiiiIIG MAC DADDY! If you've got my money, press one. If you're calling to purchase goods, press two. Wanna see my grill? Leave a message."

Yeah, the old company president had kept more powerful stuff than tequila in his bottom desk drawer.

Thinking of the message and the man who helped him record it left Geo smirking again He walked in front of the new company president's Hummer. "I'll change it from home, I promise."

* * *

"So then what?"

"I got in my Jeep and tailgated her home."

"Like *home* home?"

"Naw. Where I get off the 405 to the 101, she keeps going."

Geo leaned back in his chair and grinned at Ed Bloodworth. Geo thought of Ed as Little Eddie. Ed, Geo knew, considered Geo a rich, smarmy bastard. But fate had brought them together some seven years back. Now they met once a week for dinner. Often, as now, they went to I'll Tell Ya's, the restaurant name a play on the owner, Attalla Reznavi.

Abundant blond wood made the large rectangular room bright and inviting. Classy but friendly, not upscale, and definitely not cozy. I'll Tell Ya's had no menu; instead Attalla interviewed you and told you what you would be eating.

Eddie scooped a mound of baba ghanouj onto a pita triangle. "Where's this Baroness live?" He spoke with a hint of New Jersey accent even though he'd grown up in LA just like Geo.

"Dunno. Hell, I didn't know who she was until six hours ago. She drives this car, I looked it up. It costs nearly as much as my first condo."

"Don't tell me it's a—"

"Hummer." Geo nodded. "Open top H13 Omega in Africanized yellow with the Exploitation Package."

"What's that, like the off-road package?"

"Right. And a tailgate spare carrier and chrome everything-they-make-in-chrome."

Eddie's brow knitted. "You kinda sound like you're stalking this woman. Or at least her car."

"I used to be a gearhead is all."

"Ah, so you're jealous." Ed seemed pleased. "Speaking of jealous, your girlfriend—"

"Ex."

122

"—called me today."

"What'd she want?"

"Wanted me to pretend to be you and get some stuff out of hock or something?"

Geo explained about Anteaters' and the box by the door. "It really was an accident."

"Whatever."

"Did you help her?"

"I was down in Santa Monica. There was no way I could make it on time. But I said a lot of I'm sorries and that seemed to cheer her up a little."

Attalla came to the table, smiling as always. He wore a crisp and fitted off-white linen dishdasha. The ankle-length garment's green trim made it sporty, an image reinforced by Attalla's Teva sandals.

Usually, he started with a checklist: Are you Kosher? Vegetarian? Any food allergies? Geo and Ed were regulars, so Attalla no longer gave them this preliminary interrogation; he jumped right to the salient questions. "You are having look like good day or bad?"

Ed shrugged. "You mean by my own personal gauge or in general?"

"Ah." Attalla bobbed his head sagely. "Yes, so is bad day from home or is bad day from work?"

"Unemployed."

"Okay, bad day from work, non. And is end of month. Rent, non. Yes, I know what you need." He turned to Geo. "And you sir, Mister Geo, look like what today?"

"Never better."

"Very wonderful. Very wonderful look like for you. Okay." He pointed a stubby copper finger at Ed. "You need fried chicken with mashed potatoes, gravy, and soda. Regular, not diet. And dessert. Apple dumpling look like is best. For the very wonderful gentleman, we bring a porterhouse and a double shot of whisky. Bourbon. Is best with the grilled cow."

Attalla drifted off. Ed laughed to himself. "One day I'm gonna get that steak."

"Why not just lie?"

"I tried that once. 'I'm doing great today,' I told him. He squinted at me and said, 'Look like liar's platter!' and stormed off. Had one of the busboys bring me my meal."

"No way! What was it?"

"Mushy asparagus, overcooked liver, and instant rice."

Geo guffawed, sipped his lemon water. "Well, maybe I can help you help yourself. You said you found a new location?"

Ed sat up straight. "Have I! Spacious house, brightly lit, hardwood floor, white shag carpet."

"Nice."

"In front of the fireplace!"

The men grinned at each other.

"And," said Ed with flourish, "a private beach."

"All that house and a beach? How's the kitchen?"

Eddie nodded. "Got one of those butcher block things. Real big one. You could probably, you know, use it."

"When do the owners come back?"

"Not for three months. He just bought an island and they need to go furnish it or something."

"Excellent. You never steer me wrong, Eddie." Geo dug his wallet from his pants. "What are they paying you to housesit?"

"Nothing. They felt that letting me live there was payment enough." Ed's tone said he conceded.

Geo fished three one-hundred dollar bills from his wallet. "You'll get that doubled after we shoot. And dinner's on me."

Ed brightened at the money and the fact of a free meal.

Geo smirked. "You wanna be in this one?"

"Nope."

Geo clucked his teeth. "Waste of a good cock."

Ed always turned red at sex talk. He didn't watch porn, didn't even like cable-friendly sex. "How come everybody has this knowledge of . . . me?"

"You must have had a chatty girlfriend. So how big is it anyway?"

"I have no idea."

"Liar."

Ed flushed to crimson.

"Everybody measures it," Geo stated. "Especially our generation, we grew up with that candy bar with the ruler right there on the wrapper. And if you don't measure it, you have some crazy girlfriend that does."

Eddie stared into his water glass, stuck the fat floating slice of lemon with his fork. Geo dipped a triangle into the baba ghanouj and savored it. He had never gotten Ed to tell him, but word on the street put Ed's endowments in the double digits. All the more impressive given his mere average height. Plus how lanky he was. Lanky and pale with a mop of unruly red hair. An actual redheaded stepchild.

Or in Geo's case, step*brother*. What a weird thing to have acquired at age twenty-nine. Eddie had been only twenty-four. Looked closer to eighteen. Dressed young, too, mostly in black like tonight—black T-shirt over black jeans. Should have been on the other coast. He would have fit in; here in LA, he just seemed hostile. Ed reminded Geo of an angry teenager, the kind of sullen kid who might bring a gun to school.

Their food arrived. Ed's mountainous comfort food looked frumpy opposite Geo's tidy steak; his soda childish next to Geo's neat bourbon.

"I have something else you might be interested in," Ed informed Geo around a mouthful of chicken.

"Uhm?"

"NOx credits."

"What?"

"State-issued nitrogen oxides emission credits. Anything with combustion requires them and right now they're worth thousands each because of the energy problem."

"I know what they are. How did you get your hands on them?"

"They came as a sort of bonus."

"In?"

"One of the books I stole."

Geo took a drink of his strong, thin bourbon. He licked his lips. "You know, they're going to figure out that the guy who sat their house probably stole their first editions."

"No, no, I don't steal from the houses I watch anymore. I got nailed."

"Really."

"Yeah. Some comedy agent guy. These NOx credits came in his book actually."

"He busts you for his book and you don't think he'll miss the credits?"

"Naw, once he met me he said I could keep it. He never asked me about them, I don't think he knows they were in there. Book's got somebody else's name in the imprint."

"Only you. Of all the things to steal."

"Some of these books are worth a lot of money! First editions and anything that's signed. Books are like . . . Cinderella. They're the Cinderellas of the antique world."

"So are you done stealing them now?"

"Naw, I still lift 'em, I'm just more surreptitious now. I go—"

"More what?"

"Uh, sneaky."

"Oh."

"Yeah, I'm sneakier about it. I go to estate sales, sneak around in rooms I'm not supposed to, like libraries and offices. People blame the auctioneer, figuring he didn't tell me. Anyway, these NOx creds, you know, it's best to unload them soon, while the market is up."

"What makes you think I'd want them?"

Ed tossed a hand in the air. "You know people. You hang out with business people and stuff. People who might need these things."

"I'll keep my ears open," Geo promised, figuring he could take a finder's fee. He was also coveting Eddie's apple dumpling but didn't want to admit it. Successful people weren't supposed to desire dessert, apparently. Or maybe it was Attalla's secret way to let Ed get back at him for dinner.

Geo sipped his coffee. Eddie finished his dumpling (taking his time, in Geo's opinion), and stopped just short of licking the plate. Geo paid, left a handsome tip. Outside, the air remained thick with heat. Geo offered Eddie a ride.

"Naw, I'm gonna maybe sneak into a movie. You working tonight?"

"Yessir, and I'm looking forward to it."

"You still act?" Eddie asked around the cigarette he was lighting. "Or does directing keep you off screen now?"

"Seldom. Cameos."

Eddie laughed. "You're a porn extra. There's a job."

"Better than a fluffer."

Eddie blew a stream of smoke like a dragon. "And the money seems to be good."

"I keep telling you, any time you want to be on film, I got a place for you."

Eddie turned him down, red-faced and polite.

Geo got in his Jeep. "I'll be in touch later in the week about the new place. We'll get a filming schedule together."

"Cool," Eddie said, and Geo watched his stepbrother saunter down the dirty sidewalk like a red-headed James Dean.

* * *

Geo rested his forehead against the soothing cool of his desktop. His body ached for sleep. It occurred to him that three weeks of trying to film one movie while in preproduction for another might kill him. Thank fucking God, no pun intended, that the Palm Springs shoot was in the can. Nearly a two-hour commute each way? Screw that! Again, no pun intended.

God, he was tired.

Now he got to shoot at Eddie's new-found beach house. Shorter drive and no creepy old people who passed for twenty-something until you saw their hands. Brrrrrr!

He took a deep breath, focused on the spreadsheet displayed on his laptop. A tally, by region: sales of the Panic Bed. The Panic Bed scared him. No pun . . . yeah. What if you closed up the bed because people broke in, or they dropped the bomb, or crop-dusted the city with anthrax or whatever, you closed it but then when it was over you couldn't get out again?

Sure, the bed came standard with an air filter and two weeks' water stored in the mattress, but then what? Would it be worse to die out in the world of a fever or the inability to breathe, or to dehydrate to death in your own bed? Of course, maybe you'd just fall asleep and not wake up, given that you were, in fact, in a bed. A soft, warm, climate-controlled bed; you could just sleep forever.

Wow, that sounded nice. Sleep forever. Geo wondered idly if anyone had ever died from lack of sleep. Not from falling asleep at the wheel or getting caught in a piece of heavy machinery for lack of alertness but just plain died as a direct result of not sleeping enough ever.

Just twenty minutes, he thought, *and I'll be fine*. It didn't seem like much to ask. Hell, the plant floor guys got a ten-minute break that typically extended to twenty. Nobody scolded them. Who would notice, anyway? He stood up and eased his office door closed, the sign that his staff knew meant he was on the phone and not to be disturbed. But the moment his head lay on his crossed arms, his phone rang.

He squinted at the in-house ID. "The Baroness," it said. Not "Company President," not even her name; just her self-proclaimed, dubious title. It took less effort to push the speakerphone button than to pick up the receiver.

"Hello?"

"Wakey, wakey," the Baroness cooed. "Your expense reports are fakey."

Geo sprang awake instantly, searching for cameras and wondering aloud, "What the hell are you talking about?"

"Come see me, please, Geo. You know where my office is, right?"

He didn't, but he hung up anyway. After getting directions to her office—the old president's office—from the bemused Chloe, he pulled himself together and nonchalantly swaggered through the U of the upper floor to the end.

The president's office sat opposite the CEO's. The fact of the CEO having an office was a waste of space in Geo's opinion, since the CEO apparently lived in some other country and only came to visit about four times a year. Why not let one of the VPs have the office?

He realized, as he approached the Baroness's closed door, that he hadn't been in the room since the old company president quit. Or was murdered. Abducted? Whatever. Nervousness slowed his strut. Who worked with a closed door, anyway?

He knocked on it and the door opened slightly. The Baroness's plush voice bid him good morning. "Enter."

He did. It felt like walking into a dream. Gone was the institutional fluorescent lighting, banished were the matching non-colors; the seafoam green, the clamshell pink. Geo had to adjust to the low light—actual sunlight, filtered through crimson velvet curtains.

Having been friends with the former company president, Geo knew this office as it had been. A bigger particle-board desk than everyone else's, made with a more convincing veneer, and the bottom drawer housing a bottle of Islay single malt Scotch alongside the occasional bag of illicit white powder. Now, everything had changed. Even the carpet felt different, springy and thick.

He took a look at it. White! This chick had a white carpet on her office floor. Behind her enormous desk stood an even more imposing white bear. Its arms were up and its fangs were bared; it seemed quite angry.

The Baroness had done away with the standard particle-board office shelving, replaced it with mahogany paneling that matched her desk, and above that, from about waist-height to the ceiling, built-in bookshelves.

One of the shelves held a buzzing thing, two stiff wires meeting in a V at a block beneath them. A spark ran up the wires with a tiny zap. Like in old horror movies. Geo stuffed his hands into his pockets.

"What is that thing?"

"It's a Jacob's Ladder."

The crackling line of light made the hair on his neck stand up. He moved away from it. "Did you kill that bear?" he asked.

"No. You're in some trouble, Geo. Have a seat."

He stood next to the leather chair facing her desk but didn't sit. The Baroness stood, came around to his side of the desk. She produced a file folder seemingly from mid-air, opened it, and read for a moment, then told Geo, "Jack Hayward is a close personal friend whose thirty-fifth anniversary party I attended last summer, so I know you didn't take him to Bill's Tacky Lady." She gazed at Geo, crumpled up the report, and tossed it at his feet.

Scanning another one, she said: "T.C. Aupperle consistently pretends to be a vegetarian when he's in Los Angeles, so I'm certain it's not him you took to Ruth's Chris." Crumpled and tossed.

"And Ali Farah is a Muslim. He doesn't drink or gamble. I know some of them do, but Ali doesn't. Hollywood Park? I don't think so." This time she tossed the entire folder into the air. Expense reports fluttered down around them as she gazed at him.

"Hollywood Park isn't even classy, Geo."

"Yeah, I wait too long to do 'em and I forget stuff. I'll fix them. It's— you're—things are—why are you doing expense reports anyway?"

"Because I fired Sandy."

"Oh." He waited and she let him. Continued to gaze at him with those impossible eyes. And she smelled fantastic.

His eyes drifted to the curve of her hip, broad compared with her slender waist—oh how much he'd give to run his hand along it, run his tongue along it—*shit!* He brought himself back to work. Work and Dad Voice—flat and cool. "Is that why you called me in here? Am I fired?"

"Would you like to be?"

Their eyes locked. He counted a slow ten but then fought a smile, looked at the floor.

"I know why you leave early." She leaned in next to him, whispered her next words. "I've seen your movies." A pause. Then she drew a sharp breath. Geo steadied himself with an arm against the chair.

The Baroness moved away, taking her heat. "What you do on your time is your business." Her eyes caught his and held them. Cool as chrome in winter. "During office hours, you are my business. And at the moment, business is bad."

Geo shrugged carelessly. "I'll fix it. All of it. Gimme a week." He passed halfway through her office door before looking back at her. She remained leaned against her desk and displayed a fiendish grin.

Geo cast a hand at the mess on the floor. "I'll send Chloe to get this."

"Of course you will."

Geo made his way back to his office feeling like he'd smoked out. Time was all messed up and everything made him want to laugh. He ducked his head into the cube-farm, asked Chloe to see the Baroness for him, and then he kept right on walking down the stairs and out the door and to his Jeep, which would take him home to bed.

* * *

"It's too windy," Eddie said. Again.

This time, Geo relented. Rubbing his temples, he called the cast and crew to wrap it up and move it indoors. "We'll film the kitchen scene today."

He'd stopped at Ishmael's for a giant coffee, but the caffeine had left him more irritable than awake. He grouched to Eddie the whole trek up the wide, wooden, sandy stairs from the house to the private beach. "How can it be this hot and this windy? It's not Santa Ana season. And why won't Colleen break down and buy some tits? She's got that great pouty under-bite. Built for blowjobs. But then I always have to bring Kristin in for the money shot. That means a fluffer, which costs me."

"They're only housewives," Eddie reminded him. "If you want circus tits, hire real porn stars."

"That's the opposite of what I'm trying to accomplish here. The whole point is that they *are* real. Real bored and real horny. And real housewives."

"Real, real, real. Then Colleen's breast size shouldn't be a concern."

"You don't understand this industry, Eddie."

Ed tossed a hand in the air. "Some guys like small breasts."

"Some guys like it in the ass, too. I'm not making—what the hell's that!"

They had reached the top of the stairs, and Geo stopped, staring wide-eyed at an actor's trailer emblazoned with a five-pointed star formed by the silhouettes of two kissing go-go girls. He recognized the logo; anyone in the industry would have. Zane Frears defined the new pornography, getting as close to live sex shows as was legally possible, and in fact many times crossing the line and going to court. So far he'd won every case. Zane was a pornographer's pornographer.

He jogged to the house, muttering under his breath.

In the kitchen, sure enough, a tall, athletic man with deep maroon skin held Geo's cast and crew at bay with a frown and his demeanor.

When Geo entered the kitchen, Zane set velvety grey eyes on him. He ran a large, sculpted hand through his short, tawny dreadlocks. His other hand clutched a document which he shoved at Geo.

"You're not supposed to be here, man."

Geo took the paper, skimmed it over and noted the signature, and, when Eddie came loping through the door, brandished it at his brother like a weapon. "What the hell!"

Eddie's face widened in revelation, betraying him. "Uh . . . oh. Yeah. Mr. Fallon did mention that some people might be stopping by on occasion."

"And?"

"And that these people had free reign of the house and to just leave them alone to do their thing. Keep out of their way."

Geo felt Dad Voice rising. "You never said anything about this."

Eddie looked at the floor, worried his lip with his teeth. "I figured they'd just use the beach."

"You figured. Your math sucks." He turned back to Zane. "What are we—"

"Like you would have put the pieces together?" Eddie demanded.

Geo turned back to face him, mouth open.

"Like if I had told you," Eddie took a step closer, "about this warning three weeks ago, you would have had the foresight to say, oh, that must mean there's a film crew coming and we'd better—"

"You have clearly lost your mind. I don't know who you think you're talking to, my young friend, but he's not here. *I'm* here. And I'm not taking this from you."

Zane's slightly Brooklyn-accented voice interrupted them. "Are you two lovers?"

"Brothers," snapped Geo.

"Even worse," Zane laughed.

"*Step*brothers," Eddie specified through clenched teeth, and Geo again saw the gun-wielding adolescent.

Zane's face lit up with recognition. He looked from Geo's face to Eddie's, suddenly grinning. He turned to Geo. "You're the guy whose mom married Maureen Spencer." He laughed whole-heartedly and without malice. "You ever film her?"

"That's gross, dude. She's, like, my mom."

"She's your stepmom."

"Okay, yeah, I did. But *before*."

Zane's smile revealed his large, pointed teeth. "Is that how they met?"

Eddie cringed. "Stop!" He looked from one man to another. "How does everybody know all this?"

Zane put a reassuring hand on his shoulder. "It's a small industry, man. When your mom is a porn star," he tapped Eddie's chest, "your privates are public."

Eddie, looking now at the floor, whined like a tired toddler.

Zane patted his back. "So you got two moms and one's a porn star, big deal. This is LA." He turned to Geo. "You and me, though, we gotta chat, man."

He took Geo by the elbow and led him out of the kitchen and into the foyer. "Listen up now. I got no beef with you. But this here is uncool. If I call Sonny and tell him what's going on here, you and your entourage are toast."

Geo nodded and nodded and nodded some more. "So what is it—what do you need? What should we do? In your opinion?"

"Reparations or repercussions."

Geo blinked at him.

Zane lifted his hands in an ironic gesture of surrender. "It's your choice. Know what I'm saying?"

Geo didn't, which was actually the trouble. Reparations? Repercussions? Did Zane want money? A drum set?

"How about," Geo asked slowly, "if I move my crew out. And we leave. And we don't come back. Ever."

"That's a start."

Jesus, he did want a drum set. Geo swallowed back Dad Voice, tried to sound neutral. "Tell me what would be a finish."

"Maureen."

"What!"

Zane nodded. "Get me your stepmom for a shoot."

"You're kidding. Dude, she's, like, over fifty."

"So is every goddamn baby-boomer in the country, man."

Geo rolled his eyes. "The last thing old saggy people want to look at is other old saggy people fucking."

"Maureen isn't all that saggy. Besides, the men might all get off to Lolita, but the women? They want to see an image of themselves with some college-aged stud." Zane winked, handed Geo a business card. "Check into it and let me know. Meanwhile, get your shit out of my way. I got a movie to shoot."

So for the second time in less than an hour, Geo packed up his cast and crew. He told everybody he'd call them, except Eddie who he decided to take to dinner. On the freeway, he broached Zane's request of Eddie's mom.

"No."

"Eddie, come on."

"You ask her."

"Your mother hates me, she's always hated me and you know it. *My* mother on the other hand seems to like you more than she likes me." Geo sulked in the driver's seat. At least traffic was lean. Still, he had to pay all those people for a day's work and he had nothing in the can.

"Even if I wanted to ask my ma to do another movie, which I don't, she hates me right now too, so she'd say no anyway."

"What's she hate you for?"

"She found out about the lawsuit."

"You found somebody to take it?"

"I did. I meet with her on Friday." Eddie dug his wallet from his pants and read from a business card. "Theresa Tehzan. She's with Tehzan, Preston, and Guite."

"Wow, a partner."

"Their slogan is 'Experts in the Unprecedented.' Which I think is a sustained oxymoron."

"Oxymoron?"

"Like freezer burn or jumbo shrimp? Dude, I am *so* buying you a dictionary."

Geo shot Eddie a fierce glare. "Why don't you just steal one?"

Eddie didn't answer, which irritated Geo even more. "Just what's wrong with you anyway?"

"You mean especially right now, or in general?"

"Who sues their mother for not aborting him!"

"The unemployable, uselessly-literate, kleptomaniac son of an aging porn star. Do I need to define any of those words?"

"You wanna walk home? Cuz I can abandon you at I'll Tell Ya's. Won't be the—holy shit." He pointed to the vehicle in front of them in the next lane. A chromed-out yellow Hummer.

"Is that your boss?"

"Yup." He checked his rearview. A blue Pluto beside him, so he sped up in his own lane. He glanced left, but the little blue SUV was still there. Desperate, he put on his blinker.

Eddie cocked his head, frowning. "Her license plate is incongru— doesn't make sense."

The Pluto eased back, and Geo yanked the Jeep into the fast lane behind the Baroness. He looked at her vanity plate: ROSN80. "Why?"

"I'm assuming that it's a reference to—you're driving awfully close, even for LA, dude—to Don Quixote's horse. But his horse was all tore up and that's a new ride. That you're about to SMASH INTO! What are you doing?!"

Geo licked his lips. "It's our way of flirting."

The Hummer sped up to ninety-five, and Geo kept pace, watching nothing but the gleaming bumper.

"Geo, my ma will sue your ass if you kill me. Geo!"

He watched his speedometer creep up to one hundred. "Going that fast, she's gotta have a Turbonator in that thing."

"You wanna screw *her* or the car?" Despite his sarcasm, Eddie panted with fear. Geo glanced over and saw his stepbrother was nearly milk-white in the bright sun. He was about to tease the kid when Eddie yelped like an injured puppy, "STOP!"

The shiny bumper rose like an angry beast. Its sparkling chrome reflected the Hummer's brake lights. Everything slowed. Geo saw the tiny spattering of mud on the bottom of the chrome, made out the patterns in the plastic bumps of the brake light covers.

He yanked his Jeep's steering wheel right. A white sedan blared its horn and the driver hurled curses in two languages. Geo pitched back into the fast lane just as the Hummer sped off.

He sunk his teeth into his bottom lip and shoved his foot against the gas pedal.

Eddie punched him, hard in the arm. "Knock it off!"

When he ignored Eddie's anger it shifted to appeal. "Geo, *please*. You're going to get us killed. Or worse, injured badly. I don't have any health insurance."

He relented. The Baroness had maneuvered two cars ahead anyway, and he saw that the sedan driver was on his cell phone, so there was a very good chance that CHP would be cruising through the area shortly.

"Some day I'm going to get her." He said this through clenched teeth. And even as he said it, he knew he wasn't sure just what he meant.

SURVIVANOIA

III

The High Price of the Wild Truth

CHAPTER 9

Jackson Blake's grandfather rattled off his usual morning litany, emphasizing his imminent death and the likelihood of its resulting from the rotten food at the nursing home.

"Then they'll close all the doors, how they do. How's a closed door gonna save us from death? They don't even lock 'em! As if—" He stopped abruptly.

The old man leaned forward, squinted his wrinkly eyes, and peered at his grandson. With a concern Jackson hadn't heard since his grammar-school days nearly thirty years ago, the old man asked, "What happened to your face, kid?"

It was the third in a series of events that convinced Jackson the world was destined for swift and soon destruction. His grandfather's sudden reversal, the Perfumed Woman in the elevator, and the coyote. These formed, in Jackson's mind, an ominous triumvirate.

He raised a hand to his swollen lip and bruised cheek and eye. At least his nose wasn't broken. Jackson liked his nose. "A Greco-Roman nose," TV Guide's Adam Fitzpatrick had once said about it, "classic and expressive." Jackson was glad not to have had his expressive nose busted.

His four-year "Face of a Handsome Boxer" epithet had taken on a new meaning last night. He'd assumed his grandfather wouldn't see it, just like he couldn't see the television or the crosswords anymore. "I was helping my neighbor move."

"That's not a helping-your-neighbor-move face. That's a got-busted-with-your-neighbor's-wife face."

"Not exactly."

What to tell Grampa Pedro?

At 3:00 in the morning, Jackson had been awakened by an odd and unplaceable noise—like glass breaking in slow motion. He peered through his peephole and saw his immediate upstairs neighbor poised on the upper landing. The cement stairs led down to Jackson's doorstep, and Mel—the neighbor—clutched a giant pink crayon and gaped sadly at Jackson's door. Which Jackson opened.

"What's wrong Mel?" The giant crayon functioned as a coin bank, as evidenced by the ankle-deep pile of assorted change that cascaded onto his feet. "Mel" was Melvina, Jackson's newly dress-wearing, male-appearing neighbor who recently expressed a preference for the *she* pronoun.

"Sshhhh!" In a harsh whisper, Melvina told Jackson: "I'm sneaking out. I can't pay the rent and I don't want to be evicted."

"So you're moving out at 3:00 in the morning? You—"

"SHHH!"

Jackson whispered back, "You don't even have a car!"

"I called a cab; it's waiting outside. I'm taking what fits in it. I was going to take my crayon, you know, but . . ." Melvina gestured helplessly at the shiny mess at the bottom of the stairs.

"If you cashed that all in you could probably pay your rent!"

"I need it for groceries. Besides, I found a cheaper place. In Hollywood."

Jackson questioned the existence of a cheaper place than their fifty-five-unit North Hollywood barrio building.

"East of Vine," Melvina explained.

After making Melvina promise not to become a prostitute, Jackson helped his neighbor refill the pink crayon as quietly as possible, by first pushing all the coins into his studio apartment and then scooping them back into the bank.

"I thought you had a job." Jackson dropped a handful of coins into the mouth of the giant cardboard crayon. Its point came off, which made filling it easier. The bottom also came off, which Melvina hadn't known until a few minutes ago.

"I got fired," she sulked. "They caught me working on my novel at my desk. But I got my work done. It's not like anybody who came into the office would ever know I wasn't working on an article or something. I think it's sexism."

Jackson glanced at Melvina's five o'clock shadow and her hairy, unshaved legs, visible past her knee-length floral tank dress. Melvina wasn't what Jackson thought of as a transsexual. To Jackson, Melvina barely qualified as a transvestite. To Jackson, Melvina was simply a man in a dress.

"Sexism?"

"People think it's over, but far from it. Believe you me!" She winked.

Jackson let it go. Melvina was odd but intelligent and funny, and the only friend Jackson had made in the six months since he'd moved from bourgeois-artsy Central Coast. So he helped Melvina get the last of her few things—a suitcase and a lamp—while the cab meter ticked.

Then Jackson gave her the business card of the Perfumed Woman from the elevator, advising Melvina to be honest about why she'd been fired. "You can tell her I sent you if you want. And tell her you're good with phones. And you don't like research."

"Thank you sooo much," Melvina gushed gruffly. "I wish I could buy you lunch or something. I'll email you a copy of the novel! No one else has seen it yet, not even my agent."

Jackson agreed that'd be great.

So he had been helping his neighbor move. But that's not what earned him the shiner.

He'd tried going back to sleep, but the bar in his fold-out couch had seemed especially uncomfortable. Or maybe it was the heat. Three—no, four—in the morning and the temperature still hung in triple digits. He missed the ocean, wished he had some vodka. Or weed. Or heroin. Or gasoline.

Instead he found his book—Haruki Murakami's *Wild Sheep Chase*. Jackson had loved private investigator books since childhood when he'd read himself to sleep under the sheets with a flashlight. Tonight, though, just as the sandman came calling, another commotion dragged him from bed. This was a more familiar noise.

Tanya lived upstairs, next door to Melvina. She and Melvina swapped quick-and-easy recipes, and Tanya tried to provide Melvina tips on how to be more feminine. But while Melvina sequestered herself away (apparently to write a book), Tanya had a string of bad boyfriends. There'd been musicians, actors, a crooked judge who turned up dead, a handsome Persian prince who got deported, and a doctor who seemed promising until he was arrested for writing phony pain-med prescriptions.

Now some new clown hollered in the hallway while she shushed him. Jackson squinted into his peephole again. This time he saw Tanya on the landing, pinned against the wall by some lumbering suit. Suit's hand kept pushing her skirt up her thigh and hers kept pushing his back down. Finally she squirmed away from him. "I think it's better if you go."

Her date laughed. "We been together three weeks, and it's time I get me a little somethin' somethin'."

SLAP! "I'll give you a little something!"

Their scuffle took them out of Jackson's limited view. Should he do something? It meant admitting he'd been spying. A snippet of his TV show's opening song surfaced to memory: "*Always help the helpless . . .*"

Other guys had their college-days radio music, Jackson had his theme song. He sang through it silently, "*Always help the helpless, never fear the fearless, be doubtful of the doubtless, give the penniless your change . . .*" he hummed his way through the bridge, then heard a small whine and a dull thud followed by a chilling quiet.

He tossed open his door. "Tanya?"

He could see her legs sprawled awkwardly on the landing, the rest of her obscured by her kneeling date.

The Suit turned and snarled at him. "Mind your own damn business!"

Jackson jolted up the stairs. Some temporary insanity, the heat or exhaustion, made him grab Tanya's six-feet-plus date by his immense shoulders. He yanked backwards, sent Suit tumbling. Suit tumbled all the way back onto his feet and out the door, grumbling curses and threats.

Tanya pulled herself to consciousness. She saw a man standing over her and slugged him in the face with everything she had. That man, of course, was Jackson. And what Tanya had was a full bottle of Scotch. A kinder world would have given Jackson a new friend. One that shared her liquor. Instead, Tanya's confusion or embarrassment sent her lunging up the stairs, where she slammed her door in Jackson's face.

So what to tell his grandfather? Did it even matter? The old man believed and remembered what he wanted. That's why Jackson was the only one taking care of him now.

"I was helping a neighbor move and her boyfriend showed up," Jackson said. "They had a fight and he seemed pretty out of control."

Grampa Pedro scrutinized him again. Jackson expected the usual rattle-your-chain treatment, something like *Helping her move—is that what the kids call it these days? Ha ha! You got what you had coming, boy!* But instead, Grandpa rested his chin in his hand. "Playing the hero is stupid, kid. But real nice. That's nice what you did. I guess that's what you were known for. In your day, I mean."

Jackson wondered if his grandfather felt all right. But before he could ask, one of the nurses appeared in the doorway. "There's our Mister Sailor," she jingled. Grampa Pedro cringed at her voice. "Breakfast is ready," she told Jackson.

Jackson wheeled his grandfather to the dining room then slipped away quickly, before the horror of old age had a chance to crash over him. Once-dignified people who could no longer hold a fork, who were made to wear bibs just like babies—it struck Jackson as a cruel, nasty end to a too-short life.

The elevator reeked of whatever horrible preprocessed food they'd brought up for the residents. Not like yesterday, Saturday morning, when it had smelled sweetly musky, like sex and leather and expensive cigars, reminding him of his agent's office. Yesterday, he'd waited an extra-long time, which Jackson had found confusing since the arrow told him the elevator was headed down and his grandfather lived on the top floor. When it opened, a woman appeared. Quite a woman.

Her height struck him first, above his own five-eleven. Then her hair— wine red—and down past her hips even in a complex braid. Godiva, he thought. I've met Lady Godiva in the elevator. Jackson stepped inside, needlessly pressed the button for the lobby and then stared at the floor.

"You look familiar." Her voice matched her opulent scent.

"Maybe you've seen me around the home," he suggested.

"That's not it." Her confidence impressed him. "Turn sideways?"

He laughed but did as requested.

She squinted at him. "Say: 'Consider your ticket punched.'"

He repeated the phrase dully.

"Say it right!" she implored, and they both laughed.

"You busted me." He grinned at her.

She smiled back, her violet eyes gleaming. "That was a good show. Why'd they cancel it?"

The show she referred to was *Ferryman*. He'd played the starring role, Jared Ferryman, a hitman's hitman. His first killing had been to avenge his father after proclaiming he'd never follow in his father's gun-for-hire footsteps. Of course, one thing led to another, and every episode had him killing somebody. It was a dark comedy; Jared was a Melrose grunge kid with a tribal neck tattoo and an attitude bigger than a house.

The show predated *Six Feet Under* and *Nip/Tuck* and even *The Sopranos*, and had been a hit with critics and audiences alike. Still, "Egos got in the way. MGM picked it up for a movie, which they filmed but never released because Tommie—Tomas Jacobs over at Fox?—he just hated me." Jackson shrugged. "You know how it goes."

"What are you doing now?"

"I seem to have a penchant for getting fired."

The elevator stopped. The woman exited but didn't continue to the entranceway. "Who fires the famous?"

"Debt collectors, the *LA Picayune* subscription department, movie survey people. This month."

"Not good with phones?"

"Not good with people. After my show was canceled, I took the money and ran to Central Coast. Found an investor who keeps me in buttons and bows, and I stay up with the trees and the fish, where it's safe.

"But then Grandpa got sick, and the money's not enough to cover a place here and . . ." Jackson trailed off, at once saddened by his pathetic state and startled by his own sudden garrulousness. Something in this woman, her impossible colors and her chocolate voice, worked on him like strong liquor.

"How are you with stuff—objects? Good?"

"I'd say so, yeah."

A business card materialized. "If you'd like a job—testing things—phone me. I can use more people in R&D."

Jackson took the card, which was made to look as though it was forged from steel, complete with rivets. A sharp, raised S sat in the center, the ubiquitous S Jackson saw everywhere. But he'd assumed the company an urban myth, which in actuality only made clothing.

"Survivanoia. You make actual stuff?"

"Like you wouldn't believe." Her eyes sparkled.

"I've got a baseball cap by you guys. Lead lined, you know."

"Do you like it?"

"Sure. I haven't, like, needed it."

"You mean you haven't been shot at yet."

Jackson nodded. The fact of such a sophisticated woman so unflinchingly able to discuss violence set him off-kilter.

"Well, now you can get paid to find out if it works." She strolled out the sliding doors, leaving Jackson with alarming images of himself bent over double in his lead-lined, supposedly bullet-resistant, baseball cap while somebody took aim at his head.

Then the woman shot him a toothy grin over her shoulder that startled and shocked him. Because, what, with those perfect teeth and the red hair and that clever, daring grin, she looked just like the coyote. The coyote had started it all Saturday morning.

Saturday mornings are sleepier than weekdays. Jackson went to visit his grandfather every morning though, and always before breakfast. Sometimes, if he was feeling especially generous, he'd go in the evening as well, but he always went before breakfast no matter how grumpy he was. Jackson and the dayworkers were the only people awake most Saturdays.

Yesterday had started out typical. He first picked up coffee and a newspaper for Grampa Pedro, a trip that, as usual, brought him to the broad intersection on Ventura Boulevard right where the bookstore and Ishmael's are located.

All the lights hung red for a moment. And then, the coyote caught Jackson's eye. It strolled through the lawns of wealthy south-side residents and paused, peering up at the traffic signal. The signal changed in the coyote's favor, and the animal jaunted across Ventura and off to do business. Eat cats and carry off babies, Jackson had figured.

Jackson's now-deceased brother, Carl, had adored coyotes, said they were "really excellent." He'd once expounded on their extensive appearance in Native American mythology. At the stoplight, Jackson recalled none of it, only the pain of his loss. But seeing the mythical little beast reflected in a beautiful, enigmatic woman's face brought something back. Jokesters and creators. Creatures who would play you for a fool to teach you a lesson.

Of course, he'd given her card to Melvina. Maybe Melvina would get taught the lesson. Like don't wear Old Spice if you plan to put on a dress! Here in the elevator, Jackson laughed to himself, but then felt glum. Melvina had been his only friend, and now she was gone.

The stench of the bad food nauseated him, muddled his already confused head.

He'd seen the coyote and met the Perfumed Woman just yesterday. Looking back, it felt like weeks. Earlier in the week he'd woken from vivid dreams he hadn't shaken until well after lunch, and his sleep patterns seemed to want to reverse, keep him in bed during the day and prowling the streets at night.

He'd mentioned the dreaming to Melvina, who first dismissed it as heat-related, then reconsidered and suggested Jackson's mind was turning in on itself as a result of isolation. Jackson pointed out that he'd been previously sequestered in Central Coast.

"It's not the same. You were isolated before because there was nothing around but the ocean and pine trees. Now you're surrounded by people. This isolation is the result of anonymity of a big city."

But Jackson wasn't quite anonymous either. Occasionally people recognized him from his show. Like the Perfumed Woman. No, Jackson figured the heat was his problem, believed his planned drive to Zuma Beach would help.

He drove his red Miata up the steep curves of Topanga Canyon, top down, wind whipping his dark, wavy hair. He liked it wind-blown, disguising his greying temples. A few Harleys passed him on their way to the Rock Shop.

A group of kids on Hondas buzzed by him too, leaning so low on the curves that Jackson chewed his lip, afraid for them. Aside from helmets, the kids wore no protective gear, no chaps, not even boots. They were dressed for the most part like Jackson, in knee-length rip-stop shorts and ringer tank tops and sandals. He envied their moxie.

Once he got to the top of the canyon, a cool breeze hit him, and as he sped down the other winding side, the temperature dropped nearly twenty degrees. The chill cleared his head, and the sight of the ocean, even from so far up, soothed him instantly.

Pacific Coast Highway was jammed with cars, full of everything from movie producers and their trophy wives to minivans of fat little kids. Zuma Beach was packed too, with no open spaces on the beach road. He had to park on the highway, wait for a lull in traffic, then dart across four lanes.

The day's modest waves attracted twice the usual surfers, since newbies could catch them and not injure themselves, while veterans showed off and picked up chicks. Or guys. Jackson noted a significant number of the surfers were girls. Different from when he'd surfed. He'd never been any good but his TV self (naturally) surfed whenever he wasn't killing people or hanging out on Melrose being a smart-ass. Ah, the joy of television clichés.

Jackson stretched out on his towel and set to reading.

"Nice tattoo." A red bikini-clad girl with shoulder-length, salt- and sun-chewed hair blocked his light. "Does it mean something?"

She inspected the tribal band on his right biceps. Jackson had stolen the pattern from Jared Ferryman's neck tattoo. Superficially it appeared as any other tribal band, but closer inspection revealed the name Charon, and for the studious, the Greek version appeared as well.

"A friend of mine designed it," Jackson said. He watched her eyes steal a glance beyond the tattoo along the length of his taut frame.

She gave him a cute smile. "Anybody sitting here?"

"No, go ahead."

Jackson watched the girl—"I'm Stacey"—unroll her Spider-Man towel, and dig through a big red bag for some sunscreen. He figured her a kid, maybe twenty. Too young. Too bad. She smiled at him again, then caught sight of his left side, despite the visor and sunglasses. "Somebody beat you up. Oohhh." She pouted adorably. Jackson had forgotten the ability of a bruised face to garner attention and sympathy.

"You should see the other guy," he joked. Then added, "It looks worse than it feels," when she still appeared worried.

She frowned, unconvinced, but dropped the subject. "Whatcha reading?"

Jackson showed her his book.

"Translated! Are you a college student?"

"Naw. This is really just an old-fashioned PI novel. Well, sort of Raymond Chandler meets Don Delillo, you know? Gritty but introspective."

She cocked her head at him, like he'd triggered some memory. "You look familiar."

He just shrugged, hoping her age meant she hadn't seen his show, that she mistook him for somebody else. This was why he avoided Santa Monica; all the German tourists were just now importing early '90s American television and they all recognized him.

So did she. "You're Jared Ferryman! Ohmigawd I loved your show when I was a kid! Wow, and you're a regular guy. At the beach." She dug a pen and a notebook out of her giant bag. "So you like that writer? *Wild . . . Sheep . . .* a,m,i. What else do you read? Who'd you say, Raymond Armadillo?"

Jackson, grinning, corrected her. She charmed him. Was she by herself? Not exactly. "I'm here with my brother, but he just divorced his wife and doesn't want me around interfering with his macking."

They talked about books—she liked Candice Bushnell and Steve Martin—sunscreened each other, and bodysurfed together for a while. Jackson felt light and happy, and began to wonder if Melvina had been right, that he needed somebody to play with.

As they trundled back to shore, an enormous wave crashed over them. The rush of cool water shoved Stacey off balance. Jackson grabbed her around the waist to keep her from going under.

And then her mouth was pressed against his, soft and salty and warm. Nice. *She's too young* splashed through his mind. *This is wrong.* But it didn't feel wrong, it felt good. Another wave crashed over them and he pulled her against him.

Her mouth opened and her tongue brushed against his lips. Jackson yielded. He tugged her closer, nibbled her tongue and her mouth, felt a soft whimper escape her. Their kiss broke and she fell against him, sighed deeply, "Jared."

Oh.

In the moment, Jackson recognized the scene for the schoolgirl fantasy it was; Stacey's brother recognized his kid sister making out with some guy.

"Hey!" A gruff voice hollered over the surf's roar. Then *splash! splash! splash!* and a stocky kid with hair identical to Stacey's had her by the wrists.

But he chose to yell at Jackson—"*Leave my sister alone!*"—and all that. And she hollered back about leaving her by herself while he scoped hotties on the beach and what's good for the goose.

Though reluctant to involve himself in some obvious long-running family dispute, Jackson felt obligated to defend his would-be girlfriend. He said something about her being an adult and making her own decisions.

"An adult? She's sixteen!"

Oh . . . hell.

Jackson rubbed his grey temples and cursed God while Stacey and her burly brother packed up her things and argued their way off the beach.

* * *

"Where've you been?" his Grampa Pedro grumbled a morning greeting. "I thought you weren't coming this morning." As usual, he had wheeled himself to the lobby and vultured by the elevator door until Jackson arrived at his customary 5:00 a.m. Seemed he was back to grumpy, grouchy normal.

"I'm here same time as always. Here's your paper."

"Coffee?"

"Yeah, that too. You want to go to the big room?"

Grampa Pedro's wizened head bobbed in agreement. Jackson handed him the two coffees to hold, grasped the back of the wheelchair, and pushed slowly down the quiet length of the hallway.

The nursing home resembled a Vegas hotel with its garish carpet, gaudy wallpaper, and wall sconces shaped like different flowers. It didn't quite smell like a hospital.

Jackson wheeled his grandfather into "the big room," a sort of con-ference room for old people with two large glass dining room tables set up against each other and ringed by attractive, but uncomfortable, white wicker chairs. The room sat in the corner of the three-story building, looking out over the parking lot and the meticulous landscaping.

Jackson arranged Grampa Pedro so he could look out the window, even though the old man couldn't see past the length of his arm.

"So. How's your job going?" It was the same question Pedro asked every morning once they settled into the big room.

"Good," Jackson lied. "The same." For weeks he'd been lying, because he figured it was easier than explaining about getting fired repeatedly.

"You take a lot of orders, then?"

"Yup. Get a commission on every one."

"That's good. Not many places give a commission anymore."

Grampa Pedro thrust the paper at him. "Read me the obits, would ya? Make sure I'm still alive to drink this coffee."

Jackson dutifully read the obituary section aloud, just the names. On occasion, Grandpa heard a name he knew, and Jackson read the whole listing. Today he didn't recognize anybody.

He struggled with his coffee lid. "Hate these damn squishy Styrofoam cups."

Jackson knew he wouldn't ask for help. And since Jackson was feeling particularly dark this morning, he didn't offer any. The lid finally came off and Grampa Pedro took a long, loud slurp.

He wrinkled his nose. "That fancy stuff?"

"That's what I like."

"Waste a'money. What you pay, three dollars for these coffees? I never paid more than a dime in my life."

"And you still haven't. I have. You're welcome."

"Dinner made me sick again last night," his grandfather growled. "Beginning to think the problem is me. Might not be around much longer, you know. At my age, really, I could go any minute."

"Only the young die good," Jackson mumbled.

"What's that?"

"Nothing."

Grampa Pedro stared out the window. "Yup, dinner was downright lousy. The nurse asked me how I liked it, I told her it looked like something that the dog threw up." He continued like this. Somehow the nurses found it endearing.

Jackson stopped listening. He reflexively uhm-hmmed when pauses prompted him to do so, frowned when his grandfather's tone became especially harsh. But he was thinking about his wrist, wondering if he should have it looked at. It hurt, but it wasn't swollen. Wouldn't it swell if he'd broken it?

This morning? No. Last night. Evening, really. After the red-bikini girl had left, Jackson went to the Sunset Restaurant. The Sunset used to be the Grey Whale, a place frequented (and therefore made a popular tourist destination) by Jared Ferryman. Why did everything in LA smack of Jackson's alter ego?

The Sunset served painfully mediocre food dressed up in fancy sauces and served with flower-cut radishes and bunny-folded napkins. But the wait staff smiled and laughed with him, and at 5:00, the piano bar opened.

Like the restaurant, the singer proved comfortably predictable: in tune, mid-range versions of Billy Joel and Beatles songs designed to leave the Malibu barflies nostalgic. The atmosphere and a bottle of wine kept him warmly buzzed until the sun left only a line of violet against the black horizon of the sea.

A few songs and cups of coffee later, Jackson had headed out. The walk up the beachway seemed longer in the dark, and cars lined it only intermittently now. Toward the end, where the beach-front road met the PCH, Jackson heard a nasty argument.

"You. Backed. Over. My. Bike!" A young man's voice.

Jackson stopped in the shadows. "My bike" referred to a small bright green Honda lying next to the kid, sideways and dented. The kid, tall but thin, faced off against three well-built older looking guys whose surfboard-filled Land Rover had apparently backed over Slim's motorcycle. Slim wanted insurance info.

He wasn't getting it. "If you had a real bike instead of that Jap piece of shit, maybe it could handle a little love tap."

It always eluded Jackson when people in real life behaved the way of people on television. He searched the ground and found a piece of driftwood to serve as a big stick, then without moving from the shadows, said calmly, "Give him your insurance numbers and get off my beach."

The bullies acted according to script, playing nice cop/nasty cop, with two of them talking tough while getting in the truck to leave. But the nasty one had some point to prove and lumbered at Jackson, frothing obscenities. *CRACK!* And the driftwood busted in two over Nasty's head.

The friends rushed after him, spewing curse-spangled information. "I was fucking getting it, dude. I'm with Triple A, fuck! You didn't have to break his goddamn head open, he's just drunk..."

The driver tossed a AAA business card at Jackson, then he and the other nice guy loaded their friend into the truck. They sped off with a grind of rubber and a flume of sand.

Slim propped his bike up, but it practically formed a V—clearly unrideable.

"You need a lift?" Jackson offered.

"Naw, I called somebody." He sounded more frightened than before.

Jackson saw the glow of a cell phone and figured the kid would be fine. He handed him the insurance card, then fought déjà vu the rest of his way home.

Back at his hotbox apartment, the adrenaline must finally have faded since his hand started throbbing. This morning its ache had woken him up. But no swelling. And no health insurance. Probably it was fine, right?

A sing-songy voice tore through his reverie. "Sailor Man! Breakfast is ready!"

Grampa Pedro cringed as he always did at her effervescence. But instead of resigning himself to being wheeled down to the dining room, he suddenly turned on Jackson with the previous day's lucidity. "Why do you work anyway, kid?"

Jackson somehow managed to keep his mouth from falling open. "Uhh . . . what?"

"Didn't you make enough money being famous? What are you working for?"

The old man leaned in, his eyes glowing with concern. "Is it because you're back in LA? Too expensive here?"

Jackson stared stupidly at a man he'd thought he knew. "Um . . ." All this time he'd been lying and he could have been telling the truth? "I thought you'd want me to work."

Grampa Pedro's wrinkled face absolutely pruned with confusion. "WHY? Why work if you don't have to?"

"I'll, uh . . . quit. If you'd like?"

"It's about what you'd like." A bony finger stuck Jackson in the chest.

The same sickeningly cheerful nurse appeared in the doorway again. "Mister Sailor's going to be late. Don't want cold eggs. Not yummy."

Jackson assured her they'd be right down.

His grandfather wagged a finger after the nurse. "It's about what you'd like," he said, "with one exception." He gazed at Jackson, his eyes glowing with an immediacy the younger man did not recognize. "When was I in the Navy, kid?"

"During the war?"

"Right. I was drafted into World War II along with most of the rest of the world. And that's when I happened to meet your grandmother.

"Her parents wanted her with a Marine, not a sailor. She told them I'd proposed. They said, 'Not that sailor!' Her father called me Mister Sailor until the day he dropped dead. Four years in the Navy, no more. But guess what your grandmother made me promise to put on my tombstone?" Affection stippled his voice.

"'It's about what'd you'd like,'" he continued, "'except for the way you're introduced to the world.' That's a big truth, that introduction. Even if it's wrong! Even if it's wrong, it's a big, wild, crazy truth. Because it's how others see you. And people's opinions are their truths. Their reality."

Jackson gaped at his grandfather. When was the last time they'd spoken like this? Jackson had still been in high school. He wanted to keep it going. "What if their reality doesn't match yours? What do you do?"

Grampa Pedro shrugged. "What I did was I fought against Mister Sailor the rest of my life. I could have re-enlisted. Should have. Millie woulda been happier. But I fought it. You can fight it or you can embrace it. Either way, it's gonna come find you in the end."

Grampa Pedro stared past him, into something Jackson wasn't privy to, maybe his warm past with Gramma Millie? Maybe his cold, dark future in the ground?

Jackson, meanwhile, considered Melvina. She was certainly fighting her introduction to the world. Unapologetically! But Grandpa was right— that fighting came at a price.

Jackson realized that Melvina knew this, was well aware of that when she'd winked at him while they'd been refilling the crayon. It was a literal wink-and-nod, really acknowledging not sexism, but a different prejudice. The kind you experience when the world says you're that but you know you're this.

"Wouldn't it be easier to just find people who agreed with you?" he asked his grandfather.

The old man looked at him curiously, as if he wasn't confident about the context of the question. A pang of loss flitted through Jackson.

And what was he? Jackson? Other than a washed-up TV actor slowly slipping into obscurity in a crappy apartment in North Hollywood? Doing a poor, impatient job of helping an old man die. Just what would Jackson Blake be fighting for?

As Jackson wondered this, he watched his grandfather's face slip from alert and alive back to dull and droopy. From his jaunty, curious grandfather whom he admired, to a sick, elderly man he felt sorry for.

The old man faced him. "Hey, we'd better get down there! I don't want cold eggs. That slop is bad enough warm."

* * *

"Don't you have anything smaller?"

Jackson blinked at the clerk and the hundred dollar bill he'd handed him, then fumbled with the wallet. "I, uh . . . I dunno."

Had the kid behind the counter been less uninterested, he might have noticed the streaky fingerprints on the black leather wallet, smears of crimson that would dry to brown by dawn. But at 4:30 in the morning, Quick Mart clerks have more pressing concerns than a confused, subtly blood-stained man unfamiliar with his monies.

Jackson dug through the stranger's wallet, found a twenty and took the C-note back from the clerk. He collected his newspaper, two unfancy Grandpa coffees, and box of donuts. He got back in his car, headed to the nursing home, and the entire event went unremarked.

At a long stoplight, he flipped through the wallet to find out whose it was, maybe get it back to them. Ed Bloodworth, the guy in the driver's license photo, looked surprisingly decent. And young, especially for his Melrose address. Probably worked in the industry. Had a nice face—broad and high-cheekboned, big blue eyes against pale skin, and a red wave of hair. And this was a license photo. Whose license photo looked that good?

Jackson had pulled into the convenience store lot just as the young man exited his souped-up 1969 Mustang. Primer grey but the engine purred. The kid made the mistake of parking his muscle car in front of the store but out of the light. So he didn't see the guy in the dark alley along the side of the building. The guy who pointed a gun at him and dragged him into the darkness.

On whatever death-wish whim, Jackson followed, found a second robber back there—a thin wiry shadow. The shadow cackled profanity-riddled insults at the Mustang kid, who lay on the ground, silent, taking a beating.

"Police!" Jackson bellowed, flashing open his wallet in hopes of maybe faking himself some clout.

Wiry cursed and fled.

"*Pinche puto!*" the gun guy yelled after him in an accent that told Jackson he was white. The he turned to Jackson. "You're no fucking cop!" He displayed a mouth full of teeth. "But since you're back here, *pendajo*, what you got? Huh? Hand it over!"

The gun gleamed and its owner came at Jackson like a late train. Jackson heard the injured man stir and whimper from behind the dumpster. A pitiful, distressing sound that awoke in Jackson a righteous bravery. *Always help the helpless . . .*

Everything slowed and made sense.

Jackson landed a solid foot to the gunman's groin with his steel-toed engineer's boots. The perp fell like a sack of manure and the gun skittered away.

Jackson caught sight of the victim limping off, a dark hunch against the blossoming daylight. He kicked the robber in the face, heard a groan. He stomped on one of his hands, then snatched the gun from the ground and turned it against the perp. "Consider your ticket punched," he growled.

But he didn't shoot. The robber was already knocked out and had pissed himself either from injury or out of fear. Jackson pointed the gun at him, curious if he could pull the trigger under the right circumstances.

But these weren't them. That fact pulled him back to broader reality. He'd retrieved the Mustang kid's wallet from the alley, taken a moment to not puke by the dumpster, then gone in the store like nothing had happened.

Now he pulled into the nursing home parking lot nearly fifteen minutes late. The elevator seemed to take forever and when it finally did open on the third floor, Grampa Pedro wasn't waiting. Just an empty lobby full of oppressive furniture and plastic flowers.

Jackson headed to his grandfather's room, imagining the lecture he'd be subjected to this morning. Maybe the donuts would shield him. Yeah, they could be his excuse. They didn't have the right ones at—

Halfway down the hall Jackson noticed something different. It seemed smaller somehow. The doors were all closed, that was it. So someone had died. And here came the nurse, her face a portrait of sympathy, so Jackson knew it was his someone.

"We're so sorry . . . in his sleep . . . tried to phone you . . . wish to see the body?"

See the body? Good lord no!

"The body is a husk," he mumbled, and got back on the elevator.

It smelled like cigars and leather again—like the Perfumed Woman. The gun weighted Jackson's pocket in a hauntingly familiar way. The sensation of its weight combined with that tantalizing scent to form a forceful elixir. It solidified his sense of completion. It washed away the creeping guilt of not being too mournful about losing Grampa Pedro, of feeling his grandfather had been gone a long time already.

Jackson left the nursing home feeling content and confident, like he finally fit into the world. And why not?

Jared Ferryman didn't have any living relatives.

SURVIVANOIA

IV

(Arrivals)

Rough Passage for Biiiig Mac Daddy (Part 2)

Mysterious Bastard

Now That You've Eaten Your Own

CHAPTER 10

Geo's week passed, uneventful. **He** filmed at the home of one of his housewives. Not as elaborate as the place Eddie had found, but it had a pool and a giant dining room table, so he didn't have to change the script much.

At Survivanoia, he redid his sales reports and turned them in to the Baroness, who said nothing. He tended to find his way to the hallway when she was there and often in the parking lot, but then ignored her in his practiced, aloof way. A couple of times he tailgated her to the 405/101 interchange. She always brake-checked him. And she always outdrove him.

Then, the following Wednesday, two strange things tossed his world back into a tailspin. First, coming out of the breakroom with his afternoon coffee, he was accosted by the most eccentric woman he'd ever seen. Hairy-legged and stubbly-chinned and smelling of Old Spice aftershave, wearing a gauzy, fluttery, lavender and yellow dress.

The woman stuck out a hand, which Geo shook because it was his habit as a salesman to shake outstretched hands.

"I'm Melvina, I just started today," a gravelly, self-assured voice told Geo.

Perhaps it was the self-assuredness that set Geo's mind to wandering.

What kind of boobs were underneath all that flowing fabric? Just how strong were those hands? What—

"I understand you're my boss's boss."

"You work in sales, then?"

"Yup."

"Oh. Welcome."

And Melvina streaked off into the sales cube-farm.

Geo retreated to his office. The Baroness called as he reached for his tequila drawer, "You've got a new hire," and he could hear the grin in her voice. Then that grin faded. "And you've got a problem. Come see me."

As he approached the Baroness's closed door, he heard a man's laughter and a slight Brooklyn accent. "Good. Then I'll see you tonight."

The office door opened. A tall, athletic man with deep maroon skin stepped from the inner darkness. Geo nearly choked.

"Geo!" Zane purred. "Good to see you, man. I've been meaning to contact you." He winked and offered a hand, which Geo again shook automatically.

"I'll call this week," he heard himself saying, along with some other niceties that he supposed covered his astonishment.

The Baroness's office was brighter than before, the drapes open farther. The Baroness leaned against her desk with her arms folded across her chest, smiling like she'd won money.

Geo sipped his coffee. "What's with the new girl?"

The Baroness appeared, for the faintest flicker of a second, bemused. Like he'd accidentally done something right. Then she blinked and it was gone.

"She's bright and I think she'll do well. You and I have something more pressing to discuss."

Like magic, a certificate appeared in her hand, pale orange and slightly larger than a dollar bill. She handed it to him. "Know what that is?"

"NOx credit?"

"Know where the rest of them are?"

Geo felt suddenly cold. Dad Voice said, "Why would I?"

They stared at each other for a long moment. Geo took another sip of his coffee, gazed at the Baroness over the rim of his mug. "Why don't you take this up with our environmental compliance officer."

She leaned in close so he could smell her. "You know why."

And Geo did. He remembered Eddie asking him about NOx credits over dinner, God, *forever* ago. Eddie, who'd been missing for two days after making a point to mention that Kate had called him again and did Geo care. "Not really."

"Hmm," the Baroness purred. "Well. Figure it out."

She dismissed him. Geo trekked back to his office, poured his shot of tequila, and then in desperation called his stepmother.

"Zane is bluffing," Maureen told him, blowing out smoke from what he knew was a Salem. He heard her mixing a drink, knew it was a gin and tonic made with Beefeater. He felt lucky; she was friendlier to him when she'd had a few.

"If he was gonna cop you to Sonny," she said, "he'd'a done it first thing. Doin' it now would raise more questions than it's worth." Her thick, inescapable Jersey accent explained Eddie's, despite the logistics of his upbringing.

"Hey, have you seen Eddie?"

Maureen told Geo she hadn't. "He showed up over the weekend in some tricked-out car, some muscle car like his daddy used to drive. Seemed happy. Haven't seen him since." A pause and the tinkle of ice cubes.

Geo was thinking that the muscle car was probably Kate's, but didn't want to waste time asking.

"Maybe he's dead," Maureen said of her son. "They say suicides get happy once they make their decision. Hey, I hear you might be losin' your job."

Geo's face went all hot and prickly. What now! Did the Baroness know Eddie's mother, too? What the fuck was going on!

He took a deep breath, let it out slowly. "I'm sorry, what?"

165

Maureen drew another hit off her Salem. "That big ad in LABW. Some hotshot lawyer is suing the ass off your company—class action, baby! Some medicine youse made and won't sell. You're in sales, why won't you sell it, Jorge?"

Geo cringed at the use of his true name. "I have no control over anything here. Listen! I'm worried about Zane."

"Scared of him?"

"No." (Lie.) "We're in the same business. I don't want him blacklisting me."

Maureen smoked and drank audibly for a long moment, then conceded. "Alright, kid. The Crew hasta do a job at Tattoo on Sunday. Zane's usually there, so why'ont you go wid'em. He sees you wid'em he'll know you talked to me for real."

"Why didn't he just call you?"

"Cuz he knows I'd tell him no." She paused to sip her drink again. "Your ma says she don't want me doing no more penetration. And I respect that. Zane ever wants two old-lady dykes I can help him. Otherwise he's SOL."

"I'll let him know."

"Make sure you go wit the Crew on Sunday, call Josie. Zane sees you with the Crew, he'll leave you alone." She paused, and Geo felt she was deciding something. "I'll see if they can find Eddie for ya, too."

"Yeah. Okay, good."

"You're *welcome*."

Next he called Kate. He hadn't spoken to her since she'd moved out nearly three weeks ago. Caller ID gives your callee an unfair advantage. Kate threw attitude at him before he even said hello. "What do you want?"

"This is how you answer the phone now?"

"I'm busy? And you're bothering me?"

Her upspeak invoked his Dad Voice. "Why does my brother have your car?"

"I don't know? But he's had it since yesterday? And I haven't seen him. He was supposed to bring it back so I could go to work?"

"Are you dating?"

"What do you care? You made it clear you're not interested. Now you wanna call me and be mean for no reason?" She was crying again. Seemed like every time he talked to her, he made her cry, which was never actually his intention.

Why had he asked her that anyway? What *did* he care? He didn't have time for a girlfriend. He barely had time for a shower.

"I have to go," he told her and hung up.

* * *

Geo had at one time enjoyed being seen with the Crew—unofficially christened the Porno Mafia because they kicked ass and took names. Maureen didn't appear on camera anymore, but she was a powerhouse in the business, and her Crew protected her investments.

The Crew made an entrance wherever they were assigned—easy, since the Crew comprised mostly fetish actresses. Josie, for instance, was so thin that when she turned sideways she disappeared, but she had tits the size of cantaloupes and was perpetually dressed in thigh-high boots and some kind of cat outfit. The outfit was equally slutty and dangerous; she'd stabbed out a guy's eye with those boots.

Geo's Sunday at Tattoo, however, was not evocative in any way. Quite boring and vaguely embarrassing, actually. He'd at least been spotted by Zane, who remained seated, a calm presence amidst a storm of panic on the second floor. Seen, but not quite acknowledged by the porno legend, so that Geo still had no sense of completion, of safety. And still no sign of Eddie.

Monday night, before leaving work, Geo called Maureen again but she still hadn't seen her son. She asked him some more about the company being sued.

"I mailed the ad to you." (She had; it arrived the next day.) "Don't sweat though, kiddo. We can always get you work as a fluffer."

From work, he drove straight over the Hill, checking all the little specialty Hollywood bookshops he knew Eddie frequented. Back in the Valley, he sat outside Third Eye Books & Spells, sipped the yerba mate tea they sold in lieu of coffee, and watched the sun go down. He realized he was still in his work clothes. His stomach growled, but he hated eating dinner alone in public. Lunch alone made you a loner; dinner alone made you lonely.

Tuesday, he followed the same routine but haunted art galleries and pawnshops instead of bookstores. The only lead he got was from some surfer artist with a Viking name. The Viking asked if Eddie lived in Melrose, cuz some kid with a bloody name owed him money and the last address he had for the kid, someone else he knew was living there now.

Geo left the storefront gallery more confused than when he'd entered. He broke down, went to I'll Tell Ya's lonely, and Attalla was not fooled by his expensive suit: Geo got the fried chicken and apple pie.

Now it was Wednesday morning, 8:36 a.m., and Geo slumped across his desk as he seemed to do most mornings. He'd gotten enough sleep every night this week, hadn't hit the tequila yet this morning—though the thought had crossed his mind. God, was he depressed? Was he turning into one of those people? For fuck's sake!

He couldn't keep his cast waiting any longer, had to get back to work. What was he thinking, wasting three days like—*brbrbrrrrring*!

His desk phone lit up and the ID told him it was his supervisor, Sydney Scalinescu. He often forgot that he had a supervisor, especially with the Baroness being so up in his business as of late. Geo supposed Scally was nice as bosses go; "nice" being the word Geo used when he couldn't come up with anything bad.

"Geo, can you come see me in my office, please?"

Crissakes, what did he want? Geo felt in no shape to deal with bosses today; he might say something unrecoverable.

"You mean right now? I'm swamped."

"It'll be quick."

Now he hit the tequila. And felt much better. *Maybe I should get myself on those Xanax,* he thought. *Use this depression thing to my advantage. Depression. Ridiculous!*

He meandered partway down the hall, then thought of something, wandered back, and took Maureen's envelope from his desk. Maybe he'd pick a fight. That sometimes made him feel better. He then made his way down the hall like a dawdling child. In Scally's office—institutional and bland, the opposite of the Baroness's—he found a heavyset man sweating in a brown suit and clutching a wooden box. Both Brown Suit and Scally stared at the box and Geo felt somehow he was being made a fool.

"Geo, this is Mr. Sanchez. He's got a new little gadget he calls the poten-cho-meter. It measures the pretentiousness of people within a variable radius."

"Really."

"Do we currently have LACMA, the LA Phil, Spagos, any of those places purchasing from us, or will these be cold calls?"

What on earth was he talking about?

"I'm just trying to get a sense as to how long it will take to launch a product like this and develop a market for it."

Geo shook his head, dumbfounded. "Why would a gallery want to know the . . . pretentiousness, is that even a word? Why would they want to know that about their patrons?"

"Are you seriously asking me this? Marketing! Blah blah and yadda. . . ." That's what Geo heard anyway, because his cell phone buzzed in his pocket. He slid it out surreptitiously, glanced at the caller ID: Eddie!

Scally had stopped talking.

Geo rubbed his chin, hoping he looked thoughtful and interested. Hoping he could figure out what Scally *wanted.* "I'll look into it, Scally, and get back to you." He peeked at his phone again, seeing if Eddie had left a message.

"When?"

"When what?"

"When will you get back to me?"

"Soon," Geo assured his boss. "And I want to talk to you about this as well." He slapped the envelope on his boss's desk, then left before Scally could ask him any more questions.

Eddie hadn't left a message and Geo didn't know what that meant. He noticed it was nearly 11:00 and opted for an early lunch. On the patio of MexiCali Fresh, mopping up the last of his salsa with the butt of his shrimp and lobster burrito, he decided not to go back to Survivanoia that day.

He called Eddie's number but got shuttled to voicemail and hung up. He then called Colleen and sweet-talked her into getting the rest of the cast together. Small tits or not, the woman could start a party.

Just as his Jeep entered the 5 freeway, he caught sight of a yellow Hummer in his rearview. It crossed his mind to check with the Baroness about Zane, if things were cool. But he admitted to himself that he didn't have the guts. Then that admission pissed him off.

He kept his Jeep in the second lane, let her zip in front of him. She was on her phone but her eyes caught his and she shot him that same wicked, challenging grin.

Then she sped away, the Hummer's chrome gleaming in the oppressive sun. Geo dropped a gear, lurched over two lanes to fall in behind her. Not many cars this hour, and an easy, straight shot. Kept his eyes mostly on her tail. Shiny chrome. Vanity plate. ROSN80. What had Eddie called it? An oxymoron? He'd said it didn't—shit! Brakes!

Geo glanced in the rearview. A black SUV, but pretty far off. To the side? Enough space to maneuver if he had to. The yellow Goliath sprang away! Geo's foot pressed heavy on the gas pedal. The engine whined just a little. As they passed the 14 exchange their speed topped one hundred.

The 5 crossed into the Valley and flattened out to the 405. Chrome BUMPER! He hit the brakes, gripped the wheel. In front of the Hummer, an eighteen-wheeler. The yellow monster broke right, sped past two cars, shot over one lane, then zipped back in front of the truck.

Geo tore right. Got honked at. His exit came up. He ignored it. Fell back in behind the Hummer. Stayed what seemed like inches from that shiny bumper. At the 101/405 interchange she kept on the 405. Sped up. He followed, nearly drove over a blue Mini Cooper. Got cursed at, but fell in behind the Baroness again. He was going wherever it was she went. Straight to hell? So be it.

Traffic thickened. Inches between them. Her bumper rose. He hit the brakes. Slowed smooth, no rubber squeal. The chrome dashed away again. Geo's cell phone buzzed. *Shit!* Keeping his eyes on the road, he fished it from his pocket. Glanced at the ID. Eddie!

He flipped open the phone. "Where you been, man!"

Bumper! Coming up fast, yet slow. No mud this time. Shiny and clean. Same pattern in the brake lights. Next lane: minivan—no way out. Shit shit fuck *screeeeeeeeeee*CRUNCH!

* * *

Geo regained consciousness, still in his Jeep. He felt heavy and immobile. He couldn't feel his left leg and the toes of his right foot tingled. The alarming spiderweb of cracks in the windshield blocked his vision but he could make out some sort of chaos, people milling about and cars stopped at crooked angles on an expanse of freeway where they should have been moving, *had* been moving, moving very fast.

He swallowed, which was difficult but not exactly painful, turned his head slowly and found the Baroness standing outside his Jeep. Close to him, watching him, her eyes wide, pupils dilated.

"Don't move," she told him gently. "The EMTs are on their way."

He leaned back despite her advice, put a hand to his achy forehead. It came away sticky. Red. From the tangle of cars, he made out sounds, phones ringing, and people angry, yelling. Somewhere through the noise he heard a sound like muffled sobbing and it made him sad. He smelled a cigarette, saw that the Baroness was smoking.

"You shouldn't have tailgated me," she said softly. There was no anger in it, no mockery.

Geo gestured loosely to her cigarette, something long and oval-shaped smelling rich and decadent. "Can I get one of those?" His voice sounded scratchy.

She nodded quickly, pulled the cigarette from her mouth and placed it to his lips. He took a puff and she moved it away again. It had been nearly five years since he'd smoked and the effect was like a harder drug. It tasted wonderful, made the crash-dizziness pleasurable and floaty.

He released the smoke in a deep sigh. "Thank you."

"Of course."

Despite the pain, he turned his head to look at her. Concern furrowed her brow. Her violet eyes didn't stray from his face, regardless of the surrounding cacophony. She put the cigarette to his lips again.

"I warned you," she told him. Her voice held an odd quality, something akin to regret.

He savored and exhaled the delicious smoke. Looked into her disquieted violet eyes.

"You shouldn't have tailgated me," she said again, this time in a murmur. She placed a cool palm against the blood-wet heat of his face.

Geo swallowed, closed his eyes. "I'm sorry."

CHAPTER 11

Sydney Scalinescu stood on the corner, waiting for the light to change. Sporadic late-morning traffic kicked up grime in the hazy Bronx morning, already shimmering with heat. Southbound cleared with the streak of an angry yellow cab.

The Beastie Boys hollered from their newly-released album: "NO! SLEEP! TILL BROOKLYN!!" Their playful rage spilled out of his Walkman headphones as Sydney glanced north—red van, blue Chevy, fist full of taxis.

He frowned, peered at his watch. The fake leather band already made a damp ring around his wrist in the sticky heat, while the face told him he was ten minutes late for his first class. Second week of junior college and already he was a fuckup.

He didn't see the limo until it stopped in front of him, a slick line of black silk whose grace reminded him of a stingray. *Good driver,* he thought. *Maybe I should do that.*

The passenger door snapped open, revealing a lush crimson interior. A tall, broad guy in a dark suit came at him.

Sydney backed away, shaking his head. "No way, man!" He spun around to flee but after just two steps, knocked into the big guy's twin. "I didn't do it!" The twin shoved a pillowcase down over Sydney's head and the world went white. One of the brutes expertly zip tied his hands behind his back.

He waited for blows, or the sound of a gunshot, but the two men jammed him into the back of the car. The car moved, graceful and silent. The cool leather of the seats relaxed him a little, felt nice against his bare calves, and the pillowcase kept him safe from seeing whatever awful things shared the back of the car with him.

But he could hear. Quiet, garbled voices filled the cramped space, low and growly like a tape run backward. This made Sydney nervous, which made him laugh.

A ham-sized hand seized the pillowcase, twisted it into a tight knot around Sydney's throat. "What the fuck you laughing at!"

Sydney, smartly fearing for his life, swallowed his reply.

* * *

The car slid to a smooth stop. Rough hands pulled Sydney from his seat, something sharp cut through the zip tie, then a solid foot in the center of his back launched him from the car. He tumbled onto concrete, scraping a knee, yanked the pillowcase off his head. The car slid away, curving out of the circular driveway and into the steamy morning.

Sydney found himself at the foot of a flight of broad, shallow steps—bright white and a story high like the entrance to a museum. Two lions flanked the stairs at the top. Between the lions stood a man wearing a tuxedo and carrying a silver tray.

"Master Scalinescu, I presume," the man called. He had an accent, Austrian or something. He pronounced Sydney's name right, which was rare.

Sydney looked to the left and right.

"Yes, you, with the pillowcase. Come on up."

Sydney scratched his head, stuffed his hands in the pockets of his knee-length, black corduroy shorts, and loped up the stairs. He counted them as he went, twenty-five in all. As he approached the man with the tray, Sydney saw that he wore a blond crew cut and that his muscles bulged through his well-tailored tuxedo jacket.

The tuxedo man bowed slightly. "Do you take lemon in your Cola?"

"Nah, that's okay. I actually prefer Mountain Dew."

Tuxedo Man's lips pursed.

Sydney reached for the glass. "But thanks! I appreciate it."

The soda was nearly as cold as the ice that floated in it, and the sweat on the glass ran down Sydney's hand when he tilted it. Crisp. Bubbly. Fountain soda. He emptied half the glass, paused for a breath. His knee itched and tickled; Sydney looked down to see he was bleeding into his socks.

"Damn."

"It seems you need a bandage."

"Naw, I don't care about that. Look," he pointed to a long scuff in the tan suede of his boot. "These Timberlands are brand-ass new, man. Like, Saturday I got 'em."

"Come inside," the Tuxedo Man directed.

"And this shirt, you like this shirt?" He plucked at the short-sleeved red plaid he wore unbuttoned over his tight ringer T-shirt.

"Mister Scalinescu Senior is expecting you."

"I'm not big on plaid but my . . . Senior?"

"Your father."

"My father? No way! I live in the Bronx, man. No way anybody related to me lives here."

"Hmmm."

"My ma? She don't even speak English right. She's some kinda Romanian Gypsy or something." He set the empty glass back on Arnold's tray. "Thanks for the soda. I gotta go to school."

Sydney started down the stairs. But a voice grabbed him, stopped him, shook him.

"Sydney Ratkovitch Scalinescu!" Pronounced correctly, with the rolling

R in Ratkovitch, and said *skoo* instead of *skew* at the end of Scalinescu. Nobody did that.

Sydney turned to face a well-built man in a stylish suit. The grey pin-stripe in the man's black suit matched his wild shock of hair.

"I know because I named you," this elegant stranger said. His voice held just a dusting of an accent, but something in his diction announced him as a foreigner. "Your middle name is your mother's maiden. The rest of it is mine."

Sydney stared hard at this stranger who looked like Don Juan and sounded like a Long Island Dracula. This man who indeed seemed to be his father. And inside little Sydney, something snapped.

"Just where the hell have you been!"

"Right here."

"In this mansion. While I grew up in the Bronx?"

Sydney Senior nodded.

"That's beautiful. That's something to be proud of. You dress like that all the time? Like a goddamn mafia pimp?"

"Usually. Just as you typically dress like a stagehand."

Sydney ran a hand through his thick, chestnut hair, made a mess of it. "Some of us gotta be out in the heat, you know? Working."

His father only cocked his head.

"Fine. Enough insults and small talk. What is all this, dragging me here and shit?"

"I wanted to meet my son."

"You waited eighteen years to meet me? The anticipation was just killing you, I guess."

"What stopped you from coming to me?"

"Let's see, uhm, not knowing where the hell you were?"

"What did your mother tell you?"

"That you were in California. I'll tell you what, how about you give me some cash, we call it even? Cuz it would really help me with school, you know? You could, like, sell that tray Arnold's holding there, probably pay my whole college tuition."

Senior linked his hands behind his back. "I'm giving you nothing."

"Oh. Yeah, I can see you don't have too much to go around." Sydney chewed his lip, shook his head. "You're a real bastard, you know that? Real mysterious bastard. Wait all this time and then . . . have me brutally . . . *escorted* to your . . . *creepy* house."

A sound came out of Sydney's father, something low and mean. But a smile twisted the man's face. He was laughing. "You are the bastard."

Sydney stuffed his hands in his pockets. "That's right. That's right, I am. You abandoned me, and now I'm outta here."

He moved for the door, but two men bigger than the ones from the limo materialized, glaring. Sydney's shoulders slumped. "Now he's gonna shoot me. I wasn't killed growing up in Shitville, so now Mobster Daddy's gonna shoot me. Couldn't you at least wait till I'm sleeping?"

"You've got some amazing attitude, boy." His father sounded genuinely impressed. "Don't you have any questions for me?"

"I had one. I asked it."

"What about the money?" His father leaned in, dropped an arm over Sydney's shoulder. "Don't you want to know?"

"Let me guess. You mailed it to Ma and she refused it."

"Incorrect."

"She was your maid; you were embarrassed of the pregnancy, sent her away."

"Incorrect."

"She's not really my mother."

"That's three strikes, as they say. Come on in. Have a seat, we'll talk." Sydney Senior pulled Sydney along with him into a giant room filled with heavy, wood furniture and lined with books. An enormous white bear skin covered the floor by the entrance, its ferocious, fanged head threatening would-be visitors. The cool, dim room made the city disappear, erased the heat and noise.

Sydney ran a finger along the leather-bound book bindings. "You read all these?"

"I used to." Senior shoved Sydney into a leather chair across from an ocean of a desk.

Sydney petted the vicious rug. "How about this bear? You kill this bear?"

"Your grandfather did. My father. He hunted with Hemmingway."

Syd Senior took the high-backed wing chair behind the desk. "Let me tell you something. I'm your father. Maybe you have not seen me, but I've been around."

Sydney cocked his chin at his father.

"That's right. Who do you think got you off that murder charge?"

"What murder charge?!" Sydney's voice snapped up in pitch.

"When you inject a man with drain-unclogging liquid because he owes you money for drugs, you murder him. Are we on the same page?"

Sydney felt the warmth drain from his face, knew he was pale white. "I didn't do that! That wasn't me. That was Ian did that."

"A killer and a snitch. Bad combination."

"I'm not neither of those things. Ian ain't no pal of mine. He sells drugs to whoever, whatever age, he doesn't care. Plus, yeah, he gets nasty when people owe him dough. I don't do that. None of that. We get high together sometimes, that's it. We used to."

"And you rob liquor stores together."

Sydney crossed a leg over his bleeding knee. "It sounds bad when you say it like that."

"How would you say it?"

"Shoplifted? We shoplifted a few forties, cuz we couldn't find nobody to buy 'em for us. It's not like we took a gun to anybody. We didn't even take cash!"

"Fine, you and Ian shoplift together. You and Ian are also going to die together. Did you know that? Did you know there's a price for you?"

Sydney stared at his father for a long moment. Then he cracked a wide smile. "You're making this shit up. To scare me into doing whatever it is you want, whatever you dragged me here for. You some kinda gangster,

Dad? You trying to convince me to join your little mafia? Count me in. I want one ah them suits, though."

His father didn't smile. "The man you say you did not kill was the son of a senator. You're in a lot of trouble. Trouble I may be able to protect you from."

Sydney's grin widened. "Wait, wait . . . did the senator call you? Like, hire you to kill me and Ian? Come on, Dad! I saw that movie, too."

Syd Senior arched over the desk and slapped his son's face. "This is your last chance! I can get you out of here or you can die."

Terrible silence. Sydney put a hand to his face, more out of surprise than pain, found to his horror that he wanted to cry. He took a deep breath.

"What's the . . . ah, offer?"

"I own a company. Survivanoia. Know what that means?"

"Fear . . . of . . . living?"

"Sur, as in superior. Vive, as in life. Noia, as in mind. Superior-life-minded."

"Only the strong survive."

"We are purveyors of the post-apocalypse. We don't flinch at the wild truth. We manufacture and sell it." His father seemed to drift into sales-man mode; he stood and ambled around the room as he spoke. "We distribute some obvious things, like gas masks and civilian bio-suits."

"Civilian bio-suits are obvious?"

"Our suits are the best. They're pathogen-killing," he said with pride. "They're made of a sponge-like polymer that traps bacteria and viruses, and then disinfectants in the fabric kill them." The man's dark eyes sparkled.

"Then there's our high-tech line," he continued. "The Mighty Mass, which is a portable mass spectrometer. Amazing. They took a dragon of an instrument, bigger than my desk, and squashed it down to the size of a lunch box."

"They?"

"My scientists. My research team. Best in the world. My favorite of their inventions is the Apoc-Owlypse."

He opened a desk drawer and from it handed Sydney a small metal rectangle the size of a penknife. "Listen to it."

Sydney lifted the cool bit of metal to his ear. It hooted peacefully, like a tiny, distant owl.

"It's a single living nerve cell," his father explained. "It makes noise until something kills it. A modern day canary in a coal mine. That little scrap of metal detects and distinguishes between seventeen separate bacterial and viral toxins, including the Plague, botulism, Ebola—"

"What about AIDS?"

A soft V creased his father's brow. "AIDS is spread in a way that makes such an object obsolete."

"So how about the others? I mean have you . . . solved Ebola?"

"Touchy subject. Technically, we have. But we're one of three companies working on it. Also there's a sort of gentlemen's agreement to let the government take the credit. We'll no doubt get distribution, though. So the smart money is still on us."

Sydney suspected that people, men in striped business suits eating lobster and steak, really were placing bets. *Survivanoia, before the one hundredth death. Get me another martini, I'm hitting the head. . . .* He couldn't discern if the lump in his belly was thrill or fear.

"Where do I fit into this?"

"You'll start at the bottom, in data entry. You'll work your way up. That way you'll know all there is to know about the place. And when you're in charge, it will be because you deserve to be in charge."

"What if I don't deserve to be in charge?"

"Then you'll be in data entry until you drop dead or quit. That's up to you."

"What about school? I know I'm a fuck-up, but . . . I really like college."

"Go at night. School is cheap there."

Sydney's eyes hooded. "Where?"

"Los Angeles. The company is in Los Angeles."

Sydney flopped back in his chair. Breathed in, breathed out.

"Yes or no, Sydney. Decide."

"Can't I have, like, a day?"

"No."

"What about Ma?"

"You will tell her."

* * *

"Vat joo mean joo go! Your Da?" Zola Ratkovitch spit on the kitchen's yellowed linoleum floor. "Trash! Like in zee street!"

"But Ma, I can't—"

"Joo can shut up!"

He did. Sydney's mom stood just over five feet, more than a foot shorter than her son. She still wore the shawls and heavy dresses of her native land, still clung to the old traditions, and still carried deep-seated superstitions. When she cursed you, she really cursed you. Sydney had never shaken fully free of her mythology, and when she hollered in her native tongue—a language Sydney had forgotten on purpose in junior high and tried unsuccessfully to reclaim just after his eighteenth birthday—it made him shiver, even on a muggy day like today.

"Ma. Ma! English, please!"

She glared at him. English slowed her down, with her y's like j's, her rolling r's and her skewed th's that never came out the same twice in a row.

"Joo listen! Dis Company of his, just like gang. He tell you vat, zat joo in trouble? Zat you have to leave or joo die?"

Sydney stared at his mother, suddenly and inexplicably frightened.

"Oh, ya, joo tink joor muh-zer doesn't know. Doesn't know vat joo do. I know, Sydney. I know all about zat boy, zat Ion person."

Sydney swallowed, wondering if she knew everything. He doubted it. She'd have thrown him out if she knew. There weren't enough prayers in the world to save him from his best friend's sins. Ian oozed meanness, seeped cruelty, which Sydney's mother sensed. She'd banned Ian from the house by the time he and Sydney were twelve.

"Joor fah-zer is just like Ion. Only he hides behind his big corporation. Did he tell joo vat kinds of tings he make? Protects from zee bio disease?"

"Yeah, he told me, Ma."

His mother gazed at him for a long, silent, spooky time. Sydney glanced at the old green couch, the cracked kitchen floor, out the screenless window, anything to not have to look at his ma. Because if he looked at her face he'd see it, if he listened too closely he'd hear it, just as from across the room he could *feel* her heart break.

She nodded finally. "I am vasting vords. Please, promise. Write me to from zees California."

CHAPTER 12

"Scally" paced his new office, larger and brighter than his first apartment. Like his nickname, Sydney's new office was something to which he quickly became accustomed. His nickname had come his first day on the job, when the breakroom scared him a little and reminded him of the stories he'd been told of Ellis Island. Six different languages filled the place and nobody got to keep his name. *Poo-ah-LAH-ni? How about we call you Loni? Scalinescu? S-c-a—Scally, got it, okay. Next!* Thus he'd been christened by Mongo and Boozey, the maintenance manager and head mechanic, respectively, over sixteen years ago.

The new office had come just a few months ago as part of his new position—VP of Product Development. Along with the fancy title, they'd awarded him the center office on the second floor, overlooking the courtyard housed in the U of the new building. Survivanola engineers had designed and erected this facility especially for the company, and it couldn't have been better. The layout ensured everybody, even the production workers, a view of the outdoors. The managers, Scally included, all had balconies, in case they cared to use them.

At the moment, a Mr. Sanchez sat on Scally's balcony, slurping coffee and gazing dreamily at the garden beneath him. A wooden box fraught with knobs and meters sat on Scally's desk. Mr. Sanchez had brought it with him. Scally had recently tucked a set of plans for a similar product into a desk drawer. Those plans had come from a different man, a strange little scientist named Encludsmo Stuckhowsen who had come in days earlier to see the Baroness, the new company president.

The scientist had spoken such bad English that the Baroness switched him to German and translated for Scally. The little doctor offered pages and pages of theoretical calculations explaining how pretension could be extrapolated from changes in micro-atmospheric conditions knowing this and that and blah. He'd described in vast detail the jobs of all the individual transistors, every bit of wire, each LED in his proposed "Pretentiometer." What The Doctor hadn't provided was a prototype.

Mr. Sanchez presented the opposite situation. The stocky, brown-suited man had shown up first thing that morning, unannounced, asking to speak with anybody in the marketing group. They were about to shoo him out the door when Scally arrived, bleary eyed and clutching coffee, heard the man mumble something about "pretension meter," and saw the box in Sanchez's thick hands. Scally had swooped him upstairs.

Now he picked the box from his desk. Nailed shut, couldn't see the insides. Seemed lighter than what Stuckhowsen's plans suggested. He carried it into the midday heat on the balcony.

Mr. Sanchez smiled. "Well? Is good, huh?" He patted his pompadour, greasy in the heat.

"It's certainly a good idea, Mr. Sanchez. But I need you to prove how it works."

"You want me to give away my secrets?"

"Not at all. But I wouldn't, say, buy a car, without asking some questions, kicking the tires. . . ."

"Do you know how your car works?"

Scally paused, laughed. "You got me there. But I'd take it for a test drive."

Mr. Sanchez's face split into a wide, toad-like grin. "Oh! That is yes. We must go inside, though."

Scally led them back into his cool, crisp office. Sanchez hunched over his toaster-sized box and snapped one of its three switches. A needle on the face sprang forward and back, finally resting in the green range. "This is a prototype, you understand. The plans are for a digital one, but the money for that, I do not have."

"Understood." Scally peered at the meter. "Looks like it's reading about two and a half."

"Not bad! Most people are at least a three."

"So that's just me?"

"Correct."

"How can I get it to measure a whole room?"

"Adjust the spanning range." Mr. Sanchez snapped another knob to the on position. "It goes by feet, see? Diameter, one-to-three, that's for one person. Ten feet to measure, say, a circle of friends at a party. Twenty feet for the average living room."

"How about an art gallery or a performance at the LA Phil?"

"This one cannot do it, you'll blow out the fuse. But can be done, yes, for sure. Now. You work in a large building, there is somebody here pretentious, yes?"

"Oh, yeah."

"Can we call that person to come into the room?"

Scally punched an extension into his speaker phone.

"This is Geo."

"Geo, can you come see me in my office, please?"

"You mean right now? I'm swamped."

"It'll be quick."

Geo—whose given name was Jorge, so not only had he Americanized his name but then shortened the bastardized version—finally made his appearance nearly twenty minutes later. Even the man's walk—a loose lope that made his "hip," scruffy dirty-blond hair fall into his eyes—even this made Scally cringe.

Scally kept a close watch on the instrument, still clutched in Sanchez's hands, as the head of Inside Sales bounced through his door. The meter sprang to 6.8. He stifled a laugh; Sanchez snapped the instrument off.

"Geo, this is Mr. Sanchez. He's got a new little gadget he calls the poten-cho-meter. It measures the pretentiousness of people within a variable radius."

"Really."

"Do we currently have LACMA, the LA Phil, Spago, any of those places purchasing from us, or will these be cold calls?"

Geo raised an eyebrow.

"I'm just trying to get a sense as to how long it will take to launch a product like this and develop a market for it."

Geo shook his head, an incredulous smile spreading across his well-featured face. "Why would a gallery want to know the pretentiousness—is that even a word? Why would they want to know that about their patrons?"

"Are you seriously asking me this? Marketing! As a way of defining demographics. Maybe they've got a whole mess of low-pretension level patrons who all turn out on Thursday. They could examine what it is about Thursday and try to recreate it on other nights to pull in more of that demographic on alternative nights."

Geo scratched at his goatee for a moment. "I'll look into it, Scally, and get back to you."

"When?"

"When what?"

"When will you get back to me?"

Geo's emerald eyes widened, in a my-god-he's-serious way. "Soon! And I want to talk to you about this as well." He slapped a ratty envelope onto Scally's desk then fled.

Mr. Sanchez patted his hair again, his eyes hopeful and questioning. Scally offered the man his hand. "I'm sold. And I'm going to work on selling the rest of my crew."

* * *

"Scally. Got a minute?" The Baroness loomed in his office doorway. Her three-inch heels maximized her already remarkable height, bringing her over Scally's six-three. She was the only person in the building that had the power to make Scally feel small.

She closed his door. Sixteen years ago, really even ten, he'd've envisioned himself stripping off her black tights with his teeth—indeed could have conceived no other reason why a woman would close his office door. But now, at thirty-four, and her with that ferocity in her violet eyes, Sydney knew better.

The Baroness flowed into the chair across from his desk. The chair's claret leather matched her hair, which she wore in a soft, complicated braid ending in a fishtail below her hips. Her ruby lipstick and well-penciled eyes made her look like a movie star, a modern femme fatale. She rested her hands on the chair arms and crossed her legs at the knee and for the life of him Scally couldn't place whose gestures hers reminded him of, but it left him uneasy, that much he recognized.

"Akira tells me you stopped work on the Pretentiometer."

"That's right."

"Can I ask you—"

"Because Mr. Sanchez's design is—"

"—just who the hell you think you are?"

Scally's jaw snapped closed. He'd been expecting, obviously, that she would ask him why, not request that he justify his very existence.

He needlessly cleared his throat, steepled his fingers. "I'm the Vice President of Product Development. Nice to meet you."

"Uh-huh. Well, wise guy, Mr. Sanchez took his little three knob box with him when he left, a month ago, correct?"

"Yes, it was his to take."

"Therefore, we don't have anything of his to study, correct?"

"We'll get it as soon as we offer him a contract. I've kept in touch with him."

Her eyes narrowed. "You didn't promise him anything, did you?"

"Not yet." Which was true, though his lie of omission involved a voice-mail message to a certain small, strange scientist.

A crumpled and singed bit of paper magically appeared in the Baroness's hand. "This," she told Scally, "is all that's definitely left of The Doctor."

"The Doctor? That Stuckhowsen guy?"

The Baroness nodded. Scally blinked. Scrutiny revealed the paper to be an envelope, stamped and postmarked. "What do you mean 'definitely left'?"

"His house . . ." She paused. "His *dwelling* has been destroyed. He worked out of said dwelling, so his lab equipment went, too. Notebooks, test tubes, all of it. The only thing I did find, besides a corpse that looks too big to be The Good Doctor, is this letter. It seems to be from a sister, who seems to be psychotic."

Scally had too many questions to decide which to ask first. Why was the Baroness at The Doctor's burned-up house? Who cared if he had a sister? And was the corpse him or not, and where were the police, and why—

"We both know," the Baroness interrupted his brooding, "this Pretentiometer is a tiny little product that doesn't. Fucking. Matter."

"Yet here you are in my office."

"Right."

Scally took a deep breath. "You wanted The Doctor. Just to work for us on anything."

The Baroness smiled, whispered, "Right. He was a goddamn genius, Scally." Her smile sharpened to a glare. "How are you going to fix this?"

"Ms. Von—"

"Baroness, please. Think of it as my first name."

"Baroness. I appreciate that you're the president, but—"

"I'm glad somebody does."

"—but as new product manager—"

"Aren't you going to ask me if I am?"

"Pardon?"

"A Baroness. European landowner, or feminization of Baron, as in powerful person, like Oil Baron. Or Wine Baron. Doesn't the title intrigue you? Make you skeptical?"

Scally blinked at her some more. He hadn't considered her title. Apart from the obvious mystery of why his father turned the company over to her, Scally hadn't considered her much at all, aside from her height and that monstrosity she drove—that yellow Hummer. Rumor put snakeskin seats in that vehicle—rattlesnake hide. Looking at her, he believed it.

Her vanity plate read "ROSN80," which Scally's girlfriend had surmised was a reference to Don Quixote's broken-down horse. This Scally couldn't confirm or deny, couldn't even opine, having only loose familiarity with the Don's story or with the Baroness.

But to answer her question, "No, I guess I haven't been skeptical."

"If I were you, Sydney Junior, I'd wonder about me a lot. Because I know all about you. You and Brooklyn and Ian."

She could have kicked him in the balls. The past sixteen years of Scally's life seemed to spin out away like water in a flushed toilet. Everything fell away from him, his season tickets to the Hollywood Bowl, his membership at LACMA, his little house south of the Boulevard in Studio City. All gone.

Some primal New York instinct overtook him. It crept up from his belly and caught in his throat, made him stand up and spit some words at this sudden rival. "So what, you're some friend of the senator's? I could have you killed with a phone call!"

The Baroness stayed seated. She licked her lips, grinning. "I'm no friend to any senator."

"That won't get you far in business."

"Which business?"

"Any."

She studied him. "You say that, yet you don't practice it."

Sydney took a breath. "Who are you working for? My dad? Send you to check on me? I'm doing fine."

"Nope. I'm no friend of Daddy Paranoia-Bucks. That's okay. I'll give you another chance next time. What's your story anyway, Thug Life? Has the corporate world left you soft?" She seemed amused. This unnerved Scally and made him feel like a jackass.

Rather than sit, which smacked of defeat, he came around to the front of his desk and leaned against it. "You know my entire life apparently, why don't you tell me?"

The Baroness shook her head. "That's what we call in the business a rhetorical question."

"Why would you allow a gangster to continue working in ... *your* company?"

"Good boy. But it's not really my company and we both know that. You don't think your daddy is a gangster?" Her voice carried a sudden edge, like his cats' when they shifted from playing to fighting.

"So you do know my dad."

She uncrossed her legs, sat forward. "More importantly, do you know your dad?" She smiled, like a coyote smiles. "Heed the words your mother says. Meanwhile, come up with an amazing reason for canceling Akira's project." She stood. "Everything in Stuckhowsen's plans, as much as we were able to check before you shut the project down, clears. That little troll Sanchez gave you is nothing."

"He has a working model. How is that nothing?"

"Right. He has it. You don't. And now The Doctor is gone. Where are the plans he left us?"

"It doesn't matter. We can't use them without his consent."

"It doesn't matter anyway because what I wanted, what the company would have benefited from, is the inventor, not his invention. At least not that invention."

"So why are we having this discussion at all?!"

The Baroness grinned, apparently pleased to have riled him. "Just prepping you for the sales meeting tomorrow. Hope you have something stunning, Scally. Something truly marvelous."

He listened to her clip down the hall to her own office. Then, as he always did in a crisis, Scally went downstairs to consult the maintenance manager.

Mongo Zeneca emptied the contents of a Styrofoam carton onto a dinner plate, warmed the plate in his personal microwave. The round, jowly man set his curious eyes on Scally. "Hungry, kid?"

"Nah." Scally dropped into one of Mongo's Victorian chairs.

Mongo had been friends with Syd Senior, Scally's father, longer than Scally had been alive. People took "maintenance manager" as a euphemism for janitor when in fact Mongo held a master's in mechanical engineering. He knew every bolt and wire of the building, had access to all the engineers, and in turn, all the manufacturing lines as well as new products.

Scally wondered if such information illuminated things. He recalled his first days on the job, entering immeasurable amounts of data, much of it from the tattered, illegible notebooks of their engineering staff. Not the originals. Sydney's department got photocopies with large sections blacked out in marker. All the databases were coded by number. Knowing what his company actually developed seemed impossible. Now as the VP of Product Development, not much had changed.

Scally pulled one of the steel balls on Mongo's Newton's cradle, watched the one at the other end snap out, fall back and push the original one— *click clack click clack.* "Mongo, who's the Baroness?"

"President."

"I know that. But who *is* she?"

"Don't know."

"Come on!"

Mongo sat behind his desk, set a cloth napkin on his lap. "We don't know."

Scally gaped at him. "How … is that possible? My dad owns the company. How can he not know the president?"

"He doesn't own it by himself."

"Come again?"

"There's somebody else. A silent partner."

"It can't be the Baroness, she's my age."

Mongo pulled a bottle from one of his desk drawers, and poured himself a glass of red wine. He gestured to Scally but Scally declined.

"This silent partner," Mongo said, "never identified himself. He worked through an agent. And he appointed this president."

"She's hollering at me to reclaim a product she herself admits is meaningless."

"Probably she sees massive potential in the product's inventor. That's how you get and keep the best and brightest. You know these things." Mongo paused, assessed the younger man.

Scally's knee jimmied and he tapped his fingers like a restless musician.

"What's really on your mind, kid?"

"She knows about Ian. She mentioned him by name. Why would she know that? How does anybody out here know that?"

"Maybe she wanted some leverage."

"You saying she dug up dirt on me? To claw her way up the ladder?"

"Or maybe she's in with the senator. Could be part of the deal your dad cut."

"That was sixteen years ago!"

"You killed the man's son."

"I didn't do that!"

Mongo leveled a heavy gaze on the younger man.

Scally waved away his protest. "Besides, I asked her. She says no."

"You expect her to say yes?"

Scally let out a low, irritated moan. "What do I do?"

Mongo shrugged. "Me? I'd take the rest of the day off."

Scally generally did what Mongo suggested. When he arrived home, techno boomed from the Bose stereo, where he spotted Nike's pink MP3 player. Nike, his girlfriend, had been named after the goddess, not the shoe, by parents from the Netherlands who didn't know any better.

He removed his Italian leather shoes, leaving them in the closet-sized front foyer, and turned down the stereo. In the kitchen, Nike sat cross-legged on a stool by the marble island, poring over a hand-scrawled recipe. His two tabby cats, one orange and one grey, sat at her feet waiting patiently for scraps. When Scally came in, Nike sprang to the steel counter, spreading her arms to hide whatever was on it.

"This was supposed to be a surprise!"

"What is it?"

"Chicken *cordon bleu*. Or chicken *cordon* mess, depending on how it comes out. I got this recipe, like, six months ago, but I haven't tried it yet and the girl I got it from is some kind of gourmet chef, like, as a hobby. So it might be too hard for me. Is what I'm saying."

He slid his arms around her waist, kissed her on the cheek. "New dress?"

"You like it?" She squirmed away from him and did a little pirouette, displaying the purple silk adorned with gold and green dragons. It laced up the front like a corset, and she wore it with black tights and suede boots that came to her knees.

Scally pulled her back to him. "It's beautiful."

"I thought it looked cool with my hair."

"It does." He rumpled her short, boyish hair, which this week was cherry red with the tips dyed black. "How come you're here? Not that I'm complaining."

"I wanted to surprise you with dinner and didn't think you'd want to drive all the way to my place."

"And you're not at work because . . . ?"

"Barry's client never showed."

"Is that bad?"

"Barry's pissed. Doesn't matter to me, I'm overbooked the rest of the week. How come *you're* here?"

"Terrible headache."

"Survivanitus?"

He laughed "I think you're right, Doctor. Headache seems to have dissipated on the way home."

He kissed her again and headed for the bedroom. His little house's hardwood floors stayed cool, and he enjoyed the feel of them against his soles. After stripping out of his black linen pants and cobalt blue shirt, he stretched out to bask in the air conditioning. Morris, the orange cat, stretched out between his feet.

He hoped to clear his mind and take a nap, but how could he? It struck him, though, that the Baroness hadn't singled him out until he'd pissed her off. In her opinion, he'd somehow lost them a super-genius employee. Maybe Mongo was right, she wasn't out to get him, she was just angry. But who *was* she?

And something about Mongo nagged at Scally as well. Had the man waited a beat too long? Furrowed his brow nearly imperceptibly? Scally didn't know, but what he did know, could not shake, was the heaviness in his gut that made him think Mongo knew more than he admitted. This woman hadn't come out of nowhere. . . .

Nike plopped down next to him in the bed. "You've been in here an hour. I think something's wrong with you besides a headache."

He curled up, which sent the cat running, and lay his head in Nike's lap. "You know I hate to talk about work."

"Yeah, yeah, something about it being irrelevant and boring. Funny, I was taught that being a VP meant you were grown up and important." She kissed the top of his head. "Now vent. So we can get on with our evening."

He relented, explained about missing Sanchez and his box. "My plan was to have him appear at the quarterly meeting, box in hand. It's already built, right? Our engineering staff wouldn't need to comb over blueprints written on napkins, I'd have made a money-saving decision. Be a big hero."

"So what happened?"

"I can't find Sanchez. And the meeting's tomorrow."

Nike ran a hand through his hair. "Is that all?"

"No. Remember there was another guy with the same thing?"

"The little foreign guy with the white socks?"

"Right. I already called and told him no."

Nike shrugged. "So call him back."

"I wish it were that easy." He sighed, explained briefly.

Nike laughed, reminding Scally of a wind chime. "Why are you business guys so afraid to leave tracks?"

Scally sat up, stretching "What do you mean?"

"You painted yourself into a corner. So to walk out, you're going to have to leave tracks."

"Or wait for the paint to dry."

"Don't take this the wrong way, but I think I know what your problem is."

"Oh? The doctor is in?"

"I don't think you're enough of a bastard to succeed in corporate America."

"Funny, you're the second person to accuse me of that today."

"How'd you end up with this job anyway?"

He shrugged. "Just sort of fell into it. You know, started as a temp in the mailroom. Worked my way up."

Nike pursed her lips slightly, looked sideways at him.

"What?"

"I don't know," she said. "I just always feel like you're omitting things whenever you talk about your past. Like you've got some horrible mysterious secret you won't let me be privy to."

Scally, as he often found, was taken by her insight. It made him wonder why he didn't tell her everything. He wanted to believe he didn't like discussing work because it was boring, but the fact was discussing work meant delving into his past.

In the four years they'd been together, Scally had never revealed that the company belonged to his father, and he'd sure as hell never told her about Ian. The things he had disclosed were mostly about his mother, how poor she was, and how he'd bought her a little house in Queens (she'd refused a car) and arranged with the market to deliver her food. Once after having done all his dishes, Nike said to him, "I don't understand why you don't hire a maid."

"Because Ma was a maid. I hate to think that I've got somebody's mother cleaning my dirty drawers."

Rather than lecture him on how those women needed those jobs just as his mother surely once did, Nike smiled. "You sure love her. You think you'll ever find anyone you love as much as your mother?"

"I'm looking. . . ." *At her right now* was what he'd been thinking but he swallowed the words. It wasn't the first time he'd short-changed her. Or his mother.

There was another reason he'd chosen Sanchez over Dr. Stuckhowsen. It had to do with his Ma, and it shamed him so he didn't think about it. Instead, he ate his chicken cordon bleu and thought about how lucky he was.

CHAPTER 13

Thursday morning Scally pulled into work early. The Baroness hadn't yet arrived. Scally turned on his computer, fiddled with finished reports, kept checking her door. At 9:30, he heard her laughter.

He headed to her office, which he'd been in only once before, to interview the funny little scientist. Her office disconcerted him. For one thing, she worked with the door closed. He knocked and the door opened slightly, revealing nothing because inside was dark. But the Baroness's plush voice bid him good morning. "Come on in."

She closed the door behind him. It took a few moments for his eyes to adjust. Crimson velvet curtains blocked most of the light from outside; just a sliver crept through, seemingly guided like a dog trained to heel, illuminating a work area on the Baroness's tidy desk.

From the corner over her seat loomed an enormous, stuffed white bear. Mahogany paneling that matched her desk lined the walls to waist height. Above that stood built-in bookshelves, full. Undistracted this time by any energetic interviewees with alien-like math skills and horrible English, Scally scanned the volumes. Mostly reports, bound in three-ring binders and shelved in strict order. Here and there he saw a gap, which unerringly had a paper hanging in it with a name and date.

A curious buzzing thing sat on one of the shelves. He'd noticed it before, two stiff wires forming a V and meeting at a block beneath them. But last time it had been silent, a dumb sculpture. Now a spark ran up the wires with a tiny zap. Like in old horror movies. Scally put a hand up to it but—

"You'll get hurt."

"What is that thing?" He couldn't stop watching the crackling line of light.

"It's a Jacob's Ladder. A controlled arc of high voltage electricity."

"Amazing. Aren't you afraid of burning your office down?"

She didn't respond.

Scally tore his attention from the dangerous toy and moved to her desk. "Did you kill that bear?" he asked.

"No. My father-in-law did. He hunted with Hemmingway."

A strange, vague vertigo grasped Scally, but he couldn't identify its source so he shook it off. "I wanted to talk about finding The Doc—what are you wearing?!"

The Baroness's eyes narrowed. Scally felt his chest tighten. But he stared at her outfit. She wore a wide white jacket with a ruffled collar and fuzzy balls the size of his fists where the buttons should be. Matching white pants were trimmed in the same dark blue as the fuzzy balls. "You're dressed," he said, incredulous, "like Pagliacci."

"Oh! How delightful, an educated man who gets the reference."

"I watch *Seinfeld* reruns."

"I wasn't kidding."

"What?"

"The memo. Today's meeting will be held in clown suits. No exceptions. I'm putting corporate America back into perspective."

"My clown suit is at the cleaners," Scally stated flatly.

"You take a look in that conference room, Sydney. They're all dressed for the occasion. Rubber chickens, striped shirts, red noses. Not one of them has the guts to defy me. Are you stronger? Make me proud. Give me something to believe in."

"You're insane."

"If the clown shoe fits."

"This is madness! You're a—what? A spy? I know some things about you."

He stepped toward her; she grinned menacingly. "Yeah? Bring it on."

"You only got this job because of your connection with the owner. The silent partner."

Her eyes sparkled. "Oohh, you do know something. What else?"

"VER IS DIS SCALINESCU PERSON!" a voice raged from the hall.

Scally nearly choked. The shouting girl pronounced his name right, said *skoo* instead of *skew* at the end. Nobody did that.

The Baroness's door flew open. A girl stood in the entranceway like a scary cartoon. Her spiky hair was dyed purple, and she wore a black velvet jumper over striped tights and matching arm warmers. A girl Scally might date. If she weren't aiming a shotgun at him.

The girl's nostrils flared, eyes darting over Scally.

The Baroness's phone rang.

The Baroness cocked her head at the gun-wielding intruder.

"May I?"

"Is dis him?"

The Baroness glanced at Scally. "Who?"

"Dee man who said my brooder is not good enough. Now his house is burned to the eart, and he is gone."

"I never said he wasn't good enough!"

The Baroness sighed. "Idiot."

Then the shot came.

BLAM! SLAM! Scally fell back against the Baroness's desk. His chest splashed bright crimson. Another blast opened another fistful of gore. The Baroness shouted in German, lunged at the girl. A third horrible shot erupted and he saw the Baroness's white jacket explode in gruesome red. But she was still moving, still shouting, *"Geben Sie mir die Gewehr!"*

—I will not!

This was the girl's response, but not in English or German. Not in

English, but Scally understood it, clear as crystal. It was the language the little inventor had fallen into during their interview when he'd gotten too excited and it was the same language Scally's mother still spoke to this day. This embarrassing language was the true reason Scally had preferred Sanchez to The Doctor.

Scally crawled under the desk. The women yelled and wrestled, the Baroness in German and the punk-rock Rambo in that haunting child-hood memory of a language. Scally closed his eyes and shuddered.

He didn't hurt as much as he thought he should. In death you should feel something. His mother would be heartbroken, but she'd be okay finan-cially. She'd never know how he'd forsaken her. What she would know, what Scally now understood, was that she'd been right, that the corporate world is as ugly and cutthroat as the Bronx streets, they just put on airs of civility here.

If one was as bad as the other, then had he really stolen sixteen years? Or only shifted the location of his destiny? After all, he'd still died the death of a gangbanger. Clash bassist Paul Simonon's voice came to him, *Shot down on the pavement or waiting in death row....* Well, better the former than the latter, he supposed.

"Sweet oblivion," he whispered, "open your arms."

But he was wrong. The door slammed shut and silence filled the office. Some minutes later, when he thought he was dead, he heard the door open again, and the Baroness's bright face grinned down at him, covered in crimson smear. What was she so happy about?

She knelt down next to him under her desk. "It's paint," she whispered to him. "Taste it."

Cautiously, he set a red-stained finger against his tongue. "Bleech!"

"She shot us with a paintball gun." The Baroness laughed, reminding Scally of a tall, bubbly drink. "Clever!"

"Best she could buy on a Thursday morning, I guess," he grumbled.

"Oh, give the girl some points. In fact, take her to lunch. She might just get you off the hook."

"How's that?"

She leaned in conspiratorially, whispered, "She says she knows of some-body who can tell us where The Doctor went."

Grinning like a madwoman, she settled in next to him, there under the desk. Scally noticed that he couldn't hear any office noises. All he heard was the birds out in the garden.

"You're going to have to choose a side, Scally."

"What are my choices?"

"Me or the rest of the business world."

Scally huffed a laugh. "I don't even know who you are. *Nobody* knows who you are. How is that possible?"

"Your father is good with the media."

"Not always." He pulled a tattered half-page news article from his wallet, the article Geo had slapped onto his desk in a huff a few weeks back.

He watched as the Baroness took it from him and grinned at the half-page, three-color ad. HAVE YOUR LOVED ONES DIED FROM FLOWER FLU? it queried. SURVIVANOIA COMPANY IS WITHHOLDING THE CURE! It detailed some evidence, then provided the name and number for the law firm of Tehzan, Preston, and Guite, Experts in the Unprecedented.

The Baroness folded the ad back up and handed it to him. She looked at him carefully as if deciding something. "I hired them. That's the only reason this company has gotten any media coverage whatsoever."

"But even people inside the company don't know who you are."

"Few people here know who you are, either. Despite you sharing a unique last name with the owner. Because most people don't know the owner."

Scally nodded. "Touché. But why are you running the company like a lunatic?"

Suddenly she moved to face him, her hands taking his shoulders, her violet eyes searching his. "Do you believe that human cruelty is balanced by our generosity?"

Scally swallowed, laughed again. "Will this be on the test?"

"Do you? Have you ever thought about it?"

He looked away suddenly embarrassed.

"You haven't," she outed him. "You oversee the development of some of the most important products in the world, and you've never considered the human condition. Have you ever read a book?"

She shook his shoulders, pleading. Craving something Scally didn't think he even had. The space under her desk suddenly seemed tiny. He glanced up into those imploring eyes and something about her filled him with fear. He didn't know what and he didn't know why, only that he desperately wanted not to be frightened.

The philosophy behind his father's company suddenly seemed cruel and he wanted that cruelty to end. And then, suddenly, something about the Baroness's uncommon nonsense felt sensible.

"Is your license plate from Don Quixote?" he asked.

"Ah, you have read a book."

"Is it?"

"Yes."

"Is it true about the rubber penis at the COO meeting?"

"Yes."

"Are the seats in your Hummer really made from rattle snakes?"

"Fake."

"Are you really a Baroness?"

She paused, glanced at the floor, took a breath and held it, then let it out slowly. "The world is a very sad fucking place, Scally. And I'm either going to fix it or shoot it down in flames. If I fix it, yes, I'm a Baroness. If it burns, I'm dead and nothing like the rest of us."

"Yet you use the title. Demand it, even."

"Color me an optimist."

"Will you ever tell me who you really are?"

She smiled. "No. But if you guess I'll admit it."

To Scally's surprise, he found himself genuinely impressed. "You've got some amazing attitude, lady."

Her grip relaxed.

"You have any questions for me?" he asked.

"Just whose side you're on."

He scrutinized her carefully then, this gorgeous woman who made a mockery of hierarchy and institution. This woman feared nothing, "Not even the wild truth," as his father had once claimed of himself. And this woman had told him the truth where his father had lied. So Scally recognized where his loyalties would come down.

But he short-changed her, just as he did his girlfriend, just as he did his mother.

"Mine," he told her. "I'm on my side."

The Baroness laughed whole-heartedly now, like some dam had broken and relief had finally come. "You're a real bastard, you know that, Thug Life? A real mysterious bastard."

CHAPTER 14

Terri Tehzan **woke up and** couldn't see.

That can't be right, she thought, rubbing her eyes. Terri couldn't be blind anymore than she could be pregnant, married, blessed, or depressed. Certain ends of the spectrum were beyond certain people. And Terri Tehzan didn't get things like RV707, more commonly known as Flower Flu.

Her cat, Zippers, launched all sixteen pounds of himself into her lap as she reached to her nightstand for her saline solution. The drops stung slightly, but didn't improve her vision. Zippers shook his head with that funny, flappy sound that always made Terri smile, and she figured she'd dropped some saline on him.

Zippers had always slept on the bed, but since Terri broke up with Rabi, the big cat seemed to prefer the couch like an anxious child trying to stay up until Dad got home. Similarly, Rabi had never felt completely serene until Zippers settled at his feet. "Our little family," he'd say, and then he and Terri would doze off to the peaceful drone of Zipper's big purr. Terri had to admit she missed all that.

She rubbed her face against the creature's softness. "Hello, little traitor." He dropped himself into a furry, purring circle, resting his head on her leg, and she ran a hand over his thick fur—black-on-black stripes that she could make out only when he rested in the sun on a normal day. Today she couldn't see them at all, couldn't even see him.

She blinked at the windows, where she knew them to be, the direction the bed faced. Light made its impression, confirming what her alarm clock had shouted, that it was morning, time to be awake and out of bed, showering and eating breakfast and driving to her law office.

The heat of fear prickled its way in a rush from her belly to her face, left her lightheaded and dizzy, made her pant and fight tears. She took a long breath, counted while she exhaled. Panicking was not going to help.

She aimed her sight at the door. The room, or at least her vision, darkened considerably, a sharper discrepancy than she had ever noticed when her eyes worked right. This part was interesting. Inconvenient and frightening, yes—she could feel her heart and worried about her blood pressure. But this near-blindness was tolerable, especially compared with what came next, the rest of the disease. That, Terri knew, would be truly horrible.

Terri did what she always did in times of crisis: she called Daci. When her friend didn't answer the house phone she called her cell, which Daci answered on the second ring with, "What's wrong?"

Terri had planned to be suave and collected, *What makes you think anything is wrong?* But fear took the reins sometimes. "I just woke up and I can't see!"

A muttered curse, the briefest of pauses, then: "Okay. Lemme head back to the house, pick up my stash, then I'll be over. Gimme . . . maybe forty-five minutes. Tops."

Terri nodded into the phone, hung up, calmer. She got out of bed, Zippers jumping when she moved and landing with a thump. Thankfully, an unpretentious single story comprised her little house. No stairs to fall down.

She shuffled her way to the kitchen, running a hand along the wall and staring toward the floor. The morning light glared from the white tile there, providing a visual clue stark enough for her to ascertain even in her debilitated state. The touch of a button enabled her to get coffee brewing as she'd set it up the previous evening.

Zippers harangued her for his morning meal but feeding him involved opening a can and she decided not to risk slicing open a finger. His cries shifted from reminders to pleading to righteous indignation.

With deliberation, she managed to pour herself a bowl of puffed rice. She first opened the cupboard and felt from the bottom: the shelf, the plates—one two, six—then the bowls. She plucked the top one, brought it level with her other hand, which rested on the counter. The cereal she stored in a cabinet just below the cupboard for plates.

She held the bowl with one hand, her thumb inside it, with the other hand she located the edge of the box, and shook the box gently until she felt the cereal reach her thumb. She stopped then, taking metered breaths and fighting tears.

The concentration and resultant sluggishness reminded her of when she and Daci used to try to write with their non-dominant hands back in junior high. But this wasn't a game. She couldn't just pull off the blindfold and push her morning back into real time.

Another agonizingly slow process brought her to the refrigerator, where the milk waited on the door. Luckily, she hadn't yet shopped this week, so there was no juice to confuse it with. She used the same thumb technique to cover the cereal with milk (at which point Zippers sat at her feet purring again, hoping at least to get the leftovers).

Terri ate the rice puffs plain since she didn't want sugar all over her kitchen floor, and very slowly, so that they were soggy by the time she'd finished. Even feeding herself relied on sight! She hadn't recognized this fact. She maneuvered another bite into her mouth, recalling sogginess as the reason Daci refused to eat cereal, even as a child.

Terri had met Baroness Dacianna Von Worthington one September day as the two of them were coming off the school bus. Terri didn't yet know Daci's name, so she just smacked the lanky redhead—whose nose was buried in a book even as she exited the bus—with her paperback. "Hey! Wanna trade?"

Thus began a friendship that had withstood the cute boys, jealous girls, and too-easy, too-boring, and often irrelevant classes of Santa Barbara Junior

High, then Santa Barbara High School, where they sauntered through halls once walked by the likes of Charles Schwab and John Northrop.

Dacianna spent her summers in New York—the Hamptons, a place even more surreal than Santa Barbara. College kept them on opposite coasts, and the girls, now women, pursued different fields. Terri began her career at the Southern Poverty Law Center, while Daci had forsaken her engineering degree to conceive, start, and sell a series of successful, unrelated businesses while earning a master's in global policy.

Now Terri had her own practice, Tehzan, Preston, and Guite: Experts in the Unprecedented. Daci had just taken over Survivanoia, Purveyors of the Post-Apocalypse. Not so different on paper. Not so different at the core.

Daci's signature rapping came, three short, impatient strokes—either Daci or the police. Terri felt her shoulders loosen, her teeth unclench. Zippers lunged to meet Daci at the door and cry for food.

"That didn't feel like forty-five minutes," Terri told her.

"More like forty-five days?"

"No, actually. The individual tasks felt like forever, but now that I'm through with that minutiae, it seems like I just got off the phone with you. Weird."

"That could be the flu talking. Like when you have a high fever? Your sense of time distorts? Let me get you some water."

Terri moved to her leather armchair, felt to make sure it was where she thought it was, and sat down. "Can you feed Zippers?"

"Yes. I can see he's starving."

She heard Daci's heels click on the kitchen tiles, heard the cat food can pop-top snap open and Zippers purring around his breakfast. Everything sounded closer, clearer, like a TV turned up too loud. She heard the water run, raised her voice over it, "Hey, was there a guy washing my car when you drove in?"

"Was there supposed to be?"

"Does my car look clean?"

"Your car always looks clean."

"Right, but I never take it in. I park it and it's dirty and I get up the next morning and it's clean. But I never get out of the house early enough to catch him. I think it's the guy three doors over."

"The professor?"

"Yeah, Salvador. Turns out he's a cook, too."

"For a living?" *Click-clack-click* then soft padding when Daci hit the shag leather carpet.

"No, he's a professor for a living. I meant he's able to cook well."

"You know those Mexican guys all have three jobs. Never related, you know, *Si, Señorita, I teach calculus, operate a boiler overnight, and on weekends? I'm a valet.*"

Terri laughed at her friend's spot-on Mexican accent. "Usually they fix cars, though, they don't wash them."

"Right? Good luck finding a mechanic once Flower Flu is done decimating the Hispanic population." Daci pressed a small tablet into Terri's hand.

The comment, not flip; tinged with venom gave Terri pause. She rolled the pill between her thumb and middle finger. Tiny, like the little red sinus medication pills. Not round, though—angled, like a tiny squared football. Terri squinted at it but it made no impression against the dark blur of her hand. "What color is this?"

"Silver, what else?"

"Tell me again why these aren't for sale—or for *free*—to the public."

"It's not my decision. I just started there. Give me, like, a minute."

Daci's seeming lack of frustration sparked Terri's.

"Not 'just started.' It's been what, three weeks? A month?"

"And I've been chasing every lead I have!"

Terri flung an open hand at where she supposed Daci stood. "You're the president of the company. If you say sell the drug, it gets released."

"You know that's over simplistic. Don't feign ignorance. It's not just my company that needs convincing, there are two other corporations involved in a binding, legal agreement. And in all three companies, stockholders,

CEOs, COOs, all these jokers need to nod in unison before anything can get done. I can barely keep up with the alphabet, let alone do the right thing."

"Don't quote Spike Lee at me, you traitor." Terri stood, stomped a few steps, then thought better of it and slowed, not wanting to storm into a wall. "You need to *do* what you took over Survivanoia to do." To her relief, Terri found the bedroom, where she made her way to her clothing butler.

"I'm working on it!"

"I figured that'd be the first thing out of your mouth once you were at the helm. That's why you took over in the first place!"

A sigh from Daci. "Can we talk about this after you take the pills?"

"No! We clearly need to have dialogue. I'm not taking the pills until you spell out for me unequivocally what your plan of attack is for getting this medication into public hands. Not just those of your best friend."

"You're holding yourself hostage?"

"I'm the only clout I have."

"I'm agreeing with your mother at this point."

"What!"

"She always said you have an overdeveloped sense of justice."

"Didn't they say that about Timothy McVeigh?" Here was her bra, on the top of the butler as always. Pale peach, to set off her red-brown skin.

She fumbled with the bra until she identified the cups, distinguished the inside from the outside, put it the right way against her body. Hooking it? Shit.

"Can you help me with this, please?"

Daci arrived, took the two ends from her and completed the task. A task Terri had taken for granted every day since she'd proudly sported her training bra at age twelve.

"They gave Timmy the chair," Daci reminded her. "*Zzztttt!* Here's your blouse."

"I don't plan to use incendiary devices on public buildings."

"What about private?"

"Nope." Terri shimmied into the crisp white shirt and Daci buttoned it, leaving Terri feeling ridiculous.

"Not even mine?"

"Nope."

"Damn. You were my last hope. My Obi Won Kenobi."

"He was her *only* hope. Which would describe *you*."

"I brought you the pills."

"Me. What about everybody else?"

"Didn't we just have this conversation?"

Terri ran a hand over her butter yellow suite, a power color against her copper complexion. She rested her arm akimbo. A court move. "Give me something. Some idea, some modicum of something to impress upon me that you are serious!"

Daci gave an audible sigh. "You should take these pills now. You'll have fully restored vision by the time we get to your office."

"I'm abstaining as a means of protest."

"I guess you've forgotten that it was you who sent me on the snipe chase to determine if Survivanoia invented the goddamn flu in the first place."

"Can you walk and chew bubblegum at the same time?"

"It's a matter of resources."

"No, it's a matter of priorities. First you save the victim, then you solve the crime."

"This entire conversation is insulting!" Daci paused.

Terri couldn't see her friend's face but she knew her well enough to envision the combined rage and bewilderment. She kept the urgency from her voice. "I'm just trying to understand your *modus operandi*."

"You already know it! Setting yourself on fire is not going to speed the process along!" A pause. "You're killing me."

"Well, you're killing thousands."

"Not *me*. Syd."

"Maybe millions! Horribly, I might add."

"Can we discuss this in the car then, Gandhi? I need to stop at the desalination plant on the way."

Outside, the heat and brightness slammed into Terri like a wall, nearly knocking her over physically. She grasped the railing surrounding her little garden patio. "Are we in triple digits already? It's not even 9:00 a.m."

"9:00 a.m.? It's not even technically summer yet! Anyway, the car is refrigerated. Come on."

One, two, three steps but then Terri was at a loss. The stinging sun washed everything out, leaving her no visual cues at all. Daci took her arm and guided her to the curb and to what Terri knew was a giant yellow beast of a vehicle. "Step up," her friend warned her. "Higher." She climbed in, feeling like a child in every capacity.

The moment she was seated she felt relieved. "How is it still so cool in your car?"

Daci's door closed without slamming. "I told you, it's refrigerated. I wasn't being facetious."

Terri ignored the frustration in Daci's voice. *Let her sweat until she has an answer.* "One of your geniuses altered it?"

"Arturo. Replaced the air conditioner with a refrigeration unit."

"What's the difference?"

"An air conditioner pumps chilled air into a space. A refrigerator removes heat."

"Where does it put the heat?"

"Outside. Believe me, nobody notices."

The car moved up PCH, which would bring them to the 10 and then the 405. From there, they would take the airport exit to where Survivanoia's desalination plant stood.

Out of habit, Terri moved her eyes in the direction of the window. Pointless. Plus the brightness proved uncomfortable. She focused on the interior of her friend's giant car, and in her new weird state of aural alertness, she noticed how little noise the Hummer made.

A low hum, like a refrigerator, was all that came from the engine compartment. The soft, almost plastic *ker-chunk* of gears when Daci shifted seemed erroneously loud in comparison. Outside, the broad tires made a sticky drone against the asphalt and Terri heard each car's doppler *swish* as Daci sped past them.

She could smell Daci's coffee and feel each individual scale embossed into the leather to make it mimic rattlesnake. The ocean's salty tang felt almost tangible against her palate. Or was that saline from the engine?

"Why don't you tell anyone about this car? You know everyone who sees it thinks it's a gas-guzzling monstrosity. They hate you."

"They love to hate me. It's good to be loved." Daci's voice sounded easier now.

"If you told them this thing runs on salt water, you'd be a national hero overnight."

"Are you insane? I'd be disappeared! Troops from Ford and GM and maybe even Tesla would be at my doorstep before the press conference ended."

"Nonsense. You could start a partnership and market them."

"You are so shamelessly optimistic. Besides, if I told everybody, it wouldn't be any fun. That's my little secret. Me, Arturo Rivera, and Bucky Fuller Auto. BFA will eventually have its day on the beach."

The car stopped silently and Terri heard the key click in the steering column, though she perceived no change in engine noise. She heard the bristle of Daci's clothes against the textured seats.

"I have to drop off these sample labels so Ali can decide which ones he likes. I'm partial to the plain ones with just the big S. You want to come in?"

"I can't see anything."

The briefest of pauses. "That's your fault."

"I'd argue that it's your fault. Or your COO's faults. But my larger point is that it won't be any fun."

"Sure it will."

"It's loud."

"Only the reverse osmosis sector. The flocculation tanks are quiet as a sheep herd. Plus, you love an accent, and we now boast twenty-three languages. We hired an engineer from Bosnia and the new data entry girl is off-the-boat Romanian."

Terri got the sense Daci simply didn't want her left alone. Embarrassingly, she discovered she agreed.

Inside the plant, the air was a perfect 72. Even from the lobby, Terri could hear the rhythmic, breathy pulse of pumps forcing water through the reverse osmosis membranes. She wondered if anyone else heard it, though even if they did they undoubtedly tuned it out within a few minutes.

A receptionist whose bracelets jangled like a belly dancer and whose accent said India called Ali's office, then told Daci and Terri to go on down.

Ali, Terri knew from her visits to the plant before it was active, was slender and stooped and the color of a well-worn saddle. His English carried only the hint of an accent, "Persian," if you asked him.

"The reporters are calling again," he complained. "There is a big concern as to what we are doing with the brine."

"So tell them we're dumping it back into the ocean like every other de-sal plant in the world."

"But in fact we are not. And they don't like to hear that we are. Why can we not tell them the truth?"

Terri saw—or rather heard—an opportunity. "What's the truth, exactly?"

There was a pause then Ali explained. "All the cars in the company fleet run on concentrated saline water."

"You're shitting me."

He laughed at her expression. "In fact, no." Another pause.

"You can tell her," said Daci.

"Every employee gets a company car," Ali explained. "We are required to drive them, in fact. From the acting president on down to the secretary. We store the saline and refuel out back."

"For free," Daci added.

"All your staff cars are Bucky Fuller Auto?"

Daci confirmed this. "All the Survivanoia staff cars will be, too. And eventually, assuming the Singularity doesn't happen and the world doesn't end, all the cars in California. The trick is to make sure we have enough brine to fuel all these cars. That's why we're looking beyond water authority sales and into bottling water."

Ali's voice complained, "Bottles also terrible."

"People won't give that shit up," said Daci.

"But you're telling the press," Terri clarified for herself, "that you're dumping this horrible waste into the ocean?"

"Of course. It's free publicity when we announce that we've found a use for all that junk."

"Do you *believe* yourself to be insane?"

"Of course!"

"Alright. Then you're not. Just checking."

"Of course."

Outside felt even hotter than before.

"What time is it?" Terri asked as the tricked-out Hummer started silently. While her other senses were expanding, her sense of time seemed to have eloped with her sight.

"Not quite 10:00. I'm guessing your appointment is soon?" Vexation cooled Daci's voice.

"At 10:00. Take Vista to Pacific, we'll be fine."

"Before I take anything to anywhere, I want you to take these pills."

"Before I take the pills I want you to tell me how you're going to get them distributed."

"I'm! Working! On it!"

Terri's chest tightened and her heart rate jumped. In their twenty-five plus years of knowing each other, they had yelled at each other, seriously, honestly yelled, three times.

She and Daci had always gone at things with this childish, tug-of-war approach, at first because they *were* actual petulant preteens, then later out of nostalgia, or perhaps because it amused them. All these years had taught Terri that she could light a fire under Daci's ass just by initiating a heated, argumentative discussion.

At least that had always been the case in the past. She wondered if heading up a corporation would change Daci. Not in the common way power corrupts people by spreading avarice. Daci had her own money, so that was unlikely. But a more subtle change, a shifting in to accepting things and assuming they'd work themselves out eventually. This latent tendency of Daci's had been a point of disagreement between the two women since college. Now it seemed to define Daci's acquiescent attitude about the Flower Flu antidote.

"Standard company approaches are clearly not providing an inroad," Terri responded calm but firm. "You need—actively, right now—to use your ingenuity and resourcefulness to identify a different path, or define one yourself."

"You need—actively, right now—to take this pill before you get stomach cramps and a headache and start shitting out your own intestines! This isn't a game, Ter."

The image, and her friends vehemence, frightened Terri to the point of raising goose bumps. "That's cheap." She heard her voice crack. "Scare tactics. Beneath you."

"It's truth!"

"It would take you ten minutes!" she spat back. "Just do it, for the love of fuck! And while you're at it, drive this sheep in wolf's clothing up Vista so that I can be on time to meet my client." She folded her arms and fell back against the seat, her eyes aimed at where the light told her the window was.

Daci took in a long, slow stream of air and Terri swore she could hear Daci's heart rate increase with the introduction of plentiful oxygen. She pushed the air through loose lips making a slight raspberry. "I hate you right now."

The transmission *ker-chunked* and the car moved backward.

"Lookit," Daci said, her tone brighter, curious. "There's a car a little way down there in the parking lot. It's a white Honda CRZ. I'm pretty sure it was a few cars behind us on the freeway."

"Is there anybody in it?"

"I can't tell from here, the windows are tinted."

"You think it's following us?"

"Guess we'll find out." Daci backed her secret saline hybrid out of the space and zipped out of the lot. "So who is today's client?"

Terri laughed. "He's suing his mother."

"For?"

"Wrongful life."

"You mean conceiving him?"

"I think I'll approach it as not aborting him."

"That's . . . interesting. Have you met him yet?"

"Only on the phone."

"What kind of guy sues his mother for not aborting him?"

"He claims to be unemployable, highly literate, and kleptomaniacal."

"And the mother?"

"A porn star. And lesbian. Want to meet him?"

"The porn star?"

"The klepto. You can pretend you're my clerk. Is that car behind us?"

A pause then, "I don't see it. Or . . . well . . . there are two white cars a ways back."

Daci went silent again and again Terri could feel the strange mental static she recognized as preoccupation. Probably her friend was squinting into her rearview. For the second time that morning, Terri really wished she could see.

Her forehead tingled slightly and a headache stirred between her brows. Maybe she needed coffee? Or was this how Flower Flu progressed? Maybe this chess game with death in order to save the world wasn't such a great idea.

"Hey, doesn't Rabi drive a Honda CRZ?" Daci startled Terri out of her reverie.

"What? Oh, Rabi?" She paused then lied. "I wouldn't know."

"He didn't stop calling you, did he?"

"Once in a while."

"You've been broken up less than a month. What exactly qualifies as once in a while?"

"Like, twice a week." Terri could feel a grin spreading across her face involuntarily. Just like in high school. How embarrassing.

"I don't understand why you dumped him."

"Neither does he. I'm not sure he understands *that* I dumped him."

"So why did you?"

Terri only sighed in response.

"He's a good man," Daci opined. "He accepts your horrible work schedule and contends with your penchant for—"

"He's not very motivated."

"He owns a twenty-four hour store! A Middle-Eastern guy with a convenience store may not be very creative, but it's a lot of work."

"But that's *all* he does."

"I guess it's tough to fit the revolution in around his sixteen-hour days."

Terri sighed again. This was an old argument. Another example of Daci's complacency, a trait Rabi shared with her friend and which Daci had defended him on many times in the past.

"I like to think," Terri snapped, "that if I were from some war-torn country and made a bunch of money that I'd do something. Make some change in my homeland."

"He's a US citizen. This is his homeland."

"You know what I mean."

"Just what is it you want him to do? Maybe he should go over to his Jewish friend's house and set himself on fire?"

"Rabi doesn't have any Jewish friends."

"Maurice."

"He thinks Maurice is French. But if Maurice were part of the Israeli army, or the *president* of Israel—"

"It's prime minister."

"Whatever! If he had influence I'd support Rabi showing up with a bag of oily rags and a lighter, okay?"

"You're sick." But she could hear the touch of humor in Daci's voice.

Usually this marked the watershed of their arguments, the point where one of them burst into laughter and the other followed suit. But today she couldn't verify Daci's grin, wasn't certain. Fuck, her lack of visual clues made a mess of everything.

"Besides," Daci suddenly expounded, "he works his ass off, he brought his parents and his brothers here, and he loves you. What more do you want from a man?"

Terri held her tongue. In high school, Daci had been unaccountably pro-Israeli, so Terri found it highly ironic that here Daci was defending her Palestinian ex-boyfriend. And defending him for being apolitical.

Politics had been so important to both of them in college. But then came that bizarre trip Daci's father had taken her on after graduation, where she'd played with warlord gangsters while her father stole root stock and vine cuttings. So much exposure to such ill-gotten power. And violence. It must affect people, impress things upon them. Daci had come back much quieter about political events, much less certain of her once vehemently held opinions.

The women had been girls then, both been too young to appreciate the ramifications of that trip, and once they'd gotten older and wiser, Daci never seemed to want to discus it. It made her uncomfortable and apologetic, like the sex-heavy first film of a now-famous actress. Terri supposed this wasn't a good time to exhume the subject, though she was sorely tempted.

"I think you broke up with him because of the whole kid thing, anyway," Daci said after a lull. "You've convinced yourself it's this big political—"

"The personal *is* political."

"He wants kids and you don't, where's the politics?"

"My career is very political. Kids will get in the way of that."

Daci made a jeering sound. "Get a nanny like everyone else. You want to talk politics? Only stupid people are breeding. You have an opportunity to tip the balance and you're squandering it."

"Then why don't you have kids?!"

Daci must have appreciated Terri's tone because she reverted topics. "Do you know how disappointed Rabi is going to be if you *die* from Flower Flu?"

"Possibly enough to come kill you since it will be your fault. Are we there yet?"

"If you'd taken the pills you'd know!" Her friend's tone held less humor and more frustration. "But yes, we are almost there. Just need to park."

"Come up with a solution yet? A plan?"

"No, I've been too busy arguing with a crazy person."

"Well, when insane. . . ."

But her cheer and cleverness were pushed from her along with her breath when she overcompensated while getting out of the Hummer. She sprawled to the hot pavement. Lay there for a long moment wanting to cry like a child spilled from her bicycle. Unhurt if she discounted her scraped hands and knee but utterly humiliated. And scared.

How long could she maintain this vigil? Literally there was a tipping point. After twelve hours, even the vaccine was no use.

It was ten o'clock now, which meant three hours had passed since she'd discovered her blindness. She'd gone to bed at midnight, though, so it could have begun as long as nine hours ago. So she had only a few more hours before the churnings began in her belly and the only thing anybody could do was give her morphine.

But for most people, pain relief was the only thing anybody could do, period. Most people didn't have a secret vaccination source. This truth restored her conviction.

Doubtlessly gazing at the muscly men of Venice Beach, Daci wolf-whistled quietly. "You're missing quite a view."

"Very funny. Help me up."

CHAPTER 15

Venice Beach could always be counted on to be cooler than the rest of Los Angeles. Daci attributed that as much to the view as the water— all those guys working out on the sand like it was a gym and the surfers with their killer tats and fitted wetsuits.

"Why do you think I keep my office here?" Terri handed Daci the key, and Daci unlocked the rear door of her building, which sat right on the sand.

Terri's second-floor office window overlooked famous Muscle Beach. Clientele came in through the 17th Street entrance and contended with the hyper-efficient Isabelle. Terri loved her tesettür-hijab clad secretary as much for her beyond-stylish attire (the scarf always matched the outfit) as for the woman's complete inability to be intimidated by anyone ever.

Terri sat behind her desk, phoned Isabelle to let her know she'd arrived. She slid on a pair of sunglasses. "I'll tell him I'm staving a migraine."

"Shoulda taken the pills," Daci sing-songed. Her new tactic seemed to be feigning indifference. "Want me to go get him?"

"Yeah, go out and meet him, and have Isabelle call me and tell me what he looks like."

Moments later, Terri's office phone gave its soft electronic purr, and Isabelle's Turkish accent told her, "Man is tall, skinny, red-haired, and with big blue eyes. Scruffy but not in scary way. Kee-yute. And young. Twen'y, maybe twen'y-five. Pale! Like cheese. But has most coo-el tat-wo. Is tree-D! Ask to see."

Daci said from the doorframe, "Isabelle's got him signing preliminary paperwork. She's absolutely entranced by his tattoo. It's like one of those 3D images, you know?" She sounded delighted.

"*Magic Eye?*"

"Yeah, those."

Terri laughed at her friend. "You could never see those when we were kids."

"I still can't. Isabelle told me what it is."

"What is it?"

"I'm not saying. You should have taken the pills, you could see for yourself. He's also reading *Stand Still like the Humming Bird*. A *signed* copy."

"Henry Miller?"

"Yes, signed by him *and* by Kenneth Patchen."

"Wow. Well," Terri aimed her face at the direction of the door. "He did say he was overly literate."

"Ms. Tehzan?" Terri felt her client's substance—tall and lean—she could perceive it. Maybe the shadow that he formed? Strange to interpret the world this way, so viscerally. She usually analyzed things, distrusted her instincts unless they could be validated by some sort of external data.

Eddie moved toward her, but Daci intercepted him, shooed him into a seat.

"Your assistant told me you're about to have a horrible headache? If another time is better, we can reschedule, that's fine." His words sounded earnest, calm and without undo apology. They were also kissed by an accent.

"Are you from the East Coast? Jersey?"

"Naw. My ma is, though. So I assimilated it. Or it assimilated *me*." He gave an easy laugh. "Like those Mexican kids with the accents who don't actually speak any Spanish? I love those kids."

"That's quite a tattoo," Terri said, gesturing vaguely. "Where'd you get it?"

"Thanks. Uh, Guam I got it in. Nobody here would do it. So I went down there and this massive guy with an eye patch over one eye and a jeweler's monocular in the other did it. Took him almost nine hours."

Terri knew right then she'd take his case.

Forty-five minutes, and according to Daci a half-pad of notes in her unreadable script later, Terri sent the lanky red-head on his way.

"Is he your whole day?"

"I don't have any other appointments if that's what you mean. But I have a lot of research."

"Screw your research. You need to take these pills, so I guess we need to come up with a plan."

Terri's entire body eased up—her jaw, her shoulders, her toes uncurled—and she fought the urge to sob. Still, the tension in Daci's voice, and the clock that Terri was now quite aware of, counterbalanced that relief.

"I'll Tell Ya's is open for lunch," Daci suggested. "It's comfortable and safe."

"It's in the Valley, though."

"That's why I asked if he was your only face-time."

Daci took her by the elbow, just like a real blind person, and they headed outside to the not-unpleasant heat and cacophony of Venice Beach.

"I know that kid's mother," Daci said, abruptly like she'd just remembered. "Maureen Spencer?"

"Oh, yeah, you would because of Zane. Any thoughts?"

"She's alright. A little raw. What's often referred to as a pistol? Or full of piss and vinegar." Daci opened the Hummer door and guided Terri to step up into the vehicle. "Funny," she said, "that Eddie kid doesn't seem too angry."

"Should he be?"

"I always pictured people that are suing somebody as foaming at the mouth with righteous rage." Daci got in the driver's side, the door closing with about as much noise as a fridge door. The engine came to life, evidenced only by the soft vibration through the cabin.

"Some people are just tired," Terri told her. "Eddie clearly feels he was not given the proper skill set to function comprehensively and competitively in the world. This is, in fact, the job of a parent. We, as a society, need recourse to—"

"Hey! I'm not a jury. Take these."

Terri heard the rattle of capsules against plastic, felt a cool bottle press against her hand.

She crossed her arms and frowned in the direction of Daci's voice. "You know the rule."

"We just agreed we're working on it."

"Tell me your plan."

"We can form a plan *together* after you take the pills."

Terri sighed. "That feels disloyal."

"You do realize that nobody will know that you took these pills except me."

"And me! Myself." Terri pounded her chest with an open hand. "I have a conscience."

"So do I! I just don't like to tell people." The car careened left and sped up, entering the freeway.

"Right, your corroded public reputation must be upheld so the public can continue to love to hate you."

Daci laughed. "How else can you get ahead in this world?" She paused. "Why don't you bring *this* to the public? Survivanoia withholding the treatment, I mean."

Terri felt a wash of relief. "Ooh, I like! Elaborate."

"Say you woke—no! Say you *claimed* to have woken up blind, the harbinger to RV707. You'd heard rumors, and went through . . . channels, which led you to Survivanoia. There you discovered, as you suspected, that they do have a vaccine, so fast acting that it almost qualifies as a cure. They are not releasing this vaccine, thereby reducing the whole of the nation to the status of the Tuskegee Indians."

Terri nodded. "But at least all they had was syphilis. They had blindness to work toward, we have it as a starting place."

"Perfect!" Daci put on a reporter voice. "They were human guinea pigs for syphilis, now the entire citizenry have become guinea pigs for Flower Flu *etcetera etcetera ad naseum*."

"I'm a lawyer, though, not a journalist."

"So sue us. Even better! The journos will flock, Survivanoia will be forced to release the cure, and you can sleep better at night and not allow yourself to die of a bleeding heart."

"You think it'll work?"

"Does the Pope piss in the woods?"

"No, actually."

Terri felt but didn't hear the engine working harder, knew they were going over the Hill into the Valley. And again the mental static of preoccupation.

"What?"

"That CRZ is back."

"You certain it's the same one?"

"Certain, no. But I'd bet a few bucks. And I'd bet I know who's in it, too."

Terri heard the teasing grin in her friend's voice, decided to side step the subject of Rabi. "Do you know where I'll Tell Ya's is?"

"On Ventura and Laurel Canyon, right?"

"I don't know, I was asking you."

"But I'm not letting you order any food until you take the pills. Especially with Rabi back there waiting to kill me."

"Fair enough," Terri conceded without taking the bait. "We do have a plan. How many?"

She took one as instructed, with further directions to take one a day for the next two days.

"The virus itself is not very strong," Daci explained. "It's easily and quickly killed. The blindness is serendipitous, something triggered by the virus but not directly resultant. Once the virus actually pushes the body into gear, that seems to be irreversible."

Three pills to stop the consequences before they began. Such a simple fix to such a horrible disease. Terri still felt guilty. Traitorous. But she didn't want to die. Not even for a cause. And certainly not by Flower Flu. She'd be no use to anyone dead. She vowed, though, to hound her friend every day until this drug was marketed. Phone calls, emails, kidnap Zane, whatever it took.

The Valley radiated noon-day heat off the concrete, but inside I'll Tell Ya's she got goose bumps. Once they were seated and watered, Attalla himself arrived. Terri could hear his big grin.

He shook both their hands, Daci first. "You look like I have before seen. You..." Still holding Terri's hand, Attalla ran through his mental rolodex but clicked his tongue. "Look like can't remember," he admitted. "So. Kosher? Vegetarian? Allergic to anything?"

No, no, and no.

"Any food you not like so much, make you look like throw up?"

"Don't mix fish and cheese," Daci requested.

"Sauerkraut."

"You eat sauerkraut."

"Not in public."

Attalla laughed. "Look like funny."

He asked them a handful of questions about their day, then if they wanted to be told what they were getting or just have it brought (they chose the latter) and then slipped away presumably to the kitchen.

Out of habit, Terri glanced around. Perhaps she was filling in images but it seemed to her that she could almost make out the abundant blond wood of the big rectangular room. It seemed brighter than when she'd first come in.

"Would you think I was delirious if I said I'm seeing better already?"

"No. Like I said, the stuff acts fast. At least in the first twenty-four hours. Once that window closes, you're a goner."

"Know what I don't get? Why isn't the government doing something about this?"

Daci pushed air through her lips. "Syd says it's all legal. So there's nothing for the government *to* do."

"They could fund the vaccine research."

"They may have, for all I know. Hell, they may have paid to have the virus invented."

"Doubtful. The Republicans know they need the poor. Hell, they spent the past administration making as many as they could. Not the Libertarians, either."

Daci scoffed a laugh. "Naw, they're all about hands off, and live and let die, and fuck you here's to me."

"That only leaves one group. Liberal Democrats. Euthanizing the poor." Terri shook her head in mock incredulity.

"First Ebonics, then bilingual education, now this."

The women laughed together at their own dark humor.

"For real though," Terri said once their laughing subsided, "how could anyone purposefully design and release such an awful illness?"

"The obvious answer is money. But maybe it wasn't on purpose. Maybe it just . . . escaped? Like lions escape the zoo?"

Attalla returned, set a plate and two glasses on their table. "Here look like appetizer. Escargot in garlic, shallots, and butter. This is bread, just from oven now. This is wine. French. Look like red." He poured two glasses then departed.

Terri, with some care, sunk a fork into one of the snails. "Ooh these are good! Buttery, earthy, yummy!"

"Not chewy at all."

"No, like a good portobello."

"And not mushy." Daci sounded relieved.

Terri had a mouthful of French-look-like-red. It was smoky without being heavy and complimented the snails unexpectedly. "Guess it's good we ordered before I asked about the government, huh?"

"Right! Attalla would have brought us a gallon of ice cream and two spoons!"

Terri swallowed more wine. She definitely saw better now. Everything on the table had an individual shape. Fuzzy, but distinguishable. Not too far away from how things looked before her laser surgery.

"What if it *is* like a lion?"

"Hmm?"

"What if the research was something unrelated. The Flower Flu was discovered by accident, and the virus got out of control? Like crack. Or AIDS."

"Ooh that's a nice headline. Is Flower Flu the New AIDS? It would also help explain why I haven't found anything, if it wasn't intentional."

"You told me yourself most scientific discoveries are serendipitous."

Daci grinned at this new idea. "How did I not think of that?"

"I've always been a little smarter than you."

Daci threw the last snail at her. Terri caught it and popped it into her mouth just as their lunches arrived.

"For both of you look like same." Attalla stepped aside while a silent waiter set plates in front of them. "Lobster tails, look like giant, from Maine. Mixed vegetables and twice-baked potatoes. And with champagne." The cork popped on cue and goblet-sized glasses appeared, filled to their wide rims with gold, bubbling liquid.

"That's the great thing about this place," Daci proclaimed. "Come here in a good mood, Attalla will make you feel like a queen. Come here in a funk, you'll leave feeling better."

The door opened and sunlight streamed in like a bright flare alighting the table momentarily. And where the light had shown suddenly stood the owner of the white CRZ, and Terri could see him just fine.

Just a few inches taller than her, lean without being skinny, skin the same shade as her own but ruddier—an old penny to her coffee-with-cream. He had a constant five o'clock shadow, even at 7:00 in the morning, though it never seemed to sprout into a beard. His head was at that slight tilt that made him seem very intent, and he squinted slightly while he scanned the room.

"Rabi. What are you doing?"

His clothes suggested a hip, young golfer: well-tailored, charcoal khakis, short-sleeved button-down shirt (with a pocket) and two-tone leather sneakers. He strode toward their table, but his eyes belied the confidence of his strut.

"This morning I wash car, right? Wait for you like every morning but you don't come. Then Daci pulls up and you do come but not looking right. So I—"

"Wait, you've been washing my car?"

"Of course, who you think?"

"And then you watch me leave every day? That's sick! That's stalker behavior."

Daci set an elbow on the table, rested her chin against a curled up fist. "You said you liked having a clean car."

"I'd prefer a dirty car to a stalker."

Rabi glowered at her, his thick eyebrows knitting. "Stalker, stalker, what means this I know not, right?" He ducked his head, raised a hand to his face, and pinched his temples. An endearing affectation.

"All I want to know," he said, looking up again, "is if you are okay. You looked sick this morning. Bad, right?"

"She had a migraine," Daci said, after an uncomfortable lull.

"Migraine?"

Terri nodded at his disbelief.

"You have not migraine for almost three years. Then you break us up, you have migraine. You should put us back." He stated this matter-of-factly.

For Terri this was part of his charm, his matter-of-fact expression of emotional turmoil. He had a lot of traits Terri adored and admired, and Daci was right in saying that he worked hard, at least in the Protestant sort of way. But Terri couldn't help but wonder if she wouldn't eventually find someone whose activist zeal matched her own. And there was the kid thing. . . .

Lost in her thoughts, Terri didn't respond to him, so Rabi turned to

Daci. "We have this argument, her and I." His finger waggled between himself and Terri. "All time repeats, this argument. I tell her Palestine is not my home, I am American citizen now, right?"

"And what does she say?"

Terri clicked her tongue at the two of them. "You know, I'm sitting right here."

"She tells me I have responsibility because I originate there." Rabi went on to say how he'd brought over his family and Terri came to wonder if the two of them were in cahoots since earlier this had been Daci's argument precisely.

Terri was about to call them out on this conspiracy when Rabi suddenly turned to her. "Do you know what Mother Teresa said? About peace, right? She said to help world peace, go home and love your family. This is what I do. I love my family and I love you. This is not enough for you? The words of Mother Teresa?"

His dark, almond-shaped eyes searched her face. Eyes framed by lashes so long and thick they looked fake, and his head cocked at that angle and his full red lips not quite in a smile. His kind, open face by itself made a compelling argument, let alone his invocation of the not-quite-saint.

"I am stalk you for one reason." Rabi dipped two fingers into his shirt pocket and withdrew a small fuzzy box. Black. He set it on the table top just as Attalla arrived with dessert—fruit with whipped cream accompanied by Turkish coffee. Attalla saw the box and was delighted. "Oh look like need more champagne! Wait, I get."

Daci put up a hand. "She hasn't answered him yet."

"Oh no? Well, let's see the ring."

The box opened with a click. Inside burned a ruby sapphire, slightly smaller than a dime. Through the high, rounded surface of the gem the jagged sparks of a six-pointed star shot from the center like six lightening bolts borne of a tiny sun. The star moved when Terri turned the ring.

She plucked it from the box. The sapphire held a deep red with brighter, more fiery points that shifted and sparkled, like a glass of pinot noir held to the sunlight. Wrapped around this remarkable stone, cast in pale gold, was a lizard. His long tail formed the ring itself, while he clutched the stone between his four little feet and gazed up at her with big, onyx eyes.

"Look like not diamond."

"She would throw away if I brought diamond! She'd throw away if real ruby. Is manufactured. In a laboratory, right? No mining, nobody killed. Gold is recycled."

Attalla shrugged in surrender. "Best to give them what they want. Even if makes no sense." He patted Terri's shoulder. "So? Champagne?"

So much promise. So much energy. Held fast and tight and secure in the grip of that happy little lizard.

"Is salamander," Rabi told her when she ran a finger over its head. "Fire lizard. He defies fire, right? But also known for come out only during heavy showers and leave again once the weather is clear."

Terri gave him a quizzical look.

"That's what man at jewelry store say, right? When I tell him what I want. Uhm, also Muhammad thought they made mischief and should be killed."

At that, Daci giggled into her coffee, then guffawed openly. "That's perfect!"

"What about the kid thing?"

Now Rabi gave her a quizzical look. "We worked out other things. We will work out kid thing too."

Daci waved a fork at her. "You could adopt some Palestinian children!"

And Terri Tehzan, who had—impossibly—woken up with Flower Flu not twelve hours prior, looked from the bright hopeful eyes of the lizard on her engagement ring to the bright hopeful eyes of the man who had given it to her.

Smiling, she nodded to Attalla. "Get the champagne."

SURVIVANOIA

V

I Know How Much Hate the World Holds,
Mama

CHAPTER 16

"**G**entlemen, your new company president:** Baroness Dacianna Von Worthington."

The Baroness stepped from the Survivanoia president's office—as of that moment officially hers—into the company's executive conference room. The room overlooked a Persian garden but the drapes were drawn.

She grabbed the chain on the way past and yanked it like a kite string, zipping the beige fabric panels aside and filling the claustrophobic space with sunlight. The picture window revealed, just visible from up the road, the twin loops of Magic Molehill's newest roller coaster, gleaming in the white heat.

A murmured wave of irritation rolled across the sea of pastel, French-cuffed shirts and silk ties. The sun glinted off their diamond tie-tacks and platinum cuff links. Alas, none of them burst into flames.

"No vampires I see. Just zombies, huh?"

No response. Which only went to prove her point, she supposed. She strolled past the built-in fireplace, an absurd artifice in Los Angeles. Still, it could have added intimacy to the spacious, high-ceilinged room. If the room had been a color instead of an institutional grade of not-quite-white.

She made her way to the head of the teak, sleeper-wood conference table, where the man who had introduced her now pulled the chair out for her. He wore a suit that cost more than most people's cars, and stood as tall as she did. The Baroness's three-inch heels put her at six foot six, and she towered over many of the men in the room, but that didn't stop their hard stares and derogatory smirking.

She flowed into the chair, an overstuffed, brad-studded monstrosity whose claret leather matched her waist-length braid. "Thank you, Mister Scalinescu."

Sydney Scalinescu Senior, the man who had introduced her, a handsome man whose grey pinstripe matched his shock of wild hair, whose accent and attentions made the Baroness calm and happy, a man she loved but didn't like and was still legally married to, nodded and gave her a sad smile.

She smiled back in earnest, then set her violet eyes on each and every one of the CEOs and COOs locked in the conference room with her.

"Gentlemen. Questions?"

They attacked like stockbrokers at the bell.

"What is your overall marketing strategy for the upcoming fiscal year?" John Long could have been yelling at his eight-year-old for not taking out the trash.

Before she could finish saying that she'd hired a competent person to head marketing and that person should be consulted on this question, and that furthermore that was *John's* job, hers was to oversee day-to-day operations and bottom-line performance, Dicky Goodman tossed an imposing, acronym-laden manual in her direction.

"How do you intend to be proactive in the wake of the Enron-inspired mutual fund reform?"

"Right!" snapped Stanly "Moochie" Martin. "Not to mention recent additions to the SOX laws, which require complete retooling of our current accounting strategy."

This made her laugh. "If that's true then you'll be visiting your old company president in jail. Assuming you're lucky enough not to go there with him."

Her candor slowed them but heated them too, and more vitriolic questions were directed not to her but to Sydney. "Why do we need a new company president?" "What happened to the old company president?" "What are this woman's qualifications?!"

Jason Bell scowled at her and into his Dingleberry and up at her again. Jack Conner's cell phone rang and he answered it, informed the caller that he was in "some ridiculous meeting with some new employee," and hung up, rolling his eyes.

Moochie and Rodger Paradowski made loud jokes about how the Baroness probably wanted to be president in order to enjoy the low-hanging fruit of three-legged horses, and Dana Cinders shot Sydney Scalinescu an unveiled snarl of scorn. "Since when does your mistress get to play house with your company?!"

"Lends a whole new meaning to bottom-line performance, huh?" "Does this woman even know what day-by-day operations consist of in a manufacturing facility?"

The Baroness stood.

"Look, she's leaving already." "Gotta be tough in the business world, chicky!" "I knew she wouldn't last long, but this is a record."

She reached behind Sydney to a black-leather satchel.

"Boy I sure hope she doesn't have a gun." *Gaffaw gaffaw.*

She unzipped the center pocket and withdrew a twelve-inch, anatomically correct, soft flesh-like rubber penis, complete with molded testicles.

She slammed it against the table—"*There!*"—where it sat upright on the testicles, its circumcised tip swaying cheerfully. "Do I know everything now?"

The room went silent. Save the fleshy swaying of the dildo. *Schwep, schwip, schwep.*

"I can write my name in the snow, too," she assured them. "It's just hard to read."

She looked around the room again, but all eyes were focused on the waving rubber penis.

"Anyone with serious questions should stay. Anyone who wants to continue to embarrass himself, there's the door." She held her arm out accusingly and ominous, like the third ghost, or a Ghost of Business Future, and this time the gaze of each man met her own.

"Hmm? Free to go. Now's your chance. No takers?"

A man in the back, who she knew to be a COO named Rodney Freemore cleared his throat. "Could you, ah . . . put that away?"

"Oh? Why? Make you uncomfortable?"

"That's not really fair," said a CEO.

The Baroness leaned over the table. "Everybody. In this room. Has lost the privilege to speak of fairness."

The CFO, who to his credit had so far said absolutely nothing, raised a hand, one finger, like a British schoolboy. "With a new captain at the helm, the stockholders are going to want an official financial strategy. How soon do you think you'll be able to provide that?"

"Again, not my responsibility. But I should tell you: we're looking into re-privatization."

"I'm sorry?"

"If I'd been president six months ago, most of you wouldn't be here. I don't agree with the decision to go public. The first thing I plan to do is see if we can reverse that."

"You can't fire your stockholders Miss Vo—"

"Baroness. And don't tell me what I can't do. Because quite frankly? You have no idea."

* * *

The scientists arrived for their scheduled meeting early and curious. Dr. Krawkow came in cautiously, as though entering a cave. His blue eyes contrasted nicely with his grey elbow-length ponytail.

Egan McClure followed, his bushy auburn chest-length beard and hair making him look less like a PhD chemist than a Maine lobsterman.

Grinning, wiry Akira Nakajima wore suspenders *and* a belt, followed by

236

Rashid Bajamal who rocked a giant Fila sweatshirt and a pair of Timberlands (funky fly fresh) despite being from Yemen. Maurice Nesculescu's blue pleated pants were an inch too short and he nearly walked into the door-frame for interpreting a graph.

Rin Ping, the Chinese-Thai American, looked model-fabulous in her ripped-from-the-catwalk wardrobe. Today she sported a velvet magenta top that set off the highlights in her hair, with flowing, bootcut pants. She entered looking stern and suspicious behind the smiling, but equally doubtful, Maria Juarez, a tri-lingual, round-goddess beauty of a woman who had raised two girls around earning her PhD.

The Russians—angry, slender Alexei Balakirev and jolly, ruddy Nikolai Uliishev—came in together, in the midst of an argumentative discussion in their native tongue.

Once they were seated, Nikolai turned to Dacianna and Sydney. "He is telling me the phosphorus to fluoride ratio in line five should be reversed and I am saying he is wrong. The problem is with the acid."

Finally, in strolled Dr. Wolfy, as the Baroness called him: Wolfgang Fassbinder, who leaned against the doorframe looking like a Volvo com-mercial, smirking in his Idolater jeans and fisherman's sweater.

They quieted when she stood at the head of the table. "You are all man-agers of your respective departments," she began. "I have good news and bad. The bad news is: you're fired."

She waited but the sound of complaint was so subdued as to pass for the results of indigestion.

Krawkow's blue eyes narrowed. "All of us?"

"Yes."

Egan spoke up next. "You've made us all redundant then?"

"Not exactly. That's the good news. Survivanoia is desperately in need of scientists. It's the managers we don't need anymore."

Low grumbling, like lions thinking about getting up to hunt.

Alexei spoke while glaring at the table. "How many? Scientist? Will you do need? Ing?"

Daci took a quick head count ... eight, ten. "At least ten to begin with. But we're hoping to find about twenty before the end of the year."

Nikolai asked, "And how soon?"

"Quite. Very. Tomorrow? When can you start?"

"What about interviews?"

"You're managers, interview each other."

Dr. Wolfy had been leaning against the wall with his arms crossed. He took a step forward and addressed the white elephant. "Why is it you don't want us to be managers anymore?"

"Your degree is in analytical chemistry, yes?"

He nodded and pursed his lips. "Ja? Und?"

"Tell me how that qualifies you to supervise people."

He leaned back against the wall. "We all had to teach. Is same thing."

"By that logic every mother on the planet is qualified to run your department."

Wolfy let out a loud and lengthy breath of air. Then he chuckled. "Perhaps."

"But, please, Miss Von Baroness," Nikolai paused and blinked. "Is not bad to be scientist again, many of us do not even much like managing. But you know. We make better. Money."

He muttered this last word at the floor, then glanced up at Dacianna like a high school boy who had just asked her to the dance.

"Nikolai. All of you. I promise we would not insult you by asking you to come work for us at less than you were making at your previous posts."

Akira tapped the table. "For you to do this make you become ..." His eyes searched the room while he converted his circular language to Dacianna's linear counterpart. Then his grin flashed and he pointed a finger. "*In*sane. Then they will fire *you*."

Daci laughed as if he'd told an especially funny joke. "They can't, Akira." She turned to Sydney, still standing silent behind her. "Can you, Mr. Scalinescu?"

Sydney's eyes shot her a look to chill blood but his corporate smile and velvet voice stayed in place. "No, Miss Von Baroness. I can't."

* * *

On the rare occasions that Sydney visited Los Angeles, he insisted on eating at I'll Tell Ya's, "Because there's nothing like it in New York."

"Of course there isn't," Daci laughed as they were driven to the restaurant by Sydney's rented limo service. "You try to tell most New Yorkers what they're going to be eating and you'll get beaten. Publicly."

Sydney laughed his gracious gentle laugh. Daci ran a hand through his thick hair, pushed back and greying like a mobster Beethoven.

"You're looking very leonine lately." That shock of grey had progressed to a streak of white so perfect and stately that Sydney had, on more than one occasion, been accused of having it dyed.

He tugged gently at her complicated braid. "What about you? Dating a macramé artist these days?"

"Pornographer. But he does live in Venice, where macramé artists are wont to hang out. Peddle their wears."

At the restaurant, Attalla remembered them but not their preferences, so he started with the basics. He glanced slyly at them, first individually, then farther from the table, as if to get a view of them as a unit, a couple. "Uhm, look like yeah," he mumbled and strutted to the kitchen.

"When are we going to move on the divorce, Syd?"

"When I want a divorce. Which at the moment I do not. Especially since New York doesn't offer a no-fault divorce. I don't blame you. And I'm certainly not going to allow you to blame me."

She didn't take the bait, said simply, "I can file in California."

Attalla arrived with their food and a bottle of wine. "The reconciliation platter," he said, laying out three plates of assorted, fancy hors d'oeuvre looking things. The scents spoke of distant lands and high adventure: sharp cardamom and earthy clove reminding Daci of Arabian nights, mustard and paprika calling up the Horn of Africa. She closed her eyes and allowed the world and its culinary riches to engulf her.

Attalla's voice was low and rough, like the purring of a favorite cat.

"Look like you fight. Before. Now you finish, come here, I feed you nice meal for two." He opened their wine, let Daci sample it.

A velvety burst of fruit followed by just the slightest lingering of smoke. "Perfect," she breathed. "Dry as the desert and fruitier than West Hollywood."

Attalla filled both their glasses. "Look like good luck."

"See?" said Syd, sampling his wine. He nodded his approval. "Attalla doesn't think we're irreconcilable."

"Attalla doesn't know that we've been fighting for six years. Or that 'finishing' entailed me taking over your company." She raised her glass in a toast. "Here's to me!"

"What if you make it work? The company I mean."

"What if I do?"

"Would you stay?"

"With you or with the company?"

Syd gave her what she'd long ago termed his Unamused By The Peasants Look.

"Is that why you agreed to this arrangement?" she asked. "You think it might win me back?"

Her question was gentle, as was his response. Perhaps Attalla's sweet breads, spicy meats, and citrusy fruits had some healing powers after all.

"A woman says she is leaving because she doesn't like my business practices. Then she tells me she thinks she can fix those practices. Doesn't it follow that if she can, and furthermore does, and is able to succeed because I stood aside and allowed her to do so, that she would stay with me? Does that seem truly unreasonable?"

"Yes."

Again with Unamused Look.

Daci poured them both another glass of wine. "Your selective memory has erased the section where it's the silent partner who demands that the woman gets brought on board. Also, even if my position were the result of your forethought rather than your mere acquiescence, I decided to leave because your business practices were cruel and inhuman."

"But not unusual and therefore not illegal." He shot her a crooked smile.

She took a close look at him, searched his dark eyes, and realized how difficult it seemed to look into his face and recall the terms *cruel* and *inhuman*. Syd, the man, was neither of those.

Still. "You let yourself, or at least your stockholders, behave in a despicable manner."

"Is it unforgivable?"

Daci searched their shared platter for something especially tasty. "I don't know yet."

Syd rested his chin in his hand, then clutched his wineglass, then emptied it, and folded his hands. "Let me please tell you something. Things will often go wrong because you let them slip away from you."

"Why did you let the company go public?"

"Perfect example." He offered his sad smile. "I heeded the advice of an accountant. And he made the company money. So he did his job."

"Everybody made money but you may all end up in hell."

"With a corner office and a brass nameplate."

Daci savored a chunk of sweetly spicy meat, considered her not-quite-ex husband. "You think I'm self-righteous."

"Uhm-hmm. I wouldn't necessarily label your anger as misplaced. But you should know. These things that you learned, that made you leave, are quite small compared to much of what goes on in the world run by the moneyed elite."

"Why do you stay in it?"

"Why does your father stay in it?"

Daci paused, weighed this statement. "Meaning what exactly?"

Sydney's smile went toothy and nostrils flared. "Could be something terrible, couldn't it? Given the man's position."

And of course Daci knew that. She'd kept a purposefully ignorant distance from her father's business, especially since discovering the blood on her husband's hands. But she also knew that Sydney sometimes used that carnivorous smile just to unnerve people.

"He makes wine, Syd."

"He makes money."

"Wine money. Not blood money."

"People seem to have this idea that the road to wealth and power is mysterious and unknowable. In fact it's a scalable pyramid with well-specified means of getting to the top. And once you're at the top you don't simply decide you're through, clean out your desk, and get yourself a job stacking lettuce at the corner grocer."

"So how do you get out?"

Sydney let out his low mean growl, his Corporate Laugh. "Why don't you first worry about getting in?"

"I am in."

"So it must seem. Just recall this conversation the moment you realize that something has slipped from your control and you now must face the consequences of other people's actions." He took her hand in both of his, drew it to him, and kissed it.

"I do hope," he told her, emptying the wine bottle into his glass, "your consequences are less harsh than mine have proved."

Daci set her palm against his face. His stubbly cheek made her recall the peppery scent of his aftershave, which pulled her back to the night she'd met him. She'd been sitting in the cab of a dark blue Ford pickup, simultaneously chewing three pieces of Hubba Bubba. At age nineteen, she still liked to chew the whole pack at once, all five chunks, but sometimes that made her drool on herself and Dennis and Brian would actually be back any minute.

She wedged the gum against the back of her teeth, plied it with her tongue, and then proceeded to blow a bubble which, from her perspective, seemed as big as her head. And when it popped she grandly removed the whole mess from her face with one smooth motion and grinned at the novelty of it—in 1989 "less-sticky" Hubba Bubba was still a fresh product.

She was stuffing the mess back into her mouth when someone tapped on the truck window. She gazed past her own reflection in the glass to see a well-built man in a stylish suit. Given that he had to stoop to see in the truck, he must have been over six-six. She recalled how much this had pleased her, given her own height.

She rolled down the window and the spicy scent of his aftershave, like an exotic tea, pleasantly undercut the sugar smell her gum had filled the truck with.

"Need something?"

He identified himself as the neighbor from across the street. "I am wondering what it is you are doing out here at midnight in what appears to be a landscaping truck."

His voice hadn't changed since she'd met him either, still today it held just a dusting of a combined accent, flattened New York vowels but honed W's, like a Long Island Dracula.

Dacianna handed him a business card. "Reclamations," she told him.

He looked the card. "Which means what?"

"Depends. In your neighbor's case here, he contracted a"—she checked the invoice on a clipboard next to her—"seven thousand dollar landscape for which he provided a deposit equating to one third, roughly twenty-three hundred. The rest of the bill was never paid. Contact with him has not produced a complaint or reversal of any type on his part."

"Complaint?"

"Dying plants, algaed pond, damaged sprinklers or plumbing, or poisoned pets or other animals."

"So you are doing, again, what?"

"Taking back two-thirds of the landscape. Actually, a little more, to compensate the company for labor."

"Just what kind of person does a job like this?" He sounded curious, not accusatory.

Dacianna cracked her gum at him. "Ex-cons."

And as she said it, her crew materialized, driving across the lawn in a mini dump truck twice as big as her standard pickup. Their headlights caught her visitor and Dacianna noted that the grey pinstripe of his suit matched his wild shock of hair.

He didn't squint against the glare, but she flashed her own headlights at her crew and they dropped back to running lights.

"Just what is it you do for this reclamations company?" Sydney had asked her.

Again with the gum. She tossed the truck in reverse. "I own it."

When she'd arrived at her office the next morning, she found Sydney's voice on the machine, asking her to dinner.

Her father never stated explicitly that he didn't think their relationship would last. But the man's undisguised amusement and cavalier dealings made his opinion clear to Dacianna. In truth, she agreed. But Sydney Scalinescu fascinated her; she couldn't get enough of him and his museum-like mansion.

There were few people whose companionship she could tolerate, let alone desired. Syd doted on her almost as much as her father did, and he had money, which was Daci's grandmother's single criteria.

"It's as easy to fall in love with a rich guy as it is to fall in love with a poor one," her grandmother reminded her repeatedly. "And at least if it goes sour, and with you kids today it always seems to, you can get some money for your troubles."

So three years later, the end of summer, when she'd planned to, as an NYU graduate, get herself away from the Hamptons and back to Los Angeles, she instead found herself cross-legged on the wrap-around deck of her father's rented beach house. Every year he'd said he wasn't renting the following summer and then every summer he had, so Daci and her mother had that long, warm season mostly to themselves on the New York beach for every year Daci recalled. But this, she somehow knew, would be the last one for real.

She munched a Chewy Chips Ahoy cookie, another new product from her freshly-ended college days. Not soft in any way resembling fresh cookies, and chemical in flavor, yet she went through nearly a bag of them a day. She plucked the last one from the flimsy white plastic tray, stopped listening to the waves near her on the darkened porch and paid attention instead to the conversation indoors, between her father and her hoping-to-be-husband, Sydney.

"...just trying to be assured that you know what you're in for," her father's tone revealed plainly his skeptical bemusement. Her father looked the way Sydney sounded. His pointy beard, shoulder-length greying hair and sharpened cheekbones marked him as East European, reinforced by his being a vintner.

"You're concerned about the age difference, yes?"

"No. Yes. A little. Daci is twenty-two going on forty."

"We all know everything at twenty-two, yes? If I knew now all that I believed I knew at that age, I'd own the world."

"Not just a large paranoid piece of it?"

Both men laughed at this reference to Sydney's company, a corporation Daci did not understand and was not especially interested in.

"The difference," her father said, "is that when Daci is thirty-six, she will know everything she thinks she knows now. And she very well may own the world!"

More laughter. "All the better for me!"

"You'll never control her."

"I have no desire to."

"She might destroy you."

"What better way to be brought down?"

Her father's grin came through in his voice. "I guess you do have all the answers. You've got my blessing or whatever. Give it a shot. It'll work or it won't."

Of course it didn't. It destructed fabulously and was still in the process. Yet here they were not unhappily sharing dinner.

"You know what's weird?" she asked.

Sydney stacked the empty platters and pushed them aside. "In general or tonight?"

"We made it through the hard part. Me being away."

Sydney's face crinkled into a smile. "A lover away is an easy thing.

Especially for the one who is gone. It's when they reunite. That's what's difficult. Separated they have each created a certain perfect version of their partner. Then the real partner comes along and doesn't live up. Dismantles everything. Isn't that how it went? You thought I was a god? Turns out I'm only a man."

"I never thought you were a god, Syd. I thought, and still believe, that you're decent and good and even generous. And I can't reconcile who I believe you to be with the actions you've taken in the name of running this corporation."

"Well. Perhaps you can fix that for me."

"Reconcile myself?"

"Reconcile me."

She thought, but did not say aloud, that this was exactly what he'd wanted from her since he'd uncovered her Romanian heritage.

Sydney Elek Scalinescu had as convoluted a heritage as Dacianna herself—as most Americans. But Syd's Americanization, which made all his disparate pieces acceptable and, if he so chose, irrelevant, was newly minted—a fact exclaimed by his accent.

Despite his French *prenume,* to those with an ear for it his accent said Hungary. If you questioned him he'd claim Transylvania, now a part of Romania but at one time controlled by the Hungarian Magyars. Then he'd tell you he was Magyarian, how they occupied not only Transylvania but also Slovakia, and he'd grit his teeth and curse the Dacians.

None of this had meant much to Dacianna when they'd met. It wasn't until she traveled with her father in search of unique rootstock for his vine-yard. Her father had been nearly suicidal with grief after the destruction of his Moldavian vineyard. Rather than attempt to preserve anything within the rabid animal of Eastern Europe, he decided to collect vine cuttings and bring them to the United States. No American president would be crazed enough to burn a vineyard in the People's Republic of California.

So her father combined his rootstock quest with her college-graduation trip. In early autumn of 1992—a few days after she'd gotten officially engaged and a few months before the wedding—he took her to travel the shadows of Europe, places tourists didn't go, like the formers Czechoslovakia, Yugoslavia, as well as Chechnya, and of course Romania.

During that trip, Dacianna came to appreciate, was *made* to appreciate, that she was Dacian, the only known descendants of the original Roman Empire, and that marrying Sydney the Magyar would contaminate the bloodline.

"But so would marrying, say, Adam Brown, the systems administrator," her father had assured her. It didn't matter in the States. But it mattered, still to this day, in Eastern Europe. And Sydney-the-Magyar, in marrying her, would be taming himself a creature of stature and status to be spoiled and bragged about.

This was the fiction Sydney forged for himself about her. That she was Haute Bourgeois Romania, not a princess, but a Baroness. Certainly no American Wildwoman.

Could he be that naive? The acquisition of those rootstocks for her father's winery involved transactions with a multitude of shady men. If Sydney had ever suspected or doubted her decorum, he'd never indicated it. Never accused her of trading sex for secrets (which she hadn't—not intentionally) or her father of using her as bait (which he had).

Daci peered now at Sydney. Wondered about his comment earlier regarding her father "staying in it." The question she grappled for hadn't fully forged itself in her head when Attalla arrived with his grin and dessert—another platter for sharing.

"Here we have look like uzvar, stewed in vodka, medivnyk and makivnyk."

Sydney raised an eyebrow. "Have you gotten a new cook?"

"Oh no. Our cook cooks from all over world, Mr. Scalinescu. Look like even Slavic, yes?"

Sydney stood, shook Attalla's hand, patted him warmly on the shoulder. "Thank you, sir." He sat, took the oversized spoon, and served Daci a large portion of the fruit compote from the liquid of the uzvar.

"I mentioned to him last time he was here that my son's mother is Slavic and one thing I miss is her desserts. 'Look like sweet is gone,' he said."

Syd set a piece of each of the cakes—one honey, the other poppy seed—onto Daci's little dessert plate.

She tried a bite of everything. Liquor just permeated the syrupy rich fruit of the uzvar, the honey cake was moist and just sweet enough to bring out the harmonious tannins in her coffee, and the poppy seeds were a bright contrast to all that.

As she nibbled her sweets, she watched the gentleman across from her, refined and complicated and powerful, roll his eyes to the ceiling in silent thankful prayer, kiss his fingers and send the kiss to the sky. Such childlike glee at something so simple as a thought-gone dessert.

She dipped her spoon into the uzvar. "Sydney?"

"Ummm! Fabulous, yes?"

"Yes," she said. "You are."

CHAPTER 17

"**D**id he give you any names?"

GrandMama von Goethe, Dacianna's father's mother sounded, as she always did when discussing Sydney Scalinescu, as if she'd accidentally eaten a lemon.

Daci set her keys on the battered little table behind the couch and took from the silver dish there a wrapped candy, a caramel ring with a white, creamy center. Breakfast of champions.

"Names of . . . ?"

"Anyone! Scientists! People in the company to be wary of!"

"He wouldn't, GrandMama, he didn't vote me in. Right?"

GrandMama waved the conversation aside with a wide sweep of her flabby arm. "I already know he didn't or you would have told me. So, good! I don't have to feel guilty about giving money to those bartenders. Nothing gets staff yammering like a few free drinks."

"Bartenders?"

"I know where your Sydney is most hours of the day. And I know most of the people who own those places. I could have him assassinated at the Wolfie's if I wanted. Or if *you* wanted. Get a pen."

Daci pulled a Rotring from its space in her leather satchel, handed it to her grandmother.

"You'd better write it, kid, if you want to be able to read it. And sit down! You're making me nervous."

Daci sat on the hideous plaid couch. Orange and black mostly, in thin-line plaid. When her grandparents first bought it, sometime in . . . the '70s? Was that possible? Dacianna had thought it was awesome since she loved Halloween and the couch seemed a tribute to the holiday.

Now Daci recognized that it was *awful*, that the rust and black were ugly remainders of an ugly decade and she couldn't understand why GrandMama insisted on keeping both it and the matching chair, a plaid box worn through like the couch at the arms but whose cushions remained obstinately resilient.

GrandMama Von Goethe, once Ileana Moldovan, had built the nursing home and now lived in the facility's penthouse suite. The fancy apartment measured thirteen hundred square feet, larger than the Cape house she'd moved out of when Opa Ludwig had died and she'd discovered all that money she'd never known he'd had.

The suite included a modest but well-equipped kitchen and GrandMama had a private cook in addition to her private nurse and a driver she kept on call. She shared laundry service with the rest of the home but had her own maid. Though clearly visible from the outside, the fact of a third floor was not advertised and the staff was discouraged from mingling. A metal flap requiring a key hid the elevator button. So things would remain until GrandMama died, at which point it would be up to Dacianna's father to decide whether to preserve this family secret for their own continued use or open it to other patients.

GrandMama pulled a wrinkled piece of paper from seemingly out of the air. She set her glasses, which hung from a string around her neck and tended to collect crumbs, on her nose and frowned at the paper.

"Okay, first order of business concerns one Geo Rivera, real name Jorge, he's the . . ." She moved the paper almost to her nose. "I have some atrocious handwriting. Ah! Inside sales department supervisor. You write that down?"

"You already have it."

"If I can't read this you sure as hell can't. There's a notepad—"

"In the coffee table drawer." Daci opened the small drawer in the middle of GrandMama's hideous rectangular coffee table, found a writing tablet and jotted down Geo Rivera. She wondered if he was the same Geo Rivera she knew of through Zane.

"Does Geo make dirty movies, GrandMama?"

"He does! But that's not the problem. He was in with the last company president. Drinking and golfing."

"And hookers, oh my!"

"Mmmhmm. So you're going to want to come down on him right out of the gate."

"Couldn't I just fire him?"

"You could but you don't want to. Because you're going to want to hire his father. And even though all evidence says Geo and his father don't talk anymore, it's disrespectful to hire a man and fire his son."

She looked up from the paper suddenly, her ice blue eyes sparkling. "That's the same about Syd Junior, you know. He's probably dangerous. But if you need him gone, you'll have to make him quit. If you fire him it's the same as admitting defeat."

Daci nodded. She'd thought that situation over long and hard by herself already. "Tell me about Geo's dad."

"Him and the rest of this list." GrandMama shook the wrinkled paper in the air, "All names of scientists. I know how much you like them. So I hunted down the top thirty best in the state. Geo's father, Arturo Rivera is the first name."

"Rivera is the best?" Daci thought she should have heard of him.

"The best? How should I know? *Arturo* Rivera is the first name on the list because Arturo starts with A."

Daci laughed. She should have known. Her grandmother's address book was arranged the same way with Uncle Elwood under U, Rabbi Steinberg under R, etc.

"So why do I want him?"

GrandMama consulted her crinkled sheet. "Arturo Rivera is a desalination expert? That mean something to you?"

"Yeah! Survivanoia's de-sal plant just opened last month. Saline Solutions?"

"Okay. That makes sense. He's the mastermind behind Saline Solutions, yes I wrote that. But Survivanoia never hired him, they contracted him. And apparently that's a waste because he has a car. No!" She squinted at the paper. "No, he has a car that *runs* on waste. Runs on desalination waste. Does that make sense?"

Daci blinked. "Holy shit."

"Mmmhmm, the story is he can convert a car in three days. Okay, the next one is Bernie Goldblume. He's got a ... solar storage? System? Mean something?"

"Holy shit," Daci said again.

And on it went. A Seth Browder treating everything from autism to ulcers by harnessing the frequencies of purring cats. A physicist at JPL having success with teleportation of inanimate objects, another holed up in Riverside rumored to be levitating bowling balls and developing a perpetual motion machine. Biochemists who'd left USC after successfully transplanting eyes, and another team *rumored* to have split off from JPL, *rumored* to be growing new brain cells, and locating the origin of dreams.

"Where'd you say you got this list?"

"It doesn't matter. Syd should have given this information to you, that was part of his arrangement. I'll have him chewed out tomorrow. How'd your first day go, anyway?"

"Entertaining. At least for me."

"You don't feel overwhelmed?"

"No."

"Disenchanted?"

"No, I'm not Dorothy and Survivanoia isn't Oz, just whose side are you on here, GrandMama?"

"I got you the job, didn't I?"

True. Daci's grandmother had "pulled strings and cashed in favors" to get Daci to the president's seat. The tenacious old woman had money and, as she put it, "At the devil's table everyone may use a long-handled spoon, but they're still all spooning from the same bowl."

GrandMama knew the silent partner. Did she have something on him? Were they lovers? Daci didn't know and didn't especially care. It got her where she needed to be. Daci had done reclamations of goods and later of land. After she'd earned her master's in it, she'd taught global policy classes online to anonymous members of Congress and the UN who needed a crash course. She'd owned a pawn shop and she'd done much of Sydney's acquisition research until she discovered his corporate secret. Then everything changed. Was still changing.

Her grandmother's voice broke her reverie. "... You keep saying you want to alter the way Sydney does business, when to me it seems that how he does business is how America does business. Hell, maybe the world for all I know."

"I want something different."

"I know it. You've told me a thousand times if you've told me ever. 'A new standard by ...'—what is it you said?"

"By which to measure global entities," Daci reminded her. "A corporation whose wealth—"

"—was measured by its knowledge rather than its dollars. See? I listen."

"But you don't believe."

"Sometimes I do but not that often. It's hard to free the world, kid. Seems to me like you're a little tiny David against the Goliath of world industries. Old men who have been doing this since the dawn of time. I've told you and I'll tell you again: Men own the world. We women just run it."

"How come you got me this job, then?"

"I didn't get you this job. Your resume got it for you."

"You know what I mean. I couldn't have simply submitted my resume and gotten the old company president ousted."

"I'm talking about the stuff you don't put in writing."

The following silence weighed palpably. Her grandmother referred to her vine-collecting trip. All those countries with their men. Younger perhaps than businessmen but they too had been "doing this since the dawn of time." From the rush of memories a single image surfaced, an image actually captured on film and stored, Dacianna knew, in a box somewhere in this very penthouse.

Herself, dressed all in black, except for the Kalashnikov, a gift from the two men with her, Radu and Drakko. She and Radu were perched on the hood of his car, a battered and muddied black Land Rover. His arm cupped her shoulder with the careless possession of the young lovers they were for those few weeks; for their sunburned grins they could have been sharing margaritas.

He'd bragged openly about the theft of his vehicle from the twosome whose skulls adorned the top of its cab where mounted lights should have been. Drakko, Radu's bodyguard, loomed next to the car, grinning like the madman he was.

She'd been too young and ignorant at the time to appreciate the depths of depravity these men represented. Today she knew. Recalling the picture made Dacianna uncomfortable, like she needed to wash her hands or apologize.

GrandMama narrowed her eyes, seeming to recall the photo along with Daci. "So many places in Europe your father could have taken you."

"He was trying to teach me something."

"That's right. Few women experience war. Not like that. Mostly we wait. At home for letters or the dreaded man at the door with his hat under his arm. To run the world, first a girl needs to run with the big dogs."

Daci gave a short breath. "I ran with the wolves. My *name* is wolf."

"You kidding?" Dark laughter flapped out of GrandMama. "You walk the wolves on a leash! And that's what got you this job. If anyone can make a change, I guess it's you."

"And what if I smash it into a million pieces? Drown it in a sea of bankruptcy-red?"

GrandMama put both hands up in surrender. "*C'est la guerre.*"

* * *

A twenty-minute jaunt up the 5 took Daci from the nursing home to Survivanoia in the abhorrent luxury of her stunningly atrocious vehicle, the newest, biggest Hummer. Hers was a hybrid, but she kept that a secret, and today she planned to track down Arturo Rivera and convince him to make one run on brine for her and that would be secret too. At least for a little while.

But just this moment the tailgating red Jeep consumed her thoughts, riding close even for Los Angeles, especially given that they were on surface streets now and not the freeway.

She careened into the parking lot and slowed purposely. The Jeep followed, sped around her, and dove into a spot. Its driver, tall and slender, cute with his scruffy dirty blond hair and immaculate goatee, chattered into his cell phone as he strode across the asphalt.

Daci eased her monster into the spot next to him. She couldn't have started the day off better. The tailgater was Geo Rivera and now she had the perfect opportunity to begin taming him.

She phoned his extension, figuring on scheduling something between her morning and afternoon meetings. Grab him just before lunch, see what he was like when he's hungry and cranky.

He didn't answer his phone, instead his voicemail picked up. And it made her laugh so hard she had to call him back. Twice. Then she used her cell phone to call her friend Terri and left Geo's message on Terri's voicemail.

"You've reached Survivanoia's BiiiiiiIIG MAC DADDY!!!" He sounded utterly triumphant, like a Mexican radio announcer. All that was missing was the reverb. "If you've got my money press one. If you're calling to purchase goods press two. Wanna see my grill? Leave a message."

Charmed, Daci decided not to leave a message, just to go see him in person.

But other things came first. Like informing the sales staff that they no longer had country club memberships. "From now on instead of golfing, you'll be taking clients to Magic Molehill."

Jack Millstone complained first and loudest. "How will that make us look to important clients? How will we be taken seriously?"

"You won't, that's the point. Our products are serious enough. I think it's wholly appropriate to inject some levity in their presentation."

"Nonsense!" He banged a wizened fist against the table.

"It does seem a bit . . . unorthodox." This from frumpy Bill Teegs, whose real hair looked like a toupee and who couldn't seem to match his ties with his shirt.

Then his conspirator, red-headed and gin-blossomed Kelsey Woznyack. "Ha! Unorthodox? It's obscene. Why don't we just burn the place down, Mizz Von—"

"It's Baroness. And—"

"Who else does it?" Jules Scott's question, to Daci's pleasant surprise, was aimed not at her but at Kelsey. "I didn't mean to interrupt," he told her. "I apologize."

The pleasantly large man gave her a bright grin that lit up his big moon face, then looked over the entire table, thus including them in his argument.

"What CEO is going to forget the company that took him on a roller coaster and made him lose his hotdog-and-cotton-candy lunch?" he asked rhetorically.

"Who is not going to appreciate a break from the stodgy and predictable? I mean, wouldn't you? Just once wouldn't it be fun to go, say, go-karting, instead of taken for the predictable steak-and-golfing? Not to mention that Magic Molehill is across the street. And doubtlessly cheaper." He turned to Daci. "Right?"

"A tenth of the price."

"And you will all recall that even the old company president believed in cost cutting. As does Mr. Scalinescu. Senior."

Daci watched the men mutter in begrudging approval at the invocation of the Good Old Boys, and wasn't sure whether she wanted to kiss Jules or kick him.

Next up were the vice presidents, six in all, who she planned to inform that the quarterly meetings were to be held in clown suits from now on, just to keep things in perspective.

The VPs included Sydney's son. Daci had intended to schedule some "pre-meeting face time" with him but somehow hadn't worked it into her calendar. She had yet to see the boy—no, man, he was her age. Sydney Sr. claimed he'd told the son nothing.

But Sydney Sr. had also proven himself a liar in matters of business. Still, maybe it was best not to attract undue attention to herself by singling him out.

She pondered this while browsing the internet for acceptable clown outfits to include in her PowerPoint presentation. Her cell phone rang. Fifteen minutes before the meeting she should let it go to voicemail, but who is it calling at this—oh! "Hey Terri! Did you get Biiiiiig Mac Daddy's message?"

"Who is that, Syd Junior?"

"Nah, it's just Geo."

Terri laughed. "Well Geo made my day. And now I'mma wreck yours."

"Promise?"

"I've got bad news for you."

"Can it wait till after lunch?"

Terri, Daci's lawyer friend, shifted into mode, sounded like it was all the same to her when Daci knew her well enough to know that meant things were indeed at their worst. "It can but you don't want it to. I've got good news too, we can start with that if you'd prefer."

"Where are you?"

"I'm on my way up there."

"It's like that, huh?"

"Yeah."

"I'll cut the meeting short. You want to meet at the Austrian Place?"

"I'll swing by Survivanoia and get you."

Terri met her out front not quite ninety minutes later, driving her environmentally-respectable three-wheeled red Mini Coop with an orange, flowing sun painted on the top. Despite the crippling heat, Terri refused the use of anything beyond rolled down windows for air conditioning. Daci lunged into the car, shouting "Go, go, go! Cool it down already!"

"Very funny. I can make you walk you know."

"Nobody walks in LA. I'd drive my monstrosity. So check it out: I met Sydney."

"Little Sydney?"

"The very same."

"And?"

"He's not so little, number one. Get on the 5, it's faster."

Terri veered left to enter the freeway. Daci swore the car cooled off in logarithmic proportion to the miles per hour, and Terri shot her another you-can-walk smirk. "Syd's taller than you?" she asked.

"Yeah. Just, but yeah. Geo is comparatively short, about six feet even."

"Geo whom you have to break like a twig, as per GrandMama?"

"Yes. He's a hottie. He kinda looks like, you remember that Faith No More band? He looks like their singer. Exit here."

Terri eased the car off the ramp. "Oh, he was cute. He was the only person I ever thought looked good with an eyebrow ring."

"Geo, in fact, has an eyebrow ring."

"Does he wear it?"

"He hasn't yet but I can see the mark. Anyway, beyond his height, Little Sydney is not at all what I anticipated."

"Meaning?"

"He's ... he's modest."

"In a shit-eating kind of way? Oops, just passed it, didn't I?"

"Yeah, it's in that Western-looking building. No, not shit-eating at all. Just . . . like he wears nice fabrics but nothing showy. Geo is all about the clothes. Flashy names, little bit of cologne, touch of bling."

Terri paused at the next intersection, then pulled the car in an impossibly tight U-turn. "Huh. Yeah, that's how I pictured Syd Junior."

"Nope. Junior drives a Volvo. The new sexed-up Volvo, but a Volvo nonetheless. He's unassuming and soft-spoken and generally eager to please. Just seems to want to put in a good day's work, do something positive for the company, and then go home to live his life. You can turn here, there's an entrance."

A large parking lot appeared behind the stretch of buildings which avoided appearing like the strip mall they'd been converted to by the preserved Western externalities, including but not limited to, wood-slat walls, a steeply-pitched roof, and an old wagon wheel resting against the big oak tree out front.

Terri pulled open the swinging door and a bell announced their entrance. "So what are you going to do?"

"About Junior? I'm not sure. Maybe try to get him to come over to the dark side. You know: *I'm your stepmother, Syd.*"

A woman came to seat them wearing what could have been a can-can outfit but Daci assumed was traditional folkwear that probably nobody in Austria had worn in decades.

"It'd be like us opening a restaurant in Austria and wearing House-on-the-Prairie dresses," she'd once joked with Terri.

From an atmospheric standpoint, the Austrian Place (creatively named just that) defined *dump*. Plastic booths reminiscent of a fast-food joint, offset by dead animal heads mounted on every inch of the dark wood walls. The dead animals included a jackolope. None of this mattered, however, because of the food.

"How's your dad?" Terri asked the waitress.

"His ankle is all healed!" The svelte, honey-blonde's English carried only a hint of an accent. "He's back cooking, so your Kaiserschmarrn will once again have brandy in it. But Mom made the entrees today, so it's Fiakergulasch, you know the red goulash? Or cabbage rolls. All the usual sides, of course."

They ordered one of each, with appropriate sides and beer. Terri stood, tossed an accordion file in Daci's direction. "Oops. Fell out of my bag. Read up while I powder my nose."

Daci opened the file and read its contents. Then she read it again. She tried a third time but couldn't get her head to accept what the photocopied lab notebook pages were telling her. *"Transferable from the Flytrap to the Human."* This would not process because the date on the top of the page was nearly ten years prior.

Luckily, Terri returned.

"Well?"

Daci gaped at her friend. "Where'd you get this information?"

"It showed up at the office. Hand delivered, tucked under the door."

Daci examined the papers again, a graph, some sample data, and that significant scribble concluding *transferable from the Flytrap to the Human.*

"This means someone knew about the virus before the vaccine was developed."

"Right."

"So the virus didn't come about on its own, someone made it. On purpose."

"Right!"

Daci grimaced, shook her head. "I'd rather not be. Don't things like this usually get sent to media outlets?"

"It came *from* a media outlet. *Epstein's LA.* I know this because there was a blank sheet of letterhead in the envelope."

"Why? Why would they send you this? I'm very confused."

"What media outlet can touch it? If *Epstein's* doesn't have the resources to prove it, no magazine in the country does."

"How do you know it's authentic?"

"We've had the science verified and it checks out."

"Sure, but it could have been dummied up retroactively. To incriminate. Who are they implicating?"

"Anyone who knew this much about that virus would be able to devise a vaccine for it. Without too much trouble."

Terri peered at Daci. She cocked her head and seemed exactly halfway between irritated and sympathetic.

Daci's eyes hooded. "That doesn't match our lab notebooks."

"It might have ten years ago." Terri swiped the file and tucked it neatly back into her lawyer bag. "Who's got the best research team in the world?"

"No."

"Who's the company retroactively recognized as having combated AIDS most effectively, most efficiently, and fastest?"

Daci shook her head.

"Who's withholding the treatment for Flower Flu until other companies catch up? Face the ugly truth here! You guys made this."

"I've reviewed Survivanoia's research so extensively I could describe it to you backwards. There's nothing like this anywhere in it."

Terri leaned back in the chair, crossed her arms over her chest.

"Do you have any kind of proof?"

"No," Terri admitted. "That's your job."

"We have the smoking gun, we just need a crime?"

"We have the evidence, we need a link. Something that can confirm these notebooks came from Survivanoia."

Daci remained quiet for a long moment. Terri misunderstood. "I'm sorry," she offered.

"No, I'm wondering. Do you really believe it's coincidence that *your* law firm was given this information?"

"Is there someone you're aware of who knows both of us? Is aware of our friendship?"

Daci paused again, then shrugged, defeated. "Well, Tehzan, Preston, and Guite is a well-known law firm."

"Thanks for noticing."

"Maybe it is just chance."

"Yeah, don't get paranoid."

Their food arrived, heavy with the luxurious scents only slow-cooked, well-tenderized cuts of meat can produce. The earthy sting of onions and paprika reminded Daci of Romania and the fanned gherkin and fried egg garnishing the top of her stew made her think of the flowing sun on the top of Terri's car. Still, Terri's words weighed heavily. Daci picked up her spoon but only nudged the food a bit.

Terri cut open her enormous cabbage roll, similarly spiced as the goulash but made sweeter by ground pork and with a less earthy, more zingy sauce. She wedged a steaming chunk of it in her mouth, then immediately reached for her beer. "HOT!" She swallowed and caught Daci's glare, shrugged in response. "I told you I was gonna wreck your day."

Daci sulked at her goulash. "You could have at least waited until after we'd eaten."

Not quite an hour later, after Terri finished her cabbage roll and Daci had her lunch wrapped to go but did indulge in a cup of coffee and some freshly-prepared Kaiserschmarrn ("Like a funnel cake with brandy-soaked raisins," she'd once described it to Terri, who had then tasted it and said dreamily, "Oohh, just the soft, fluffy center of the funnel cake!"), Terri stopped her Mini neatly outside Survivanoia's front entrance. She snapped her fingers, "Oh! Hey do you wanna go on *Queenie*?"

"Queenie Winspear?"

"Is there another?"

"Why, is she doing a show on best friends who make you want to eat your own head?"

"Something about strong women who have turned their lives around. Or some shit."

"My life has always been fabulous."

Terri sighed. "Wait, let me get this right." She rolled her eyes heavenward. "Women who . . . recovered from life after divorce." She paused, looked back at Daci. "Or some shit."

"You need to tell me for sure before I decide. I can't be going on some whine-and-weep kinda show, you know. I have a heartless bitch reputation to uphold."

"Oh for the love of fuck! It's some show about strong women doing stuff most women don't do—would you just *go*? I'd go, but they don't want me but I'd love to go. I love Queenie! Just go!"

"Okay, fine! Shit."

CHAPTER 18

Daci wrestled drowsiness for the remainder of the afternoon. She tried amusing herself with emails from the VPs—the fallout from the morning meeting.

The VP meeting had gone more smoothly than she'd anticipated. Most of the VPs had long ago been browbeaten into deferring to whoever was in charge and if what she thought they needed was clown suits to raise the profit margins then by golly so be it.

At least that had been the consensus at the meeting. Her email inbox greeted her with a bucketful of kindly worded complaints expressing concerns over the clown suits. These ranged in nature from simple lack of vision regarding the clown suit ratio gain to safety issues regarding the flammability of most clown suit fabrics.

Normally she would have savored these emails like a substitute teacher savors letters of apology from the bad class. But she found the information Terri had shared with her at lunchtime, combined with her emerging headache, left her simultaneously glum and angsty. She determined this as the perfect time to pick a fight with Geo.

Geo's office displayed the same worst-of-both-worlds afforded by most bachelor pads; utilitarian but inefficient.

"Is someone trying to kill you?" she asked him by way of a suggestion.

"Because this is not very inviting. I've got a designer coming...."

He fumbled not-so-surreptitiously for his cell phone, babbling something incongruent about *if you want to leave flyers*. Then he tilted his head and a lock of his dirty-blond hair fell into his eyes.

Daci found him appealing but affected. She watched him look her over without realizing he was, gave him the time to do it, leaned against his desk, crossed her arms, and gazed at him evenly.

He fumbled with his cell phone again. Daci, growing bored, sighed evenly and when he looked up this time she glowered just slightly.

"I won't countenance being tailgated," she told him.

"Countenance?"

Oh no, a dummy! "Tolerate."

"Oh."

Well, at least not proud to be ignorant. Might make him easier to train. "Running your Jeep into my vehicle would be equivalent to driving into a stopped train. If you're going to continue to drive like that, I'm hoping you're insured."

Geo responded, in a low, flat voice Daci knew boys used when they were finished with the conversation. "This is Los Angeles. Everybody tailgates."

She responded cheerily: "Not me they don't," then left, smiling sweetly over her shoulder.

But she didn't feel any better. In fact she felt exhausted. Keeping up any façade for the rest of the day was impossible with Terri's strange mystery haunting her. Daci decided to leave until normal business hours were finished.

Geo found her in the parking lot. This pleased her, proved he was just that easy to manipulate. He flirted with her and she stepped just to the left of her business composure knowing it would keep him electrified. Then just before leaving, she sterned up.

"I expect you to change your outgoing phone message. Today. Before you leave." She had to hide her smile at watching him blush in the heat.

She drove down the 5 to the 405 and then took the Santa Monica

Freeway into Los Angeles, caught an early dinner at the Mint, watched the jazz band there for another hour, then headed back up the freeway over the Hill and to Survivanoia.

Survivanoia's manufacturing areas ran all three shifts but no other department did. This gave Daci plenty of time to creep around after hours. Tuesday night revealed nothing, so she stayed late on Wednesday, after more board meetings and phone calls and irate emails, spent Wednesday night into Thursday morning checking CAD drawings, sales logs, accounts payable . . . but just what she expected to find she didn't know, which may have contributed to her not finding it. Time to try something different.

* * *

"Sure," her father said. "It seems like one of those things you'll know when you see. But they say that about embezzlement, too, and plenty of people get away with *that* every year."

He deftly clipped the empty tangled mass of vines to all but the twin root and the horizontal cordon, leaving a T with five buds for next year's growth. "Don't feel bad," he said.

"Okay. But that doesn't solve my problem, Daddy."

The regal man moved down a few steps and adroitly took on the next tangled mass unconsciously, like tying his shoes. Her father was catalogue handsome no matter what he wore, but Dacianna had always liked him best when he worked the vineyard. That's when he seemed, to her, the most dad-like.

He wore flannel shirts and boots, and with his wave of hair, neat goatee and sharp, Slovak face he always seemed to her like a person who could protect her from anything. A creature of the land and the forest who could survive in any climate, coax food from any soil, and converse with wolves.

She knew differently now, had had these delusions shattered during their trip abroad, but she still loved to see him at work in his rustic clothing. It brought a wave of nostalgia and longing. For the briefest instant she returned to being thirteen and safe and responsibility-free. So unlike today.

"I'm not convinced it *is* your problem," he said, retrieving the moment.

"I'm the company president. If something illegal is happening—"

"I don't think it's illegal. Research escapes laboratories like lions escape the zoo."

"Immoral then, okay? Are you convinced that you think it's immoral?"

Her father looked up from his pruning.

"They should have alerted the public!" Daci took a deep breath, annoyed with her own frustration.

She had flown up to San Jose, then driven a rented car just an hour down the 101 then east to a space between the Diablo Range and the Coyote Rez, to her father's modest but prized and award-winning California vineyard.

The better known wine regions—Napa, Sonoma—were farther north. But her father grew grapes thought to no longer exist. He was a legend, an inverted myth. Not a household name—except in households where it truly meant something to be so.

But just now he was the concerned father of a corporate executive. He closed the pruners and latched them. "Tell me again what you suspect is taking place."

"Someone researched and produced Flower Flu. It didn't just occur as some abomination in nature. And there is evidence that Survivanoia did it."

"So you're attempting to verify or disprove."

Daci nodded.

"Any researchers come to mind who might have been involved?"

Daci had already performed this exercise, considered her scientists: arrogant Wolfy and jowly Nikolai, rustic Egan and ever-amused Akira and Maria who had taken the day off to help with her daughter's science fair and . . . "No."

Her father nodded like she was a schoolchild who'd offered the correct answer. "Likely the research was being done off-site. Survivanoia is contracted with external labs for round-robin requirements."

"Right. It'd be easy enough to contract experimental work as well."

"Check those records. It could also be the work of a disgruntled ex-researcher. You did say the notebooks were old, so the timeline would be correct. It serves to explain the whistle-blowing."

Daci nodded. "I'll check HR. See who's been fired or whatever."

"Also examine the pollution records."

"Why's that?"

"I can't pour a bad batch of wine down the sewer without advance clearance from the state. I'd imagine there are similar regulations in place for deadly viruses." He frowned into the distance.

Lost in thought, her father needed to move. He flipped the wire holding the pruners closed and went back to the drastic clipping of his cherished vines.

Ahead and behind him, between the rows and rows of trellises, Daci watched his staff, largely Mexican but a few Romanians as well, dressed in jeans, high rubber boots, and big sombreros, quick and precise in the late-morning heat. Usually the air still held a chill through noon, but this morning all the workers had already stripped to shirt sleeves.

"How's it look this year?" Daci asked.

He shook his head and sighed. "We're going to have to move it. All of it. Within a few years. The growing season has gotten too long and the day-time temperatures too high. Especially for these little guys. They're the vines from Romania, everything from the fence over."

"England?" She knew he'd been looking into land there.

"Looking more like central Canada. Everyone else is flooding into Britain, driving up prices. Canada is also less of a commute. I've got a realtor. Should have a firm answer by the end of the month."

"What about genetically engineering a different rootstock?"

Her father smiled his endearing I'd-like-something-but-am-in-no-position-to-request-it smile. "What about it?"

"I'll see what I can do, Dad."

"I assumed you've checked your lab records already?"

"Everything that hasn't been archived."

"Where are the archives?"

"Underground salt mine."

"The Hutchinson facility?"

"No, it'd be easy enough to fly to Kansas. Praid."

"Salina Praid? In *Romania*?"

Daci nodded, empathizing with her father's bewilderment since it had been her own reaction upon discovering that any documents older than seven years and considered out of service were shipped to an archive located somewhere in Romania's famous center for speleotherapy.

"Only Sydney," her father sighed. A pause. "Don't you think it's likely that Sydney is the person behind the design of this disease?"

"I don't want to believe that."

"Maybe you should ask him."

"This is a pretty serious offense, you know? I'd like to have more conclusive proof before I accuse him. And yes I realize the catch-22 that I'm in."

"Fair enough. It could also be the old company president. They're cousins, correct?"

"Yeah."

"That will make it difficult to get information of any kind about him. Sydney is very protective of his family. As you well know."

He glanced at her, then turned and gazed at her intently, his eyes the same impossible violet as her own. "What about the Flower Flu vaccination?"

"What about it?"

"It seems to have fallen from importance, yes? Taking second place to the origins of the virus?"

"No."

"Will finding who invented it force the treatment to market any faster?"

She hadn't actually thought about that but didn't admit it. "Daddy, I've been there a week!"

He nodded. "Just don't let the weeds get higher than the garden, as they say." He turned back to his empty vines. *Snip, snip, snip.* "You planning to visit your mother? Since you're up here?"

Daci crossed her arms. "It's just as easy for me to drive up to Cacophony from LA."

Snip, snip. "So you'll be doing that, then?" *Snip, snip, snip.* Rhythmic, like a song.

"Yeah, Daddy."

Snip, snip. "When?"

"Soon."

"Promise."

"I promise."

Snip, snip, snip.

* * *

Zane Frears yawned like a big cat—all bright teeth and pink tongue. He folded down the waistband of his plaid pajama bottoms, stretched his trim, toned, six-feet-seven-inches first left then right, accompanying this stretching with a series of huffs and satisfied groans, finally scratching a hand through his short, tawny dreads.

The coffee maker hissed and spat, signifying that his coffee was ready. He pulled the carafe from the hotplate, stepped three paces through his kitchen to the marble center island where he folded himself up onto one of the spinning stools, and poured a third of the coffee over his big bowl of frosted corn flakes.

Daci admired all of this from the other spinning stool as she sliced cheese and apples and drank her French press coffee.

"Were the funnies ever funny?" She tossed the colored comics from the *LA Picayune* aside.

"Who says 'funnies' anymore?"

"Me. And all the cotton tops. Then there's this article about how there's too much sex now in the Army."

"Between soldiers?"

"Right. What did they expect when they upped the enlistment age to forty? The only thing hornier than a nineteen-year-old boy is a thirty-six-year-old woman."

Zane grinned over his corn flakes. "You're living proof of that. I can't keep up with you."

"Sure but you're nearly twenty-nine yourself. That's old as boy-toys go."

"Time to retire me, huh?"

"Maybe I'll join the Army. There's a movie you could make! *Paris Does Parris Isle.*"

Zane laughed around a mouthful of cereal. "Parris Isle is the Marines."

"Don't spew coffee through your nose. Why are you eating business breakfast on a brunch day, anyway?"

Zane's velvety grey eyes widened. "I told you?"

"Told me what?"

"Fuck, I didn't, did I?"

"I don't know, you haven't told me what it is you haven't told me."

"B.C.'s coming over."

"Bag *of* Chips?"

"Yeah."

"Is that what's on his birth certificate?"

"I'm thinking no."

"But you don't know? He's your friend for eight years. You don't know his real name?"

Zane shrugged elaborately.

"You're lying," she said giggling.

"It's biblical, his name. I took a sworn oath not to tell anybody, under penalty of death. Then his ex let it out of the bag anyway."

"I'm going on *Queenie* with her."

"Queenie Winspear?"

"Is there another?"

"When is this?"

"Tuesday."

"Like in two days Tuesday?"

"That'd be the one."

"Don't they film in New York?"

Daci nodded. "The show's paying the airfare and the Paul Klee exhibition is still up at MoMA. Want to come with?"

"I can't. I'm interviewing leads for *OPV.*"

"Really? That's awesome! Why didn't you tell me that?"

"I didn't want to tell anybody until afterwards. It's cursed or something, I swear. God only wants me to make porn for the rest of my days."

OPV—Other People's Violence—was definitely not porn. Zane wanted to be a real filmmaker and he'd written a script, complete with storyboards, which Daci had read. It told the story of a man whose addiction to hope led him to put himself in the center of other people's violence in order to stop it, not through force or persuasion, but simple presence, like a port in the storm.

The story and the proposed cinematography had impressed her enough to give him a grant. A month later, they had lunch, where they went over details and signed contracts; then they went to the beach and accidentally had sex in the back of Daci's Hummer.

Zane yawned again and wrinkled his nose. Loose-limbed and grinning, his physical presence mirrored his demeanor. Zane was easy. Easy to smile, easy with his touch. Bright-eyed and hopeful but without expectation or demand. Generous—arguably to a fault. Watching him always gave her a sense of reverse déjà vu; she could see her future self looking back to these moments and knowing memories of this boy would always make her smile.

"What does Snack Foods need from you today?" she asked, smiling at her future memory.

"He wants to get some girls for the new video, plus I told him I'd help him location scout since Stella ditched on him."

"So it's a workday is what you're saying."

"Right." *Crunch, crunch, crunch.* "Are you mad? You could go with us if you want."

"Boy stuff bores me. Besides, Bag of Chips is not one of my favorite people, really. I mean, he's well-mannered, I'd never bar him from my house, but I don't want to waste a whole Sunday with him."

Crunch, crunch. "I'm sorry. I really thought I told you."

"S'alright, I'm going to see GrandMama anyway. Will you braid my hair, though?"

"Of course."

It took Zane twenty minutes to put Daci's claret red hair into a loose two-sided French braid that joined in the back and fishtailed open at the bottom. She could do it herself but it took her twice as long and never held as well. Besides, having someone else do her hair relaxed her. Hypnotic. Like a good massage therapist, Zane didn't talk.

Once her hair was braided, Zane rolled his hands over her shoulders, bringing heat and loosening the tension there. He wrapped his arms around her and nuzzled her ear.

She responded with a deep kiss, running her hand along his jaw and pressing her fingers through the thick, nappy hair under his tawny dreads. He murmured in appreciation, moving a hand underneath her robe but, "We don't have time for this, baby," she reminded him. "You have to meet Slim Jim, remember?"

He laughed and kissed her nose. "When do I get to see you next?"

"The week's going to be crazy." As she acknowledged this, she felt the tension creep back into her shoulders. "But, you know, sometimes I like it when you just sleep beside me. Midweek-ish."

He kissed her again, gently, ran a finger along her lips. "I promise," he said smiling. That reverse déjà vu caught her again, made her smile back.

* * *

Geo's Geo-appointed secretary poked her head into Daci's office. "Geo sent me down? For some forms?" She squinted just slightly as her eyes adjusted to the light, then pointed at the stuffed white monster looming over Daci's desk. "Cool bear! It's like the Addams Family or something. Except theirs was on the floor I guess. Anyway. Forms?"

Daci pointed a finger at the floor, circled it around. "Geo had a little accident."

Chloe sighed, rolled her eyes. But she squatted without complaint and began collecting Geo's forged expense reports from off the white rug of Daci's office.

"I saw you on Queenie Winspear a few weeks ago," the girl said. Well, 'girl' was a bit of a misnomer; Chloe was Zane's age. "They should have showed this office! That would really tell people you mean business. Like, business *your* way." She paused and looked up. "I gotta tell you: I think you're pretty cool."

"Thank you. The office wasn't finished at the time, though. You're friends with Vonnie."

"Yeah. How'd you know?"

"I talked with her. Just a little. She mentioned that she had a friend who worked here."

"Really?"

"Uhm-hmm. She doing well?"

Chloe, still collecting papers from the floor, raised a shoulder and let it drop. "Yeah, actually. They finally decided to get officially divorced. And now she hardly even tells any jokes about him. Got her life back or whatever."

"I followed the interesting fiasco the night she played Purple Dot. Or tried to."

Chloe collected the last of the papers from the floor, rose to a stand. She pointed at the wire V on the bookshelf with a thin spark running perpetually up it. "I made a Jacob's Ladder once for a science project."

Daci smiled. A smart one—how refreshing! Unlike her boss.

"Geo Rivera is your supervisor."

"Yeah?"

"I'm curious if you've witnessed anything corrupt. Sordid."

"Witnessed? Or been subjected to?"

Hmm. Not the intended direction. Daci had long recognized Chloe's crush on Geo, figured this emotional tie would be easy to exploit, but hadn't predicted the girl would be so forthcoming about it. She delicately clarified. "Witnessed. Anything questionable from a business standpoint."

Chloe set all her weight on one foot and linked one of her hands through her belt loops. "Uhm, lookit, I'm not trying to get fired, for, like insubordination? But if you just tell me what you're actually looking for, this will probably go a lot faster."

Daci inventoried this young woman. Watched her unabashedly to see how she addressed scrutiny. Chloe held her gaze for a respectable moment, then dropped her eyes to the floor. Daci saw her shoulders tense as she fought the urge to tap her foot or sway or whatever. Chloe glanced up at her again and Daci rewarded her with a smile.

"Alright." She pulled a rectangle of thick, clothy, orange paper, just slightly larger than a dollar bill, from her top desk drawer. "You know what this is?"

"No."

"Have a seat."

Chloe did as instructed, examining the orange certificate.

"Those are called NOx credits," Daci informed her. "NOx is N-O-X, it's a chemistry term. The N is for Nitrogen, the O for Oxygen, and the X is a variable, most often a 1 or 2, at least in atmospheric chem. You follow?"

"So far."

"You can't physically manufacture anything without generating nitrogen oxides as a side-product. And they screw up the environment."

"Greenhouse gas?"

"Themselves, no. But they oxidize carbon monoxide and hydrocarbons, which produces more ozone and that affects the radiative balance."

Chloe squinted slightly. "You're close to losing me."

"NOx impacts climate change. Adds to global warming. It's also part of smog and acid rain. It's not friendly stuff. Hence, we can't generate NOx emissions legally without permission to do so."

"So each of these coupon thingies is a certain amount of NOxes?"

"Exactly. And we seem to be missing quite a number of them."

Chloe frowned at the paper still in her hand. "What's that have to do with Geo? I mean, he's a sales guy."

Daci paused. She liked Chloe but didn't know her, could only trust her so far. What this *really* had to do with Geo was that in the three weeks she'd spent snooping and digging after most everyone else had gone home, those were the only things Daci successfully uncovered—Geo's screwed up expense reports and missing NOx credits. Nothing related to research, firings, or disgruntled employees, just these stray pollution credits. Had she not been scrutinizing every used tissue, she probably wouldn't have even noticed they were gone.

But the fact of those two items being the only anomalies among the immaculate books, coupled with Geo's relationship to the former company president, well . . . like her father said, it may have been nothing more than a meaningless act of spite. But who knew?

Daci certainly didn't, and this is part of what drove her decision to obfuscate. "It's complicated," she told Chloe. "Geo has a history with other employees that might have made him privy to information. Most likely they've been misplaced. We are proceeding as if that is indeed the case. If we need to report them as missing we can, but that involves fees and fines we'd rather avoid."

"Oh." The girl ran her fingers along the thick orange paper, her brows knit and her mouth slightly pursed.

"I'm not asking you to go through his desk." Daci said this with a laugh to sound light. "I'm perfectly capable of that myself. I'm merely requesting that if you do see something odd or suspicious, be it regarding Geo or any other employee or department, give me a heads-up, yes?"

"I guess so. I mean, yeah, of course." The young woman gave another half-shrug.

Daci knew Chloe was wondering why she'd been singled out. Doubtlessly the girl also recognized the veiled half-lie she was being told. Daci's hope was that she'd interpret it as a privilege, an act of trust. She waited, watched Geo's employee sigh and squirm with the unasked question.

Chloe eventually looked earnestly into Daci's eyes, but what she finally inquired, still clutching the NOx credit, was "Can I keep this?"

Daci suppressed a smile. "Sure."

* * *

The week skimmed by in a patchwork of meetings, arguments, and phone calls by day, stitched together by long nights of digging through lab notebooks and breaking into everybody's C drives in search of archived data. Apart from the missing NOx credits, Daci had found no evidence of anything in the research or manufacturing departments. So it was time to follow the money. This posed more of a challenge. Computer hackers and scientists populated Daci's world heavily, but accountants and auditors proved an underrepresented demographic.

Zane found her a young woman supposedly named Laurel Johnson who claimed she could not only account, but could skip-trace. "That's what I did before I got into the business," she told Daci in the informal interview. Daci had seen the girl's sparkling new truck, recognized the bling around her neck as Tiffany's, knew the tracksuit Laurel wore cost close to four hundred dollars: didn't have to ask why Laurel hadn't gone back to skip-tracing.

She hired the girl for an hourly fee high enough to keep her from talking but short of making her want to quit working for Zane. Not one to worry over problems other people had been hired to fix, Daci finally could return her efforts to the Flower Flu treatment. But sometimes a neglected pot overboils.

Friday morning, everything came to a screeching halt. The same kind of awfulness where you sit tense waiting for the sudden, sickening impact of metal and the shatter of glass.

Daci was heading to work, approaching the 405/101 interchange, sipping a French press coffee and listening to Rahsaan Roland Kirk play three horns simultaneously when her cell phone rang. Few people phoned her before 9:00 and those who did were important. This morning's important person was Terri.

"I just woke up and I can't see."

And everything stopped. "Shit," Daci whispered, then promised to be there soon, cure in hand.

As she exited the freeway and got back on in the opposite direction, horrible images filled her sight, visions of Terri in the hospital, shitting out her own intestines, pink foam of her destroyed stomach frothing from her mouth and ugh. *Brrrr!*

Because that's what the Flower Flu did. Despite its innocuous media name, the retro virus RV707 had originally been transmitted from the Venus flytrap. No researchers had yet pinpointed the source of the morning blindness, but it served as a miraculous harbinger. The virus's mechanism ultimately caused the human body to digest itself from the inside out.

But Survivanoia had the cure. A tiny pill, smaller than aspirin, on a three-day regimen beginning within twelve hours of the onset of morning blindness, and the victim recovered completely. This little miracle was the thing Survivanoia withheld, waiting for their co-conspirators to catch up. And this withholding had served to crack open her and Sydney's already stressed relationship.

The circumstances had led her to take over Survivanoia and if getting this pharmaceutical to the public meant destroying the company then so be it. Sydney had been oddly acquiescent to the arrangement. But, Daci knew, he believed she would fail and in the process learn what drove had driven his decisions, thereby enabling her to receive his apologies, recognize the situation as inexorable, and everything would go back to the way it was.

She shoved the key into the lock of her door as her rotoscoper neighbor came stumbling up the stairs clutching a paper coffee cup and looking like she'd been mugged by death. Brianna, that was her name. She raised a hand in hello.

"How long this time?" Daci asked.

"Three days. Well, sixty-eight hours. But it looks awesome. I'm gonna go pass out now." The petite blonde opened the door to her place then paused. "You alright? You look a little rugged."

This coming from a woman who had just worked three days non-stop.

"A friend of mine is very sick," Daci told the girl.

Brianna offered condolences and a soup recipe. Daci thanked her, dashed inside, pulled the pills from her fireproof safe, and sprinted out again.

Normally the view of the marina and the lazy boats buoying on the water calmed her the moment she arrived home. Today she didn't even see them. Back in the Hummer she checked herself in the rearview and saw fear and worry describing their tell-tale lines in her visage.

From Marina Del Rey up PCH to the Palisades. Twenty minutes that felt like twenty hours and her mind going nonstop the whole time. She still had no plan to accomplish her main, original goal—getting the drug released. Sydney offered no help, believing such backroom deals to be the insurmountable means by which businesses survived. His first lecture had been an explanation of how Survivanoia's arrangement was with not one but two other firms, both of them Big Pharma.

Daci failed to see how such a bargain benefited Survivanoia monetarily.

"If we hadn't been the first," Sydney explained patiently, "we would have wasted enormous dollars in research. This arrangement makes for a more conservative investment. It guarantees returns regardless of who discovers an antidote first."

"But Survivanoia always discovers everything first," Daci had protested.

Sydney dismissed this as dumb luck.

Daci figured as company president, she'd simply break the deal, sell the drug and accept the consequences. But: "They can take a lot more than just the company," Syd had assured her. "And *you* will go to jail."

"Me?! You brokered the deal."

"The *deal* is legal. Breaking it means breaking a legally binding contract. I also can promise you that once you are in jail it's unlikely you'll make it out again. Big businesses these days are better connected than gangsters and warlords. And their tolerance for traitors is lower."

This last sentiment quieted her for a few days. Daci never surmised when Sydney alluded to warlords if he intended a double entendre. Eventually, though, her righteousness eclipsed her consternation, and she approached him again.

"Is there a time limit for these other companies to develop their cures?"

Sydney, she remembered, had smiled like the father of a teenager caught drunk. "Yes," he relented. "Three years."

"What if they realize they can't do it in that time frame?"

"There's a forfeiture clause in the contract, certainly." He paused, shot her that toothy grin that disconcerted people. "Sabotaging a lab would, of course, be life threatening to the scientists who work in it."

She'd feigned indignation, but was once again caught off guard by Sydney's uncanny ability to predict her motives. Only Syd and Terri—no one else had such insight. Maybe that's why she couldn't quite let him go, not completely. There is unmatched comfort in the luxury of being understood.

Daci made the right onto Entrada, then left onto Mesa, and finally left again onto Amalfi, where Terri lived. The little house had both ocean and mountain views and typically screenwriters haunted the neighborhood, walking around Will Rogers State Park mumbling to themselves. Today the area seemed still and empty. Post-apocalyptic. Daci found herself spooked.

She took a deep breath, cleared her mind. No point in running into Terri's in a panic—doubtlessly her friend would already be frightened. Best to play it cool, nonchalant, like RV707 wasn't really that big of a threat and the treatment was on the brink of mass distribution anyway.

Sure.

She took another deep breath. Exited her modified Hummer, got nearly slammed by the morning's heat. One thing she knew, Terri would help her find a solution, develop a plan. And as she knocked on her friend's door, she realized how focused she'd become, felt a clarity of vision that had heretofore escaped her. Because now, more than righteousness drove her. As of that moment, the fight became personal.

CHAPTER 19

Melvina Mills stood six-two and carried the body of an aging line-backer. Melvina spoke in a husky, confident growl, smelled pleasantly of Old Spice aftershave, and at the time of the late-morning interview, five-o'clock shadow just blossomed on Melvina's cheeks and chin. This same Melvina sat in the chair opposite Daci's desk, sporting a floral print caftan accented with a tunic-length blue blazer.

The caftan and the A tacked to the end of Melvina's otherwise decidedly-male name led Daci to suppose that Melvina's pronoun of choice would be she. But it hadn't yet come up during the interview. Which impressed Daci, as self-confidence always did.

Sick to death from the boredom brought on by listening to executives and sales people chastise each other while aggrandizing themselves, Daci had fired half the HR staff just to give herself an excuse to regularly meet people from the outside. So far, interviewing had proven the most enjoyable aspect of running the company.

"Documentaries are formulaic," Melvina was saying of (presumably) her old job. "It was like somebody designed a video template, then we entered the topic. Also these supposed documentaries told the viewer how she should feel about stuff. You know: Wars, a Necessary Evil."

"Is that why you left?"

"Uhm ... not exactly." Melvina glanced to the side as if weighing the advice of a friend. "I got away from the *documentary* department for that reason. I preferred the infomercials, at least they were an honestly-titled product.

"I fact-checked copy from the scripts against what was provided by the manufacturer. We were trying to sell commercials to the captive audience market. The TVs in the subways or in the supermarket lines?

"But I couldn't get over the fact that I was writing commercials for commercials. It gave me vertigo. Like being trapped between two mirrors. And it really got me thinking. I started jotting ideas down then typing them up ..." She scowled at the floor as if she'd confessed something embarrassing.

Daci raised an eyebrow. "You were writing a novel while you were supposed to be working?"

"Yes. But my work was done. On time. I never blew a deadline. That's the truth—you can call and ask. Also, I worked for *Epstein's LA*, she'll give me a sparkling reference."

Daci's ears pricked right up at that. "*Epstein's*. Really?"

"Three years. It's on my resume."

"I didn't read your resume. Why'd you leave?"

"It's a small magazine and, well. . . ."

"Money. Or lack thereof."

Melvina nodded. "I hated to, she's great. But she's down to publishing once a month now. The online edition is still weekly."

"Do you list contact information for her?"

"Yes! Like I said, her reference will be stunning. I'd love for you to talk to her!"

"Oh, I don't need to," Daci assured her. "When can you start?"

* * *

"*Epstein's* is under investigation, though." This was Zane's response Tuesday evening when Daci shared her news.

He closed the book he'd been reading, set it on the night stand, and snuggled under the sheet. The breeze from the marina shimmied the curtains, necessitating a sheet and quite possibly, later, the cotton blanket folded at the bottom of Daci's bed.

"Under investigation for what?"

"Tax evasion. Probably trumped up charges, but it'll keep her quiet."

"Melvina said she's still publishing on the web."

"Sure, her and every college kid in the nation. How many people consider MySpace the go-to place for investigative journalism?"

Daci bugged her eyes and went slack-jawed. Zane apologized. "I just don't want you to get your hopes up like last time."

"Last time" referred to her and Terri's apparently failed plan. By Sunday evening, frustration had extinguished Daci's shiny new vigilance. Terri had called the big local media outlets, but not even the major alternative press wanted her story. None of them claimed not to believe her, but they all expressed concern over the liability of running a story like that without hard evidence and sources willing to be revealed and quoted.

LA Bi-Weekly let Terri run an ad, stating she was planning a class action against Survivanoia and inviting anyone who had lost friends or relatives to Flower Flu to contact her. So far, though, it seemed as though the only people she'd gotten calls from were the lonely and/or schizophrenic deviants who read *LABW* for the sex ads in the back. Neither of the two mainstream papers would accept the ad, again citing liability.

Daci sighed. She leaned her head back against the velvet back of her sleigh bed. "Once again I am out of ideas."

"That's not completely true. You just don't like your options."

"Sydney has a point, okay? Torching a lab has potential consequences beyond those intended."

"Off hours."

"A lot of places run twenty-four seven. And even if they don't, there can always be the stray researcher whose burning question has him performing solo vigils. Also who knows what else they could be doing in there that could be unleashed on a hapless public."

Now Zane sighed. He draped an arm around her hips, ran his hand over her taught stomach. "Desperate times...."

"What is it with you and Terri and these bumper sticker quotes? Destroying a research lab is at cross purposes with my intentions. Besides, I've got other conundrums to attend to. Who developed the virus? And the missing NOx credits?"

"Laurel is working on that stuff for you, girl, remember?"

"Is she getting anywhere?"

Zane's hand stilled. He tapped his fingers against her belly. "You are sure fighting an awful lot of battles."

"Is that a no?"

He pulled himself up, bent an elbow, and leaned his head against it. "I'm positive she is, and I trust she'll be in touch when she has something conclusive. I'm not using her for my current project, so your assignment is all she's working on."

"Speaking of your current project, just when are you going to get back to your *movie* movie? You said you had all the actors in place."

"I do. Now I need the money in place."

Daci borrowed a phrase from her father, "Weeds getting higher than the garden?"

Zane flashed his broad grin. "You mean did I forget that I want to make a real movie?"

"Life can get on top of us all. I've been hearing from you for over a year now about this art film, but all you've done is churn out more porn."

Zane dismissed this with his deep laugh. "Porn makes me money, and I plan to use that money to make art." He tapped his forehead with a finger. "The diamond is still there. For me, fewer battles, more wins."

"So you're saying I'm spreading myself too thin?"

"I don't know how you work, I only know what works for me. And what I observe. From here you seem to be digging trenches with your spinning wheels but not actually getting anywhere."

Daci glared at him.

He gave her another big grin. "I could be wrong!"

"I just had this conversation with Terri four days ago."

Zane blinked his big grey eyes at her.

She paused then relented. "It's just that I feel I can make some progress on the other issues. Especially the NOx credits. I just know it's got something to do with Geo."

"I crossed that guy's path today."

"Geo? My Geo?"

"Yeah. He was shooting in the Danhill house."

"Where you're filming?"

"Yeah. Apparently he thought he was filming."

"Did you kick his ass?"

"Nah, just used big words. Scared him good!"

Daci laughed and Zane kissed her.

"He owes me something, though," he said. "A connection. I suspect he's going to try and blow me off."

"Come visit him at work! That'll shock him good. Make it look like coincidence. You can take me to lunch!"

"Oh I could, could I?"

"Speaking of coincidence, you'll never guess who I met in the elevator at GrandMama's."

Zane yawned his sleepy yawn, different than his morning yawn, finished with a satisfied hum. "Then just tell me, love."

"Jared Ferryman."

"*The* Ferryman?"

"Yup. He's still just as cute."

"Isn't he a little young for the nursing home?"

"You are so funny, I forgot to laugh."

"Oh, I'll make you laugh." He came at her, fingers wriggling.

"No tickling!" Daci shrieked, lunging from him.

"All's fair in love!" Zane snatched her around the waist again, fingers wiggling against her belly and sides. Daci fell into a giggling heap against his chest.

Zane kissed her again and she returned it in kind, pleased that he'd spoken of love, and happy that his affections were borne of his appreciation for her, as a person, as a flawed individual struggling with immediate problems. These things drew Zane to her. Not her heritage. To Zane, she was a simple woman to be loved, not a mantelpiece trinket to grant clout to his muddied bloodline.

Daci kissed her lover more deeply. Shoved everything else out of her dizzy head. For the first time in a long time, she dropped all her problems and enjoyed her moment.

CHAPTER 20

Of all the interviews Daci had conducted in her six weeks—six weeks that seemed like months on the good days and decades on the bad—and all the scientists she'd met, this little man was her absolute favorite.

The fact of his umbrella—full-sized, traditional black with a curved wood handle—this device alone in the stinging heat of Los Angeles told her much: That he believed in himself and his own superstitions for one thing. That he was not uncomfortable standing out as an obvious foreigner for another. And, Daci suspected, his insightful recognition that a large inappropriate tool could be used as an effective weapon by a small obvious foreigner, if necessity dictated, with little legal consequence.

His madman's haircut and unique mangling of the English language fascinated Daci and endeared him to her further. But he was unable, really, to express himself in English and somehow fell into German even though that wasn't his mother tongue either. Daci spoke German, so it worked.

Encludsmo Stuckhowsen had phoned Wednesday saying he would like please a speaking session with the Baroness Von Worthington. The remaining employees in HR had been instructed to turn all resumes from scientists over to the Baroness anyway, so they forwarded his call.

She understood that he invented things and had invented something perhaps her company would be interested in purchasing from him. She scheduled him for her earliest available appointment.

He knocked on her office door just after twelve noon on Friday as Daci poured herself a glass of wine to compliment her lunch of roast pork with grilled asparagus.

"I am sorry to be early," he said, hesitating in the doorway. He stood nearly a foot shorter than Daci. His cuffs didn't quite graze his ankles, revealing sparkling white socks. "The schedule of bus is . . . ah . . . confused?"

Daci reassured him, offered him some food or a glass of wine, both of which he politely declined. She poured him half a glass of wine anyway. He took it from her amid protests, which tasting halted.

"Is Romanian, yes?"

He'd folded an ankle on top of a knee, displaying even more sock, and now leaned a tweed-jacket patched elbow against the horizontal knee—the quintessential professor.

Daci confirmed the wine's origin, showed him the bottle.

"This serve they where I eat. Romanian restaurant. Difficult to find. The wine, I mean."

Daci had never heard of a Romanian restaurant in LA and asked him about it. The little scientist was not quite sure of the address but gave her good enough directions that she felt confident she'd be able to locate it. He raved about the food, claiming it to be authentic, made by the wife who cooked as if she were cooking for family and said, "I am supposing they have some family member traveling and fetching wines and vodkas.

"Also there is California company making Old World wines. DVG, they are called. From where they access vines I know not but *scheint authentisch.*

"Seems authentic," he'd said in German and she responded in this language as well.

"*Ich bin mit dieser Weinkellerei vertraut.*" *I am familiar with this winery.* She proceeded in German, "The owner believes these grapes to be the best in the world and made a point to preserve them before the regions were devastated by war." Because DVG was, of course, her father's winery—Dragomir Von Goethe.

She poured The Doctor another half glass of the ruby liquid.

"I'm very fond of Romanian wines," she told him in German, "but the Georgians are too sweet for me."

The Doctor told her that Stalin's favorite wine had been Georgian, and they laughed together at the irony. They spoke of tannins and the influences of the regional soils. How great it was that someone had had the foresight to conserve this important piece of history. The two proceeded with their conversation in German.

"But climate change threatens all the California wineries now," Daci related. "They are seeking to genetically modify the grapes to prevent the necessity of uprooting the vineyards."

"Modification could be done, for sure. But to ensure maintaining authentic flavor, it's better probably to graft. Also better to alleviate public fears and preserve mystique."

"Not as fast, though."

"*Das stimmt.* (That's true.) Much slower, yes. But with the rise of your Flower Flu, people have become quite wary of anything that changes genetic structure of plant material."

Once he got on this topic he rode it: "*Bitte erklären Sie mir* (Please explain to me), plants have 40–60% of the same genetic material as humans, which of course enabled the spread of Flower Flu. But it also narrows down the areas of research for treatment. How is it there is no treatment or vaccination yet found, when it seems fairly simple a thing to identify?"

His insight struck Daci like an oncoming train. She needed this scientist. Whatever he was selling, she would buy it.

"Tell me about your invention," she suggested.

In addition to his umbrella, Dr. Stuckhowsen had a briefcase, from which he now retrieved a ream of notes, drawings, and theoretical calculations for something he termed a pretentiometer. This little device apparently gauged changes in microatmospheric conditions to assess heart rate, body temperature, electromagnetic activity, etc. Pretentiousness, as a measure of deceit, could then be used to estimate future levels and likelihood of deceit in a person or group of people.

Daci stopped him halfway through and he blinked at her, started to pack up, blank faced. "*Nein, nein, nein,*" she assured him. "I have a colleague who should hear this for himself!"

A tentative smile graced The Doctor's face.

Daci called Scally, Sydney Ratkovitch Scalinescu, her one-time stepson. He'd somehow made his way to the VP of New Product Development. Daci knew Syd Senior well enough to know he wouldn't help his son; if the man was there, he deserved to be. About that, she felt confident.

Daci could hire The Doctor blindly, but with Scally's buy-in she would have the camouflage of legitimacy. Scally would give him something banal and corporate to work on while she secretly steered him toward developing, or re-developing, a cure for Flower Flu. Syd Senior had no control over anything discovered while she sat at Survivanoia's helm—that was part of her contracted agreement.

Scally loped in, loose-limbed and open-faced, and any animosity she'd contrived toward him faded. Syd Junior seemed to have inherited only the positive aspects of his father. Humble, hardworking, eager to learn and to please.

She got him seated, explained about The Doctor without mentioning the Flower Flu business, and had Dr. Stuckhowsen start at the beginning. Daci translated his German into English for Scally, who frowned in thought and nodded in understanding.

"I'd be more confident with a prototype, is all."

"Can't you assess from the plans whether it's workable?"

"Uh, I'm not that good yet."

Daci appreciated both Scally's honesty and the confidence expressed in his qualifier. "We can have Akira build a prototype in time for the next sales meeting."

Scally shrugged, noncommittal and hard to read. For Daci it

constituted one of those rare moments when she wished she didn't intimidate someone.

She requested that Dr. Stuckhowsen leave them enough data to build one of these analyzers, with an agreement—in writing—that both the data and the completed prototype were his property should Survivanoia choose not to purchase it from him. She then sent him on his way with a promise to respond in a few weeks' time.

* * *

"It can't be that easy." This from Terri, five days later.

Daci pressed her phone against her ear with her shoulder, lowered the volume on Charlie Parker, and shoved the Hummer into a higher gear as she entered the 5 Freeway from work.

"Are you and Zane in the same club? Are you now going to tell me that Encludsmo Stuckhowsen is under investigation for tax evasion?"

"From what you've told me the government probably owes *him* money. But don't you think it's a little too convenient? Did GrandMama's roster of scientists include this guy?"

"No," Daci admitted.

"So where'd he come from?"

"Under the 110 and 105 interchange."

"Get serious!" Terri snapped. "How do you know he's not a spy? Working for Sydney? How do you know he's not the very same guy who invented Flower Flu in the first place?"

"If he did develop the virus, or discover it or whatever, then I'd say he's probably the person who can treat it the fastest, don't you think?" Daci cursed, nearly dropping the phone as she dodged in front of a black SUV. "My internal radar says he's innocent," she assured Terri. "And I've checked said radar several times."

She had, because Daci had felt a shiver like someone walked over her grave, and all the suspicions Terri now vocalized had erupted in Daci's head during her interview with the little scientist. Daci had repeatedly reviewed every vocal intonation, hand gesture, and facial twitch. Nothing suggested that he had any agenda, ulterior motives, or secret spy plan.

"I also checked UCLA," she said, "and he did in fact graduate from there."

"Then why hasn't he been working?"

"He doesn't speak English."

"Please. This is LA. And the university alone will hire any scientist they can get their hands on. He could speak Martian, they'd find him a grad student to translate. Something's fishy."

Daci suppressed a sigh, annoyed at the constant argument her life had become. Earlier in the phone call, she'd argued with Terri about the NOx credits that had shown up yesterday. Chloe brought them into Daci's office with little in the way of explanation, just that some guy she went on a date with had them in his wallet. The girl had handed them over, wallet and all.

Instead of being happy or even intrigued at the mysteriousness of the situation, Terri started on a tirade about Daci's "distraction from her main purpose!" Daci never even got the chance to inform her that the name in the wallet was her new client, Eddie Bloodworth. Also Geo's brother. Halfbrother. Step? Something.

And think of the devil there, he was, his red Jeep gleaming in her rearview.

"... So now we're back to our original problem," Terri was rallying yet again. "Even if you have this man develop some new, different treatment which blah crr and blah. ..." Daci couldn't take it anymore.

"Ter, I gotta go right now, there's something going on the freeway." She hung up without saying goodbye and chucked her phone into her purse.

Somewhere after that motion and before she managed to find her sunglasses, Geo smashed into the back of her Hummer and racked up an estimated seven additional cars after him.

* * *

Later on she would look back and recall how things didn't slow down for her the way she'd always been told they would. One minute she was tearing down the highway with a little red car on her tail, a split second later they were piled in a rumpled heap by the side of the road.

She couldn't recall how they got there, not the details. Only that she'd brake-checked him before she had her sunglasses . . . or was it after? And this time he didn't respond, didn't slow, plowed his tiny, insubstantial toy car into the yellow brickwall of her modified Hummer. The ensuing pile-up was being blamed not on them but on a pair of rubber-neckers who slowed down to look for blood. This at least lessened her guilt.

In the emergency room, she wished they'd crashed sooner; Valencia, where they worked, was a monied suburb with decent hospital care. Here in the Valley, the EMTs were your only hope. They hauled Geo off the freeway to some hellhole of a hospital where they left him on a gurney outside what appeared to be the laundry room because he was "*not all dat in-yured, main.*"

At his request, Daci unstrapped Geo from the gurney. The EMTs had evaluated him, seemed unimpressed, hadn't put a cervical collar on him, how bad could it be? He sat up, making a noise.

"I don't think anything's broken," he assessed. "I'm still a little dizzy. Do you have any ibuprofen or anything?"

"There are painkillers you're not supposed to take when you're injured. In case of—"

His dark look stopped her.

"You want a soda to wash it down with?"

He smiled at her through his bangs, like some kid brother who'd hurt himself running with scissors. "Please and thanks."

"Alright, let me find a vending machine. If they move you, call my cell."

He promised and she headed into the foray of the bloodied, the self-bandaged, the shrieking babies with no other way to express their dis-comfort, and the lonely old people convinced they are dying because this conviction guaranteed them a modicum of caring, human contact at least for today.

At the soda machine, she realized that she hadn't asked him what kind he wanted and that furthermore she probably didn't have any cash. Conveniently, the ER offered an ATM, where for a mere three dollar courtesy fee she could get money from Bankzilla, which would charge her its own fee. She did this, and then stared blankly at the twenty dollar bill the machine spit at her. Because of course *this* wasn't any good in the vending machines either.

"I got fifteen dollars for who needs change."

Daci looked up to see a man dressed like he used to be somebody. Crisp shirt, tailored pants, shined shoes. But a gleam showed in his eye, announcing the lunacy to which he had finally succumbed.

"What if I need change for a twenty?" she posited.

"I got fifteen."

"Singles?"

"Four singles and a ten."

"That's fourteen."

The man blinked, a gesture that somehow reminded Daci of an owl whose head had twisted that strange, impossible way they do. "I got fourteen dollars for who needs change."

Daci marveled that this man wading knee-deep in madness still appreciated his own need for money. She asked to see the dollars he was selling and he produced them, so she traded her useless lone sheet for his utilitarian four and the stray ten-dollar bill. She suspected that if she later needed to change the ten, this same man would have eight dollars for whoever needed change.

She purchased two sodas, deciding on Pepsi because that's what all the Romanians drank, despite their inability to pronounce it. "Pep-shee"

"Pep-*see*."

"This is what I said. Pep-shee."

Back in the dark corridor, someone had joined Geo at his gurney. The two men chattered fast and quiet—co-conspirators. Geo's companion stood, pale limbs lean and lanky, in a hospital gown, its blue set off by his curly tangle of red hair. A few steps closer revealed the blur of a tattoo that displayed a 3D image if looked at the correct way.

"Eddie."

He turned and set his blue eyes on her. The rest of his face hurt her to look at. Bruised on the left, stitched together down the side, and distorted with swelling.

"Let me guess, I should see the other guy?"

"Ah, no, I'm pretty sure I *am* the other guy." He held out the wrong hand for shaking, the right one encumbered by a short cast. "I remember you from my lawyer but I'm bad with names, I apologize."

Geo made a noise of distress. "You know her?"

Daci offered Eddie the spare Pepsi. He declined, and while he explained to his stepbrother how the Baroness had been at his lawyer's, she opened Geo's Pepsi and gave him some ibuprofen.

Geo popped his pills then frowned at the floor. "That's weird."

"You don't know the half," Daci assured him with a chuckle.

Eddie set those eyes on her again. "Say, can you get me out of here?"

"You need a cake with a file in it?"

"They won't let him out without a chaperone," Geo explained. "Someone to sign for him, so if he croaks it's not their responsibility."

Daci looked around the gloomy hallway. Nurses scurried in both directions but no one stopped to ask if they needed help or even to accuse them of something. "Funny, they won't let him out—they won't let you in."

"I don't have any clothes, really, is the problem," Eddie explained. "I guess they cut them off me after . . ." He trailed off and a grimace of humiliation shadowed his face. Geo patted his stepbrother's shoulder. It seemed awkward for both of them, uncharacteristic, but gauging by Eddie's face apparently needed and appreciated.

"I can run out and get you sweats," Daci offered.

Eddie looked to Geo. "I don't have my money."

"I can loan—"

"I have something of yours," Daci interrupted. She pulled Eddie's wallet from her purse. He squinted at it until she opened it, revealing his license and a photo sans bruising and stitches.

"How'd you get it?" he asked. Not a hint of accusation, pure curiosity.

Daci considered this. "Circuitously," she finally said. "You can have it back, your money's still in it, but you need to explain something first."

Geo flopped back onto his gurney. "A condition to get his own wallet back, isn't she hilarious?"

Eddie winced at his stepbrother. "I think he may have a concussion."

Daci ignored the both of them. She pulled the folded, dull orange certificates from the wallet. "Tell me about these."

"Oh. They're pollution credits. So companies can—"

"I know what they are. I want to know how you got them."

Geo sat back up now. "She thinks I stole them."

"Geo? No. I . . . acquired them from a guy whose house I watch when he's away."

"Who?" Daci asked him.

Geo moved to kick his stepbrother but missed. "You tried to sell those to me."

Daci looked from Geo to Eddie, raised an eyebrow at the redhead. Eddie stammered in response.

"Just tell her," Geo cajoled. "She probably knows already anyway."

Eddie glanced from Geo to Daci and back again. Geo rolled his eyes, turned to Daci. "He house sits for people and he steals stuff from 'em. Only he's too dumb or too much of a snob to steal stuff that's actually valuable. Well, one of the things he stole had those inside it. He tried to sell them to me, figuring we might need them at Survivanoia. I guess he didn't realize they were ours to begin with."

Daci took a hard look at Eddie, who nodded and shook his head at the same time.

Daci laughed, then considered all she knew about Eddie. Recalled the signed Kenneth Patchen. "It's books," she said, gently. "You steal books."

He flushed, bringing out his freckles. "Yeah."

"Good for you. Nobody reads them. Whose book were those credits in, do you know?"

Eddie gave a loose shrug. "I know what house it came from. But he's an AR guy for comedians and stuff. Not a business guy, know what I mean?"

She did. No manufacturing connections. No need for pollution credits. "Did he ask you about them?"

"No. But he did ask about the book. Maybe he didn't know they were in there."

"Do you still have the book?"

"Yeah. I went to give it back to him but after he met me he decided I could keep it."

Someone pushed a giant canvas bin in their direction, spotted them, and hollered as he ran off, "Go back to your rooms please!"

The bin smacked off Geo's gurney and bounced against the wall before stopping. Eddie peered inside. "Hey!" He pulled a neatly-folded pair of pants from the bin. "Scrubs!"

"Guess that saves you a trip," Geo said. "Say, can you get me out of here too? I'd do it myself but I think my car is broken."

Daci laughed again. "You mean don't want to go back to your room?"

Geo groaned at her. "I'm going to die waiting for these people to check me in."

Eddie looked up from the bin where he had finally found a pair of pants long enough for him. "Why don't you go up to my room? I'm already checked in. Besides, the Baroness needs that book from my apartment."

Geo gazed at the redhead like he'd spoken Swahili. But then a grin spread across his face, erupted into laughter. "Why not?" Geo said. He turned to Daci. "My brother—he's a genius, huh?"

Geo said this without irony and Eddie's abused face blossomed into a smile. Suddenly, Daci wanted to cry. Stress? Something else, she thought. Guilt? Frustration?

No. She watched Eddie hide his happiness by looking at the floor, saw him swallow hard, and she understood that neither of these men had ever referred to the other by that unqualified term before. Never felt of each other that way. What had transpired between them to produce that shift? Daci was not privy to that. She wondered if the men themselves were aware.

Eddie needed Geo. The older, more grounded, more established brother. Geo's approval had served Eddie the immediate relief that a life raft serves a drowning man; this despite their aura of competition. The people who help us the most are not always who we'd have predicted.

People close to Daci had tried and they had meant well. Her father and Terri, believing that she was being derailed, nagged her persistently in order to help keep her on track. Her grandmother thought Daci needed to be reminded of her strengths, so she gave her pep talks and brought up the ugly, raging waters she had successfully navigated in her past.

But none of these people had what she needed.

Daci had scolded her friend for playing dice with death. But it seemed to her now that Terri's folly intentionally mirrored her own. Daci was making a similar mistake, not realizing herself that this was a dangerous game she was playing with this company and her not-quite-ex, not accepting that the stakes were in fact quite high, and finally believing herself removed from the competition and its consequences, when in fact her own fate was tied to that of the company. Syd's company.

The only person Daci had with the strength or knowledge she needed was the very man she struggled against. Whose approval she needed as well, not just emotionally but in a very tangible, business-based respect. Had she grossly mis-tread? Was she putting out fire with gasoline? Perhaps she should be fighting *by* Sydney, instead of opposing him. Some bulls are too big to be taken by the horns.

Daci put a hand to her forehead. This mental laundry needed to be sorted over a glass of wine and a relaxing soak, not after a horrible car crash. She didn't cry. She followed Eddie's lead and took a moment to recoup with a deep breath and long glance at nothing. Humility felt to her increasingly like a warm bath.

"C'mon genius," she said. "Let's get your brother upstairs and get you home."

CHAPTER 21

The daytime skies eased from blue to orange and the hills from green to a scrubby struggle of brown as LA's August heat battered the shrubs and long grasses. Weeks eased along, too, in a flurry of redundancy and absurdism, punctuated by the occasional relevant conversation with the occasional sane individual. They seemed progressively more rare in Daci's world as the days passed. She began to wonder if she'd be selling money in emergency rooms soon, especially since even the sane folks seemed to bring only bad news.

The first had been Zane. Despite her consuming work schedule, they made and kept a date night once a week. The summer daylight ran long enough that even with her corporate hours, most nights she could still watch the sunset while dining on her porch. The boats slowly congesting the harbor like an oversized family at Thanksgiving filled Daci with a sense of happy longing. Later in the evening, the dark masts would stand stark and foreboding, and on nights when the sky was more fiery, they appeared sinister as crosses.

Zane arrived while the sky was still blue, clutching a good bottle of pinot noir that he nearly dropped in his fluster.

"I don't believe this," he started. "But you probably will. You've made a liar out of me."

"Another notch in the bedpost," she responded with a grin.

"Laurel came up with nothing."

"Nothing?"

"Every cent Survivanoia has taken in can be tracked and all to completely genuine expenses. Of course there's the overpriced sales dinners, that sort of corporate nonsense, but nothing like what you're looking for." His big hands turned palm-up, surrendering a shrug.

Daci cut the foil wrapper from the wine, then handed the bottle to Zane. "Syd's probably funding his operation out of his own pocket."

"Beat you to the punch on that one, girl: Laurel checked the man's personal finances. But they look clean too."

"'Look' being the operative word."

"Laurel's sources are good." Zane twisted the corkscrew effortlessly, yanked out the cork with a satisfying pop.

"How good?"

He splashed a mouthful into her wide, bell-shaped glass for her to sample. "Unless the man is hiding information from his own accountant. There's no existing shady fronting operation of any kind, and again, the money is all traceable. A few dimes and nickels maybe but not enough to make anybody go hmmm."

"So not enough to fund a microbiologist research team expertly skilled in virus technology."

She twirled the wine in her glass, not feeling nearly as anxious as she would have ten days prior. Granted, humility's warm bath had quickly turned tepid when contaminated by the reality of approaching Sydney. Not so much for the reason of admitting defeat as her uncertainty of what his response would be. Would he take back the reins? Shrug and smile? She supposed she wanted his help, but she found that difficult to envision. The logistics seemed unlikely.

"You alright?" Zane remained poised with the bottle.

"Yeah." She sipped the wine, bubbling it over her tongue and then letting it sit on her palate before swallowing. "Oh, very nice! Everything a pinot should be."

"Which is what?" He poured her a full glass. "Full of leather and oak?"

She cuffed him on the hip but laughed. "With an overtone of rusty nails!"

Zane poured himself a glass and settled next to her as they waited for the duck to finish roasting. The thick scent of it wafted onto the porch from the condo while they watched the bay buzz with activity, all the ships coming in as the orange sun sank into the dark ocean.

"I thought you'd be more agitated."

"Me too."

But she wasn't. Not by the bad tidings and not by the stagnant, fruitless day-to-day stuff either. Meeting followed meeting just as changes followed meaningless changes, most of them strictly for her own entertainment. Her policies left some people happy, a lot of people angry, and everybody confused. Days not wasted in meetings were consumed by phone calls and sidestepping inane arguments from her CEOs and COOs and SOBs.

Daci wished it was the scientists her job forced her to interact with. She had little valid reason to associate with them. They seldom had meetings; instead they held impromptu problem-solving sessions. On days when she couldn't stand the clichés and chatter of the business end, she'd trump up an excuse to be in the labs.

The Russians argued over who was the better of the Mighty Five, Rimsky-Korsakov or Borodin (an argument Rin ended by floating the proposal that the Mighty Five were an inherently synergistic fraternity). Wolfy flirted with Daci and sometimes played chess with Dr. Krakow. Akira sang along to his Van Halen CDs in accented and often incorrect English.

Akira was the second sane but discouraging conversation, only a few days after Zane. She'd requested that he perform a literature search on the development and/or discovery of Flower Flu. It had by then occurred to her that none of the scientists working for her seemed conflicted, suggesting either that some of them were selfish and evil, like businessmen, or none of them knew the flu had a treatment, a vaccine. She hoped to out any moles by going to them for aid.

None of them changed their attitudes around her. And her gut said they really didn't know. So who did? Somebody invented this vaccine . . . but Akira, like Laurel, came up blank. Not a single peer-reviewed science or medical journal made mention of this virus that was supposedly manufactured. If the notebook pages Terri had received were authentic, they were proving to be the world's most underground laboratory in the history of laboratories!

"What is very . . ." Akira paused, searching for the English equivalent of his word: ". . . Weird! What is weird is that most private research is opposite, will announce discovery before is proven. To not announce at all . . . so strange."

Daci only nodded. Had Akira been just a modicum less earnest he would have been suspect.

"So sorry," he said in response to the face she must have made. Akira spoke with a thick accent but a precision to his words, reminding her of the clack of an old typewriter. "Oh, and since pretension meter project on hold, I have much free time, now. Perhaps you can fill?"

"On hold?"

"Yes, Scally-san come and say to wait until August sales meeting."

"Really. Did he say why?"

"Something about new prototype. Already complete. Does not need this one, only needs approval." He gazed into her eyes, awaiting instruction.

Already complete? What did that mean? The past three weeks she'd been killing time, waiting for the sales meeting to bring The Doctor on board. Apparently she'd wasted those weeks, should have just hired him on her own accord, legitimacy be damned.

She promised Akira she'd provide him a new project and wandered out of the lab. As before, though, she wasn't as agitated as she would have expected. In fact, she admitted to herself as she made her way up the broad staircase and to her office, she felt relieved. Because if she had truly lost the little scientist, then she had done everything she could, and if that were the case there would be no shame in approaching Sydney.

On her desk, her phone's red light blinked, telling her she had voice-mail. She dialed the mailbox and found two messages. First Terri asked if she wanted to have lunch. "No news, so we can commiserate while you're waiting for your little scientist to come save us all." Terri laughed cheer-fully. "Call me," she sang and hung up.

After her, a monotone voice delivered her a message so deadpan it made her laugh. "This is Barry Brownstone, calling at the behest of that Eddie Bloodworth boy. I do recall the book. I never read it. It was left here by a friend who's since moved away." A pause, as if deciding then: "His name is Remington Rendor. Yes, really. I made him show me his birth certificate. I can have him contact you. I guess. If you want."

He left three phone numbers but Daci didn't write them down. She knew now where the NOx credits had originated from. Remington Rendor was second-generation Hungarian. He was Sydney's cousin and right-hand man. He was also Survivanoia's old company president.

Terri would have to take a rain check for lunch. Daci picked up the phone and called her not-quite-ex husband.

* * *

All his money and that vast ocean, yet Sydney chose to live in the hills, not on the beach. Kanan Dume Road wound its way up and over the Santa Monica Mountains, connecting the pricey southwestern edge of the Valley to the Pacific Ocean. At the peak of the mountain, the ocean sprawled out in front of a driver like infinite opportunity.

Sydney lived in a tucked away Spanish Colonial, whose red roof and white walls appeared out of place against the surrounding greenery. The quaint house seemed antithetical to his Eastern-European sensibilities, but consideration made the differences superficial; tile abounded on the stair-cases, kitchen, and bathroom, in place of the marble gracing Sydney's New York mansion. Instead of rich velvet, heavy canvas draperies hung from ornate metal rods, blocking light from the round-arched windows. And the round tower of the asymmetrical Colonial certainly called to mind castles and turrets.

Like his New York home, the little house quietly displayed enormous wealth. Unlike his New York home, the grounds here offered a sprawling, untamed garden. Sydney's trees grew dates, pomegranates, blood oranges, and of course plums. He'd agreed to meet her but here and only here, in his garden, among the shade of his fruit trees.

When she arrived, the quiet of the garden made the place feel empty, abandoned. Peculiar, it had always been so inviting.

Daci gave the wooden windchime a gentle shove to announce herself. She wandered to the dining table by the side of the house, a round, marble monstrosity with mosaic inlay. On it she found a bottle of wine, two glasses, and a decanter. A huge, hand-carved wooden bowl lay in the center, filled with fruits both from the garden and purchased; mangoes and kiwis shared space with the plums.

The wine turned out to be one of her father's. Believing that the best wines have the simplest labels, her father kept things traditional, used his initials. A thin, scrolling font (that thickened at the bottom and didn't quite remind drinkers of Dracula) read DVG. Where customarily a drawing of rolling hills or an estate would act as the background, her father's wine displayed a sketch of the Carpathian Mountains.

She sat in one of the six wrought iron chairs flanking the marble table and peeled the metal wrapper from the green glass. As she screwed the waiter's pull into the cork, Sydney appeared, carrying a cheese tray.

"You never have my father's wine."

"During your phone call you suggested that this was a . . . significant occasion."

Daci handed him a glass, took one for herself, and raised it in a toast. "To you!" she proclaimed, clinking her glass against his.

Something felt unfinished and she realized she was waiting for a hug. Odd; they hadn't shared physicality in greetings since she'd been assigned head of the company. Even goodbyes were generally limited to smiles. Daci recognized where this put her emotionally, this need for grounding. A rare want that Sydney used to fill. Would he today?

He took a slow sip, savoring the wine, bold and jammy without the cloying sweetness of so many Romanian wines. "To me," he repeated her sentiment. "What is it you need?"

Daci smiled, sampled a piece of tangy cheese, smooth textured like mozzarella, but sharp on the palate like a cheddar. "Things have gone a bit sideways."

"Imagine."

"You were right, Sydney, it's hard. Harder than I believed. I don't know what to do."

"What to do about what?" He ran one thumb through the belt loop on his opposite hip, held the wine glass in the other like a shield.

"The Flower Flu treatment."

Sydney cocked his head at her and Daci felt something foreign, some distance she'd never had to cross before.

"The vaccine and the NOx credits, alright? I don't know what to do."

Sydney took a deep swallow of wine, swirled the remaining bit around the bottom of his globe glass. "You certainly seemed to know when you had your mutiny."

"Sydney, please. I've searched for a loophole, some way I can use my new presidency, the fact of it, or my naiveté and newness, to set the situation straight but I'm ... overlooking something?"

Syd blew breath through his nose like a dragon. "You're assuming I have an answer to this conundrum. Which mandates that I myself consider the situation something in need of correction. An abhorrence."

Daci gazed at him, scrutinizing. She could not find it in herself to believe that he would let people die in order to make a profit, and she told him so.

Sydney smiled and Daci caught a glimpse of the man she knew.

"Look," she said, "maybe there are things you couldn't do because of your status or certain alliances to other companies, whatever. I'm fresh and new and relentless. I can get away with anything.

"But I can't figure out what it is I need to get away with! Excepting the case of a buy out, the contract holds. There seems to be no option that doesn't break it. Short of black marketing the stuff."

"And would you do it? Sell it illegally?"

Daci hesitated. She'd considered it. The logistics gave her pause but she was acquainted with enough people who hustled for a living that she knew she could put the necessary pieces together. The consequences of getting caught—that was the unknown variable.

"It's a last resort."

"Ah. So your altruism has a limit."

"Did I ever claim it didn't? I'm no saint, Syd."

"No. Of this much at least we have proof and can agree." The sudden razor in his voice combined with his insinuation made her mentally flinch. Her bewilderment read in her face apparently, since Sydney responded with his toothy grin.

"You tell me you don't think I would allow people to die in order to profit. You say with the intention of flattering me. But I don't care. I suppose it's not a choice I would consciously make. But a committee made this choice, this decision to bind our companies together, and a board at someone else's company approved it. By the time it got to me, saying no would be useless and confusing."

Not too many months ago Daci would have protested, accused him of corporate negligence or old-fashioned lying. But today she understood.

"Am I to recognize that there is no legal way out of this arrangement?"

"As I expressed to you a long time ago."

So what was it to be? Manufacture the treatment and sell it on the streets? And what of the NOx credits? Syd hadn't made mention of them. His silence and his strange, uneven keel struck her, suddenly and subtly, like when she'd mentioned the Flower Flu cure and he'd cocked his head at her. And he'd corrected her when said she didn't believe he'd let people die to make money.

All of this forced through her head cyclonically and conveyed itself before she could select the words in a precise statement spoken without animosity or vehemence.

"You're lying," the cyclone concluded.

Sydney didn't quite smile. "Good to see your bold candor hasn't abandoned you."

When she didn't respond, but held his gaze, Sydney moved to the table, finally joining her.

"I am going to tell you some things," he said. "And when I've finished, if you still want my help, I'll give it to you. With just a few conditions."

Daci gazed at him, her husband of nearly two decades who at one time worshipped her, maybe still did. What could he be about to tell her? Her father had researched him completely before they were married, and afterward he'd been transparent to her.

"I'm waiting," she said.

"The NOx credits were misplaced by Remington, who is a brilliant man but a foolish drunk. He stole them for exactly the reasons you suspected, so that we—he and I—could start our own side business. Which we have."

"Making what?"

"Flower Flu. The treatment was developed before there was a disease to treat. A lot of drugs are developed from simple curiosity about a biological mechanism. Such was the case with the Flower Flu treatment. But nothing in nature had yet crossed the line between plants and humans. We had to give Mother Nature a little shove. The flu—"

"Wait, who all is pay—"

"They're all paying us. All three pharmacy companies pay Nommasto to keep Flower Flu in circulation. Don't interrupt. Plants share—"

"Plants share 40–60% of their genetic material with humans, enabling the spread of Flower Flu, and don't talk to me like I'm a child."

Sydney looked amused. Not baffled, not angry. This frightened Daci.

"Who told you that? One of your pet scientists?"

"Someone who is going to deconstruct your cure and find his own. He's a genius, Syd. Smarter even than you and in my employ."

"That's not completely true. You had a man you were looking to hire and he went missing."

"If you say so."

"I still know what goes on inside the walls of my company. And it is still *my* company. Where things like nepotism make for certain obligations."

Daci called his bluff. "You barely spoke to your son the entire time we were married—"

"We are still married."

"We have a piece of paper with our names on it. And if you're so interested in staying married to me, why are you sabotaging what you perceive as your last chance to keep us together? Why don't you just tell me? How to launch the treatment? And stop making the flu for fuck's sake!"

"If you have someone in your employ who is capable of designing his own cure, why are you here pleading for my assistance?"

They glared at each other for a heavy, silent moment. Stalemated. Sydney finally offered a mild shrug and reached for the wine, refilled both their glasses.

It was Daci who broke the silence. "Why didn't you just say no to letting me be the president? You needed to see me fail?"

Syd displayed his nasty smile, the one that frightened people. Daci hid a grin. William Congreve believed Hell hath no fury like a woman scorned? Congreve never met a Romanian.

"If I set you up for failure," he said, "it's because you let me. But why would you not? It's how you were raised. Your whole family has set you up to fail or to be used for the entirety of your life."

Daci shook her head. "I've never been set up for failure by anyone, at least before now, and I've certainly never been used."

Syd nodded, took a slow, savoring drink of her father's wine. His nasty smile stayed. He rested his elbow on the table, gently twirling the ruby liquid at the same level as his dark eyes.

"You seek shelter from me in the bed of a man you pay. Ostensibly to make a movie, though by all accounts there is no start date set for this project, let alone a completion time. You don't believe this man uses you for your money?"

Daci opened her mouth to respond but paused. Zane's motives for being with her had buzzed through her consciousness on occasion but she never got that sense from him, so the thought never lingered. As to what Sydney knew or should know? "That's not really your business," she said.

"It is absolutely my business what my wife is doing."

"Also, you've never met Zane. Anything you think you know about him is hearsay." She recognized she was protesting too much, wondered what Sydney had tapped into, wasn't sure she wanted the whole truth.

"I know *you*," Syd asserted. "I know you better than you know yourself because we have been together more years than you were alone."

Daci laughed gently at Sydney and his strange tactic. "This psychoanalysis you're doing doesn't cast *you* in a particularly flattering light. If Zane has possible hidden motives, then you've probably got some yourself."

"I never veiled my motives for wanting to marry you. Yes, I found you intriguing and beautiful. But your bloodline couldn't be ignored. Would I have been as vehement if you'd been more of a mixed breed? A more truly American girl? No. And if you believe anything differently, then you're even more naive than I've been taking you for all these years."

A quick, sharp intake of breath and Daci cleared the sting of Syd's statement. "Let's get back on topic here. I asked you a straightforward question, and you've strayed completely."

"You made an accusation. Which I am not denying. I'm explaining. Demonstrating a pattern—your pattern. How your decisions get you into situations, and how the root cause of these poor decisions on your part is traceable back to your upbringing."

"That's ridiculous." But it wasn't, and Daci knew it, and Daci knew just where Syd was going with his argument.

"Recall that trip your father took with you. Supposedly a graduation gift for you, in actuality a business trip for him. Who brings their daughter on a business trip to a politically unstable country full of men with guns?

He didn't care enough about you to leave you at home. Because he knew what would make Radu happy. He had the perfect distraction for that filthy war lord. The perfect bribe."

Her throat constricted further and this time she did hesitate, fearing that if she spoke she'd cry. The truth, if that's what he was telling her, was uglier still than she even knew. *If. . . .*

She took a deep breath, said without quavering, "What makes you think any of this is true? You weren't there. Again, it's hearsay."

"I don't think, I know it all to be fact." His face was blank as he watched her, but his eyes, deep and serious with the slightest hint of regret, told her that his words were fact. He did know. He'd always known.

She looked away. "If you knew all this why'd you want to marry me?" Water brimmed her eyes now, unstoppable.

Sydney put his hand to her face, wiped the tear from her cheek with his thumb. "No, darling, you have it backward. It's because I wanted to marry you that I know all this. Your father wanted something, and I knew the people he needed to get it. I sent Dragomire to Radu. And I told him to take you."

Daci put a hand to her head and the other to her gut. She felt ill, sick like with a significant hangover, all jittery and drained, rolling stomach, pounding head.

She felt Syd's hand on her shoulder. She lurched away from him. But his touch broke something deep down inside, and when she moved, an animal cry escaped her followed by relentless sobbing, the depth of her sorrow racking her body. Merciless like she'd never believed. More corrupt than she'd ever admitted. A stupid pawn in a game of men, used as a plaything, and worse: willingly.

Hadn't she suspected it? That her father had brought her on purpose, that some dark deal worked on in the shadows while she cavorted around like some gruesome princess?

No, actually. She'd never believed that her father purposefully aligned himself with suspected warlords, no. And she'd absolutely never inferred that he'd brought her along to prostitute her.

Likewise, while she'd been aware of Syd's fervor regarding her Dacian background, it had never occurred to her that this fact alone comprised his main motive in his desire to wed her. More naive than he'd believed. All these years.

She took a deep, shuddery breath. Where did all this leave her? *Really?* Most people's childhoods didn't lend themselves to any idyllic delusion. It equated to believing in Santa Claus. Her husband was a selfish schmuck? That made her normal, not unique.

She thought of Chloe; she knew from conversing with Vonnie that Chloe's mother had died at birth (and the unspoken details seemed to be sinister) knew too that the father and stepmother had died recently and within a year of each other. Nothing about Chloe suggested any of that. Funny and smart girl. Happy and brave. Sweet and vicious.

And Vonnie, whose husband had privately and publicly abused and humiliated her. She'd flipped the script on him. Funny... brave... no wonder her and Chloe were best friends. And these friends faced their responsibilities without the luxury of resources Daci had been privy to.

So where did Daci's shattered illusions leave her? In exactly the same position as when she'd entered the garden, so full of the absurd hope that Syd would help her. She still sat in the helm of a powerful, corrupt company, people were still dying needlessly, some scientist had intentionally developed a horrible virus, and Daci still felt an overwhelming obligation to help.

And the difference between her and people like Chloe and Vonnie, Geo and Eddie, and even Zane or The Doctor was that Daci was in a position to help, make a change on a national, if not global, level. Shouldn't that responsibility be the price of wealth and power? That's why she took Survivanoia from Sydney!

So what did it matter, saint or slut, so long as she charged ahead and made her difference? If people were rescued?

Daci wiped her eyes. She was still Dacianna Von Worthington, and her dubious, absurd name still made her smile, at least internally. She blew her nose into a cocktail napkin and fanned her face while she got her breathing back to normal.

"Okay," she said, and her voice was steady. "You've said what you have to tell me. What are the conditions?"

Sydney grinned in a quintessential villain-like way. "Alright," he said by way of admiration. "The first is that you find out who the silent partner is. The person who put you in power."

"You have more than enough resources to identify him yourself. You've just contrived an elaborate snipe hunt to keep me busy while you wait around for other companies to develop a cure for your virus."

It occurred to Daci that perhaps Sydney himself sent Terri those notebook pages. That his intention was to sabotage his old company. But it also occurred to her that everything he was telling her was contrived. An intricate ... Sydney was talking, apparently had been.

"I already know who the silent partner is," he was saying. "I want you to discover it for yourself. I'll even give you a hint, condition-free: Ask GrandMama."

* * *

"Well, I didn't expect to see you today." GrandMama smiled, proudly displaying teeth that were still her own. "Something good or something bad?"

Daci had to grin at the woman's insight. "Never could keep anything from you."

"Old people know it all. Now tell me something new."

"I've been talking to Sydney."

"That's not new."

"It was all new to me." Daci relayed what had driven her to Sydney, and his chilly, sadistic response. She divulged the details in full, about the NOx credits and Barry and Remington, how he claimed to have invented Flower Flu and she'd lost track of her little scientist. And she told her grandmother of Sydney's nastiness, his cruel joy at her failure and his absolute refusal to help her or his own company.

Then she paused. Searched for the way to ask her question without being overly dramatic.

"Just spit it out, kid."

"Sydney threw it all back at me. He blamed Dad. For taking me to Romania, saying Dad traded his little girl like so much cattle, for some black market connections. Said my whole family has set me up for failure from day one, why should I expect anything different from my husband."

"Ex-husband."

"Yeah, well tell him that."

Another pause. Followed by another prompting from GrandMama. "You still haven't told me what brought you here. To me."

Daci looked at every other thing in the room, then finally met her grandmother's expectant gaze. "Who's the silent partner?"

GrandMama ran her thumb along the hangnails of each finger, making a dry little scratchy sound. "Why?" she finally barked.

"He says the partner is part of this unconscious conspiracy as well."

"I'm the silent partner. And that's a line of crap."

Daci was surprised to find that she wasn't surprised. "Of course."

"Of course." GrandMama nodded. "How else could I have gotten you into that position? Nobody has that many strings to pull."

Daci pondered the ramifications of this strange, wild fact for a long, silent moment. "But if I drive the company broke," she said quietly, "I take you with it."

"So? I'm old! I've got a place to live, whether you shut Survivanoia down or blow it up, makes no difference. The corporation is its own being. It doesn't affect my money in my bank." She pointed a crooked finger. "I checked."

"When? Did you enter into this partnership, I mean."

"Syd wanted to expand. And he wanted to marry you. And you seemed to want to marry him. So talk of you stretched to talk of him and his company. And, as you know, I had just come into some money around then."

Daci hoped her face didn't expose the sense of betrayal she felt. Not nearly as deep or as intentional as Syd had indicated. But perhaps that was merely a matter of perception. Or yet another example of her own willful ignorance, like not catching onto the obvious fact of Flower Flu being purposefully developed, or refusing to recognize that of course GrandMama had to be the silent partner.

Despite some trepidation, Daci asked the begged question. "Why? Why the company, why me as the president? I don't know what I'm doing, you knew that."

Her grandmother folded her lips over her teeth the way only old people can. "You ever see that movie *GoodFellas*?"

"Isn't that a little violent for you?"

"I'm over seventeen, they let me in. Nothing you can do about it. Anyway, you see it?"

Daci nodded.

"The one guy, he says, 'You light a match.' And kid, I knew just what he meant. Torch the place. Burn the company, hell, the whole damn economy! To the ground and make money on the way down.

"I watched the super-rich make a profit off of the Great Depression. Made me sick. But what could we do? Sydney comes along—and for the record I never liked him. But he had this piece of wealth and power that he wanted me to invest in. And he's a lot of rotten things but he's a savvy businessman. I gave him some money and he made me more. Lots more.

"You threw a monkey wrench into things, coming here and telling me about that cure he won't release, and saying you should just take over. Got me to thinking, maybe she *should* just take over!" GrandMama waved a hand. "The rest, you already know."

"But then . . ." Daci took a deep breath. "How is Syd wrong?"

"First, in thinking that I wanted you to fail." GrandMama brought a fist down against the arm of her Halloween couch. "You're my only grand-daughter, I want you to be the Queen of the Goddamn Universe!

"Second, in Sydney's mind, if you don't make money, you failed. I don't agree with that. If you don't try the best you can, if you don't follow your conscience, *then* you failed."

The same strange humility overtook Daci that overtook her that night a few weeks back at the hospital with Geo and Eddie. Still so vivid it felt like yesterday.

She wanted to say something, preferably something funny—GrandMama was not usually so candid or so earnest. But Daci knew if she tried to talk, her voice would shake and those tears rimming her eyes would spill down her cheeks.

GrandMama saved her by speaking first, more calmly this time. "You're upset for the wrong reasons, kid. And at the wrong people. You need a good meal and a night's rest. Go see your father tomorrow when you're head is screwed on straight." She laughed gently. "Don't see him like this, though, you'll kill him."

She uncharacteristically gave Daci a hug goodbye.

In the elevator, a nurse reviewed the nighttime meds with an aide. "Mrs. Sanchez won't take a sleeping pill, so tell her it's a laxative. Don't let Hollister drink these down with that rum she keeps. And make sure you get Mrs. Ogden's teeth out tonight. She convinced the last aide they were real and then nearly choked on them."

Daci was happy for the levity.

Outside, thick heat slowed her, radiating off the parking lot's blacktop like an invisible curtain. Daci decided GrandMama was correct; she did need a good meal. And this fact conveniently coincided with the one last stop she had to make before she could relax.

If Sydney wouldn't help her get the Flower Flu treatment released, then she *had* to find an answer on her own. With her ignorance and shortcomings having been splayed out this evening like so much meat at a butcher, it seemed "re-discovering" the Flower Flu vaccination was her best option. If the wheel's inventor refuses to let the device be used at any price, then it's certainly worth reinventing.

Daci recalled that The Doctor had said he walked to the Romanian restaurant. And he'd given her a solid idea of where said restaurant was located. Logic dictated if she could find it, she could find him.

Instead of exiting at the 90, she stayed on the 405, which took her to the 105. There she headed east, into uncharted territory, parts of LA that seldom made the silver screen: cloverleaf junctions and green line metros running down the center of the freeway and little Romanian restaurants housing mankind's hope.

The restaurant proved elusive, having no sign. But The Doctor had described the odd building housing it, a long white box with a sharp-peaked roof. Daci drove the three square-mile area surrounding the 110–105 interchange, making an ever-widening circle. Eventually she spotted it, about three blocks from the exchange.

Luckily, Romanians are late eaters; even on Tuesdays the kitchen stayed open until 2:00 a. m. She had a fantastic meal; the menu proved much broader than she'd been led to expect. She started with a plate of cheeses and cold cuts and a bottomless glass of *țuică*, Romanian's potent plum brandy. She followed this with a tripe soup and then *nisetru la grătar*, grilled Black Sea sturgeon, paired with the black vodka of which The Doctor had spoken. She finished with a chocolate-filled crepe and more *țuică*.

Daci brought the check to the front register herself and asked the hostess who had doubled as an attentive waitress about Dr. Stuckhowsen, as if inquiring of an old friend.

The girl, Sorina, consistently replied in English to Daci's Romanian. Pride at having grasped this monkey-puzzle of a language? Rebellion against her off-the-boat parents? Most likely some of both with the ratios shifting when the weather changed.

Sorina recognized The Doctor's description almost immediately. "Yes, he comes and uses telephone. He was here tonight, you just missed him."

Daci asked if Sorina knew where The Doctor lived. She didn't, but a thin man in cuffed trousers and a llama wool sweater looked up from his book to interject. "A mile that way," he said pointing. "Off the road a bit.

Probably is best not to go alone." He grinned in a volunteering kind of way, but Sorina agreed to go and convinced him they'd be fine.

"He is lonely," she told Daci once they were outside. "But harmless."

They took the Hummer the short trek, found a dirt road leading to a clearing literally under the overpass, and now the two women stood side by side looking at . . . Daci wasn't sure.

"That," Sorina pointed at the giant panel of metal impaling the little box that presumably had been a house, "used to be a billboard."

The sign had come down in not-quite-the-center of the house, flattening one side while leaving the other largely intact. Oddly, wood covered the windows. Impossible for emergency enclosures to have arrived already. They must have been boarded up before the sign crushed The Doctor's house.

"I wonder if he's in there," Daci pondered aloud.

From her peripheral vision she caught Sorina's shiver. She watched the young woman, saw her pragmatic, flippant American upbringing wrestle with the dark superstitions carried in her bloodline. Her eyes narrowed. "I don't believe that he is."

"I need to check," Daci told her. "You don't have to come."

Sorina nodded. "I'd prefer not to," she admitted. "Something is off, is bad."

Daci suggested that she wait in the Hummer with it running. But they had to keep the headlights pointed at the house, as neither of them had thought to bring a flashlight.

The headlights made stark contrasts in the destroyed abode, splashes of blinding white against spots of unknowable darkness. The front door hung half open, stuck there on busted hinges in its crumpled frame.

Just past the threshold, a sweet, coppery stench took hold. A smell humans are hardwired to recognize: blood. Her breath quickened and she felt her heart do the same. She saw a flashlight in the stinging glow of her car's headlights, but that smell made her think twice about touching anything.

And there he was. Just to the left of the doorway, glassy-eyed and horrible, a dark chasm where there should have been a white, fleshy neck. Daci stepped away, shoved a hand in her mouth to keep her from screaming. They made it look much easier on television, accepting unexpected corpses.

It didn't look like The Doctor. Seemed outsized to be the little scientist. But she needed to be sure. She stepped back inside, forced herself to take a good look at the dead man. Large indeed and with a dark smear of hair. Not pale, either; this man had been Mexican or Latino. Not The Doctor.

She looked away into the dark recesses of the house. She supposed she should check them. But they weren't very well lit. And she really didn't want to. . . .

As if in response to her ruminating, the sign shifted and creaked, leaned another few inches and brought the house down that same distance. Daci ducked and covered—earthquake training. The creaking stopped. Dust and debris rained from the ceiling, rattling through the house.

Daci found herself half under an end table, crouched against an overstuffed leather chair. An afghan had been draped over the chair; she clutched it in one of her hands. Soft. Hand knitted. She spotted a small horse head on the floor, a knight from a chess set. All very depressing. And dangerous. The debris slowed, too quiet now to be heard over the cars above, though she still felt them landing on her face and in her hair.

As she stood up straight, a patch of angular brightness on the floor caught her attention. An envelope. It protruded from under the overturned coffee table, stark white in the murky darkness. Daci delicately withdrew it. The postmark said Pennsylvania, some town Daci didn't know. Neat but severe and very slanted lettering—half cursive, half print—graced the front and the return address carried the name Lucretia Stuckhowsen. Mother? Sister? She couldn't make out the date on the postmark. She slid it into the pocket of her pin-striped pants.

Daci took a deep breath, scanned the broken house for any sort of clue. It offered none. And the dead body at her feet suddenly frightened her completely; images of the dead man rising up shrieking and moaning filled her vision unaccountably.

She spun and fled. The glare of the headlights forced her to squint, and she shielded her eyes with an arm. Sorina, smartly, saw this and switched the headlights off, mercifully leaving just the running lights.

Daci lunged to the car and yanked open the driver's side as Sorina was moving to the passenger seat. The girl assessed her. "Something is bad."

"Somebody is dead."

Daci sat panting for a time, realized to her embarrassment that her hands were shaking. She raised one to show Sorina. "Americans," she joked. "We're so sheltered, a little death and we fall apart."

Sorina scrutinized the house, dark and distant in the reduced light. "It's not The Doctor." She said this, did not ask it.

"No. Too big."

Daci put the car in reverse and the engine growled while the tires spit rocks and dirt. She paused a moment, hand on the wheel, took some measured breaths. Back in control again. Car in gear and out of the clearing.

Sorina remained silent the duration of the short drive back to the restaurant. Daci pulled to the curb and put the Hummer in neutral, put the brake on. "Thanks for your help."

The girl's eyes hooded again. "I believe The Doctor is alright. You will find out." She hopped from the vehicle and closed the silent door, not looking back. Daci kept watch on her until she was safe inside the restaurant.

She took another measured breath, whispering as she let it out, "I hope so."

CHAPTER 22

The universe is a weird place.

This thought summarized all the disjointed static buzzing in Daci's head as she assessed Lucretia Stuckhowsen. With her spiky purple hair and striped tights and arm warmers, the girl appeared for all the world like a petulant teenager. Her vehemence matched this facade, but her methodical stated logic implied something more complex; a mature but cracked psyche.

It occurred to Daci that Lucretia's thoughts regarding her likely mirrored her own, given that Daci currently wore a wide white jacket with a ruffled collar and fist-sized fuzzy balls for buttons—a Pagliacci clown suit. She'd worn it as a courtesy to her VPs after requiring them to dress appropriately for their monthly meetings, to demonstrate that she'd never demand that they do something she herself would not.

Lucretia had just shot one of Daci's VPs and said VP happened also to be Sydney's son. Lucretia had also shot Daci. Luckily for all parties involved, the girl's chosen weapon was a paintball gun.

Daci had wrested the gun from the girl, who had proven deceptively strong. Slender but taut, all muscle and sheen like a cheetah or a serval. She'd hustled her out the door, away from the terrified Scally, who, given the color of the ink and how much the damn things stung, could not be blamed for believing himself to have in fact been shot and dying this very moment.

Now the women sat in Scally's office—Lucretia in the guest chair and Daci on the desk.

"I received a note from my brooder. He was very upset." Lucretia's accent was more pronounced, but her arrangement of words more correct than her brother's. "He interviewed at dis place, your place, was told one ding by a woman and later dismissed by a man. On the telephone, a message, not in person. Den I go to his house and find it is destroyed. What would you feel?"

Daci shook her head. "He wasn't in it. I know, I checked."

"Den where is he?"

"I'm trying to figure that out myself."

The girl's storm blue eyes drilled her. Used whatever irregular standard to size Daci up. "Der is a man who verks here. He sent my brooder here."

"Who? I'll find him."

The woman stiffened, probably thinking she was about to betray something. Daci appreciated, not for the first time, that political fears are as deep seated as religious superstitions.

"If you'd prefer I can give you our phone list, you can call his extension. I'll even leave the room."

Lucretia's eyes narrowed and her lips pursed. Cheekbones like razors and eyes such a vivid blue . . . Daci thought the girl should remain in LA and take up modeling.

"Where are you staying?" Daci finally asked.

Lucretia looked away, feigning boredom. She raised a hand by way of a shrug.

"Let me put you up. It's the least the company can do."

"I suppose dis is true."

Daci called Geo, asked if he could spare Chloe for an afternoon. "Tell her ten-sixty-two," Daci said and this made Geo laugh.

Remington—ex-company president—had commandeered the police

code for Meet the Citizen to mean befriend the client. Befriending, for Remington, had involved spending money and eating well on the company's dime. In other words, shower the client with gifts and goodwill until they begged you to take their money. Daci didn't want Lucretia's money, but knowledge is its own currency.

Besides, she felt bad for this off-kilter young woman. To come all this way and find her brother's house looking like a crime scene. Also, Daci admired the girl's utter contempt for social taboos. If she wanted to shoot somebody, there was no one gonna stop her.

She'd have Chloe take the girl shopping, sightseeing, Disney, whatever. She arranged for Geo to bring Chloe, come meet Lucretia in Scally's office, then she went back to her own office to check on Scally.

Pitch quiet. Was he still in there? She ducked under the desk. Sure enough.

"It's paint," she told him, unable to hide her grin. "Taste it."

She explained about the paintball gun, then settled in next to him under her behemoth desk. Somehow, forces had brought her exactly the moment she needed with this man. She had no idea where Sydney Junior's loyalties lay. Sydney Sr.'s proclamation was not entirely convincing, nor was it simply dismissible.

Beyond merely wanting Scally on her side, though, Daci genuinely liked the man. She knew his dealings by virtue of having been married to his father. So she knew things like that he had taken care of his mother, had a steady girlfriend he adored, and kept two cats, one of which had cost him eleven hundred dollars in emergency medical bills.

But Scally still had Sydney for a father. Would he pledge allegiance to all Sydney represented because of that tie? Out of perceived obligation?

"You're going to have to choose a side," she finally told him. It was the distillation of her labyrinth of questions.

He parried, asking how he could side with her when he didn't even know who she was, then asking about Terri's ad, even pulling a tattered copy of it from his wallet.

He finally stripped it down to his own essential question. "Why are you running the company like a lunatic?"

Now it was she who couldn't answer directly. She couldn't tell him about the divorce and the Flower Flu vaccine and development, not without first being absolutely certain: Did Scally think for himself? Did Sydney have so much as a single hook in this man, his son?

Daci sat up, faced him, took him by the shoulders. How to ask what you're not supposed to know? Scally had sent away the funny little scientist for his funny little language, the language they shared—that's what Daci thought. It had nothing to do with business and everything to do with personal.

She looked at Scally hard and long, searching for an in, what to say, how to phrase . . . "Do you believe human cruelty is balanced by our generosity?"

The question surprised her as well.

Scally made a joke that frustrated her, then threw a flurry of questions which she answered bluntly, hoping the grace of honesty would act as persuader.

"Do you have any questions for me?" he finally said.

"Just whose side you're on."

He scrutinized her and she felt she knew what was churning through his head. His eyes shifted as he watched her, like the moment in lovemaking when lust gives way to intimacy.

"I'm on my side," he finally told her.

But his eyes had already revealed what he attempted to veil with his words.

Daci grinned, then laughed, the big round laughter of relief. "You're a real bastard, you know that, Thug Life? A real mysterious bastard."

He laughed back and all tension left. Daci was certain that from here forward, she would always know where she stood with Sydney Junior. And it was a good place to stand.

* * *

Late in the afternoon, Chloe gushed into Daci's office like a drunken clown.

"Lucretia is about the coolest person I've ever met. Despite being an economics professor. Thanks sooo much for letting me hang out with her!" She dropped into one of Daci's leather chairs.

Daci inventoried Chloe but didn't know her well enough to ascertain if the girl was drunk or simply exuberant. "Did you drive?" Daci asked.

"No, Geo did. She runs like five miles a day," Chloe continued about Lucretia. "Every day. And she drinks vodka for *breakfast*. Not straight but fifty-fifty with water, because I guess they can't drink the water where she's from?"

This made Daci smile. GrandMama did the same thing for the same reason. "Where is she from?"

"Pittsburgh. Kidding! No, I don't know, she told me but it's some place I've never heard of. I actually accused her of making it up, but she showed it to me on a map."

Daci wondered vaguely where they were that there was a map handy but she had a more pressing issue. "Where *is* Lucretia?"

"Oh, she went home. But she gave me something for you." She pulled her messenger bag onto her lap—fuzzy and blue with yellow skulls—riffled through it.

"Home? Back to Pennsylvania?"

"Yeah, she had us take her to LAX."

"How'd she get a ticket?" Daci wondered aloud.

"Lucretia is very convincing." Chloe smirked.

Daci nodded, grinning. "I suspect that I'm sorry I missed it."

"Here you go." Chloe pulled a folded sheet of green striped paper from her fuzzy bag. "Lucretia said not to read it and for the record, I didn't. Now I have to go," she said, rising. "Geo is waiting for me. He's taking me home."

"Are you alright with that?"

Chloe paused to consider this, her simple act inadvertently informing Daci that yes she was drunk, that there was nothing going on between her and Geo (at least from Chloe's perspective), and that she wasn't threatened by him. So all was well with the world.

"Yeah, I'm good," Chloe decided. "Thanks again!"

She whirlwinded out, leaving Daci with the ledger paper.

So that was it. Lucretia had come and gone, like a shadow at daybreak, allowing most of them to perceive her as a caricature. An economics professor? Not too surprising. It explained her rigid logic, if not its peculiar application. Lucretia seemed to take things to their logical conclusion, and then take two steps left. The plodding, the patience, appreciating that it's no fault of the numerals if they don't add up but rather the error of the accountant. Lucretia took umbrage with those accountable.

Daci unfolded the green striped paper. In the center of needless columns, Lucretia Stuckhowsen's neat, severe, print-cursive hybrid said only two things:

Tyson Woolritch

CHAPTER 23

Daci awoke Friday before the alarm; remarkable as the thing was set for dawn in August. She snapped it off and set it on the nightstand, moving slowly so as not to wake Zane.

She watched him in the pale dawn light, stretched out on his side, breathing rhythmic and calm, mirroring his sixty-beat-per-minute heart rate. That's why she picked him: he calmed her down, kept her grounded. She didn't need a port in the storm because with Zane she didn't see any storms.

Daci set a hand on his back and he sighed softly. She kissed him on the temple, then nudged him until he woke.

"What's up?" he whispered.

"Would you rather have the land or the view?"

Zane took a deep breath, answered on the exhale. "The view."

"Why?"

"Too many people been treated wrong over land." He said this around a yawn.

Daci nudged him again. "If you were stuck on a deserted island and could only bring one thing with you what would it be?"

"A boat."

"Very clever but that's not what you're supposed to say."

"What am I supposed to say?"

"You're supposed to say *me*."

"The boat would bring me back to you. And you said one *thing*." He rolled over and curled against her, mumbling into her lap. "Maybe you should let people wake up. Before you … *yawn* … profile them."

"What if I totally screw up Survivanoia, get disowned by my family, and go completely broke?"

"Then you'll have to move in with me. Milo won't mind."

Milo was Zane's beta fish. And his only consideration, apparently. Nothing about "Oh your family wouldn't disown you" or how she'd never be broke. Nothing money oriented.

"One more thing."

"Whats'at?"

"Would you braid my hair?"

"Of course."

Three hours later, Daci munched on the little bit of heaven that was Roscoe's famous waffles. "Sydney was wrong about Zane," she proclaimed, stabbing a piece of chicken.

She'd taken off the tailored duster she'd worn to meet Tyson, and the crushed pant-suit as well, traded the impressive business gear for a pair of denim capris, a linen vest, and a pair of leather sandals. Now she enjoyed the chicken—and the weather—freely and with abandon.

Terri swallowed a giant mouthful of crispy-top homemade mac and cheese. "Of course he was wrong about Zane. He's wrong about all of it, I'm sure. Put the chicken *on* the waffle. It's better. How'd it go with the Woolritch guy?"

"So-so."

"Hence the scoop on Zane? Giving me the good news first?"

"He says he'll think about it, and if he decides it's a possibility then he'll get in touch with The Doctor, give him my contact info."

"Did he give you an idea time-wise?"

"Nope." She followed her friend's directions with the chicken and found them to be correct. Even better when she dipped it into the bowl of onion gravy.

She went to Roscoe's seldom enough that she rediscovered the amazing food each time she visited. Daci was finicky about waffles but these were perfect—a thin crispy layer surrounding the fluffy inside. Whoever thought to pair these with crispy chicken and onion gravy was a genius and should be sainted.

"Tyson is in the same position as Encludsmo's sister. Afraid of betraying the man. Unfortunately, I don't have a Tyson-appropriate version of Chloe to help convince him that I'm not the devil."

Terri swayed gently to the soft rumba playing through the speakers. "You don't think an outing with Geo would loosen him up?"

"An outing with Chomsky maybe. Geo is a bright enough guy—"

"If you say so."

"—but he applies his smartness to diversions. Tyson, in comparison, he reads and studies languages and for him that *is* a diversion. That's why I decided to approach him with the truth."

"The whole truth?"

"Mostly. I exaggerated a little about the sister, made it sound like she was still here. I also commandeered Chloe's sudden deep friendship, referred to Lucretia in the diminutive."

"So what did you tell the truth about?"

"I spoke allegorically about the Flower Flu situation. I told him about my dad's vineyards."

"In Moldavia?"

"Yeah."

"Wow, you really trust this total stranger."

"Sometimes strangers are more trustable than family."

Terri mopped up the last of her mac and cheese with a big biscuit. "Are you going to the vineyard today?"

Daci nodded.

"Are you ready?"

She finished the waffle and chased it down with a long swig of Eclipse, one of Roscoe's signature fruit drinks. "It's like Richard Wright says: if I wait until I'm ready I'll never go."

"Will you see your mom, too?"

"I guess that depends on what my dad says."

"Well, tell them both hello for me."

Outside, the morning haze still lingered, not yet completely blasted off by the midmorning sun. Terri bought a pack of strawberry incense from a supposed Jamaican on a unicycle who'd set up unofficially outside the restaurant.

"I still can't believe you drove here all the way from the Valley," she told Daci, "just to turn around and go back up north."

"There's no Roscoe's in the Valley. If I have to go over the Hill anyway, I may as well go to my favorite one. My car runs on salt water! It's not like it's costing me anything."

"Okay, calm down."

"I'm nervous."

"I know. But like I said, Sydney is wrong. About everybody. God, what did he say about *me*?"

Daci thought and was struck by an odd fact. "He didn't mention you. Or my mother. He alluded to GrandMama, but vicariously."

Terri laughed. "This is like in high school, when boys say you're beautiful and so funny and so nice, until you dump them, and then suddenly you're a slutty bitch and so are all your friends."

Daci smiled vaguely. Her friend wanted her to feel better, she knew. And Terri's statement held truth, but unfortunately some of what Sydney said did as well. He was not, as Terri asserted, wrong about everything.

Terri gave her a hug. "Call me if you need to."

Daci agreed, but as she climbed into her reengineered Hummer, she felt unequivocally alone, in the primordial sense of life and death. She turned off the Charles Mingus CD once she got on the freeway in order to revel in the bright sun, the salty air, and her own, deep solitude.

331

* * *

She hadn't told her father she'd be coming. It didn't matter; he'd be where he always was among the vines, seeing to the grapes, attending the foundation of his passion. Did she envy him that? Her entire life nothing had ever taken her over completely. Not a subject, not a cause, not a person. What did it feel like? Was this envy the reason she liked researchers so much?

The grapes were changing from bright green to dark purple so that the vineyard looked like a painting, the clusters of grapes picture perfect like a tchotchke. She found her father weeding along with his crew. And because she didn't know where to start, she started in the middle. "Sydney is of the opinion that you should have taken me to see the rest of Europe."

And because he was her father, had forged and formed her like a lump of conscience coal, her abruptness failed to fluster him. "He's wrong," he replied simply.

"I told him that at first. I told him you were trying to teach me something and you probably figured I'd see the rest of Europe by myself. And I told him I agree with your philosophy that there is more value in seeing people whose lifestyle is inarguably different than yours. Especially when you are related to them in some capacity."

Daci's father frowned at her. For the briefest moment he seemed a stranger.

"That's not what I meant," he said quietly. "I meant that he was wrong in saying 'the rest.' That's the only part I should have shown you. Paris and Berlin and London. I shouldn't have taken you on that trip at all. A better father certainly wouldn't have. But you were young and eager."

"By eager do you mean in heat? And you needed that woman's touch?"

Her father glanced at the ground, then squinted at her with confusion but not anger. "This was fifteen years ago. And you wanted to go. Why are you just now irate about it?"

"What were we doing on that trip?"

"We collected over thirty thousand cuttings. We built this." His arm swept wide to include the vineyard in all its dark green glory, decadent against the 9/11 sky.

Daci gazed out over the vines but couldn't see them. Instead, her mind cluttered her vision with Kalashnikovs and landmines and smelly, unshaven thieves.

"What did we trade for it? Besides me, I mean."

Her father closed the pruners. He crossed his arms and set his weight all on one foot, spoke with deliberation. "I never asked you to entertain those men."

Daci, suddenly humiliated, gazed at the ground. But her question held. "What did we trade for those cuttings?

"What are you asking me?"

"What or why?"

"What exactly are you accusing me of? Let's settle that first. Then we can discuss the whys."

"Sydney tells me you traded weapons for your rootstock. He says the whole vineyard is blood money."

"Sydney lies."

"About some things, yes. What about this?"

Her father took a deep breath. "Did you ever see me with any weapons? Let alone duffel bags full of them?"

"No."

A long pause and Daci's heart pounded its way into her belly. Balanced on the precipice between relief and anguish, embarrassingly similar to when she'd been fifteen and confronted Jamie Radcliffe about Becca, that girl from the dance, had he? Had they?! *Please say no.* It was so important then, so immense, Christ the sky should've cracked open and rained frogs on Becca's house, the earth could've split and swallowed Jamie whole. What she'd give this moment to again be so sick with agony over drunken groping. Would the vineyard rip itself in two and swallow her father?

She watched him sigh and uncross his arms. He stuffed his hands into the back pockets of his canvas work pants, rocked back on his heels.

"Sydney. I see. Playing Sins of the Father."

"It wasn't just you on that trip, Daddy."

"Please. Sexing up a few rag-tag warlords is a far cry from distributing nuclear warheads. It's a long way from distributing canned foods intended for relief to black marketers, like the UN in Bosnia. It's not as bad as purchasing automotive vehicles for militia men to strap machine guns to and then writing off the cost of those bribes as technical expenses, like the Red Cross in Somalia."

"What about the Kalashnikovs?"

Another deep breath. Her father's round, steel-toed engineers' boots kicked the soft, fertile ground with an imploring thud. *Please say no.*

"Yes. Yes! Yes, I arranged the sale of some crappy, outdated Russian rifles to a handful of over-zealous gangsters-cum-warlords in exchange for the theft and delivery of a sizable supply of Eastern European grape cuttings."

Daci tried to form a question but the words wouldn't come. Just unspecified accusations punctuated by anguish. "Aren't you ...? Doesn't it ...?"

"The transfer of a few hundred half-broken guns made little, if any, difference in any of those wars. And I got to preserve the history of those areas. They can burn down the libraries and plunder the museums and commit all other forms of memoricide.

"But wines will tell the story of regions destroyed. Even if the flavors fade with time, as they may, vintages from certain grapes will always tug at the drinker intellectually. In wondering about the flavors and the soil and the climate, a drinker of these wines will recall the region from which they arose and in that way recall the past. So no, I am not conflicted. The history of those places exonerates me."

Daci gazed evenly at her father. She realized it hadn't been Sydney she'd fictionalized, but this man. "You sound like Daddy Machiavelli."

"And you behave like a Benita Mussolini, whose namesake famously stated that fascism should more properly be called corporatism because it is the merger of state and corporate power."

"No! That's exactly why I took over this company—to put an end to those kinds of practices."

"Which you have yet to accomplish. Which it seems to me you have yet to even address. And while we're on the subject tell me: what are you doing to Sydney to provoke this?"

"I went to him for help. He absolutely refuses to help me distribute the vaccine."

Her father rocked on his heels and gazed into the deep blue sky.

She watched him and waited. Because Sydney had told her something her father hadn't: who'd put her father in touch with all those grimy gangsters in the first place. Which was Sydney himself. Sydney had sent Daci's father in search of Radu. Yet here her father stood, not pointing his finger. Not casting blame. The bigger man.

His violet eyes caught hers and held them. "What else?" he asked.

"He claims he started another company with the missing NOx credits, that he developed the Flower Flu on purpose. His new company distributes the virus in a controlled fashion that keeps the research funded. Then once the other companies catch up, they'll basically all keep each other in business."

"And he's telling you that you've got nothing to say about it because your father is a war criminal and you behaved like a wicked slut up in that den of wolves."

Daci felt herself blush, looked at the ground. "Yes."

"I see." He pulled his wallet from his back pocket. Once black, now worn brown and smooth, and Daci thought it might disintegrate to a pile of dust before he could get it closed again; but then the wallet went back into his pocket and she found a business card in her hand.

The card displayed a stylized dragon, the name Balaur Radu Tepescu, and a phone number preceded by an 818 area code. Daci's brow knitted and she looked to her father nonplussed.

"War criminals are much frowned on when the war is over," he told her. "They often get put on trial in a public court—"

Daci scoffed. "The same type of international institution that let them rise to power in the first place."

"Yes. And *you* became an active, responsible part of that international nexus when you took the helm of Sydney's company. Radu—now Balaur—wanted only to come to the States and drink Pep-shee."

Daci ran her fingers over the cheap, thin business card. Wondered what kind of business this vicious man had found for himself here. "He lives in the Valley?"

"Valley Village. He has a pre-teen son named Zalmoxis, and his wife Elena makes the best mititei this side of the Danube."

"And?"

"He still speaks fondly of you. And I'm sure he'd be interested in knowing that Sydney Scalinescu is spreading rumors and lies about him."

"Interested?"

"Uhm-hmm."

"How interested?"

"Don't call him unless you're quite serious. As I said, Radu's wife makes the greatest mititei. Sausage, too. She makes them in bulk and sells them at one of the little local delis."

Daci looked carefully at her father at this hardness she had never seen, did not recognize. She'd not understood him capable of such cruelty. Her heart pounded again, this time in her ears, the rush of blood momentarily muting the laughing chatter of the workers. She recognized it—fear. She saw her father in an entirely different light and was afraid of him.

Which, she understood, had been Sydney's goal.

* * *

Terri's voice down the phone asked—reasonably, "How is killing Sydney—and having him eaten apparently—going to help things?"

Daci tried to explain, more to herself than to her friend, what she believed were her father's motives. "He's saying to watch myself. And that if I need help—you know, drastic help—that this man will help me. And that Sydney is maybe dangerous and—"

The words didn't make sense or convince even herself.

"You know what's really going on here, right?" Terri, grounded queen of sensibility. "It's as old as the creation of Earth. Or at least of man."

"Sure. Sure, these men are attempting to hurt and destroy each other and I'm caught in the middle."

"Oh honey. You're more than caught in the middle. They're using you against each other."

Daci's nose stung and her eyes filled with tears. "But that's my dad," she croaked. And the sound of her own weak voice embarrassed her.

"I know. But, as your mother drilled into us, he's still a man and still a human and like the rest of us sometimes must bow to the demands of the species."

"I have to go now."

"Stop and see your mother!"

"Exactly."

* * *

Cacophony, California lay across the beach from the overrated drive that was Highway 1. It claimed neither Northern or Southern California but Central, that wild, largely unknown stretch where Hearst built his castle and the pine trees kissed the ocean.

On the service road running parallel to Highway 1 stood a sign with white letters on a green background: CACOPHONY, CA, POPULATION 35. Somebody had used reflective tape to change the 35 to a 38.

Dacianna's mother, Jillian Rogan Worthington, had kept her studio here for nearly a decade now. Santa Barbara had become too much for her at some point, with its unusable beaches and drunken college-kid surfers. She'd openly envied Daci's father for his vineyards, about which she intentionally maintained a romanticized vision. In the interest of continuing to preserve this idealized image, she'd never spent more than three consecutive days at the vineyard, a practice Daci herself followed and also applied to Las Vegas.

Daci's father had hired an architect to fashion a studio from an old barn. Her mother would have preferred a Cape, but Capes are notoriously small. The idea of a studio space worked at cross purposes with the dimensions of a Cape Cod–style house. This little dualistic want had come to characterize Jillian in Daci's comprehension of her. Jillian wanted to live on the beach but not get a tan, wanted a husband and child to love but not be responsible for.

And the marvelous thing about Jillian Worthington, the thing Daci admired and sometimes envied her mother for, was that she usually managed to finagle a solution, some third way which satisfied her seemingly irreconcilable demands.

The barn, for instance, still rectangular and blocky from the outside, had been reworked so that the second floor studio had the pitched roofs and dormers characteristic of Cape, while the monstrous space afforded by the building's actual architecture remained preserved.

Another marvelous thing about Jillian Worthington was that despite being a vintner's wife, she enjoyed the bubbly sweet flavor of sparkling boxed wine, especially when paired with Twinkies and Doritos. So Dacianna made a stop at the local market to get some along with a Hershey bar and the latest copy of *Cosmo*.

At the barn, the Hummer crunched over gravel and Daci left it to rest in the shade of a pine grove. A mural graced the side of her mother's barn studio, reminiscent of those along the Venice Beach boardwalk—stars and planets and lions and dolphins and a little girl in a green dress poised on a rock, staring out at the wide world in wonder and amazement.

Daci had witnessed her mother paint these images. Otherwise, she would have questioned the claim. Because Jillian's artistic mainstay—her fairies—were painfully mediocre at best and occasionally reached the point of being laughably embarrassing.

Daci walked along the mural to the back of the house, where renovations to the barn reminded visitors of a secluded forest cottage. The entire second floor of the back was comprised of wide windows and opened onto a redwood deck. As Daci came around the corner, she caught sight of her mother on the deck, her grey hair sparkling in the sunshine while she cradled a giant orange cat in her arms. She peered into the forest, frowning.

Jillian had hair that rivaled her daughter's in length and wildness. Medium height and build, but with the body that ninety minutes a day of Ashtanga yoga earns a sixty-six year old woman. Despite the Twinkies. She left her waist-length hair down, crowned with a thin braid. The only thing brighter than the sheen of that hair was the sparkle in her yacht-blue eyes. Her clothing accented the lines of her body without being teenager-tight or showing an inappropriate amount of skin, and she wore her laugh lines with dignity and pride—a veritable poster child for graceful aging.

The stripy monster in her mother's arms purred so loudly that Daci heard it before she reached the bottom stair leading up to the deck. Her mother held the contented animal upside down and rocked it gently like a baby.

The snap-snapping of Daci's sandals against her heels echoed as she made her way up the sturdy wood of the staircase, and a generous smile wiped clean all traces of her mother's creased brow. "Hi sweetie! It's great to see you." As if Daci had been expected. But, Daci knew, she was always sort of expected.

Her mother jutted her chin at the thick forest in front of them. "I've misplaced Thing. I'm afraid he's run off."

"Is Thing the white one?" Daci scratched the big orange cat on the head and it nuzzled her appreciatively.

"No, the white one is It. Thing is the grey one."

"How many have you got now, Mom?"

"Just the three! I know your father believes that I'm slowly deteriorating into the crazy cat lady down here but I find homes for all those strays." She once more searched the perimeter of the tree line around the house, then hunched her shoulders in a shrug.

"Probably he'll turn up. Come inside."

The deck led directly into the second floor studio, through one of the flared gable dormers. Three of these little rooms projected from either side of the barn's sloping roof. The one directly across from the deck's foyer held a veritable jungle's worth of plants and a sliding door separated it from the rest of the house, allowing this sunroom to serve as a proper greenhouse.

In the small, pale pink room to the right of the greenhouse, books spilled out of old white bookshelves and two Adirondack chairs with ottomans and puffy blue and yellow pillows invited guests to waste a day reading. The dormer left of the greenhouse held a daybed and an oversized velvet fainting couch. Both pieces shunned the classic burgundy, sporting instead pink and yellow with lace accents and striped pillows. The ultimate in by-the-sea princess furniture couture.

The two dormers shared the side of the house as the deck and foyer held her mother's art supplies, and central to all these miniature rooms lay the studio, its enormity disguised by the lowered, pitched ceilings and warm, caramel-painted walls. Littered throughout the studio, grouped loosely by color palette, were the fairy paintings. Rendered with a childish over-simplicity and fragmentedness, Daci had never appreciated them and had on more than one occasion suggested that her mother choose an alternate subject matter.

"I'd probably do a better job painting them," her mother once confided, "if I believed in them. Or for that matter *liked* them."

Regardless, they apparently sold: Her mother had paid all the expenses for the barn renovation. A few of the paintings had been purchased for use in a TV series, which no doubt helped, between the obscene prices Hollywood paid for even the tiniest of details and the subsequent residual sales to people who just absolutely had to have that painting Jezebella the Werewolf Huntress had hanging in her living room.

Her mother brought a bowl for the Doritos and glasses for the wine.

"Lunch of champions!" she said.

They settled on the redwood deck, under the shade of a green-striped picnic umbrella. Birds called their separate, distinctive songs; Daci made out four. A hummingbird buzzed to the feeder, its constant motion keeping it in one place. Daci relaxed. She didn't feel like talking.

Her mom, being a mom, let her get away with this for a bit, munching snacks and drinking wine and occasionally calling attention to some nearby bird or animal. When the Doritos were about two-thirds gone, though . . .

"Your father called me today," her mother told her. "Right after you left the vineyard."

Daci, despite being in her thirties and regardless of running a company, felt herself pout. A grown woman and this was her response, what she reverted to in the presence of her parents: a pout and the tightness of yet again fighting tears.

"It's cooler in the house. Why don't we go inside for a bit?"

Her mom swept up the snacks and her wine glass, floated through the sliding doors with her long flowery skirt trailing behind her.

They resettled in the room next to the greenhouse, her mother on the daybed, folding her knees up "Indian style" as Daci had called it growing up. Daci opened a bottle of her father's wine and poured a full glass, then stretched out on the fainting couch.

Her mother sensed when she was once again at ease and took a different approach. "Funny," she started, like easing into a swimming pool. "You've never liked people very much. Always enjoyed the offerings of being alive, but people you could take or leave. Yet you continue to live in Los Angeles. Where there are so many people."

Daci shrugged. "I live in the snobby section. Bohemian snobs. We all keep to ourselves."

"You are somewhat elitist. In your way."

Daci couldn't deny that.

"You're intellectually elitist and you don't like people, but you do care about them. Even for them. Curious. I'm happy about it—it shows you have compassion, so I must have raised you right." She gazed dreamily at the greenhouse.

"But?"

"But it confuses me as to just why it's so important for you to get the Flower Flu treatment released."

"People are dying, Mom. I'm not especially fond of alligators, but that doesn't mean I want them exterminated."

Her mother shrugged, placid. "From what your father told me, from what you told him, the treatment will eventually meet the market."

"It could take up to three years!"

"Is that too long?"

Daci paused; her mother had asked this in earnest and Daci had to admit she'd never seriously considered it. Her knee-jerk response was to get it out to the public immediately, and besides, "Flower Flu isn't an accident. Sydney had somebody design it. On purpose! It's murder, Mom. Would you wait three years to stop a psycho killer?" She stopped, realizing she sounded on the verge of panic.

"I'm not asking you to justify yourself, sweetie. I'm just curious is all." She gave what Daci's father called her Serenity Smile. Half-closed mouthed, half toothy, with her head cocked. Simultaneously acknowledging and dismissing all the world's awfulness and cruelty.

"Your mother will smile through the apocalypse," Daci's father used to say.

"I heard about the flu being invented," her mother said.

"Horrible!"

"Mmm. But a lot of cures have been developed and then a disease had to be found to apply them to. Also, is there any evidence that what he's told you is true? Are you certain?"

"I'm not. I don't know. And I've lost the only person who can tell me for sure. And that person could develop his own cure, too."

Her mom smiled again, soothing like a summer shower. "You always have admired scientists."

"I appreciate devotion to specialized knowledge, I guess. They also seem resistant to nostalgia. And unlikely to commit murder."

"I always figured you simply admired their intelligence."

"I guess. But the stuff should be taught in grade school, the concepts anyway. ABCs, unified field theory, counting, quantum mechanics, reading, nap, snack."

"You know what's terrible? I don't know either of those things."

"You don't know your ABCs?"

"Nope, those either. For instance, I don't actually know what E equals MC squared *means*."

"Oh. It's part of the theory of relativity. It just says that energy, the E in the equation, can be expressed as a product of mass and the speed of light. So energy and matter," she rapped her knuckles against the arm of the fainting couch, "are different manifestations of the same thing. Kind of like steam and ice. Both water."

She stopped, pausing to listen. "Do you hear that? It sounded like the greenhouse door."

They listened, but the sound didn't repeat.

"Alright. Anyway, that famous equation is a part of his, Einstein's, theory of special relativity. The theory of relativity basically says that space and time are the same thing. The fourth dimension *is* time."

"I've heard that discussed, yes."

"That theory explains the nature and behavior of everything that we can see."

"Except junior high school kids."

"In physics, a 'field' is just an area under some force. You know, like how the Earth has a gravitational field? Unified field theory simply posits that all the forces like gravity and electromagnetism are actually manifestations of one field."

"A force field?" Her mother sang the original *Star Trek* theme song.

Daci threw a Twinkie at her. "I think teaching you is like teaching junior high school kids!"

Her mother giggled. "Why didn't you stick with science, anyway?"

"I'm too mentally lazy."

"Shame," her mother said, unwrapping the Twinkie. "You'd've been good."

"You don't think I'm a good business person? I mean, Survivanoia is a bad example, but I had a lot of successful businesses before."

"It's not about you it's...." Her mother paused, cocked her head slightly. "Women seldom thrive in the business world. They may make money, as you did, and climb the ladder, as you have. But they don't flourish."

"Meaning what exactly, Mom?"

Her mother squinted into the distance. "Too many women get into the workplace and ... try to become men. We have different sensibilities. We should try to apply them. I think." She eased from the loveseat. "I'll be right back, sweetie. You need anything while I'm up?"

Daci shook her head and her mother floated off to the bathroom. The door to the greenhouse shook again, this time hard enough that it rattled and Daci was entirely sure of it.

Rats? There were three cats in the house; it seemed unlikely her mother would have rodents of any type, but it was a big old barn and they were in the middle of absolutely nowhere.

She got up from the couch, picked up a broom and crept across the studio to the greenhouse door. *Rattle rattle rattle.* Louder and more persistent and it crossed Daci's mind that maybe the Romanian was here; her father had phoned him and he'd come up to make her some horrid offer or, fuck, maybe it was Sydney!

Rattle rattle thump! Sydney knew where her mother lived. What if he'd somehow been tipped off about Radu and come to gain a bargaining chip or seek some kind of revenge or *rattle thump MEOW!*

"Oh for fuck's sake." Daci laughed at herself and unlatched the greenhouse door. When she slid it open, a streak of grey *whoosh*ed past her and into the supply dormer across the studio. "Thing! C'mere kitty."

344

She followed him. He let out another meow, sounding happier this time as she pushed the curtain aside.

"*Er-gnow*," Thing said, his odd foreign meow ringing from the depths of the dormer. Paintings filled the room with a few on easels, seemingly in progress. But not paintings of fairies. These were cats: one orange, one white with blue eyes and too many toes, and a sizeable but svelte grey one with white-tipped feet and a white bib—Thing.

Daci scooped the cat up from the floor and he made his funny noise again, then bumped his head against her cheek and purred. She studied the paintings. Cats all angular and sinewy, drawn from thick, simple brush strokes. Simplicity—that they shared with the fairies. But where the fairies came off as childish and nascent, the simplicity of the cats lent them elegance and splendor.

"Oh, here you are," her mom's voice indicated she'd been searching.

"Mom, what are these? Why are you not selling *these*?"

"They're the works of a friend."

"But they're *your* cats."

"Of course. She comes here to paint. You don't think I need this enormous studio all for myself, do you?"

Daci considered this and the fact of her mother *designing* this studio for herself, and started to express this thought; but her mother spoke first.

"Oh, know what, she's in Santa Barbara today! She wanted me to meet her but you know my aversion to driving. But you're here... maybe we could go? There's an arts fair. Food and music and some kind of poetry reading. Plus you can meet Bridget."

Slender grey Thing wriggled happily in her arms. "*Er-gnow*."

Daci shrugged. "Okay."

* * *

Santa Barbara always made Daci happy. Its crescent bay and single pier brought back a rush of childhood memories so varied and pleasant that she had a difficult time imagining growing up any place else.

Its heart held a college town, but the setting was what people thought of when they heard the Beach Boys sing; sandy beaches and hilly streets full of young people in shorts and sandals. No one ever seemed unhappy here. Nobody ever seemed to rush. No traffic jams or chain stores. Just ninety minutes outside Los Angeles but a planet away in soul and texture.

Being by the ocean kept temperatures down and the salty breeze coming off the bay seemed more pristine than the one at Daci's condo. This despite the oil rig off in the distance. She'd long admired the refusal of the Golden State's residents to exploit their waterfront property, but oil rigs could be seen from most of the central coast.

As with any time the town hosted an event, parking proved a challenge. They'd taken her mother's car, a 1977 Corvette with the original 8-track tape player and not quite forty-thousand miles. They'd found it in the barn when they started renovations. Smaller than the Hummer and far easier to park; Daci found a spot near the Mission and they walked down to State Street and the festival.

The festival had the feel of a street fair, all bright colors, big smiles, and good food. Vendors hawked churros and fruit pops while clowns, acrobats, and even a fire-eater lurked through the crowd granting impromptu performances to anyone who expressed interest.

Tents lined the west side of State Street, sheltering artists and craftspeople. Jewelry, watercolors, clothing, stuffed animals, birdhouses made from beer cans, and in the neighboring tent, birdhouses made as tiny replicas from *Architectural Digest*. At El Cabrillo Boulevard, where the streets gave way to sand, a tent full of wind chimes added their music to the surf and breeze.

"I want to see the beach," Daci said.

"Blech. Too polluted. I'll meet you by the churro stand in, what, an hour? I'm sure I'll be hungry by then." With that her mom drifted off again, her flowing skirt in her wake.

On the beach, a dozen or so teams were participating in the ephemeral and therefore arguably fruitless art of sandcastle competition. Gorgeous, impossible constructions and no two alike. One reflected a Scottish fortress, flat and squat with anchoring turrets and even a moat for monsters. Next to that configuration, another more square and symmetrical, mansion-esque, like Windsor Castle.

Farther along the beach, a threesome used utility knives and masonry trowels to put the finishing touches on a French motte-and-bailey, a horseshoe built onto a mound of earth. A fourth person followed behind them, spraying something from a bottle, presumably some sort of glue to keep the thing together.

Daci stared in awe at the open, functional archways and painstakingly rendered bricks, even a flag on the top; how long had these folks been at this? Further along were two Asian structures, a Martian castle, a Dali-inspired castle, even an Escher castle, all sculpted from the sea's abundant clay.

Speakers from somewhere nearby sent out a wave of electronic feedback, followed by a man's voice: "Sorry! We're still mastering the art of sound here."

Across El Cabrillo, Daci spotted a stage flanked by plastic lawn chairs and heard the announcer introduce someone who received an impressive round of applause. A woman stepped forward, tall and curvy in a bright red T-shirt dress. A thick cluster of micro-braids fell in a ponytail halfway down her back, and the noonday sun made the woman's skin glow bronze.

The woman took a long slow breath and began, not reading or even reciting, but almost singing; there was so much rhythm to her poetry. "Slam poetry" people had called it when Daci was in college, and she'd never been a fan because the poets invariably struck her as self-righteous in bearing and mediocre in talent—too lazy to write a real poem, too isolated to write song lyrics.

This woman impressed her, though. Daci couldn't make out the words, but there was undeniable power and presence in the poet and—whatever her statement was—an allure that pulled Daci toward the end of the beach.

At the far end, a group of five thirty-somethings struggled with their sand replica of Neuschwanstein. They'd done a commendable job with the foundation and upper courtyard, but the thin, flanking cylindrical towers and spires would not cooperate. From watching the others, Daci had the suspicion that they'd approached it backwards, trying to add things when they should have carved them from the original lump of sand. Or perhaps they'd changed their minds halfway through a different concept.

Suddenly a little girl came running, shouting the name of one of the women. Caramel skin and a pink short-sleeved dress like the one worn by the woman on the stage. Two big, puffy pigtails held in place by old-fashioned two-ball hair bands. The girl's exuberance took her right through the Neuschwanstein's courtyard. She came to an abrupt halt, her eyes big with worry. She looked down at what she stood in. "Oops."

A moment of quiet from the group. Then one of the guys, more appropriately than he likely knew, burst into "Ride of the Valkyries." Laughter and joking about a German Godzilla, then the woman the girl came for knelt so she could carry the child piggyback. "Let's go listen to your mom."

The group made their way up the beach and across the boulevard to the stage. Daci followed them. They moved right to the front of the raised platform while Daci stayed at the perimeter.

She caught sight of a tent she'd missed on the walk down—though seeing it now, missing it seemed impossible. Paintings filled the tent, paintings of sinewy angular cats painted in simple, elegant strokes.

Just as Daci mentally shrugged, *Mom really* must *have a friend who paints her cats,* she caught sight of her mother. For the briefest of moments, she saw her mother as she understood other people did: an attractive, fit, artistic hippie who lived by the sea. Likeable through and through, if none too smart. Pleasant and ditzy—don't expect too much. Delusional painter of ugly fairies.

She watched her mother chat with the woman in the tent, point to a few prints like she was discussing a painting technique. They laughed together, the woman nodded, and they continued talking as the woman counted sales receipts and pulled cash from a lockbox, handed it to Daci's mom.

"Well butter my ass and call me a biscuit." Daci blurted this outloud, sparking laughter from a couple seated nearby.

Daci apologized for distracting them. Happily stunned, she dropped into one of the plastic chairs. Here, her mother could paint after all. And pass herself off as a charming little fool.

What else had Daci picked up from her parents without being fully aware? Because she certainly, at this moment and never before, appreciated the origins of her own talent for social camouflage. What of her father? She thought of GrandMama, who only seemed to want change, no matter the means and without necessarily giving complete thought to the consequences. Did this describe Daci's father?

From the stage the rhythm changed. It caught Daci briefly, significantly, the poet's words like a consultation.

I know

Am well aware
Of the despair
Caused by
The sterile debate
While in the streets the hate
Is driving us to kill
Instead of commiserate . . .
But Momma . . .

Daci was at the bottom, she realized. Everything had spun from her control; she'd lost her tools and mistreated her beasts with the road still uncompleted. But it didn't feel like the bottom. More like the beginning of something, just as each valley leads to a new mountain.

Why did she like science? Because she saw it as a unifying force in a world that increasingly dehumanizes us. Because it balances and validates the inner problems of life and thought with the outer problems of matter and death. Because it gives us meaning in a way that does not require murder or cruelty.

Which is why, yes, three years was too long to wait for a cure that was ready now, today. Yes, if Sydney's claims were true, he needed to be stopped. By hook or by crook, as the saying went. By whatever means necessary.

She took a deep breath, suppressing her rising anxiety and accompanying short, shallow breathing. No need to panic. . . .

She made her way to the churro cart to meet her mother. The business card her father had given her seemed to burn from inside the little pocket of her linen vest. Menacing.

As menacing as Sydney's virus. Could it be true? Why would a person lie about something so thoroughly reprehensible? This wasn't enforced absurdity or pretending to drive a gas guzzler. This was people being killed. *Murder.*

The way to stop the virus was to stop its cause and its cause in this case seemed to be Sydney Scalinescu. She dug her cell phone from her purse—this one a small colorful bag made from an old sari. Took the card from her vest. Stood staring at it. *Torch the place* . . . Radu's number, *818-612-080.* . . .

He still speaks fondly of you, her father had said. *His wife makes the best mititei* . . . So he'd been there. From the sounds of things, the men were quite friendly. Wasn't her father therefore equally remiss?

People kill people and they use guns to do it and what was the difference between supplying guns and developing a virus? Violence is its own disease. Keep fighting fire with fire and eventually you'll scorch the entire Earth.

"Fuck."

She pressed cancel on her cell phone.

Her mother caught sight of her and waved, then raised a finger to indicate she'd be a moment. Daci waved back, recalling now her mother's words: *We have different sensibilities. We should try to apply them* ... But how did this philosophy translate tangibly? How could her sensibilities be forged into actions? They only seemed to guide her as to what *not* to do, not provide a solution.

The little girl in the pink dress suddenly bounded across the stage, just as the voice of the poet rose over the noise of the crowd, blending with the warm smell of cinnamon and fried dough to forge one of those isolated moments that Daci recognized, even as she lived, it would stay with her until death. And the poet's substantial, alluring cadence:

But Momma ...

The sky

Is not falling
Not hauling
Its ass toward Earth
Not even bending
Does not need mending
Just looks that way to you,

Momma

Because

You are

Ascending

Clapping, hollering of appreciation, even a small group in the back corner standing. Daci clapped too, around the card and her cell phone, but then the phone rang. H. SANCHEZ, the caller ID told her. A 310 number.

Where'd she know that name from? Her mental rolodex spun but came up blank. Still something nudged her and she took the call.

"The Baroness here."

"Ah, Baroness! This is Dr. Encludsmo Stuckhowsen. I am servicing you."

END

ACKNOWLEDGEMENTS
(Second and First Editions)

The acknowledgements for help and advice with the second edition of this book should be read in conjunction with those of the first edition. These former thanks are clearly still relevant and are shown below.

For this specific edition, I am indebted to fellow writer and candid critique partner Gage Chenier, and also to Ashley Lauren Rogers, an instructor at Writing the Other. This organization is an invaluable resource for writers, so if you are one, check them out online.

Thanks to the supportive fellow writers I've found in Western New York especially Gary Earl Ross and Jon Elston. It's nice to make friends in the asylum.

Finally, shout-outs to all my friends who don't get to see me while I'm writing and are still friends when I'm not. I owe you all drinks.

ACKNOWLEDGMENTS
(First Edition, 2011)

This book has been nearly a decade in the making from conceptualization to this ink-and-paper reality. Suffice it to say the entire list of people to thank is too lengthy for inclusion . . . you know who you are! I am, however, *especially* grateful to Matt Brownlie—without whom Encludsmo would not exist, to CJ Lyons for believing in me even when my belief had faltered, to my Editor-and-Mom Dr. Beverly Richards-Smith, and to Bruce-my-Bruce Weinheimer, Sr. for being infinitely patient and generally spectacular.

ABOUT THE AUTHOR

Baroness Melody Von Smith wrote her first story when she was six. Everybody died in the end. It was a comedy. She is the author of the play *And Where Will You Put the Things You Save*, and the short story collection *Roadless Homelands*. She currently spends most of her time in Western New York, where she shares her home with two cats and one husband.

For more information, go to:
www.baronessvonsmith.com

ALSO BY THE AUTHOR

"Von Smith is a wildly talented writer with a keen grasp of personality, an ear for dialogue, and a razor perception of the thread-sized intersections that lead to trouble. The Art of the Short Story is alive and well."

Gary Earl Ross
(*Blackbird Rising, Mark of Cain*)

In this wry collection, the Baroness explores our need for a place to call home, and how this need is tied to our identity.

In "The Ocean Doesn't Want Me Today," it is a physical place—Downeast Maine—that provides solace for a young woman contending with her mother's suicide by learning to be a lobsterman. In "The Snows of Jake Manjaro," it is Jake's all-consuming vocation. "Yes, This is a Fine Promotion" features a young man who meets himself on a subway train in Chicago, while in "The High Price of the Wild Truth," a beach bum slowly transforms into his once-famous television character, a hired vigilante killer.

These stories—blunt, funny, and deceptively simple—showcase the Baroness's knack of capturing the wonderful ridiculousness of being human.

Order direct from Burning Giraffe, and take 25% off.
Enter Coupon Code **SURV2** *at checkout.*

COMING SOON

THE ACCIDENTAL DESPOT

A deep-sea diver starts his own country, to which a brilliant scientist rebelling against Nomnasto, the corporation that once employed her, defects. She is subsequently chased by one of the high-ranking officials of Nomnasto. Among those coming to her aid are the Landfill Miners of Long Beach, a virtual tagging crew known as WHOM, and a strange little scientist with a giant black dog and very confused English. But will these ragamuffins be enough to battle Nomnasto's Green Ops?

Jodi Summerscales comes off his latest underwater welding job—six weeks at six hundred feet—to be informed that the oil rig he'd been working on has been decommissioned. After thirty seconds of deliberation with his dive team, Jodi formally declares the oil rig the City of Mayor's Income, California, and is promptly elected mayor by the city's other six residents (Jodi voted for Moochie Cohen). He soon discovers that declaring a city involves things like proposals and referendums and it's much easier to start your own country. So he does. *On the same day that . . .*

Verisimilitude Skrlnmacher definitively assesses the results of her most recent experiment. She is beside herself with glee! As she makes her way to her boss's office, she dreams of all the papers, the patents, the professional indulgences including her *own* lab, run by *her*. Except that she is fired. Frog-marched out of the building in fact and not to her car, either, but to a nearby bus stop because her car has been seized as company property. So has, she soon discovers, her house, her bank account, and her electronic data body. Her lawyer's advice? Flee to another country . . . there's one you can swim to. *Verisimilitude is fired on exactly the same day that . . .*

Lyman Odd signs the paperwork for his freshly-minted LLC, Terra Safe Inc. He then transfers his personal ownership of a large, kelp-covered swath of ocean floor to this nascent company. Nomnasto needs the kelp for their Meat Fruit project, and being that Lyman Odd is the face of that company, known in fact to the public as *Mr. Nomnasto*, it seems reasonable to assume that he would want Nomnasto to have the kelp. But he doesn't. He also wants Jodi off the oil rig and seems to want Verisimilitude dead. Why is such a man being supported, then, by the zealously virtuous likes of Terri Tehzan?

Join our mailing list to have access to pre-order specials and unique offers
www.BurningGiraffeBooks.com

www.ingramcontent.com/pod-product-compliance
Lightning Source LLC
Chambersburg PA
CBHW072321280626
47159CB00027B/253